Tangled PAST

TANGLED IN TIME BOOK 4

CAROLINE CORVIN

First published in 2024 by Grenwyvern Publishing

Auckland, New Zealand

Betrayal

University of Edinburgh, Scotland - November 2017

THE WORDS FLOWED LIKE an enchantment, the man's voice casting its spell. It captured Cassie in velvet handcuffs. She made no attempt to resist.

"Full house," he said, staring out at the crowd with wide eyes, as a woman fumbled at his lapel, adjusting a tiny microphone. "They must be in the wrong room."

The self-deprecating comment; the flush that crept up his neck as he realised the microphone had thrown his words out to the entire lecture theatre; the embarrassed smile; all these small gestures immediately endeared him to her and others in the audience.

Yes, his observation was correct: there *were* a lot of people in the lecture room, and they *were* all here to see him. At least a hundred had voted against making a run for home before the threatened early-season snow coated Edinburgh so they could listen to his words. With a rustle of papers and a click of a pointer, he began.

"So, good evening ladies and…." He hesitated for a moment. There wasn't a single man in the group. "…ladies." The melodic rise and fall of his accent caressed the ears of every woman in the room, and their collective silent sigh washed across the space.

The title slide 'Outlander With The Castle Hunter' featured a larger-than-life portrait shot that only confirmed he was a good-looking man, although in real life less severe than the image on screen. Her eyes followed the sensuous curve of his lips that relieved an otherwise angular face. The straight nose, slash of cheekbones, and pale skin were unlined apart from a crinkle at the eyes that held a suppressed smile. That smile seemed to lie in wait, ready to spring forth in delight at the effect of his next utterance on the assembled women.

"First of all, I'll apologise in advance for disappointing you—I'm not a Fraser or a Mackenzie. Not even a Fitzgibbon." Laughter rippled across the room, warm waves radiating towards him. "For this final session of the day, you'll have to make do with me—Simon Buchanan. And as you can probably tell from just looking at me, I'm no brawny Highlander."

Another small titter of amusement bubbled in his direction. Not a sturdy red-haired Jacobite warrior as described in the books or brought to life in the TV series, but a mid-thirty-something university lecturer. His athletic build and sleek wave of hair as black as the heart of an English garrison commander completed Cassie's assessment: Doctor Simon Buchanan was strikingly attractive. She wondered if he knew it. Surely a man of his age would have heard it, seen it reflected in the admiring eyes of women. But even if he was aware of the effect of his appearance, his humble manner of speech and a slight awkwardness projected back at the audience suggested a refreshing lack of arrogance.

"However, I do know a thing or two about castles," he smiled. "So, come with me on a journey."

In that moment, Cassie decided she'd be perfectly happy to go anywhere this stranger led. She envisaged him a Pied Piper, a long line of women following, mesmerised—but with her elbowing past, determined to be first.

Another click and the screen behind him sprang to life, video images taking them soaring high above castles and lochs before diving low to circle ancient battlements.

"Nothing is more romantic than a castle. When writers, and indeed filmmakers, take us to a castle, they're tapping into our fantasies of times past, of bold heroes and despicable villains, of sworn enemies and passionate lovers."

His eyes met hers, and Cassie gulped in air. Did she imagine it, or was his direct gaze deliberate? Did it linger a moment longer than it should? She forced herself to study the cover of her notebook. *My Secret Thoughts Lie Within These Pages*. The playful gold letters stared back. Even the 'Duly Noted' stationery chain had conspired against her. Maybe it was a small sign from the universe legitimising this sudden instant attraction she felt for a stranger, despite eight years of marriage to the one man who had ever made her heart lurch at the sight of him—until now. She risked a surreptitious glance and let out her breath in relief that his gaze fell elsewhere.

But it was only a temporary reprieve. Simon Buchanan's sweep of the room turned back in her direction and again they made eye contact, and this time she was sure of it—a hint of that unexpected chemistry projected back at her.

She could just get up and leave. No. This close to the end of the day, she must complete her mother's assigned mission: attend every session of this one day exploration of the history behind a much-loved series of books. Blair had read the first when it came out, back in 1991. Now battling cancer, revisiting the fictional world of her favourite author and repeatedly watching the spin-off TV series, gave her mother respite from thoughts of an uncertain future.

There was no way Cassie could bail on this session. Besides, seated in the middle of a row, leaving the lecture theatre without creating a disruption was virtually impossible. The last thing she needed was to draw attention to herself. So she vowed to tough it out, no matter how uncomfortable.

An hour of exquisite torture followed. The startling sensation of having Simon all to herself took hold, making her feel like the other hundred women in the room didn't exist. A flush of embarrassment surged across her neck and face each time he made eye contact. Surely it must be obvious for all to see?

The pleasure of basking in his presence mingled with thoughts of future pain when confronting the empty notebook pages, reminders of her failure to completely fulfil the task. Discomfort niggled her, as she anticipated the awkward scene to come. What reason might she offer her mother for her paralysis? Detailed notes of every other session filled the book. The pages allocated for this one lay bare, the blank lines an accusation of negligence. And oh, how her mother loved those castle scenes. With three weeks left before she'd have to offer up the notebook, she might find time to read and research—bury herself in the library, scour Google for obscure facts that might replicate the musings of a Scottish castle hunter.

Stabs of guilt assaulted her at the thought of Nik, her husband. She could still hand on heart, say she loved him. She didn't doubt he loved her. Although, it was no longer the wild, tumultuous love of teenagers. Facing the inevitable changes as they'd grown into adults wasn't easy; they were such different people from the two naïve kids who'd pledged a lifelong commitment. Even now, they were determined to honour that commitment, but both would admit they had struggled lately. It wasn't only the emotional challenges of their evolving selves. Weathering the shitstorms that had come their way, rather than drive them closer in solidarity, had caused them to pull apart.

Physically, they had barely spent a day apart in a eight whole years. Not healthy probably; and it made this separation hard. But she'd had no choice but to remain in Scotland on her own. Nik had already abandoned his work for two months to be here with her. She couldn't object when he'd asked to return early, making his own family pilgrimage along the way.

Meanwhile, she sat here focused on this academic eye candy. Unbidden, but certainly not unpleasant impulses circulated deep down in her centre. Nik was the only guy who triggered this lustful longing in her loyal body. Now a stranger had provoked the same. Nik was the only person who understood her, with an instinctive deep knowledge that seemed to touch her soul. Now another man had brushed against it.

Was this cheating? If Nik should pick up the damn notebook and flick through it, would he see those pages and know that in her mind, in her heart, in her soul, she'd cheated on him? Were these blank pages evidence of betrayal?

As the lecture ended, she rose from her seat. Her eyes met Simon's again in a brief glance—of what? Attraction? Knowledge? Recognition? Whatever it was, she knew she had to leave, abandoning that sweet carrot of possibility dangling in front of her. She forced herself to go, moving in mechanical steps towards the door. His smile just for her now turned to the throng of women who'd poured from their seats. Some thrust copies of a book at him for signing.

Walking through the vaulted ceilings of the cloisters, she reached for the swirl of emotions that circled the corners of her mind, separating the strands to examine each more closely. Shame that she'd even allowed herself to give in to this crazy instant infatuation. Fear that it was a symptom of some hidden flaw within herself. Dread that it was a warning one of the numerous tiny fissures in her marriage was about to rupture, unleashing devastation. Regret for something that might have been. And a sweet melancholy that she must leave Simon Buchanan behind.

And leave him she must, relegating him to a surreal temporary insanity best forgotten; the product of an overactive imagination, as she clutched at what was real.

Stepping out into the chill night, she shook her head free of the disturbing thoughts. She recognised the fresh sniff of snow in the air, familiar from childhood winters in New Zealand's deep south. She rummaged in her tote bag for a hat, pulling it on to contain the strands of her hair whipped by the icy wind off the cobbles. Cursing the absence of her gloves, left behind in her hurry this morning, she plunged her hands deep into the pockets of her coat. With her phone still on silent, a vibration against her fingers signalled an incoming call. She pulled it free to peer at the screen. Blair Tremayne.

"Mum?" she asked. "You're up early. It's only six a.m."

"Oh darling, I couldn't sleep with the excitement. How was it?"

"It was fabulous, Mum."

"And you took lots of notes, I hope? And maybe a few photographs? I want it all."

"Yes Mum, of course I did," she lied.

"Thank you, my darling. It will be almost as good as being there." Cassie caught the faint hitch in her voice. An unexpected thread of worry surfaced.

"Mum? Are you OK?"

"Of course, yes. I'm just a bit tired." She unleashed a girlish giggle. "You know me, never been a fan of early rising. But today I had a reason."

There it was again—the faint tremor in her mother's voice hidden under a cheerfulness so bright it didn't ring true.

"I can't wait to see you, Mum. It's been amazing here. I'm proud of myself for doing this. But I'm ready for home."

"I think Nik's ready for you to both be home, too." She could hear her mother's smile across the miles at the mention of him. Her so-called 'second son', they talked often. "He's not happy about having to leave you there on your own."

Guilt at her crazy preoccupation with that man in the lecture theatre slapped hard at her again at the mention of Nik. What the hell was wrong with her? The pressure of this last couple of months weighed heavily. But with the retrospective exhibition of her mother's art coming to an end, the worst was over. All that remained was to oversee the packaging of those precious pieces that would never be for sale, ready for their journey home. Perhaps she wasn't coping with that final responsibility as well as she'd thought. Whatever the reason, she needed to bury the whole shameful hour deep down in the past. It was time to focus on more important things: the safe return of the paintings, and getting back to her life.

"Yeah, I know Mum. I hate it too. But it's not for much longer." Her voice echoed off the stone buildings flanking her.

"Are you outside?" Her mother's concern for her child sprang forth, even though thousands of miles separated them.

"It's OK, Mum, they're predicting snow, but it's not here yet."

"I'll not keep you talking then. Get yourself back to the apartment before you freeze. Talk to you tomorrow."

"OK, love you Mum."

Her mother's call had pulled her part way back into normal life, but to secure herself there, she must talk to Nik. She flicked her phone to the World Clock. What would he be doing at eight o'clock on a Saturday night in Dubrovnik?

Most guys of his age would be tourists checking out the bars and the pretty girls, hoping to hook up for the night. But he would more than likely be sitting in a little house in the old town, making stilted conversation with his grandparents. Yes, while Nik unselfishly spent his time doing something for his family, his wife walked the streets of Edinburgh fighting off treacherous thoughts of a Scottish stranger who, for some inexplicable reason, had forced his way into her mind.

With one last firm shove, she pushed Simon Buchanan away. She turned her focus to the most important contact in her phone and dialled her husband's number.

PART ONE – HERE

Chapter 1

Fight

Auckland, New Zealand - January 2009

"Fight, fight, fight."

The chant echoed off the red brick-walled buildings of the quad. An untidy ring of boys clustered around invisible combatants, urging them on with feral whoops of encouragement. Yelps and gasps sprang from the mouths of the wide-eyed spectators excited by a first day of school brawl.

Cassie swore if she was any closer, she'd see the waves of testosterone wafting off them. Their uniform grey shorts revealed both hairy legs and their lowly status in the secondary school pecking order. She gave an involuntary snort and shook her head disdainfully. Having a younger brother left little tolerance for the immaturity of the average teenage boy.

Archie was already a right pain in the arse and spent an inordinate amount of time further perfecting that skill. He infuriated her, using her as a testing ground for his annoying habits. One advantage of completing her final year at this large city school was her path and his were less likely to cross. Back at sleepy little Mackenzie College with a roll of two hundred, it felt like he was everywhere and knew everything.

Getting off the bus this morning, she'd immediately lost him in the tide of fifteen hundred students pouring through the gates of Valley High. She'd savoured the sense of anonymity as she too plunged into the crowd, a welcome contrast to the scrutiny of small town life where knowing everyone else's business was an acceptable local pastime.

Apart from Archie, she knew only one other person here. Grace lay on her stomach on the bench seat beside her, head buried deep in one of her favourite smutty romance books. The book rather resembled her new friend, a steamy world hidden inside a discreet flowery cover. Propped on her elbows, her expression lay unfathomable behind a spiralling curtain of mahogany hair. No one would suspect sweet wholesome-looking Grace harboured a secret life with an array of lusty book boyfriends.

Cassie put down her own book, one of Grace's recommendations, pulling herself away from the story of a turbulent relationship between fictional teenagers to survey the very real trouble drawing more spectators to the far corner of the quad.

Now it had escalated beyond a momentary scuffle, a ripple of interest rolled across the remaining seated students, breaking the languid mood of a stinking hot summer lunch break. Anything to distract from the merciless sun beating down was welcome, even the spectacle of some junior kids scrapping. Cassie wiped a pearl of sweat from her lips, shading her eyes as she peered through the glare.

A couple of boys lolling against the fence near her straightened and ambled towards the ruckus. Clad in t-shirts and jeans, their dress marked them out as Year 13s, like her. The lack of uniform and a separate common room were privileges bestowed on senior students. Not to mention a daily timetable starting with a free period that allowed her to sleep late if she wanted. That is, if she could convince her mother to drive her to school rather than take the bus. Yes, there was a lot to like about Valley High.

"Take a look?" asked Grace, her interest piqued not by the fight itself but the particular older boys who'd sauntered over to investigate. One of them, Liam, had melted Grace into a puddle simply by speaking to her outside the beach cafe last week. With a knowing smile, a lean shirtless body and sexy hair that brushed low across molten chocolate eyes, he'd remained the subject of her endless boy-focused chatter ever since. She watched Grace's eyes track Liam's progress across the yard. Following them, she had to agree with Grace's earlier assessment—he looked equally hot with his t-shirt on.

"Yeah, OK," Cassie said. She let the book fall onto the seat beside her and strolled over to squeeze in between the row of Year 13 boys. A faint smell of sweat mingled with the overpowering odour of cheap spray-on deodorant.

"Who is it? Do you know?" Grace directed her questions toward Liam, using her difficulty in seeing exactly what was happening amongst the crowd of onlookers as the perfect excuse to strike up conversation.

"Dunno," he said. "But it looks like the little red-headed kid is giving as good as he's getting."

Red-headed kid? A jolt of concern urged Cassie forward, jostling her way through with elbows and shoulders. It wouldn't be the first time a certain red-headed kid had ended up in a fight. Archie wasn't one to go looking for trouble, but when you were a scrawny, pale stick figure with a face pepper-potted with freckles so thick you could hardly draw a line between them and a shock of red hair that acted like a beacon for bullies—well, trouble often came looking for you.

"Shit." She recognised the flash of hazel eyes, glinting with adrenaline, in between the flurry of fists and feet and flailing limbs. First day in their new school and bloody Archie was on a one-way trip to detention at least, or at worst a summons to appear in front of the school board. What if they kicked him out? God, her mother would be furious.

Blair, desperate to take up the artist in residence position, but secretly reluctant to leave her children behind, had argued that the experience of life in the big city would do them good. Meanwhile, her father, Daniel, thought it best they remain with him, in sleepy little Tekapo, offering a more settled environment for Cassie to finish her final year of high school. But given the choice, she'd leapt at the chance of escape from the boring sameness of small town life. Now her dickhead little brother was jeopardising everything.

She felt a twinge of guilt at the purely selfish thought. Just as she still felt uneasy with the selfish choice to leave her father behind. The decision still gnawed at her. Forced to choose, she'd chosen her mother. But not for the right reasons. This choice meant a way out of her dreary, narrow life; escape to the possibilities of a city with nearly a million people.

Her heart thumped against her ribs, hammering as if it too wanted escape. Her brain frantically assessed the wisdom of intervention. Rooted to the spot by uncertainty, she found her voice, the only suitable weapon to wield against the pair.

"Stop it!" she screamed at the two enraged boys. But her cry was lost in the buzz of the onlookers. Needing to do something before that happened, she pushed through the rows of spectators, stumbling into the middle of the circle.

The boys continued to wrestle untidily at her feet, oblivious to Cassie. She stood over them, hands on hips, unsure of her next move. As she debated whether to yell some more, or make an attempt to grab Archie, a sudden hush descended on the crowd. The students' chatter cut off with an abrupt hiss of surprise.

In front of her, the cluster of bodies parted as if a giant hand had slashed the group in two with a sword.

An enormous young man strode along the wide path cleared simply by his presence. With his bulk reminiscent of a front row rugby player bursting through a tackle, he thrust himself past the inner circle of spectators who, unaware of his arrival, still urged the boys on.

It seemed luck had run out for Archie and his nemesis. The broad-shouldered warrior lunged for the pair, gripping each by his shirt collar and hauling them to their feet. With one dangling from each of his huge hands, he surveyed them calmly. Archie, now wide-eyed with fear, swallowed audibly. His dark-haired opponent appeared less intimidated, twisting his mouth into a crooked scowl.

"What the fuck do you little turds think you're doing?" The older boy's question held a thinly veiled menace. "Well? You going to tell me? Huh?" He glared at the boy. "Time to start talking, Moffat." A rough shake followed for emphasis.

"Fucking ginga kneed me in the balls." The boy thrust his chin forward, unrepentant.

At that, Archie's eyes flared, the flush on his face turning a deeper shade of scarlet, subduing his freckles even further. "Arsehole," he spat. "And I'll do it again too."

He writhed against the hold on the scruff of his neck, fists clenched in fury despite his helplessness to make good on the threat. Like a mongoose, fearless against a cobra, Archie would always stand his ground. And Cassie knew when provoked, he wouldn't hesitate to fight dirty; whatever it took to survive, to fight another day.

"You, you're new?" asked the older boy, cutting off Archie's struggles with a jerk of his arm.

"Yeah," Archie replied, his tone wisely a little less belligerent.

"What's your name, new kid?"

"Archie Tremayne."

"Arc-tuuuurus." Opposite, Archie's unrepentant tormentor rolled the name around in his mouth with a sneer. A snigger escaped from someone in the crowd.

"Shut your fucking mouth." Archie's voice rose in indignation, his face reddening again as one fist flailed uselessly towards the boy held out of his reach.

"Ahhh, I see what's going on here," said his captor with a weary grin. Without warning, he dropped Archie, who stumbled onto the ground. The other boy remained dangling in midair, his toes just brushing the concrete. "Moffat..." He eyed the boy with a scornful glare. "It's about time you shut that smartarse mouth of yours or it's going to get you in a lot of trouble," he said before abruptly releasing Moffat, who fell to the ground in an untidy heap. "Seems to me you need a swift kick in the arse. I promise you'll get one if you don't stop this crap. If there's one thing I can't stand, it's fucking bullies." His head swivelled to Archie. "And new boy, this little fucker gives you any more shit—let me know."

He extended one huge hand to Archie, and when her brother reached for it, his defender rolled him onto his feet, with an amiable expression. Archie's eyes remained wide, fear wrestling with curiosity at this surprising gesture of solidarity. The older boy swivelled his large shaggy head, eyeing the onlookers with a threatening expression, before he gave his orders. His voice came low and calm, but still harboured a hint of menace.

"And as for the rest of you, piss off back to where you came from. Show's over."

For a moment, a pair of blue eyes met hers, cool with a self-assured ease in their gaze. She was certain a twitch of amusement lurked at the corners of an otherwise terse mouth. He acknowledged her with a subtle lift of his chin, as if silently reporting a job completed to a superior, before striding off. His large form disappeared around the end of the quad with an unexpected casual grace.

"Who the hell was that?" The question leapt to the front of the queue of a hundred all fighting their own battle in Cassie's head.

"Nik Francovic," Grace replied. "You know, I hadn't noticed before, but he's quite good-looking. Especially when he's mad."

"You *know* him?"

"Sort of. I think Mum went to school with his dad. She's not close to his parents, but she knows them. They're all part of the bloody Dallie mafia. Can't get away from them in this part of Auckland. You know, Croatians," she said.

Of course Grace's proudly Croatian mother, Marija, would know them. The vineyards, and wineries, market gardens and roadside stalls of Dalmatian immigrant families from Croatia dominated the rural area around this part of the city. The signs for their family businesses were everywhere: Babich and Boric, Selak and Soljan, and dozens of others, all affectionately known as 'Dallies'.

"Us Dallie kids get dragged along to all their festivals and music evenings. Boring shit like that. So yeah, I know him. He's OK."

Tucking away this information about Archie's surprising protector, Cassie turned to see her brother's small figure retreating as quickly as he could, attempting to flee the scene without appearing to run.

"Archie." She called at his back and the brief flicker of his head told her he'd heard but chose to ignore it. She considered going after him, but the bell jangled, signalling the start of the last period of the day. Cassie and Grace joined the rivers of reluctant students heading to overheated classrooms.

They poured outwards in reverse when the three-twenty bell blared, offering back a little more of the freedom they'd tasted all summer. Cassie trudged after Grace, her small backpack weighing heavy on her shoulder. From the tired exterior of classrooms untouched since the seventies, Valley High might not look like a school focused on academic success for its students. The swag of homework from her every single class on day one argued otherwise.

Restless lines formed by a queue of buses. Cassie took her place beside theirs. It sported the destination 'Waitakere' in bland black lettering on an old-fashioned sign propped in the window. They might officially live in the city, but out here on the edge of the farmland and bush-clad hills, flash buses with electronic signs were as absent as the one that had transported her from her home in a tiny tourist village to her last school in the nearby larger, but still sleepy, town of Fairlie.

She was grateful for a friend to navigate these new routines. While they weren't yet the besties their mothers were—you couldn't instantly replicate a friendship carved out over thirty years—she and Grace fitted together with an unexpected ease. Maybe they too were destined for a similarly enduring friendship.

Her own mother, Blair, the flighty turbulent artist, her eyes forever turned to the stars, clung to her bohemian dreams at nearly fifty. Grace's mother, Marija, the practical lover of all things green, still found happiness with her hands in the earth. To outsiders, they might appear an unlikely pairing, but the fact they'd remained close, although separated by distance, spoke to the strength of their bond.

Cassie was sure that Blair finding out she'd be based at a small cottage buried deep in the bush-clad Waitakere Ranges, only a few narrow winding driveways away from Marija's organic farm, had given her the final push to accept the year-long position of artist in residence. Thrown together again, the two women had fallen back into the comfortable ways of old friends, while looking on with knowing smiles as they saw the growing closeness of their daughters.

"Must be a union man," Cassie said, with a nod at the grumpy-looking driver of their bus. "Working to rule."

"He's just a bastard," Grace grumbled under her breath, the uncharacteristic curse falling from her mouth as she glared up at him lounging in the driver's seat, an unlit cigarette between his lips. "He never opens the door until exactly three-thirty," she said. "Just ignores us out here frying. Same in winter. It'll be bucketing down and he still makes us wait, getting soaked while he sits inside in the dry."

They slouched in the queue, tucking in close to the side of the bus, seeking the narrow band of shade. The moving line of students entering the next bus parked ahead suggested a more charitable driver on the Henderson Valley run.

One figure towered above the rest, not necessarily the tallest but certainly the one who dominated the crowd by his solid bulk, and the broad shoulders straining against his grey t-shirt. As if feeling Cassie's scrutiny, Nik Francovic turned, and seeing her, his wary eyes transformed in an expression of friendly recognition. He wore his hair long on top, swept back, with an unruly strand flopping over a strong arched brow. The shade of blonde stubble made him look older than his years. Except for the fact he was about to board a school bus, you'd never pick him as a secondary student.

He lifted one hand in a wave, the faintest hint of a smile lurking. Grace was right. Not only did Nik Francovic project a rugged attractiveness, something compelled you to notice him. Perhaps his sheer physicality made him stand out. Or perhaps the confidence, even a veneer of arrogance, set him apart as someone not to ignore.

As the line moved, he offered a salute before disappearing up the steps. Cassie found her own hand rise, returning the gesture in a spontaneous wave, her mouth involuntarily moulding itself into a grin.

"Hmmm, I think you've got an admirer." Grace breathed a suggestive hiss in her ear.

"Maybe," Cassie offered, desperate to appear noncommittal. She summoned a casual tone to mask the unexpected thrill provoked by thoughts of his interest. And to disguise the niggle of worry how she'd handle that if it was true.

She tried to push away the thoughts of the last time she'd let a boy in close to her, and the frightening night when he'd expected to take things from her that she wasn't prepared to give. She shuddered at the memory of his insistent hands, his determined mouth, and his vile words. It was almost a year ago, but every so often something triggered the remembered fear, and the terrifying spectre of 'what ifs' reared up in her mind.

Since then, she'd succeeded at putting up a protective barrier between herself and boys. Adopting an aloof outer, making wise choices about where to go and who with, and then the fortunate opportunity of this move north had conspired to give her what she needed: space to mend. Hiding behind that cool wall had served her well. She wasn't sure if she was ready to take it down just yet, or if Nik Francovic was the sort of guy she could trust with what lay behind it. But maybe it was time to find out.

Chapter 2

Dallies In The Valley

Auckland, New Zealand – February 2009

Cassie's muscles screamed from the effort as she stumbled the last few hundred metres. The box held twenty jars of Marija's manuka honey. Under its weight, she swore her arms had stretched to orangutan proportions on the hike from the van. Grace's gasps of breath and faint groans from behind suggested she wasn't alone in the struggle. At least there would be two of them. Twin long-limbed freaks collapsed on the grass of David Lukić Reserve.

Marija strode ahead, looking every bit like one of the puffed up bantam hens she allowed to free range all over her property. In her colourful traditional Croatian dress, with flowing floral sleeves and pleated skirt billowing in the breeze of her brisk steps, she led the way from the van, pausing now and then to check on her unruly brood trailing behind, each one burdened with their share of the items. Unperturbed by the weight of the enormous plastic storage container in her own arms, she responded to Grace's noisy faltering progress with a theatrical roll of her eyes.

Blair hefted her load with ease, two of her trademark bright landscape paintings, one stashed under each arm, while Archie toted a third larger one balanced on his head. Two of Grace's brothers each carried a pair of unruly easels, their unwieldy dimensions causing the boys to lurch from side to side as if a little drunk. Grace's father came next, bumping a wheeled trolley over the uneven ground of the pathway, accompanied by the faint clink of eight dozen bottles of extra virgin olive oil hand-pressed from Marija's grove of organic trees. Bringing up the rear, Grace's youngest brother followed Archie's lead. He crouched under a tall sign on which Blair had neatly painted a list of the produce for sale.

Marija navigated through hordes of similar groups converging on the row of red and white tents. Finding her allocated booth, she beckoned them across. She took a moment to greet her immediate neighbours in a flurry of hugs and double-cheeked kisses. Then, surveying the space, she began firing directions at her exhausted crew.

In less than two hours, crowds of people would pour into the reserve for the annual 'Dallies In The Valley' festival. A hum of excitement filled the air, as these descendants of earlier immigrants to the valley busied themselves at the colourful stalls.

Within fifteen minutes, neat pyramids of jars and clusters of bottles lined up with military precision waited on a tablecloth made from a huge Croatian flag. Blair's paintings provided a colourful backdrop. She didn't expect to sell any, having offered them simply to give the stall a splash of colour and a point of difference from others in the row. Cassie noted the glow of pride as her mother arranged them, the huge iridescent southern landscapes captured in wild swirling brushstrokes filling the space.

It wasn't likely that many people with enough money to buy a Blair Silvestri original would be in the crowd today. Still, Cassie knew a sale would make a welcome addition to the weekly household income and boost her mother's mood. While they might live rent free, and her father sent generous support from his modest academic salary, an artist's earnings, even those of an established one like her mother who could command high prices for her work, were unpredictable. In response, and perhaps fuelled by memories of the time when she actually was a struggling artist, Blair had cultivated a frugal approach to life over the years. Cassie found her harping on about money being tight, even when it wasn't, to be one of her more annoying habits.

"Right, my darlings," said Marija, surveying the stall with approval. "Why don't you run off and get yourself something to eat? If you get in now before they let the public through the gates, you'll have your pick."

They needed no encouragement, drawn to the bustling food area. Cheerful recorded folk music blaring from a set of speakers hinted at the live bands to come. Beneath the shade of a large marquee, laden spits rotated lazily over smouldering coals, under the watchful eye of two grumpy looking chefs. The tantalising smell of roasting meat drifted across, eliciting audible growls from Cassie's stomach. Roused early by Blair's way too cheerful voice, breakfast was now a distant memory.

"I'd never admit it to Mum, but it's actually quite fun," Grace said, as they strolled towards the food stalls that were already doing a brisk trade.

"The best thing is, once she gets here, she pretty much forgets we even exist. Not that you can get up to much. Someone will always report back through the Dallie grapevine. Always too interested in everyone else's business," she said with a sigh.

Grace led the way to a stall, where already a small queue had formed. "These are the best," she said. "Fritule, a Croatian version of a donut." A sweet aroma drifted from the pan of bubbling oil, and Cassie, already drifting in a haze of longing, startled at Grace's sudden hiss in her ear. "He's here."

"What?" She turned, scanning the people milling around like ants. "Who's here? Liam?"

Grace's summer crush showed no signs of abating. Spurred on by their brief conversation that first lunchtime, crowded around the fight, Grace had firmly set her sights on Liam Keenan. Since then, they'd spent a large part of each day stalking the poor guy, creating a detailed outline of his timetable and artfully engineering 'chance' meetings. But a traditional Croatian festival seemed an unlikely place for Liam to be spending his Saturday morning.

"*No*, Nik Francovic," she said, voice secretive, as if lining him up as the next target for their private investigator activities.

"So?" Cassie glanced across, following Grace's gaze. Nik stood behind the counter of a wide booth under a banner that read 'Francovic Wines'. His family must be one of the swag of Croatian wine-makers who had made their homes in this valley, with its unique climate perfect for growing grapes. Nik's muscular arms flexed as he worked. He arranged bottles of wine in neat rows, some dark bronze, others a soft delicate green. White labels with an intricate red and gold logo wrapped around each. Even amongst what she presumed to be the Francovic family, he stood out, with his large frame and shock of blonde hair at odds with the cluster of finely built, dark-haired people milling around him in the tent.

"So, don't you want to talk to him? I think he likes you." Grace shot her a sly grin.

"I don't think a smile and a wave getting on the bus is enough to say he likes me." Although she outwardly scoffed at Grace's suggestion, the memory of the look in his eyes accompanying that small bit of attention told Cassie that Grace was right. Even after such a brief meeting, Nik *was* at least a bit interested in her. But if he was, he hadn't followed up on it. "And I haven't seen him since. If he liked me, don't you think he would have made the effort to come and talk to me? After all, he's had four days and I'm not exactly difficult to find."

The Year 13 group tended to stick to themselves, hanging out in and around their common room. In the entire first week of school, she hadn't seen Nik there once.

As if sensing their attention, Nik looked up from the stack of cartons he'd unloaded and zeroed in on them. Uncanny how, in the growing crowd, his gaze should fall right on her. The tilt of his chin in acknowledgment and the lazy smile that crept across his face brought unexpected tingles. The possibility that he might even speak to her triggered a delicious ripple of excitement.

The circumstances of their meeting and his mysterious absence from school life imbued him with a certain roguish appeal. That should be a warning in itself. For some reason she didn't understand, Cassie found nice guys boring. Not that Tekapo or Fairlie were overflowing with rebels, but she'd always been drawn to the boys that her parents and even her friends told her to stay away from. And that had led her close to disaster once already.

Nik gave off the same suggestion of danger that never failed to ignite a spark of interest on her part. But her wiser self recognised it and hopefully knew better how to deal with it. And the bold confidence with which he'd waded in to break up the fight suggested a basic underlying decency.

Certainly, he'd dealt with Archie and the other boy more fairly than she'd expected. She hoped Nik's family didn't plan to keep him busy all day. Then, maybe, he'd prove wrong the doubts she'd voiced to Grace, and seek her out.

With tubs of donuts warming their hands, Cassie and Grace found seats under a huge pohutukawa, its gnarled spreading branches providing welcome shade from the blast of sun. The colourful bean bag chairs scattered underneath the tree looked like giant toadstools in a bizarre fairy ring.

The donuts were as delicious as Grace had promised; crispy on the outside and a fluffy cloud-like interior, sweet with a zing of zesty lemon. Cassie scoffed half of her tub in minutes. As she greedily reached for the next, a hand snaked over her shoulder and lifted one out.

"Hey." She turned an indignant face on the thief, expecting to see Archie. But instead, Nik Francovic leaned over her, offering a teasing grin as he popped the donut into his mouth. It disappeared in one swallow while he licked powdered sugar from his fingertips.

"A bit bloody cheeky," she said, unable to prevent her own matching grin.

"Just call it payment for saving your little brother," he said. "My services come cheap."

She suppressed the sudden urge to wipe off the white smudge of sugar on his lip, but seeing her stare, he stretched out his tongue and swept it away. That small gesture set off an unexpected flurry of butterflies in her stomach that grew into a frenzy as he tossed a beanbag chair on the other side of her and folded his large body into it.

"So, how do you like it so far?" he asked.

"What? School? Auckland?"

"Well, those too. But how do you like our big day out?" He waved a hand at the line of stalls and the floods of people now pouring through the main gate.

"Loving it—up until some guy mugged me for my donuts."

With a smirk, he reached over and took a second. "Better get myself another before they're all gone."

She lunged at the donut, but he held his arm high in the air. She scrambled helplessly as he taunted her, waving his hand just beyond her reach, but failed to prevent him from dispatching it between two rows of even white teeth.

"I thought you fought the bullies, not that you *were* the bully." She slumped back into her seat, crossing her arms, and twisting her mouth into a mock pout.

"I hate to tell you, but you look kind of cute when you're pissed off." His laugh matched the sheer size of him, booming out from deep in that broad chest. A pair of eyes sparking with trouble looked down at her from under a wayward swathe of hair. As he pushed it back with one sweep of his large hand, she caught a flash of metal.

A black leather band sat tight against his wrist, similar to those she'd seen other guys wear. But a piece of glinting silver encircled it, unlike anything she'd ever seen before. The intricate form of a dragon rested against the leather, wings furled against its body, the long reptilian tail curled in a neat spiral. Seeing the direction of her gaze, he let his arm fall to his side, obscuring her view. And before she could ask about it, Grace broke the moment, rising to her feet, her empty tub cast onto the ground.

"Want a drink? I'll shout you a Coke," she offered.

"Sure. Thanks. I'll get the next one." Even the shady tree provided no relief from the rising temperature. A cold drink would be welcome.

"Back soon. You kids behave," she said, waggling a finger at them.

Cassie relaxed back on her beanbag, eyes hidden under her sunglasses, wondering now she had Nik all to herself, what the hell was she going to say to him. Luckily, he solved the problem for her.

"I presume your brother's keeping out of trouble?" he asked. "You haven't needed to wade into any more of his brawls the rest of the week?"

"No, he's been lying low. So, why'd you do it?" Cassie said, rolling up on one elbow to face him. "Break up the fight?" She'd thought about it often since. Why did a senior bother to step into a fight between two Year 10 kids? It wasn't as if there were even prefects or anything. The school had a fairly relaxed attitude and its students tended to match it.

"Like I said to that little shit who was thumping him—I can't stand bullies. When you've been the kid getting thumped, you can't just stand by and watch."

"You?" she choked out in disbelief.

The vehemence in his voice and the dark look in his eyes suggested more to the story. But surely no one would pick on such a huge guy. Seeing her frown, and the way her eyes roved across his thick muscular arms pressing hard against his t-shirt, a smile broke free of his scowl.

"Yeah, I grew. But it wasn't so many years ago that I don't remember what it was like to be on the receiving end of bullies. It's only a matter of time when you're a teenage boy with a girl's name."

"Nik?" she asked, her frown deepening.

"Nikola." He said it 'Neee-ko-la', with an exotic rhythm. "Or 'Nicola' to the average New Zealander. The teachers don't bother to say it right—and bullies don't care if it's spelled with a 'k' or a 'c'. Being born here, my father at least should have been smart enough to know that some Croatian names don't work too well in West Auckland."

"No, I can imagine. Neither do ones from Greek mythology—like Arcturus."

"Yeah," he said. "I felt sorry for the kid. What were your parents thinking?"

"That's what happens when your dad's an astronomer and your mother is a hopeless romantic. You get named after a star."

"But you got lucky. Cassie's pretty normal."

"Nope," she said, unable to prevent her mouth pursing tight, her instinctive reaction to any discussion of her name. "It's short for Cassiopeia. Also Greek. Archie got a star. I got a whole constellation."

"That's not so bad. Sounds sort of cool. Cassiopeia." He rolled the word around on his tongue, experimenting with the syllables. It slipped from his lips in a gentle flow, with a delicate cadence she'd never heard before. Hearing her name anew in that deep voice triggered a flutter in her stomach. She wanted to hear it again, watch his mouth say the name she'd worn for all those years, and hated for most of them, to hear it offered in a way that lent it an unexpected beauty. As if reading her mind, he said it again. "Cassiopeia. It's pretty." He hesitated for a moment, a hint of shyness in his eyes. "It suits you." He flushed a little, but didn't look away.

Under that steady blue gaze, heat washed up her own cheeks. As always, she was unsure of the compliment. She didn't see herself as pretty. Yes, her deep copper hair, a far less riotous shade of red than her brother's, might be the sort of colour other girls looked for on the supermarket shelves. She'd spent afternoons with friends, helping them apply cheap hair dye, seeking to add a flash of warmth to their own less attractive brown shade. She supposed she should be grateful that nature had chosen to give her a colour that others desired. Just as she thanked the genetic lottery for the faint smattering of freckles inherited from her mother, unlike Archie's excess, that often attracted unkind taunts. She didn't consider herself vain like her mythological namesake, but nor did she dislike the face that looked back at her from the mirror.

And the way Nik stared at her in that moment left no doubt he liked what he saw. She broke away in confusion, awkwardness at witnessing his blatant attraction competing with the sensations bubbling up from low in her body.

"So, that's your family you're helping out over there?" she asked, attempting to steer the conversation back to safer territory.

"Yeah, my grandparents started the business, but now it's my dad and my uncle. They grow the grapes, make the wine; use us kids as cheap labour." He laughed. "In the big picture, it's not a huge day for them. Most of our wine goes to wholesalers, a bit at the cellar door. But they love it. Wouldn't miss a chance to catch up with all their Dallie mates."

"Are you on a break, then?"

"Nah, once we're set up, I'm off the hook for the rest of the day. Not old enough to sell alcohol legally."

"Convenient."

"Very. What about you two?"

"Same, unless they sell out and we have to help load the van, I think." She tossed a questioning look at Grace, who stood over them, passing an overfull cup that rattled with ice, the foam of Coke lapping at the brim.

"Doesn't matter if they do," Grace replied. "No way Mum's going anywhere early."

Nik laughed. "Yeah, they'll all sit around after the public has gone and sing and talk and get pissed. Hate to tell you, but you'll be lucky to get home before dark."

"God, last year Mum drank so much rakija she could hardly stand. Dad tossed up about putting her on the trolley to take her back to the van. And I swear I heard her throwing up in the middle of the night." Grace wrinkled her nose in distaste. "Gross."

"Oh yeah, I heard Marija was the life of the party. That party anyway." He flashed an enigmatic smile.

"What Nik hasn't told you is, while he's not legally allowed to *sell* the alcohol, it doesn't stop him drinking it. Or giving it away." Grace shot him a knowing look.

"Gracie," he said through a laugh. "You know you want to join us again. Come on, bring Cassie with you." He turned to Cassie. "What Grace hasn't told you is the best party happens down at the river. About five-thirty. Gives the oldies time to get to the point they don't care what the hell their kids are doing." He nodded towards a small sign that pointed towards a bush track. "Take that path over there." The words read 'Fairy Pool, 5 Minutes'.

"Don't worry, we'll be there," Grace promised, not giving Cassie any say in the matter. But she would have agreed, anyway. They couldn't let the adults have all the fun. And although she wouldn't admit it to anyone yet, not even Grace, Nik had definitely got her attention. No way she'd turn down an invitation from him.

"You better or I'll come and get you." He rose to his feet, shooting a two-fingered guns out gesture at them. "Right, I should head back. They can always use some help behind the scenes. Five-thirty. Don't be late," he called over his shoulder as he ambled across the grass.

Cassie lay back on her bean bag, her stomach clenching as dark-winged moths of fear battled with whirling butterflies of anticipation. She'd allowed Nik Francovic to step inside the wall, and she didn't want to push him back outside. This was the first small risk she'd taken in over a year, and still it felt huge.

CHAPTER 3

Rescuer

Auckland, New Zealand – February 2009

AROUND FIVE-THIRTY, THEY SLIPPED away along the wide bush track. It took a meandering path along a high bank, then narrowed, plunging steeply downwards towards the water below. Lush ferns sprouted on either side, surging over Cassie's feet. They also masked a hidden hazard, the network of twisting tree roots that criss-crossed the path, as if seeking to trip or trap them. The damp mustiness of the forest floor drifted up to meet her with each careful step.

"Whatever you do," Grace warned as they grew closer to the voices that echoed off the banks, "if someone offers you rakija, *do not drink it.*"

"I don't even know what it is."

"Like rocket fuel. A kind of brandy. Favourite Croatian booze, but it's *really* strong. I swear you do not want to even try it. Don't worry, you'll know. One sniff of it is enough to burn your nose hairs."

Cassie hoped she wasn't about to look stupid or immature, arriving with a bottle of Coke clutched in one hand. Without advance warning of this party, it was her only option. Apparently other kids came prepared, lifting booze from their parents' stalls or stealing it from home liquor cabinets. With a mysterious smile, Grace had assured her it would be fine.

The last few wooden steps cut into the bank were as steep as descending a ladder. Grace stretched up a hand to help Cassie down to the sand where a wide beach bordered a large, deep green pool. Here the main course of the river veered away around a bend, leaving this abandoned patch of stillness.

To their right, a cluster of boys sat perched on rocks, their eyes firmly fixed on a single girl who sat in their centre. Her long dark hair trailed in waves down her back and she tossed it in time to the rhythm of tinkling laughter, one dark brow quirking up in playful amusement at something one of the boys had said. Noticing Grace and Cassie's arrival, for a moment the boys' attention turned their way, but seeing nothing more compelling, every pair of eyes flickered back to the girl—except for one. Nik nodded towards them, as if marking their presence with approval.

They hadn't seen him all afternoon, and Cassie suspected that although he hadn't been selling the wine, he had kept busy helping with the family stall. He hadn't come back to join them under the pohutukawa where they'd spent the afternoon happily gossiping, while Grace went on missions to return with one after the other of Croatian foods to tempt her.

Cassie inwardly groaned, thinking of it, the uncomfortable, overfull feeling still pressing against her stomach.

Grace led them further down the beach to where a group of girls sat on another tumble of rocks. Cassie recognised a few from school. They met Grace's exuberant wave with familiar murmurs of welcome, suggesting she knew them all.

Cassie hung behind Grace, shy under the inquiring gaze of the group. She was suddenly acutely aware of her 1950s style playsuit with its scarlet bottom and halterneck top of a jaunty cherry-patterned fabric. This morning, looking in the mirror, she'd thought it such a cute outfit for a summer day. Now it simply marked her as the odd one out amongst all these girls in shorts and t-shirts.

"This is Cassie," Grace said, "my friend who's just moved up from the South Island." Another round of greetings came her way, accompanied by unexpected friendly smiles.

"Hi," she replied, exhaling in relief. It wasn't usual to find this ready acceptance in a new group of teenagers. School had been tricky even with the support of Grace's friendship. Navigating the inevitable hidden undercurrents of the teenage social scene presented an ever-shifting challenge. But these Dallie kids seemed different; as if like a huge extended family, they willingly included everyone, no matter how small or distant the relationship.

Grace clambered onto an old log lying next to the rocks, patting the space next to it, indicating room for Cassie. Slipping off her backpack, she rummaged inside ,producing two plastic cups and an aluminium drink flask.

"Here, hold these."

Cassie took the two cups in exchange for the bottle of Coke. Grace wrestled with the bottle lid, trying to loosen it off at the same time as preventing the ominous fizzing of its contents, shaken up by the walk, from becoming an explosion. Even so, it foamed dangerously close to the rim of each cup as she poured their drink. Next, she grabbed the flask and added a careful slosh of amber liquid to each cup.

"Coruba. Rum. And yes, you guessed right—I pinched it from home. Mum and Dad never drink it, anyway. I'm sure someone left it behind after a party one night."

"Are you sure? I've only ever drunk wine and beer."

Cassie's parents had a liberal attitude toward alcohol. She'd tasted it from an early age, and while she didn't drink it often, she accepted the offer of a glass of sweet bubbly at Christmas or a tumbler of her dad's beer around the family barbecue in the summer. But never spirits. She cast a wary glance at the dark mixture, wondering about the possible effects, as a whiff of alcohol drifted in the air. Grace, seeing the doubt, rushed to reassure her.

"Don't worry, it's only a little to liven things up a bit."

"Probably just as well we've loaded the van already?"

"Nah, you'll be fine. Honestly, it's only a splash. You won't get drunk on that amount. Besides, if getting off your face was the only objective, I'd have brought vodka. Cheers." Grace tapped her cup against Cassie's.

It wasn't strong; in fact, the rum added a delicious, sweetly spicy depth to the Coke. After a few mouthfuls, she also decided Grace was right: she couldn't feel anything remotely like inebriation sneaking up on her, only a pleasant warmth that might be as much from the company of these chattering girls as the drink.

However, it wasn't long before another more nagging sensation pushed its way forward. No matter how much she tried to ignore it, her bladder became more and more insistent, reminding her of all the liquid she'd consumed over the last few hours while warding off the heat of the afternoon.

"Grace." She leaned in close to her friend's ear. "I need to pee."

"Just go in the bushes." Grace's casual suggestion brought a rush of horror. "That's what everyone else does."

"I'm *not* peeing in the bushes. What if someone sees?"

Grace sighed. "Well, it's a long walk back to the loos. And all uphill."

"Yeah, I don't think I could hold on that long, anyway," she said as her need rapidly edged towards physical pain. What was it about the urge to pee? Somehow, the moment you thought about it, your body became desperate.

"Look," Grace said, sensing her distress, "go down the beach a bit, round that little bend, and then duck into the bushes. If it makes you feel better, I'll stand watch on the sand." With a sigh, she rose to her feet. Propping their cups against the log, they set off on their mission.

Afterwards, as they strolled back up the beach, echoes of raised male voices bounced off the river banks. Rounding the curve, the source of the uproar came into view. Nik Francovic towered over another boy, his fist curled tight around the boy's shirt, his face contorted into a snarl. By his feet, two plastic cups lay on their sides, their contents already soaking into the sand. He gave the boy a shove, sending him sprawling.

Interrupted by their approach, Nik looked their way. The boy, sensing an opportunity from this momentary distraction, gathered himself up, raced to the base of the steps, and began climbing, hurried on by Nik, who whirled to take a last threatening step towards him.

"Oh, my god. What the hell is going on?" Grace stared down at the mess of their spilled drinks. Every other face turned towards Nik, all seeking an explanation.

"Little bastard spiked your drinks. With this." He reached over to pick up a narrow bottle from where it lay discarded behind the log. "Rakija. The pair of you would have been off your faces if you'd drunk that."

"Don't you think we might have noticed? I mean, we're not exactly stupid, Nik." Grace had a point. They'd have noticed something off for sure.

"Even so, he shouldn't be *doing* shit like that." He jabbed an indignant finger towards the track where the rustle of the undergrowth marked the path of the fleeing boy. "Tonight he does it to you. Next time it might be someone who doesn't notice. You don't *do* that." Nik glared at her, adamant. "Not when I'm around, anyway."

"OK, I get it." Grace's appeasing tone seemed to soothe him, his face relaxing back into a more neutral expression. "Thank you for looking out for us. You're right, it is a shitty thing to do." She retrieved the two cups, brushing off the crust of sand on their rims and set to refilling them with Coke.

Cassie watched Nik stomp back towards the other group, pausing to lock eyes with her for a moment, a shy smile spreading across his face. He took his place on a rock at the edge of the circle, a bottle of beer in his hand, staring out across the river while the conversation restarted around him. A moment later he lifted the bottle, downed the contents before casting it into a box where it clanged against the other empties. Without a word of farewell, he set off up the stairs towards the reserve.

"Well, that was a bit of excitement for the night." Grace giggled as she rummaged in her pack for the flask. "Nik Francovic, to the rescue of the Tremayne family twice in a week." She wiggled her eyebrows in amusement. "Although, tonight he definitely came to *your* rescue."

"I don't think that was about me," Cassie huffed in disbelief. Nik had an obvious sense of right and wrong and wasn't averse to handing out his own brand of justice to people who stepped over the line. No, he would have nabbed that guy, no matter whose drinks he'd been doctoring with rakija.

"Oh no, you're so wrong there." Grace shook her head, her grin wide. "Cassie, that was *all* about you."

As she watched his large form disappear into the trees at the top of the stairs, Cassie sipped at her drink, mulling over Grace's words and washing down the faint taste of her disappointment. The exuberant butterflies in her stomach quieted and while the sun still gilded the leafy branches high above their heads, somehow the shine had gone off the day.

CHAPTER 4

Mother

Auckland, New Zealand – February 2009

NIK NUDGED OPEN THE door, feeling like he should have knocked first, despite this being his own home. On nights like this, when his parents sequestered themselves in the tiny bar room off the main lounge, it sent an unspoken message that he and his five siblings all understood: keep out unless the house is on fire or someone needs an ambulance.

However, tonight, while there was no immediate emergency, his questions were too important to be left for another time. He wouldn't sleep until he had definite answers. His mind buzzed with a plan, but to make it work, first he needed to confirm his father's agreement that, since he'd helped at the festival all day, he didn't need to make up his usual Saturday hours in the winery tomorrow. And more importantly, and more difficult to achieve, he needed his mother's permission to use her car.

While she usually begrudgingly agreed to let him borrow it, Sundays came with special conditions. On Sundays, to emphasise the point that she would prefer he'd accompany the family to Mass at St Joseph's in Henderson first, even though he'd long abandoned the weekly ritual, she insisted that he couldn't have the car until after the traditional family lunch. And usually he accepted that without argument. But this Sunday was different. He wanted to make an early start, leaving the whole day open to possibility.

It had been less than a week since Cassie Tremayne had fallen into his life, but she occupied his every waking thought. Images of her played in his head on repeat; the sight of her shoving her way through the crowd of feral school kids while attempting to rescue her brother; stretching out those satin smooth golden legs in front of her as she lay in a beanbag, with dainty feet tucked inside little red shoes; descending from the steps out of the bush, dressed in those odd colourful clothes, like some exotic species of bird that had lost its way, coming to land amongst a flock of squawking pigeons; her tumble of dark hair, neither red nor brown, bouncing on her shoulders as she walked away along the sandy riverside.

He wanted to make more of those movies in his head. He wanted to feature in them alongside her. And where better than at the beach on a summer Sunday. Not just any beach, but Karekare, with its spectacular crashing surf and sparkling black sand. It was beautiful there, and being more remote, often near deserted.

He cringed at the thought of taking her somewhere, only to run into others from school. He was hungry for time with her on his own, didn't want to share her with anyone else, didn't want other guys talking and laughing with her; didn't want other girls, not even her friend, Grace Taylor, competing with him for her attention.

It could have waited until morning, but now was the perfect time to ask something of his mother—because his normally authoritative and rather formidable mother was drunk. And Antonija Francovic was a happy, benevolent drunk.

It was a windfall that after her hard work in the heat of the day down at the reserve, his mother had decreed his father, Ivan, should be the sober driver while she had a few drinks with her Dallie friends. Returning from the river, Nik knew she had a good few glasses of rakija on board the moment he saw her laughing and singing, one arm draped around the shoulder of her best mate, Millie Vella.

He'd realised just how far gone she was when they arrived home. Vision blurred by alcohol, his mother had to look twice to work out which of his younger twin brothers was still lolling on the couch next door instead of following her directive to go to bed.

And Nik knew, even though it was rare to see her like this, alcohol also softened her normally abrasive attitude to the world. This was why she didn't reprimand him, as she normally would for his intrusion. And why he chose to make his request now.

As he moved towards her, the distinctive smell of rakija drifted on the air. A glass of the pale golden liquid sat beside her. His father clutched a beer, the condensation sitting in jewel-like beads on the bottle neck. The windowless room felt thick and heavy with the remnants of the day's warmth.

"Nik, darling," she cooed at him. She lay along the couch, her feet resting across his father's lap. She stretched her toes, with their scarlet painted nails, like a cat flexing its claws. "Come and sit with your mama."

She swung her legs down, patting the space next to her. He did as she said, trying to recall the time in his life when she'd been like this all the time, not just when basking in the glow of alcohol. Back when he was small, he had vague recollections of this softer, kinder version of his mother showing up without assistance.

Like all children, he had only hazy memories of those early years, before his next two siblings arrived, a sister two years younger than him, then, a year later, another. But he had this sense that even as the family grew, things had been fine, happy even. He even suspected that things had still been OK when the twins were born, and he was five.

But at age nine, when baby Lana unexpectedly showed up, he was old enough to remember clearly, and knew that was when things had really gone awry. At first, after bringing the new baby home, his mother had existed in a sad, vague bubble, often languishing in her room, only leaving it when necessary, and going through the motions of motherhood like a robot.

Then his father had summoned Aunty Svetjlana, who swept into their home like a tornado, taking over care of her tiny namesake, bottle feeding Lana, ordering around the rest of them like a drill sergeant, and exerting her method of tough love on her sister. He could still hear the conversations; remembered the tense scenes.

"Antonija, get up." He'd watched Aunty Lana tear away the sheet, glaring at her sister huddled beneath it. "Toni, you're not staying in bed all day. I am not your servant."

And under the relentless barrage, slowly, Toni Francovic emerged from the shadows. But it was a different woman than the one they had known. It seemed from that time on, his mother only coped with life by putting on a suit of cold steel, going on the attack rather than waiting to defend, and wielding her sharp tongue as her weapon of choice.

The last few years, she'd become worse. His father let her foul moods slide across him, passive in his acceptance, spending most of his time at the winery beyond her temper. Ivana and Mila, the older of his sisters, clashed with her daily, muttering behind her back about hormones and menopause, but not offering her a drop of feminine understanding if that was the reason. He and the twins, Marko and Viktor, generally adopted his father's approach, trying to stay out of the line of fire. And Lana, well she'd had it the toughest, Toni picking relentlessly at her youngest, as if she blamed her for everything that was wrong in the world.

As his mother lay against him, pulling him close, her head on his shoulder, he waited, breathing in the familiar perfume and revelling in the unfamiliar warmth, not wanting to break the moment.

"Did you have fun today?" Her words slurred in his ear, the lingering smell of the spirits on her breath.

"I did Mum. But not as much as you, I think."

She giggled girlishly. "You're a good boy Nik. Helping your mum and dad today. Thank you."

"Yeah, thanks son," his father added, while smiling across at his wife in amusement. "Toni's right. You're a good kid."

Here was his moment. "Dad, do you think I could leave dealing with that back storeroom till after school on Monday?"

"Sure, I think we could all take a day off tomorrow."

"Take the day," his mother echoed, stroking his hair absently. "Go have some fun."

"OK if I borrow the car tomorrow morning, Mum?"

"Of course," she said. "You're such a good boy."

He felt a slight twinge of guilt at taking advantage of her state, but he pushed it aside with thoughts of Cassie. Whatever it took, even conning his drunk mother, he needed to see her.

Bit by bit, the caress of his mother's hand slowed and then stopped, her body growing heavy against his. He turned his head to his father, who quietly sipped at his beer.

"Dad," he breathed, not wanting to wake her, "I think Mum's ready for bed."

"Yeah," said his father, smiling across at her, as she let out a tiny snore. "You wanna take her?"

"Sure."

Nik gently slid an arm beneath his mother's tiny form. It felt like he was the parent and she the child, as he lifted her effortlessly and carried her down to her bedroom.

He pulled up a sheet, adjusted the pillow, and arranged the covers over her legs. He stood for a moment, examining her features in the glow of the bedside lamp. She was still a beautiful woman for her age, especially sleeping like this, with no trace of the world weariness that usually haunted her face. Nik loved his mother, even though she wasn't an easy person to love, even though he very often didn't like her. He suspected she felt the same about him in return.

CHAPTER 5

Friend or Foe

Auckland, New Zealand – February 2009

CASSIE'S FINGERS FLEW ACROSS the keyboard. She'd never admit to anyone, not even Grace, that she loved homework. Well, not all homework, but English homework. Especially when it coincided with doing the thing she loved best in the world—writing. One day, this was all she'd do. Visions of feeling the weight of a real life book in her hands, reading her name across the cover, spurred her on.

She'd managed to suppress a smug smile of delight at receiving the first assignment of the year on Friday—surrounded by a chorus of unimpressed groans from her classmates. 'Dallies in the Valley', and her mother's insistence they help Marija, had thwarted her enthusiasm to start on it straight away. So now, on Sunday morning, she'd only just begun. But already a page of carefully crafted words stared back at her.

Her English teacher had given them free rein with this one, a chance to show what they could do and what they enjoyed. So that's what it was: fantasy with a medieval feel, although she wasn't sure about the romantic subplot that two of her main characters seemed to be hatching without her permission. She smiled to herself and kept typing. The *Twilight* soundtrack drifted through her headset, setting the mood, while drowning out the irritating cicadas who had kept up their raucous celebration of summer since a little after dawn.

"Cassie?" Her mother's sharp voice penetrated the music. "Your friend's here."

The words jolted her out of her work, provoking an immediate question—which friend? The only person she could call a friend so far here in Auckland was Grace, and surely she would have come straight in. The two families had already got into the habit of treating each other's neighbouring houses like an extension of their own home. Archie had already made the trek down their long twisty driveway and up the next, joining Grace's brothers in saving the world by killing zombies on the PlayStation, leaving her own house blanketed in blissful peace.

So if it wasn't Grace, who was it? Torn between reluctance to leave her writing while the words flowed easily, and curiosity about her 'friend', she sat for a moment, listening for a clue. Her mother's purposeful footsteps bounced off the wooden boards of the ground floor in the direction of her studio. While helping Marija yesterday had required a sacrifice of time on Blair's part, she had made an unexpected sale of one of her bold oil paintings. Today, in a cheerful and productive mood, she had dived straight into work.

As the flapping of Blair's Birkenstocks faded to nothing, a faint impatient tapping echoed through the empty house. Whoever it was, she'd better not keep them waiting any longer or the annoying rhythm might interrupt her mother's work for a second time and she would not be happy. She closed the laptop with a click and headed downstairs.

Pausing at the lounge door, she peeked through the gap. She glimpsed a large, hairy male knee protruding from a pair of shorts. It jiggled up and down, tap, tap, tap, in a nervous staccato of bare toes on wooden floorboards. She pushed the door wide, and its owner swivelled a tousled blonde head towards her.

"Nik." The intriguing Mr Francovic perched on the edge of an old orange paisley moon chair. He not only overflowed the seat, he dominated the tiny lounge room of the cottage. Surely her mother should have pointed him at somewhere more suitable. Unless she'd deliberately thought to prevent him from getting too comfortable. Anything was possible with Blair.

"Hi," he said, his voice soft and hesitant. That awkward smile bloomed on his face at the same time as a wash of colour rose up his neck. This guy was such a contradiction. Twice now she'd seen him in the role of fierce avenging angel, powered by a barely restrained aggression, unafraid to wade right in and deal with a situation. And yet, in his encounters with her, she'd sensed this underlying current of shyness. It pushed forward now, even though he abandoned the agitated fidgeting.

"Hope you don't mind me just turning up like this. I was just driving past, and I heard you lived next to Grace." He took a cautious tone. And so he should when he was already telling little white lies. *Just driving past?* There were only a handful of houses beyond hers on this road that wound up into the Waitakere ranges.

"Where did you hear that?" She tried to make it a casual inquiry rather than a suspicious question.

"From her mum. Marija called over to have a chat with my parents at the stall yesterday. They asked about your family. They always have to know everything that's going on out this way. So I kind of overheard."

"And so you told my mum you were my friend, and she just let you in?" She couldn't help but smile. A move to the big, bad city had done nothing to alter her mother's relaxed attitude. Unlike most parents, she hadn't stopped to interrogate the enormous young man who'd shown up on their doorstep claiming to be a friend.

"Well, we are sort of, aren't we? We know each other. You couldn't say we're enemies. Unless you've got a thing about donut thieves."

"No one in their right mind would want to be your enemy." The laughter tumbled out unbidden, a vision of Nik throttling the drink-spiker dancing in front of her. "I've seen what happens to those."

"Yeah. We possibly haven't got off to the best start." He dropped his head, and his leg once more began to move of its own accord. "You might find it hard to believe, but I don't go around looking for trouble." Another faint blush accompanied his apologetic tone.

"It just finds you?"

"Sometimes, unfortunately." He let out a resigned sigh. "I suppose I'm one of those people who can't let arseholes get away with bad behaviour. Life would be easier if I could ignore it. But I can't." His posture straightened a little, as if confidence grew from defending his position.

"Maybe you should join the police," she joked. "You've got the build for it too." She couldn't help her gaze drifting across his muscular chest and broad shoulders, barely disguised by his t-shirt. "Hey, I get it. The world would be a better place if more people were brave enough to face down bullies and jerks." She had to admit to her gratitude for his intervention on both occasions.

"And like you," he said. "I saw you step into the middle of that fight at school. I'd consider that pretty brave."

"Not really." She snorted, dismissing the compliment. "All I did was stand there and yell, and that didn't work. Besides, he's my brother. I kind of had to try."

"He's a lucky kid to have a sister like you who would try. My sisters sure wouldn't."

"I imagine your sisters don't need to."

"Well yeah, being the oldest, and a fair bit bigger than them, I do tend to fight my own battles."

"How many sisters do you have?"

"Three. And two brothers. A great big happy Catholic family of six."

"Wow, that is a big family." She couldn't imagine what it would be like to have a pack of siblings. One was more than enough.

"Yeah, my parents were slow starters, but once they found out where they were going wrong, they didn't hold back." The tight set of his jaw matched the bitter tone. For a brief unguarded moment, emotion flitted across his eyes; a glimmer of pain, or maybe sadness. But it disappeared in an instant, as he drew down the blinds, shutting it away behind hooded lids.

"Anyway." He flipped to a new, less troubling topic. "I came over to see if you might be brave enough for something else." He arched a brow, tossing another one of those enigmatic smiles that surfaced without warning.

"Depends what it is. I can tell you now I'm *not* into adventure sports, so if it involves heights, high speed or anything dangerous, count me out." While new places and people excited her, she'd never understand the thrill of physical danger. She'd even shunned the roller coaster at Rainbow's End, holding out against her little brother's jeering sneer.

"Nah, not dangerous. Not unless I fall into that category." His mouth turned up in a lopsided grin.

It was an innocuous comment to anyone but her. Even though Nik's sheer physical size made him intimidating, emphasised by his proximity in this cramped room, that wasn't what bothered her. Spending time with Nik meant she must grapple with the fear that simmered away beneath the surface. She'd tried to bury her mistrust of guys. They weren't all like the one who'd pinned her beneath him in a car in a remote spot, who had come close to hurting her, who had left her scared and wary. Everything she knew about Nik so far suggested he definitely wasn't like that, and if he was, surely Grace would have warned her off him. Even so, her guard flew up, a reflex reaction.

"I don't know…"

"Look, it's not a big deal. I'm just heading out to the beach and I thought you might like to come for a drive."

"The beach?"

"Yeah. Karekare. It's not far from here. Have you ever been?"

"No. Only Piha and Muriwai over the summer."

"This one's much better than either of those. Fewer people. More beautiful. A bit wild for swimming, but good for a walk."

She'd known this day would come, when she'd need to step outside her small safe bubble. Curiosity about Nik was the extra nudge she needed. She wasn't sure she liked him, but couldn't say she disliked him either. He'd caught her attention. And, as Grace had correctly observed, his interest in her was obvious. Why else would he turn up unannounced with the proposition of an outing? Suddenly, her writing no longer held its previous attraction.

"Sure. OK, I'll come." She said it with more conviction than she felt, pride in her courage at taking this step still mingling with doubt that she was ready.

"I'll just let Mum know."

"Grab a sweater too," he called after her. "It can be a bit breezy out there."

She told her mother simply as a courtesy. Once immersed in her art, Blair blithely gave permission for virtually anything her children asked as long as it didn't interfere with her work. Cassie and Archie played it for all they were worth, carefully choosing to bring up tricky questions while their mother was preoccupied. Blair wouldn't be the least concerned about her daughter hopping into a car with some young man she'd only laid eyes on once, and only for a moment at that.

Of course, she'd be far more protective if she knew how one of those occasions had turned out in the past. But Cassie had resolved not to tell her, not anyone, in fact. No matter how much the school counsellor had assured her it wasn't her fault, she still bore the shame of her own stupidity. She didn't plan to share what had happened with anyone, not even her mother.

With a deep breath, she stepped out the front door, closing it behind her with a definitive click of the old lock. Nik stood alongside a modest hatchback. This car definitely wouldn't stand out here in the wild west; not amongst the local guys who made a sport of illegal street races. On Saturday nights, out in the empty industrial areas, they'd bring thumping V8s to war with others driving screaming rotary-engined relics or the latest howling Japanese beasts. She wouldn't have picked Nik for a boy racer, anyway. He didn't look like the type to need a testosterone-laced vehicle to boost his ego. He wore his masculinity with graceful maturity.

Some of that grace seeped away as he folded himself into the confines of the car. His large frame overflowed the seat, filling the space with his presence. It reminded her of her dad in the dodgem cars at the Fairlie A&P Show, hunched over the wheel as he pursued a giggling Archie while she screamed encouragement, and her mother's rippling laughter spilled across the track. A little knot of melancholy twisted inside her as she accepted those days were gone.

Seeing her glance at his knees knocking against the centre console, Nik broke into a smile. "My mum's car. My parents believe in encouraging self-sufficiency. Won't buy me one until I can save up half of the money. Driving this sure gives me some incentive. That and having to face old St Chris everywhere I go."

He tapped a finger on the bling suspended from the rear-view mirror. A large St Christopher medal with a particularly ugly representation of the saint twirled hypnotically.

"At least you know how to drive." She couldn't prevent envy from creeping into her voice. "Until I learn, I'm stuck here dependent on the mum taxi. Which operates on a limited schedule."

"I'll teach you," he said. "It's easy. Especially in something like this. Any time you want, let me know. We'll go to one of the business parks. Big empty car parks on weekends. Nothing to hit."

"I might take you up on that," she said. She had lived the last nine years in a town so small that you could walk everywhere in ten minutes. Now finding herself stuck out in the country with no transport, always relying on her mother to go anywhere had started to wear thin. It was a long way from what she'd imagined when she'd chosen to move to Auckland.

He planted his foot on the accelerator and the car leapt forward with an unexpected spurt of speed, spraying gravel from the unsealed driveway before bursting onto the narrow road towards the coast. As they took the next sharp turn left, in the tight space, his shoulder brushed hers, heightening her awareness; close enough to touch, close enough to smell a faint fresh maleness; close enough to feel the warmth radiating off him. Feeling a slight intoxication at all the sensations swirling in the confines of the vehicle, she tried to drag herself back onto safer ground.

"Your mum wouldn't mind? Me learning in her car?"

"My mum won't know. But I doubt she'd care. It may come as a surprise to you, but she considers me her responsible eldest." He snorted a laugh.

"Oh yeah, tell me about it," she said, unable to repress a knowing sigh. "Me too. Unfortunately, that means they expect you to pick up responsibility for the rest as well."

He gave a resigned nod of agreement. Being the eldest of two was bad enough, but the eldest of six? That had to be tough.

"Hey, are you up for a game?" he asked, as he tossed the little car around the tight curves with a relaxed confidence. The question caught her by surprise. Playing word games in the car to pass the time? Not exactly what you'd expect from this big macho guy sitting next to her.

"Why not, as long as you're prepared for me to win? I hate to lose." She grinned at him. She loved any chance to test her quick brain against someone else. Even in sports, she made up for what she lacked in natural skill by sheer determination. Nik was in for a shock if he thought he'd easily defeat her.

"Challenge accepted," he said, matching her grin with his own confident smirk. "I hate to lose, too. So this game is perfect for us—even if you lose, you win."

"Sounds like my sort of game."

"OK, it's simple. You tell me something about yourself. I decide whether it's fact or fiction. If I'm right, it's a point to me, otherwise it's a point to you. We take turns. You keep the score so you can't accuse me of cheating when I win."

"Oh, I see, and along the way you'll have also tricked me into revealing all my secrets."

"You could say that. Or you could say that I'll have gotten to know my new friend a little better." His new friend. Interesting. She wasn't quite prepared to reciprocate with that label yet.

"You go first."

He didn't hesitate, of course—it was his game; he'd already have his facts and fiction lined up. "My five siblings all have dark hair, brown eyes, and olive skin."

"That's not a fact about you," she protested.

"Well, it is. Because they are *my* siblings and you can see that I'm blonde and blue-eyed. It's totally related. So what do you think?" He shot her a challenging glance.

"Fact." Disappointment at the speed of her reply showed in the immediate downturn of his mouth. "I know I'm right," she said. "It wasn't beginner's luck. I saw them yesterday." It was only fair to admit it.

"Ahhh, should have thought of that. But you know, I have to go easy on you at the start," he lied. "Yeah, you're right. I bear absolutely no resemblance to any of them." His words had an odd tone, like an off note in the middle of a piece of music. She glanced across, recognising that expression in his eyes again, a hint of sadness at the mention of his family. Strange, therefore, that he should choose this as his opening gambit. Like scratching at a scab that wasn't healed, perhaps it brought a strange satisfaction.

"I'm adopted."

They sat in silence, the only sound the hum of the little engine and the whirr of the air conditioning. That was a very personal fact for Nik to share with someone he barely knew, and she wondered if he regretted it. She didn't really know what to say. As if sensing the awkwardness his revelation had thrust between them, he moved on.

"Looks like it's first point to you. Now it's your turn."

"OK." She didn't pause to mull over the possibilities. Deciding not to overthink it, she went with the first thing to come into her head. "I've wanted to be a writer since I was five years old."

"Fiction," he said without hesitation.

"Bzzzt." The sound leapt from her mouth on impulse, a reflex reaction from her dad's compulsory family trivia nights. She and Archie had outwardly moaned, but secretly loved them. She never realised how much she'd miss them till they were gone.

"What the hell is that?" His choking laughter was enough to distract him from the road, almost causing him to run off it as the car swerved wildly in a patch of loose metal.

"The buzzer telling you that you're wrong," she said quietly as the car stabilised. A spontaneous bloom of heat flared on her cheeks. Something about this guy was bringing out an embarrassing touch of crazy in her. "Bad idea, seeing the effect on your driving."

"No, no," he said, still laughing. "It was cute in a weird kind of way. I'm tempted to come up with more wrong answers just to make you do it again."

"I think I value my life too much to do it again."

"Yeah, sorry about that. Don't want to kill off the author of the world's greatest ever novel before she's written it." He slowed the car making a visible effort to take the corners with more care. "So, that's what you were doing upstairs this afternoon? Writing?"

"Yup. That surprises you?"

"Not really. I only said fiction because of the way you dress. I had you picked for a future fashion designer or an artist like your mum."

His words and the quick sweep of his glance triggered a sudden self-con-sciousness. Her outfit of vintage fifties style shorts and matching floral crossover top weren't your average Westie teenager outfit. But damned if she would swap them for the weekend uniform of most girls out this way: denim cut-offs so minute their butt cheeks hung out and equally scanty tops. She hunched herself into the seat as if it might somehow provide a reprieve from his scrutiny.

"Being a writer is a great ambition," he said with a reassuring smile in response to her obvious discomfort. "Although I like how you dress, too."

By the time he'd nosed the car into a small parking area, Cassie knew that Nik was a Kiwi music lover who could rattle off random song lists and concert dates about every major band of the past twenty years. He'd also revealed himself as a reluctant rugby player. After five seasons of playing in the forward pack, hearing his neck creak with the strain of a scrum, he'd now abandoned the national sport. His death row meal choice would be macaroni cheese, and he spent his evenings listening to his favourite band, Shihad.

Meanwhile, she'd shared her obsession with *The Hunger Games*, her hatred of cockroaches, that a bearded dragon called Snoopy (who helpfully ate cockroaches) was the only pet she had ever owned—and given him no choice but to declare her the undisputed victor in his game, beating him seven points to four.

They found the bush-shrouded parking lot empty of other cars. To have a beach all to themselves so close to New Zealand's largest city would be an unexpected pleasure. She'd spent enough afternoons on bustling city beaches this summer. On the whole she found Auckland a refreshing change—its diverse population, the ability to blend in if you wanted, the anonymity of a crowd—these things appealed.

But sometimes she craved the solitude of the South Island. And thinking of home—because that's what it would always be—made her feel a little sad. She sat unmoving, wondering what Dad would be doing. There, in their house, without them. Strange, this bleak unhappiness washing over her, because he'd always travelled so much for his job, research taking him all over the world. Her whole life she'd been used to it, her, Mum and Archie in the house without him. Birthdays and Christmas phone calls from some remote dark-sky country, anywhere from the Arctic to the southern tip of the Americas. It shouldn't be any different, with them doing the same here in Auckland, carrying on life without him. But it was.

"You OK?" Nik's gentle query jerked her back from her thoughts. He leaned forward, studying her face, blue eyes alight with concern.

"Yeah, I'm OK." His penetrating gaze told her she wasn't at all convincing. Something about him made her decide to own up. Perhaps it was the honesty about his own family, his own unspoken sadness that allowed her truth to spill out. "I was thinking about my dad."

"Is it weird? You two and your mum here, and him there?"

"Not weird. Just kind of sad."

"But you'll go back. Won't you?"

She shook her head. "No. I don't think so."

"I'm sorry, I had no idea that they were like, separated," he said, his face a mask of apology.

"Well, they're *not* really. I dunno." And she really didn't. Because her father had travelled so much for work, her parents had always spent time apart, but this time it felt different. "Mum's got this one year artist in residence thing. She's loving it. So, I'm just not sure that she'll go back at the end of it. And I'm not sure Dad realises that."

She couldn't work out what it was about Nik, that somehow he'd invited this from her. Opening up about the nagging worries of her parents' complex relationship made them seem a little less frightening. It felt good to voice them out loud, confide in someone.

"And you?" he asked.

"No. It'll be uni for me. Victoria. They offer a Masters in Creative Writing. Not that I've even been to Wellington, but it's where I need to go." His nods of encouragement stalled and his smile dimmed a little at her mention of a move to the capital. "So no, I won't go back to Tekapo." And that admission didn't trouble her at all. She'd moved beyond the confines of the little town already and she wouldn't let it reclaim her.

"Well, I hope your mum and dad work it out," he said, as if he'd sensed the pain their possible separation caused her.

"Me too," she said, trying to smile, although still not buoyed by the kindness in his blue eyes. She clicked her seatbelt undone and shoved open the door. No need to ruin a beautiful day by moping about stuff she couldn't change.

Chapter 6

Karekare

Karekare Beach, New Zealand – February 2009

WITH A BEEP OF the remote, Nik led off into the overgrown entrance of a track. Without even a signpost, she'd not have found it by herself. They followed a winding bush pathway, emerging from the gloom into blazing sun.

The sandy beach spread before them, a glittering black carpet, bordered on one side by relentless surf. Giant waves pummelled the shore, releasing a strident, salty tang. At its other edge, rugged headlands soared skyward. The spectacular scene had a surprising familiarity, despite her never having been there before.

"Why do I feel like I know this place?" she said, tossing her question against the wind that blasted off the sea and peppered her bare legs with small sand flurries.

"*The Piano*," he said. "The movie. They filmed here."

"Ahh, of course," she said, stooping to remove her sandals. With every step across this strip of soft sand, rivers of fine grit flowed through the gaps, trapping the searing granules against the soles of her feet. Shoes clasped in her hand, she ran after him on tiptoes, seeking refuge on the cooler and more solid, wave-dampened sand. "Mum loves that movie. If it's ever on TV, she insists on control of the remote. Way too moody and brooding for my taste."

"Yeah, mine too," he said, wandering ahead of her towards the roiling sea. He ventured into the water up to his knees. Even there in the shallows the violent foam surged around him.

Cassie made her way to join him, seeking a reprieve from the heat of the black sand painfully searing her bare feet. Edging into the water, she closed her eyes in bliss as the cool wash of the first wave swept around her ankles.

The second larger wave caught her by surprise. She shrieked as it wet her shorts. Leaping backwards, she dropped one of her sandals and watched as the receding wave carried it away. She lunged towards the bobbing shoe as a third enormous wave swept in, knocking her off her feet.

She sat in shock, and too late attempted to scramble upright. The powerful backwash took her with it, sweeping her away from the shore. She could swim reasonably well—in a pool—but living all her life about as far away from the sea as was possible in New Zealand, she had little experience of the ocean. Fear erupted in her chest.

People drowned at these West Coast beaches. She'd watched *Piha Rescue* on TV enough times to know the danger. And even greater danger loomed here, with no surf patrol ready to leap into the water after her. The beach dropped away steeply and even now her feet barely touched the bottom and each successive wave broke over her head until finally one toppled her again. In the midst of the tumbling surf, spurts of rank tasting water penetrated her mouth. Stinging droplets forced their way beneath her squinting eyelids. Water found its way into her ears amidst the pounding roar of the relentless swells coming at her.

"Cassie!" His voice beside her ear held an edge of panic. A powerful arm wrapped around her chest, dragging her roughly backwards. At first she continued to struggle, in an instinctive fight to stay upright. "Just relax. I've got you," he yelled over the thundering surf.

She registered his words and, despite the gripping fear, succumbed to his strength and let him tow her into shore. Once free of the biggest waves, he scooped her up, staggering clear of the water, and deposited her in a dripping heap on the sand.

Her breath came in ragged gasps, and a hiccup of salty bile spilled from her mouth. She wiped it away with the back of her hand and sat there, too shocked to speak. Nik dropped with a thud beside her, rapid breathing and white-faced.

It had all happened so fast. The sea was an untrustworthy friend, extending a hand of welcome one moment, turning on you without warning in another. She knew that. How stupid of her to forget, especially here on a coastline renowned for tragedy. And she'd not only put her own life at risk, but his too. So many times she'd heard it in the news. A rescuer drowned while saving another. Today it might have been him. And how could anyone live with the guilt of that?

Tears of shock and shame welled up and trailed down her cheeks in a hot stream. "I'm so sorry. I'm so sorry."

A large finger swiped at her cheek. She opened her eyes to see his stormy blue ones inches away. "It's OK. You're OK. We're OK."

"I know, but we nearly weren't, and it's all my fault." Pain stabbed at her chest, her heaving lungs competing with the wrenching pain of realisation—her carelessness had been the catalyst for a near-tragedy. All over a stupid shoe.

"Hey," he said. "It happens." The large arm, only a minute ago so fiercely clutching her to him, now wrapped around her shoulder. With a gentle pull, he gathered her against his chest. "I'm fine." She could feel his breath against her hair. "Remember, I'm a big guy. We were never in any real danger." The thudding of his heart against her back said otherwise. "And if it's anyone's fault, it's mine for going into the water in the first place. Shit, it's wild down here today." As if in response, the wind whipped loose tendrils of her wet hair against her face. He reached across his free hand to tuck them behind one ear. "This beach is treacherous and god knows I've been here often enough. I should know better than to go into the sea when it's like this."

She nodded, although she wasn't prepared to relinquish full blame. "Hey, it happens." She managed a weak smile, echoing his words in reassurance. "But thank you for saving me. That's twice in one weekend. You'll be thinking it's me that attracts trouble." Despite still feeling shaky, a brittle laugh bubbled out. What a crazy couple of days.

"You're welcome. Any time."

"Hopefully not anytime soon. That was definitely enough drama to last me a lifetime. But thanks, it's nice to know someone cared enough to leap in and grab me."

He stiffened a little against her. As if her words provoked sudden awareness at the intimacy of their bodies, he carefully unwound his arm and shuffled away a little. She immediately missed his comforting, damp warmth.

"I suppose we should go, get you home." His eyes roved over her dripping clothes, the shorts clinging to wet legs, and the vintage cotton of her top heavy and sodden.

"Yeah, but what about your mum's car? We're soaked." The pristine pale grey fabric seats wouldn't cope with wet, sandy bodies.

"Oh, yeah," he said. "I haven't got a towel or anything. You OK to sit and dry out a bit first?"

She nodded. "Aha." Unable to form proper words, she braced her teeth to stop them chattering. But goosebumps prickled as the stiff breeze met her damp skin. She tried to push away thoughts of cold, but shivered anyway. He reached out a tentative hand, resting it on her forearm.

"You're freezing. Let's move up the beach out of this wind, and I'll go and get your jumper." He found a spot on the springy seagrass where she could tuck in beside a broad pohutukawa tree. The maze of tortured branches still allowed patchy sunlight to filter through. Nik left her sitting there soaking up the warmth while he disappeared into the mouth of the bush track at a jog.

When he returned, he'd swapped his own wet t-shirt for a thick hoodie. As he leaned down, her jumper dangling from his outstretched hand, her eyes couldn't help but land on the little fuzz of chest hair and follow the line of the gaping v-neck. He wasn't wearing anything underneath. What might a bare-skinned Nik look like? Probably rather hot, judging by the sight of his muscled chest straining against his t-shirts.

She blamed Grace's influence for her own growing interest in the male physique. Of course, she'd been interested in boys before, taken notice of them, but not really *noticed* them, not their bodies, not like this. Fuelled by her friend's obsession and Nik's very real presence, her mind wandered down all kinds of tracks, providing disturbing although thrilling images. Heat surged in her cheeks at the thought, despite her attempts to push away those thoughts and focus on his hand.

"Thanks." Now she had a problem. She saw little point in pulling on her jumper over the wet top—it had to go. As if sensing her dilemma, he took a tactful step to the other side of the tree, leaning his back against the trunk. He directed his gaze back down the track.

"Go for it," he said. "I'll keep a lookout in case anyone else arrives while you change."

She stripped off her top. One of her favourite vintage store finds, it now lay on the ground, a sad bundle of wet fabric. There wasn't time to stand here and mourn for it. Nik waited on the other side of that tree and she stood here in only a bra. She tugged her jumper over her head, relishing its immediate warmth.

"Done."

He emerged from behind the tree. "Great. That better?"

"Much better, thank you."

"Well, we can go, anyway. Come on, I've worked it out."

Back at the car, he produced one of the tartan picnic rugs that virtually every Kiwi family owned, folding it to cover her seat.

"Found it in the back," he said. She carefully slid onto it. The scratchy wool, although uncomfortable against her bare legs, would protect the seat from her still damp shorts. Meanwhile, on the driver's side, Nik flung the door open. He slipped off the hoodie, draping it across the seat, before climbing in. She couldn't help it, allowing her gaze to sweep across the bare body so close to hers. The lightly-tanned muscles of his broad chest glinted under a haze of golden hair. In the chill of the air, his bronze nipples stood erect. Cassie took a deep breath. No longer under any illusions about what an unclothed Nik might look like, she prepared to suffer the twenty-minute drive home beside him. She sucked in another breath and fixed her eyes firmly on the road ahead.

CHAPTER 7

Teacher

Auckland, New Zealand – February 2009

"CASSIE." SHE JUMPED IN her seat, startled as a face loomed over her shoulder.

"Don't *do* that Mum. I just about wet my pants." She yanked off her headset, frustrated by the interruption. The line she'd been typing lay incomplete, the next words evaporating from her mind as she turned her attention to her mother.

"Well, you will insist on sitting up here with those damn headphones on."

"They help me concentrate on my work."

Her mother spluttered. "I don't know why you can't leave them off. It's not as if it's exactly noisy here. Only the sounds of nature. That's why the trust bought this place for an artist's retreat."

"You might find the blaring of those cicadas soothing, but they are downright annoying. And how can you not notice the rosellas in the trees out front? They squawk their heads off all day." A cottage in the bush conjured up idyllic visions of peace and quiet, but in reality, the whole of nature seemed determined to sabotage her writing.

"I think you're being a little precious about it, my sweet." Her mother's amused smile infuriated her almost as much as the wildlife. "But if listening to loud music is what it takes my tortured writer child to weave her magic, then I suppose it's what she has to do." She resisted the urge to flick off the hand tousling her hair. Sometimes her mother treated her like she was still five. "And how about from now on you tell your friends to just come on up? That way, my art won't suffer the interruption."

"Someone's here?"

"Yes, that lovely boy Nik again. I'll send him up." She disappeared in a swish of her calico wrap pants before Cassie could protest that her room was in no fit state for accepting visitors. Especially not boys. Especially not Nik.

She flung herself on the pile of discarded clothes lying by the window, heaving them into the wardrobe. Sweeping up a wayward bra and crumpled pair of knickers, she deposited them on top. She tried to close the door on the shameful evidence of her slovenliness. Glancing down in irritation at the pair of Doc Martens wedged in the gap, she berated herself for not taking her mother's less than subtle hints to tidy up.

The Nicholson Arts Trust members were coming for morning tea on Monday, ostensibly to check on Blair's progress with her work towards her first exhibition of the artist in residence programme. With less than a month to go, Cassie bet they'd be more interested in the contents of the studio, not her teenage children's bedrooms. But Blair refused to take any chances, adamant that they'd need to pass her inspection on Sunday evening. The threat of all privileges being revoked, including the internet, hung over them. The prospect of losing his precious PS3 had motivated Archie into an unusual burst of activity. On finishing, he'd escaped to the neighbours' place.

But on a Saturday morning, two whole days stretched out before her. She saw no urgency to attend to domestic tasks over the pleasure of her writing. The short fantasy story she'd written for school last weekend had spurred her on. A second in the same world with new characters had already taken a satisfying shape on her computer—until now.

At the steady tread of heavy footsteps on the stairs, she made a wild grab at the covers. Too late to make the bed properly. But as the only option for a seat, if she had no choice but to invite him to sit down, she threw pillows into an untidy row and dragged the duvet up to meet them. The tangle of sheets from where she'd tossed and turned in last night's humidity remained an accusing lump beneath it. Maybe she'd be safer to offer him her chair. She snatched at the tired stripy pyjamas trailing from beneath the duvet and stuffed them under the bed just as a polite knock came on her door.

"OK if I come in?"

His large shape filled the doorframe as he waited awkwardly for her invitation. Trust her mother to have left the door wide open. Closing it might have bought her extra time to hide the embarrassing row of stuffed toys that she could never bear to part with. Acutely aware of their button eyes staring pointedly at this newcomer, and Nik meeting that stare with an amused smile, she wanted to wipe the stupid grins off all of their faces.

"Sure," she said, waving her hand at the vacant computer chair and taking a seat on the still dishevelled bed.

"Sorry," he said, glancing at her screen. "I've interrupted your writing."

His eyes widened as he followed the lines of text there. At once she regretted the large font size she'd chosen—and why, oh why, had she never bothered to change the lengthy default settings on the screensaver?

'His hand trailed through her hair as he leaned in, lips parted'

Nik tore his gaze away from the screen, the colour rising in his face a mirror to the sensation she could feel in her own. *Oh my god, kill me now.* She squirmed uncomfortably as his eyes met hers.

"Yeah, working on some fantasy." She shouldn't be ashamed—it was perfectly OK to write stuff like that. She'd read *way* steamier. But for him to read it, in her presence, knowing these were the thoughts running through her mind mere minutes ago—that made her cringe.

"Fantasy?" he said, his smile widening into a grin.

"Definitely," she said. May as well own it. Too late for anything else. And then change the subject quickly. "So, I wasn't expecting you today."

"Yeah, I need to get your number. Then I won't keep turning up unannounced like this."

He slipped a phone from the pocket of his jeans and handed it to her. *Keep turning up.* The words swirled in her head while she keyed her details into his phone. He obviously planned to continue these visits. And unexpected as it was, in honesty, the thought didn't trouble her. Apart from the near-drowning and the awkward drive home with his very real, very muscular, very naked torso so close beside her—even now the image caused heat to rise inside of her and threaten to flood her face—she'd found herself more comfortable with him than most boys of her age; probably because he wasn't like most boys her age.

"There," she said, offering it back.

"So, if you're not busy today…" he stared cautiously back at the screen, "like you could get away from your writing? I was thinking about…you know, you said you didn't know how to drive? Do you want me to give you a lesson?"

"As long as you're happy to risk me crashing your mum's car."

"You are *not* going to crash the car. I swear. It's so easy. Can you ride a bike?"

"Yeah, of course, although I haven't been on one for a while."

"Well, it's way easier than that. But put something decent on your feet." He glanced down at her bare feet and she reflexively curled her toes, self-conscious of the bright pink chipped polish on her toenails. If hanging out with boys was to be part of her plans here in Auckland, she should devote more time to her appearance. "A pair of trainers would be good. No jandals or anything." Seeing her raised brows, he added, "It's safer. My grandmother took out the wall of the garage because she got her Croc stuck under the accelerator."

"I guarantee—no Crocs." She couldn't think of anything more hideous. "OK, I'll be down soon."

He took the hint and left, allowing her to open the wardrobe door and find footwear without his scrutiny. No way she wanted him to see the untidy mountain of clothing stashed inside. She sat on the floor lacing her shoes and wondering at how she'd suddenly found herself tied up with Nik.

That wasn't necessarily a bad thing, not when she checked off the list she'd been mentally compiling of things to like about Nik Francovic. Good looking, but seemingly unaware of the admiring stares of girls. Didn't feel the need to run in one of those intimidating packs that most teenage guys clung to. Respectful of her—she hadn't realised how that sense of safety made her relax and be herself in a way she'd never done before. There had only been a few guys she'd hung out with enough to be considered friends; even fewer boyfriends. There had been a couple who'd been way too forward. And then, of course, the one who'd genuinely scared her with his assumptions as to what she'd allow him to do with her. Nik showed no sign of any creepy behaviour.

In addition, he was polite to her mum—that always made things easier. She'd seen him give up a Saturday to help out his family, suggesting kindness and an admirable loyalty. The list was longer than she'd realised.

And oh my, didn't he smell good? She closed her eyes a moment, breathing in the scent of him that still lingered in her room. That musky male smell overlaid with some kind of deodorant. Not the hideous Lynx spray in all its revolting variations that was every teen boy's go to; slathering themselves with vast quantities of it from the moment their parents suggested paying better attention to bodily hygiene might be a good thing. This far less strident, spicy, woody aroma still hung in her room. And now she could look forward to savouring it for at least the next couple of hours while she had her first driving lesson.

The anticipation of spending time with him competed with her nervousness. Not being the most practical person, there was a fair chance she'd make a right fool of herself. She took a deep breath and headed downstairs, hoping they both wouldn't regret this.

Two hours later, with quiet smugness and welcome relief she parked the car neatly between two white lines, stopping a metre short of the towering grey wall of an industrial building somewhere in the depths of Henderson. Nik was right—driving was easy. Now she'd mastered the final challenge of the day, not that there was too much challenge parking in a carpark empty of other vehicles.

"You're a natural," Nik said for about the tenth time.

To start with, she'd seen the tension in his body, hands poised ready to intervene if necessary, surveilling her with an intense scrutiny that didn't make the task easy. But as he'd observed her growing competence, he'd relaxed into enjoying the role of driving instructor he'd volunteered for.

"You're a good teacher."

"Maybe it's St Christopher watching out for us both, eh?"

He gave the shiny medal a flick with his fingers, sending it swaying wildly. The movement drew her eyes to the band on his wrist. She'd wanted to ask him about it, but each time he'd seemed hesitant to let her look at it more closely.

"That's an amazing design," she said. "I've never seen another one like it."

This time he didn't draw his wrist away, rather offered it up for her to see. The silver dragon's sharp claws clasped the black woven band beneath, as if, having alighted on the diamond-patterned bark of a tree, it now clung to a branch. Its head swivelled in the opposite direction, perhaps in search of prey. A pointed tongue flicked across triangular teeth. The neat rows of scales, etched into the metal, reflected the light like the facets of a gemstone.

"That's because there isn't another one like it." He dropped his head shyly and sat for a moment, as if deliberating whether he should share more information. "I made it."

She could sense a quiet pride in his voice. And there should be, if he had in fact made the intricate creature clasped tightly around his broad forearm.

"For real? *You* made *that*?"

"For real."

"I can't imagine how you'd even begin to create something like that. It's beautiful."

He paused a few beats, as if mulling over some weighty decision.

"I can show you. That's if you've got time."

"Of course I've got time. Yes, show me."

"OK, well, first thing is we need to get you out of the driver's seat." He reached for his door. "You might be doing well for a new driver, but you're not ready for the road to the studio yet."

"Bet you didn't know there was anything more up here," he said, as she frowned at him. They had retraced their earlier journey, winding past her place, then Grace's, heading for the mysterious studio location.

"So, it wasn't a lie when you said you were just going past my house last weekend."

"No. Not exactly," he grinned. "I knew you didn't believe me. But yeah, I'll own up—I planned to call in at your place, anyway. Even if I hadn't needed to come up here."

Beyond the seal, the road narrowed, climbing higher in ever more tortuous twists towards an abrupt dead end, deep in the bush of the Waitakere Ranges. A faded red letterbox with the name 'Dravitski' in pale but neatly hand-painted letters gave the only hint of a dwelling beyond the overgrown entrance to the property.

"Dra-vit-ski." She tested out the syllables. "More Dallies?" Her words hiccupped out as the car bounced up the rutted driveway.

"Polish. Got to get your Eastern Europeans sorted. The 'ski's are always Polish. The 'vic's usually Croatian."

"Who'd have thought? A whole other country out here in the west."

"Not really. Only the one Pole as far as I know. His first name is Jan. Spelled J-A-N. But you say it 'yarn'."

"As in, like telling a yarn? Or knitting wool?" An odd name, but presumably Polish too.

"Yes. Don't ever call him 'Jan'. One of many things he and I have in common—a girl's name in the wrong hands."

Around a last twist of the driveway, a house came into view, its weatherboards bare of paint and curling at the edges. With a thin coat of bright green moss and a frost of lichens along the windowsills, it blended into the surrounding bush.

A man burst from the door as Nik parked. Bare feet poked out of a pair of faded jeans. His blonde hair streaked with silver trailed in a long braid down his back. The compact and sturdy body gave an impression of strength. Muscled arms protruded from the rolled sleeves of a plaid shirt. The hand he extended to Nik glinted with an assortment of heavy silver rings, and a pendant of gold peeked out of the v of his shirt.

He pulled Nik into a hug, and Cassie noted a gleaming engraved band around his wrist. A face of leathery tan crinkled in a welcoming grin, deeper wrinkles edging a set of intense blue eyes.

"Nik. Wasn't expecting you till tomorrow, man." He spoke with a heavy accent, the words thick and clipped.

"Hope you don't mind. Thought I'd bring my friend to see the studio. Jan, this is Cassie."

"Any time. Any time."

She offered him her hand, and he pumped it up and down with enthusiasm. His abrupt manner of speech belied the warmth of his welcome.

"What you up to, Jan?" Nik asked. "Studio free?"

"Ya man, you know me. Usual Saturday. Watching the ponies."

"Making you rich?"

"Not yet. But this next race at Ellerslie. Got a bit riding on it. You go ahead. I need to get back inside. Don't want to miss it." He glanced at a heavy gold watch.

"Thanks Jan."

"You know I mean it, man. Any time. And bring your girlfriend any time too," he said. "Nice to meet you, Cassie. Gotta go." He hurried back into the house where the distinctive pre-race patter of a racing commentator drifted from the open window.

"Loves his horses," Nik said, with a grin at Jan's swiftly retreating back, while pointedly ignoring the 'girlfriend' reference. "Grew up on a farm in Poland. Still gets his fix of them on the racing channel." He motioned her towards a small path to the left of the sagging porch. "The studio's this way."

He led them along the uneven path, where cracked concrete jutted up in dangerous wedges.

"How did you meet him?" You didn't stumble across jewellery makers every day of the week, let alone convince one to let you become his apprentice.

"Jan's a friend of my dad's. Worked on the vineyard when he first arrived from Poland. Dad and my uncle were doing the same. My grandfather believed they needed to do every job themselves if they were to take over the business..." He winced. "Just like Dad would have me do when I leave school."

"But you don't want to."

"No. Let's just say it's not in my blood."

"What made you start on the jewellery?"

"Firstly, Jan's always been like one of the family. Great to us kids. Sort of another uncle to us. So I knew what he did. And then—well, you've seen his hands. Even as a little kid, they fascinated me. He was so different. There was no other man I knew who wore stuff like that. Anyway, my interest grew. He noticed. Offered me a chance. I didn't hesitate."

Tucked against the rear of the house, the studio stood in stark contrast to Jan's dilapidated home. The modern corrugated steel shed, painted a jaunty brick red, glowed brightly against the backdrop of bright green bush. Nik produced a key from his pocket, unlocking the sliding door before ushering her inside.

Lights flickered on, illuminating work benches and shelves of neatly stacked tools. The pine-scent of the wood-lined room overlaid a faint chemical tang. Above the benches, pin boards papered with sketches fluttered in the breeze. One board bloomed with images of flowers and foliage, trailing ribbons of vines, and lacy ferns, interspersed with birds, a bee, and a delicate butterfly.

Nik opened a drawer in the bench and lifted out a black-covered spiral bound sketch book. His large hands reverently peeled back the cover, and he slowly leafed through the pages with gentle care. They swarmed with images, similar to those on the wall above but reimagined as pieces of jewellery. Views from different perspectives showed how each might look from every angle.

She had spent her whole life immersed in a world of art, grown up surrounded by it, both pieces created by her mother as well as that of artists Blair admired. Even to an untrained eye, the exquisite level of detail left no doubt about the talent of the artist.

"It's fucking amazing, isn't it?" Nik's eyes glowed with admiration.

"It sure is."

"But this is only the beginning. Come and look at what he does with these sketches."

In one corner of the room stood a large wooden cabinet, two tall doors with little dangling handles, and an old-fashioned key lock. Nik reached in behind it, retrieving a small brass key and turned it in the lock. Behind the doors were layers of drawers.

Nik pulled one open, and, nestled against the black velvet base, lay rows of pendants, the plants and animals of the drawings brought to life in silver, the light and shade of the gleaming metal imbuing them with a surreal beauty. In another, rings of an endless variety lined up in neat rows, sticky labels with letters denoting the sizes.

Bracelets and bangles filled the third drawer, some like Nik's own, crafted from a single shape—perhaps a plant that would curl vine-like about the wearer's wrist. Others were solid bands etched with spiralling floral patterns.

"That's what he's teaching me," he breathed, awe in his voice despite having seen these before, perhaps many times. "You want to be a writer. I want to be a jeweller."

"So, did you make any of these?"

"No, no, these are all Jan's work. Here's a few of mine."

With a shy smile, he pulled open the bottom drawer. A second silvery dragon band, similar to his own, lay surrounded by four pendants, each a shiny sea creature. An octopus cradled a tiny pearl in its tentacles. Two seahorses reminiscent of those she'd seen bobbing placidly at the aquarium faced each other, their single eyes small glinting diamonds. And a fish with overlapping scales and a hook in its mouth hung from a silver chain.

"They're amazing, Nik." Her voice came out in a whisper, as she looked in awe at the delicacy that he, although still a novice, created with those huge hands.

"There's a long way to go before I can produce stuff like his, but I'm working on it." He moved back to the second bench. "I'll show you."

She'd been so focused on Jan's talent, she hadn't noticed the drawings of lizards and dragons, mixed with sketches of extravagant sea life pinned to the smaller board above it. The resemblance to Nik's bracelet was unmistakable.

"So you start with sketching. Let your mind roam. Then, once you have something you like, you think about what it suggests. This sounds weird, but sometimes a drawing tells you how it should be shaped." Her eyes fixed on a sketch of a dragon and he followed her gaze. "Yeah, that's my first sketch for this one," he said. "And here's the working drawing."

He pulled out his own sketchbook, flipped over a few pages and there it was, the dragon band brought to life in soft pencil.

"But how do you go from that—" she said, pointing to the sketch, "—to that?"

"Very slowly." He laughed. "Well, I do. Jan is incredibly quick, given the detail of his work. Come through here."

In an adjoining room, more benches flanked the walls, each peppered with small metal pots filled with tools, some curved, others pointed.

"We use a process called lost wax casting," he said. "You take a piece of wax, like this." He produced a small lump of blue wax from a container. "And you carve away the design." He picked up a scalpel-like tool and with a few deft swipes, the cube of wax already sported delicate curves.

"Blue wax for something less intricate. And this purple stuff—" He tossed another bright lump her way, and she caught it, surprised to find it hard to the touch. "It's for the really detailed pieces. Jan pretty much always works with the purple."

"Then," he said, "you make a cast of it. Put it inside here." He held up a small pot. "Pour in plaster. After it's set, you heat it in that oven. The wax melts away—that's why they call it lost wax. And you're left with the cast."

"Wow. All that work carving it, then it's gone."

"Yeah, the final step always feels like a bit of a leap of faith. Did your mother or grandmother ever have one of those old-fashioned jelly moulds? Or a fancy fluted cake tin?"

She nodded.

"So that's what you're left with. You pour in the liquid metal. And it's done."

"You make it sound so easy."

"Oh, no." He shook his head, biting his lip. "It's far from easy. But I love it. I'm up here three or four days a week. More if I can."

"Is that why I never see you round school? You're here?"

He nodded. "In my favourite place. I've got Jan to thank for that. He convinced the school to agree to a special Gateway programme for me. You know the work experience thing. So I go to my classes, but the rest of the time I'm here. And on Sundays too—despite my mother thinking I'm going straight to hell for missing Mass."

"So, what subjects are you taking? I haven't seen you any of mine."

"Sculpture. Jewellery falls into that. Printmaking, because there's heaps of drawing. Technology. And English—" He grimaced at the word. "—which I'm already regretting. I did OK with it up till now. But this year...I feel like I'm doomed to fail."

"You could drop it. Lots of people only take three subjects."

He shook his head. "Not possible. I need to pass the Scholarship exam and I need it in four subjects. Otherwise I'm fucked."

"But why? Even for uni you don't need *any* Scholarship subjects. And why four?"

"Because Fieldcrest Art School has the only proper jewellery making qualification in the country. The fees alone are huge, and of course, when your materials are precious metals and gemstones... I need that scholarship money. And even that won't be enough. I have to chase more. There are a couple of art trusts who give out funding. But it's super competitive."

She understood perfectly. Sometimes her mother spent more time chasing the money to allow her to be a working artist than she did creating the art.

"Earning Scholarship marks in four subjects would give me an advantage. I need that funding or it isn't happening. And in that case, I'll have to get a job for a couple of years and save every cent."

"And that's not an option?"

"No." He gave an emphatic shake of his head. "Not unless I'm desperate. But I might be. Defeated by Year 13 English."

"No." Cassie shook her head. "You won't be." Something about the way his animated face had fallen into a resigned slump tugged at her heart. She thought of the dragon band; the row of shiny pendants. Someone with his talent deserved to follow their dream. And she knew how to help. "We are *not* letting that happen."

Chapter 8

Stargazing

Auckland, New Zealand – March 2009

NIK HAD THE ODD sense of being watched and it wasn't only the beady eyes of the ridiculous row of stuffed animals upon him. He glanced up and Cassie jerked her head back to the screen. He smiled to himself as he went back to scrawling notes in the margin of the book on his lap.

Better hold up his end of the bargain and finish this chapter. And not let her know that he saw the way she looked at him when she thought him too preoccupied with work to notice. And also not let her see what her discreet surveillance did to him. Best he kept this book very firmly covering parts of him that demanded his attention at the sight of her; fuck it, even at the thought of her. She invaded his thoughts all the time.

Only the prospect of earning her displeasure damped down those thoughts and relieved some of the pressure of his rampant dick, now pushing a little less insistently against his jeans. That and the dull words that occupied the page in front of him, taking up more space than they deserved. Nothing could kill a hard-on quicker than Shakespeare.

He'd always found an escape in books, and considered himself reasonably able to string a sentence together, but fuck, he hated English. The school curriculum writers had conspired to take a perfectly good subject and devise ways of using it to torture unwitting students lured by the promise of something that should be interesting. His brain didn't work in the way the teachers wanted.

Luckily, Cassie's brain did. Like using a translator, she guided him to understand a language he knew snippets of but couldn't assemble into coherent speech on his own. Each week, she applied that sharp mind of hers to dissecting the latest assignment, serving it up to him in chunks he could manage. He'd chew on the words and spit them back out in an acceptable form.

In only a month, he'd made a dramatic improvement in his marks. He'd never aspire to be a straight-A student like Cassie, but he was more than happy with the solid Bs and the occasional B+ that he achieved with her help. And in some back-to-front way, the nightmare of Year 13 English had delivered this—an excuse to spend several hours each week hanging out with her.

He justified avoiding Saturday work at the vineyard by claiming he had to study with a friend, an acceptable excuse. It wasn't a lie. But he'd omitted to tell his parents exactly who his study partner was. A 'sin of omission'—that's what the priest called it, droning on from a perch at the front of the classroom of his Catholic primary school to a captive audience of bored ten-year-olds.

If it was a sin, it wasn't the only one he was guilty of. He felt fairly certain 'impure thoughts' qualified, and he'd defy any teenage guy to spend time with Cassie and not have his mind drift in that direction. It was inevitable when sitting in this tiny bedroom, the air heavy with the sweet girly perfume that hung in a fragrant cloud around her, and wafted back to tantalise his nostrils whenever he followed along behind her. He stole a look at her, so beautiful with hair swept back behind one ear, dark brows knitted in an adorable frown of concentration as her eyes moved across the screen, and felt another lurch of his dick.

Thank god for stupid fucking Jackson Moffat and his choice of Archie Tremayne as his first—and hopefully last—victim of the school year. Maybe he and Cassie would have found each other, anyway. He'd like to think he'd have noticed her in the crowd. Of course he would have—hair a rich chocolate, almost red but not quite, and the brave style of clothes that marked her as different from the other girls. He'd have noticed.

But seeing her standing in the middle of that brawl like some warrior princess, that's what had ignited the instant spark of attraction that grew brighter every minute he spent with her, even minutes like this while wading through the world's most boring study guide.

And now, he spent every Saturday here; lounging in her bedroom; sitting on her bed. The only thing wrong with this picture? She wasn't sitting on it with him. He knew that day would come. But he wouldn't push it.

Despite the fact that they talked lots—with his next closest siblings all girls, he was a better talker than most guys his age—there were still some secrets Cassie held close. Most of the time, things were so easy between them. They'd chat away, their hands would brush, or their bodies collide, as they fell about laughing at something one or the other had said, and she'd appear so relaxed and happy to be with him. And then a word, or a touch, and she'd pull away and shut down tight. Never for long, but it bothered him.

The first few times he'd leapt to the assumption he'd said or done something to trigger it, and sat there stunned, desperately trying to understand so he didn't repeat his mistake. But then, in an instant, she'd snap back to normal. He'd come to realise there were simply things about Cassie he didn't know; things that in brief moments stole away this bright, sparkly girl that he couldn't get enough of. She trusted him with so much of herself; he knew that one day she'd trust him with the rest.

"Want a break? I'm over this." She sighed as she slammed shut the book beside her in uncharacteristic frustration. "My mind's not on it today. In fact, why don't we call time on it, if you're OK with that?"

"You forget who you're talking to here. More than happy with that suggestion."

He grinned at her, tossing the tedious analysis of *Richard III* across the bed. It could wait. Outside, a brilliant autumn day beckoned. Maybe they should get out into it and find something to do to lift her mood.

Cassie had seemed off all morning, right from when he'd sprinted up the stairs, expecting to see her in her usual spot. Most days he'd find her already seated at her laptop, tapping away, usually engrossed in whatever latest fairy tale she spun on the screen. That was another thing about Cassie that got him horny—wondering if the sexy scenes he'd caught glimpses of were figments of her imagination or reworking of things she'd already done with boys, or—even more tantalising still, things she'd *like* to do with boys. If that were the case, he wouldn't hesitate to volunteer.

But this morning, she hadn't even made it to her desk yet. He'd discovered her sitting on her bed, huddled under a sheet with only her eyes showing. Fixed on the ceiling in a glassy stare, as if she wasn't quite present in her body.

One other Saturday, he'd caught her still in her pyjamas, albeit already typing with furious fingers, desperate to get an idea down. Possessed by the writing muse, she'd simply not made time to dress. Embarrassed at him catching her out, she'd shooed him downstairs while she chucked on jeans and a t-shirt. Today, on seeing him, the lack of reaction surprised him the most.

She'd offered a mumbled, "Sorry, I overslept," and swung her feet onto the floor with a tired thud. Like a sleepwalker, she'd pulled on a robe and headed for the door, leaving him sitting there bewildered. And then returned five minutes later, fully dressed, a mug of hot chocolate in her hand and acting as if nothing had happened. But something had. And he still wanted to find out what, to ease the niggle of worry.

Having made the mutual decision to abandon homework for the day, he gathered his things and followed her downstairs.

"Want a sandwich?" she called from the kitchen.

"Sure. What you got?"

"Healthy shit, of course."

She opened the fridge with a flourish. Blair's determination to steer her offspring away from poor food choices stood before them. Neat rows of organic vegetables, oddly shaped tomatoes, an extremely ugly red pepper, frilly hydroponic lettuce and a bunch of contorted carrots filled the plastic chiller bin. Cassie produced the remains of a roast chicken in a zip-lock bag, still proudly sporting a label announcing its free range status. He almost closed his eyes in blissful appreciation of the smell as she cut big slabs off a loaf of homemade sourdough. Healthy never looked so good at home as it did here.

The food seemed to pull her out of her brooding, so in between mouthfuls, he decided to venture a question. He wasn't sure why he'd developed this protectiveness towards her. She was bold enough not to need him to fight her battles. But if there was something wrong, and it was in his power to do something about it, he would.

"So you want to talk about it?" he said. "Whatever's upset you?" He'd learned from his sisters that, for girls, talking was good. God knew he'd provided a listening ear often enough for their constant string of minor problems grown huge in their minds. And he'd watched his dad coax his mother out of a bad mood, simply by inviting her to vent about whatever had pissed her off over the dinner table. Surely it would work on Cassie, too. He didn't like seeing her less than her normal self, hated seeing that mesmerising glow dimmed.

Eyebrows raised, she stopped mid-chew, frozen by the unexpected question.

"I suppose," she said slowly, after swallowing down the bite of her sandwich.

"Well, I don't think it's me—this time, anyway." That produced a small smile. "But you can tell me. If you want."

She sighed, putting down her food. "OK." She took a breath. "I know I shouldn't let it worry me, but it was Archie's birthday yesterday and Dad didn't phone. If he's not with us on the day, he always phones and we do this thing."

"This thing?"

"Well, we do it if he's with us and if he's not, we do it over the phone."

"You're not making a lot of sense here."

She shot him a smirk. "It might sound a bit weird. But, we go outside, and we lay on the ground. And look at the stars. And we always find his star. Arcturus. It's easy to find because it's big. A red giant."

"Red, huh? Your brother is well-named."

She let out a giggle. "Not sure he'll ever be a giant. But he was born with a red fuzz on his head and it only got worse from there."

"So, your dad didn't come through this year. Is Archie upset?"

"Don't think so. I mean, he's a kid. A PS3 game arrived in the post. Dad got that right. And Mum handed over money for a new pair of Nikes. So he's happy enough."

"But you're not."

"I tried to tell myself that maybe Dad thinks Archie's too old for it, but…" Her lip quivered and her voice grew hoarse. At that moment, he felt a flash of dislike for this unknown man, letting his kids down, hurting her like that. "It just feels like as a family, we're done. We're here, he's there, that's nothing new. It's been like that our whole lives. But this… it feels different. Like we've come to the end."

"Families," he said. "They can get to you." God knew he understood that. For him, staying out of their way whenever he could helped make them bearable. Obviously, it wasn't the same for Cassie. He fumbled to reassure her, unsure of what to say. "If Archie's OK, maybe you should just let it go," he suggested gently.

"Maybe I should. I know it's strange that it bothers me. It's not as if it's *my* birthday."

"You do the stargazing thing for yours, too?"

She shook her head. "No point," she laughed. "You can't see Cassiopeia."

"Wrong time of year?"

"No, you can't *ever* see it. Not here. It's a northern hemisphere constellation. From New Zealand, the tilt of the earth blocks it. One day I'll get to see it. When I go travelling." Her eyes had a wistfulness that made him want to buy her a plane ticket right now, and both of them get out of here. "Besides, my birthday's in August. Lying on the ground outside might not be so much fun when it's still practically winter."

"Maybe not." He wasn't about to give anything away, but the thought of lying next to Cassie, winter or not, sounded totally fine to him. Especially in winter, huddled under a blanket, with her pressed up close, needing his warmth. The way she stirred him up, there'd be no risk of cold. He'd be hot enough for both of them. And that thought stirred up the beginning of an idea.

Chapter 9

Universe

Auckland, New Zealand – March 2009

As he cut the engine, a curtain pulled back. The light spilling from the window framed Cassie's silhouette. She peered out, and he could just make out her features. Her mouth shifted from an 'O' of surprise at a car in the driveway at nine o'clock at night, to turn up at the corners as she recognised him heading up the path. She opened the door before he reached it.

"Hey," she said. A warmth spread through him at the welcome in that one word.

"Hey," he offered back.

Now he was here, shyness crept up on him as he wondered what she'd think of his idea. It had seemed such a good one as he loaded up the car right on dusk and headed back to the Tremayne house. But now, standing on her doorstep, while she waited for some explanation for his sudden appearance, the words eluded him.

"Come in," she said, filling the space. In the lounge, an annoying KFC advertisement blared from the television. The chewed-out crusts of one of those supermarket frozen pizzas lay on plates on the coffee table, accompanied by the smell of slightly burnt cheese. Cassie flopped onto the couch and he sat beside her, close as he dared, but not too close.

He saw no sign of Blair. "Home alone?" he asked. Cassie had told him her mother only ever painted in the day; something to do with the natural light. So she wasn't in her studio.

"Not quite. Archie's upstairs."

"On the PlayStation."

"Of course. Mum's gone into the city. Left me to cook dinner." She rolled her eyes and cast a glance at the dried out pizza remains. Cassie made no secret of her total lack of talent in the kitchen, although she made a pretty decent sandwich. "One of her friends had an exhibition opening tonight. She'll stay down there. So she can enjoy the champagne."

He couldn't imagine his parents leaving them overnight like that. But then, in almost every way, Blair was a very different kind of parent to them.

"Don't worry, she won't mind you being here," she said, misinterpreting his expression.

Blair trusted him, a reassuring sign. Although, when he'd come up with this plan, he'd assumed she'd probably be *with* them. She might trust him in the house, but he wasn't so sure her trust would extend to him driving her children over to the east coast after dark late on a Saturday night. But she wasn't here. If she was pissed off when she found out later, he'd have to talk his way out of it then.

"Do you think we can drag Archie off that PlayStation?"

"Maybe. Depends what for."

"We're going stargazing."

"Stargazing?"

"Yep, if I did my research correctly, we should be able to see Arcturus coming up in the horizon in about an hour from now. And I think we should all go and watch."

She broke into a grin. "You mean it?"

"Yeah. Of course. Grab a jacket. I'll go get your brother. It might not be his birthday any more but we are still doing this."

He suspected separating Archie from his PlayStation might prove difficult. It helped that the memory of their first meeting still loomed large in the kid's mind. Nik stuck his head around the corner of the door and, too intimidated to do otherwise, Archie meekly agreed.

Within five minutes, they'd bundled Archie into the cramped rear seat of the tiny hatchback while Cassie sat in the front, almost bouncing with excitement. Even in the shadowy light, her face, framed by the upturned collar of a puffer jacket, glowed with life. Something inside him twisted and turned at the sight of her, growing out of the knowledge that he could trigger this happiness, in contrast to her earlier sad mood. Waves of anticipation filled the space as they sped off into the night.

***

"Here," he said, extending a hand to clasp her smaller one in his, as he helped her down the low bank onto the sand. She didn't appear to mind that he didn't release his grip as they strolled further along the beach. The comfortable ease of her walking with him hand in hand encouraged a little flicker of possibility. He was obsessed with Cassie Tremayne. The only time she didn't fill his thoughts was when he got busy in the studio, and even then sometimes she crept up on him.

Here on the east coast, a wide bay opened out in front of them, the glow of the city no longer visible. The soft hiss of the waves lapped against a deserted beach. Archie, freed from the confines of the car, bounded along in front of them. At this age it didn't take much for him to drop the demeanour of jaded disinterest in the world that all fourteen-year-olds were determined to cultivate and fall back into taking childish delight in simple things, like a walk on the beach after dark.

Cassie called him back to where they'd spread out the rug and they seated themselves facing the sea. A slight breeze off the water brought a chill. Grateful for its prompting, as she snuggled in closer to him, he wrapped an arm across her shoulder. Overhead the stars whirled bright against the sky, the absence of streetlights magnifying their beauty. The unfathomable number of them, thousands, millions, billions—that alone made locating only one daunting.

"There it is," Archie said, pointing off to the north, unable to contain his excitement. "See, it's kind of orange."

Nik followed his outstretched hand and sure enough, low in the sky, a shadowy orange star glowed amongst the strings of twinkling white and blue. He breathed a sigh of relief that his afternoon spent poring over star maps and deciphering unfamiliar terms, like 'right ascension' and 'declination', wasn't a waste of time. It would have been gutting to arrive and find he'd fucked it up.

"Dad's favourite star," Archie announced.

"Yeah, but not because of you." Cassie grinned at Archie. "Tell him."

Archie sighed. "Because it's most likely to have life around it."

"Pretty cool, eh?" she said. "Out there somewhere, living things."

"Yeah," Nik agreed, although right this moment, the only life that he cared about was this girl pressed close under his arm. He couldn't imagine finding anything he liked more anywhere in the universe.

It was too big to comprehend, really. The vastness of it all. And them, their lives so tiny and insignificant by comparison. But not to him. This girl, and the feelings he had for her, seemed to spiral out into the void, filling the vast expanse with something that glowed as much as the light of a million stars.

Within a few minutes, Archie, bored with simply gazing at the sky, mumbled something about going for a walk, and ambled off down the beach, his hood pulled tight against the breeze.

Cassie lay back on the blanket, pulling one edge up over her. He mirrored her, lying in silence, the ceiling of the sky sprawling above them. When her hand once more crept across to find his, a current of electricity sprang from the touch. He tried not to let it show, not wanting to mess things up. Something in his gut told him to take it slowly, play the long game. He could be patient.

So he lay there accepting that offer of contact, while she murmured in his ear the names of the constellations above. He let the peaceful hum of her voice wash over him, their heads turning in perfect unison as he followed her outstretched hand, pointing up into the night sky.

The sprawl of the Milky Way resembled one of Blair's more abstract paintings, swathes of silver and gold swirling across a black canvas. As Cassie said each name, he echoed it back at her, marvelling at her knowledge. Of course, he'd heard the names of the constellations many times before, but he'd never truly looked at them. Tonight he imagined it a game of join-the-dots on a cosmic scale; the shapes drawn from the musings of ancient peoples: Orion, the hunter with his belt and sword; Scorpio with the sting in its curved tail; and, of course, the Southern Cross, its beauty only revealed to those in this part of the world. Cassie made things he'd seen all his life become new in his eyes.

"Nik?" She swivelled towards him a little, letting her head flop against his shoulder. They'd been lying in silence, lost in the brush of the waves, the blanket a warm cocoon and neither concerned that the small glow of a cigarette down the far end of the beach was the only sign of Archie.

"Yeah?"

"Can I ask for something for my birthday?"

His heart did a small lurch of pleasure as his mind made the link—her birthday in August and she expected him to still be in her life. But he wasn't sure the part he envisaged for himself in her life was the same as hers. Yes, right now here she was lying next to him, like she'd be open to something more, but he knew that could evaporate in a moment. He'd seen it happen, just a word or a look, and she'd draw back into herself, leaving him standing alone out in the friend zone.

"Oh, so I'm getting you a birthday present now, am I?"

"A-ha." He could feel her smile against his shoulder, her breath warm against his neck.

"Better tell me now so I can save up."

"No need. Can we just come here and do this again?"

The answer was always going to be yes. "Sure," he said. "You know it'll be freezing, right?"

"No, it won't. Not when you're here," she said, looping an arm around his waist as she snuggled into him. He drank in the press of her warm, soft body. Like a faint star bravely twinkling out on the furthest part of the horizon, a small glimmer of hope stirred inside of him. He grasped it tight, knowing that she held the power to snuff it out.

CHAPTER 10

Constellation

Auckland, New Zealand – March 2009

NIK'S SATURDAY MORNING NO-SHOW pissed her off. They'd agreed on nine o'clock to look over the latest assignment. Nik was already spinning out about it, so she couldn't believe he'd just not turn up. With no sign of him by ten, Grace's invitation had come as a welcome diversion to lift her mood. Now close to twelve, back at her house, the empty space out front where he always parked the car riled her. Still no sign of bloody Nik, not a word of excuse from him—of course she was upset.

Running one hand over her sleek hair, she wiped away her annoyance, smiling at the success of the morning's unexpected opportunity. Grace's pestering for a set of GHD hair straighteners had fallen on deaf ears until now. Marija had stood strong with her argument—probably valid—that no girl of their age needed to spend that amount on her hair. But finally she'd relented, parting with a substantial sum of money for Grace's eighteenth birthday.

Cassie paused on the landing by the hallway mirror, examining her reflection and taking time to admire the way her hair now brushed her shoulders in a smooth, coppery curve. Her life had descended into one continuous bad hair day since arriving in Auckland. The humidity played nasty tricks. Some days it tugged her hair into face-framing wings reminiscent of her mother's seventies high school photos. Other times fine strands erupted in all directions, and a Medusa stared at her from the mirror. But not today, thanks to the magic of modern technology.

"You look great."

The low voice from the direction of her bedroom startled her. She turned to face Nik, who lounged comfortably on her bed, a sketchbook open on his lap, her pillows stacked behind him. At least he'd taken his shoes off. And thankfully, the socks and trainers scattered on the floor didn't smell like a piece of pungent French cheese. Archie's made her want to puke.

"You're only saying that to keep me from asking where you've been. You said nine o'clock."

She knew her voice sounded whiny, but she couldn't mask her annoyance with him. Never mind that he'd come every Saturday for eight weeks straight without missing a beat. Never mind that his lateness had worked in her favour. Never mind that she was pleased to see him now, even late—she had long admitted to herself that she looked forward to spending time with him. Despite all of that, she fought against her instant instinct to forgive him. Today, disappointed at his no-show, she wasn't about to let him take her for granted.

Unperturbed, he just grinned back at her, eyes flickering across her with an appreciative gaze. "Even if I was trying to sidetrack you—and I wasn't—your hair still looks great. GHDs?"

"What the—"

"Three sisters. Remember? I know more about hair styling than any guy should have to. It's the topic of conversation at the dinner table every damn night. Unless it's make-up. Or skin care. I try to zone out, but..." He gave a helpless shrug.

"Yeah. GHDs," she said. "But back to the question of where you've been." She wasn't going to let him off that easily. Inside, her determination melted a little under his scrutiny. If she didn't hold strong now, the last of it would trickle away, leaving her with no defences against him.

"I'm sorry," he said, a look of genuine remorse in his eyes. That was perhaps the most disarming thing about Nik—his honesty. Despite her teasing otherwise, she never sensed other than the truth from him. "I had to go up to Jan's for something, and then Mum's fucking car wouldn't start again. It's the second time this week." He shook his head, mouth a tight line of frustration. "I've told her she needs a new battery, but she says she'll take care of it and then doesn't. Anyway, Jan went to see if he could find some jumper leads. And you know..."

He finished with an exasperated huff. A vision of Jan's ramshackle garage mingled with a whiff of understanding of his plight.

"Yeah. I know. How is it a guy whose jewellery studio is so tidy and organised should live amongst a rubbish tip? But there is such a thing as a phone, Nik. I sat here for an hour."

"No coverage up there."

"There's coverage here."

"Yeah, well, by the time Jan dropped me here—he's taken the car up to Wellsford, giving it a good run to recharge the battery—well, I figured you'd be so mad at me I'd be best to wait and own up in person." He stood, looking sheepish, one hand buried in the pocket of his jeans. Her last shreds of resolve to grill him until sure he was absolutely sorry drifted away. He was so easy to forgive.

"OK," she said, letting her hands drop from her hips. "Maybe that was for the best."

"Look," he said, taking a slow breath as if summoning courage. "I need to show you why I had to go to Jan's in the first place." He unfurled his fingers, revealing a small black box in the centre of his palm. "For you." He extended his hand with a shy smile, while his eyes darted nervously from his hand to her face.

"Hey, but it's Grace's birthday, not mine." She frowned, uncertain at this gesture.

"It doesn't need to be your birthday for me to give you something." The words stumbled out as he thrust it towards her.

As she reached to take it, realisation dawned: that sort of box usually came with something significant inside. A knot of nervousness tightened in her own stomach as she balanced it on one hand. She tugged at the snugly fitting lid and a metallic jangle echoed from inside.

He watched, brows furrowed, eyes of intense blue focused on her, while he bit at one lip. Beneath the lid, a circle of gleaming silver nested in black tissue. She lifted the pendant by its fine chain and it twirled in her hand. Stretching out her finger to still the movement, she saw the sparkle of gemstones.

"Nik... Oh my God. You *made* this? For *me*?"

Captured inside the circle, five tiny pale blue stones were arranged in a wide 'W' shape. From each stone, intricate lines etched into the silver gave the impression of starlight extending out into space. Five stars, a constellation. Her constellation, Cassiopeia.

"Did I get it right?" He worried at his lip some more, eyes searching hers.

"Yes," she breathed, "of course you got it right." His body visibly relaxed and his mouth curled into a relieved smile.

She flung herself at him, unable to repress the sheer joy. This had to be the best, most thoughtful gift she'd ever received. His happiness radiated in warm waves as she pressed against the broad chest. When he hugged her to him, resting his chin on her shoulder, the soft brush of his breath against her ear sent a small tremor down her spine. Eyes closed, for a moment she took in how good it felt, to be pressed against the length of him, before he released her carefully, dropping his chin as an embarrassed flush crept across his face.

The small involuntary movement they'd both felt, the quickening of his desire, might have repelled her a few months ago. But the slow, careful building of trust between them had created a broad divide between her disturbing memories of the past and this present.

"Check out the back," he said, braving eye contact, his expression enigmatic.

She turned the pendant over and saw what she'd missed; the words inscribed in neat letters. She read them out loud.

"We are all in the gutter, but some of us are looking at the stars." She knew those words. Lyrics of a song, from a band she'd discovered in her mother's old CD collection.

"The Pretenders, isn't it?"

"No," he said, with a light laugh. "Well, yes. They borrowed it. I thought you were the one who knew your English literature?" He taunted her with an amused grin, relishing her blank look. "Oscar Wilde," he said. "But I think it sounds a bit like us. Not quite in the gutter, but definitely going for the stars."

"A lot like us," she agreed.

"I'll help you put it on." He held out his hand for the pendant, and then motioned her to turn around as he looped the chain behind her neck. His large fingers rested at the nape as he deftly secured the clasp. Surely he must feel the tiny prickle of sensation that rippled across her skin at his touch.

Nik's hands were soft, in contrast to the suggestion of his physical appearance. A big strong guy like him conjured up images of manual labour: a tradie, or a farmer, with skin roughened by hard work. Not the gentle fingers that caressed her neck as he stepped around and straightened the pendant to lie on her collarbone. Not the deft hands that created jewellery like this.

"Just the right length," he said, with an approving pat.

"Oh, I must see." Stepping out into the hallway, the mirror should have reflected the same girl as two minutes earlier. But it didn't.

It wasn't only the pendant gleaming at her throat, or the way her mouth curved upwards. It was the hand resting lightly on her shoulder, the face of the young man staring back at her, their eyes meeting, and the suspicion that in those few minutes her world had changed forever.

"It's so beautiful. I can't believe it. How come you made this for me?" His answer would tell her what she needed to know. Hope and fear mingled, swirling in a nauseating battle in her stomach.

"To say thank you." He paused. "For helping me out of the gutter. Well, at least out of failing English," he added with a smile. "And because you're my friend." The smile broadened and then faded. She saw his throat pulse as he swallowed, and his hand dropped to take hers, giving it a slight squeeze. His words were low and cautious in her ear. "And because I wanted to make something beautiful for the person I hoped might be my girlfriend."

Their eyes met in the mirror. It wasn't bold, confident Nik who stared back at her. This Nik wanted something from her, but handed her the power to decide. In that moment, she knew she'd overcome the terrifying evening of almost two years ago. She'd been a stupid sixteen-year-old impressed by an older boy's interest. To know that it didn't have to be like that; she was in control; she could decide. And with Nik, the decision was easy.

"I think I might like that," she said. "Yes, Nik, I'll be your girlfriend."

He leaned in over her shoulder. He hadn't bothered to shave, and the stubble of his cheek brushed against hers.

"If it's really yes, can I kiss you?"

"Yes. And yes," she said.

He gently turned her towards him, their bodies close, but not yet touching. She placed her hands against his chest, feeling the warm bulk of him under her palms; so familiar but now suddenly so strange. They'd sat side by side often, wrestled playfully on her bed, laughed and touched. But not like this.

Tilting her chin upwards, his finger lightly supporting it, he scanned her face, his eyes darting, as if checking he'd understood correctly.

His lips parted a little, and she caught the slight nervous flick of his tongue between them. She'd thought about this—often. And now here he was, wanting to kiss her, and it sent a shiver of anticipation. She wanted to kiss him, too.

Not waiting, she closed her eyes, slid her hands into his hair and pressed her lips to his. She could tell he'd expected hesitation, but there was none. Only certainty—she wanted this. It seemed the firm pressure of her lips caught him by surprise at first, but his tentative response soon became urgent, the warm softness drawing her in, his mouth growing bolder. His tongue traced the space of her lips, tasting her, seeking her hungrily. Now he covered her mouth with his, demanding more, and she willingly complied.

When he finally pulled away, she felt the loss. Wanted his mouth on hers again. Wanted the probing of his tongue and his teeth lightly grazing her lips. But there was time. After this first kiss, there would be more; many more.

She stood clasped to him, his head on her shoulder. In the space of minutes, her world had changed. Her friend Nik was now more than a friend. Although she'd probably known that for a while, but had hesitated, waiting for him to make the first move.

The faint slap of a sandal caught her attention, and she glanced towards it. Her mother stood at the foot of the stairs, her upturned gaze meeting Cassie's. And the smile on her face—it wasn't merely pleasant, but *pleased*—signalled her approval of the scene. She turned and headed away, whatever her reason for being there shelved for another time.

"Come back in here." Her bedroom offered privacy from a lurking mother. Cassie took him by the hand and led him inside, closing the door firmly behind them. He lay back on her bed, drawing her down beside him, already seeking her mouth.

CHAPTER 11

Sex Ed

Auckland New Zealand – March 2009

"How did she know?" Nik said under his breath, while Blair rummaged in the kitchen. "I mean, the first time I kiss you and suddenly your mum needs to talk to us about 'our relationship'. Is she psychic?"

"No, thank god," Cassie whispered. "But she saw us kissing on the stairs—I should have told you. Damn her, she's developed a new ability to sneak around the house. Normally you can hear her sandals flapping before she gets that far, but today she caught me out. I suppose I was a little distracted." A nervous giggle escaped.

"So," Blair said, eyeing them with a too bright smile, as she strolled from the kitchen, placing two glasses of water on the table before them. She slid onto the couch opposite, elbows on her knees, leaning forward, chin on hands, taking an expectant breath. "As I said, I think it's a good time for us to have a chat and make my position clear."

Cassie grasped at a glass and slugged down a few mouthfuls, hoping the icy liquid might cool her flaming cheeks. Less than an hour into this new direction in her relationship with Nik and her mother intended to have a sex talk with them. This might be the end before it began. What guy would hang around when she had this mad woman for a mother?

Nik cleared his throat and opened his mouth. "Mrs Tremayne—"

"Please, call me Blair. Mrs Tremayne's my mother-in-law and—close your ears, sweetie." She gave Cassie an apologetic look, "—and despite being a wonderful grandmother from afar to the kids, in person she's a right bitch."

"OK, Blair—" he said.

But she pounced, giving him no time to continue. "When I was your age, and I know, don't remind me..." she admonished with a wave of her finger. "... it seems like the dark ages to you..." she chuckled to herself. "... I was backpacking around South America. And spending time with boys. I met some rather gorgeous young men in my travels. And had sex with them, too."

Cassie bit at her lip, cringing down into the couch, wishing it would swallow her between the lumpy cushions. Heat flared, and she felt the blush right down to the roots of her hair. What kid wanted to think of their mother having sex? Even if it was thirty years ago with some gorgeous Latino man; that was not an image she wanted darting around in her head. Nik swallowed audibly and tried to look anywhere except at her mother.

Blair, as always oblivious to her effect on others, continued. "Look, I wanted to say that, if you are, or when you do decide to have sex, please promise me you won't park up in a beach carpark or down some remote forestry road over at Riverhead. Apart from being very uncomfortable, it's not safe."

"Mum, what *are* you saying?" Cassie frowned. Was her mother really suggesting they should just do it here? In her bedroom? And this talk of parking up in cars. If she only knew how sick that suggestion made her feel.

"I'm saying—and Nik, your parents may have a totally different view-point on the matter—there's no point in pretending that young people won't be having sex."

Inside her head, Cassie groaned in agony. Oh, if only she'd stop saying that word over and over.

"But safe sex is more than just condoms. Though I expect you'll use those too. It's so good they teach all of that in school now. Anyway, I'd much prefer if it's happening, that it's here at home where I know you are OK."

Cassie heard Nik gulp air. Her own mouth fell slack in disbelief. She wanted to say it but couldn't: Yes, you're right Nik. My mother is actually saying we can have sex upstairs in my bedroom while she sits in her studio painting and Archie plays video games.

The sound of a car engine saved them from any more of the excruciating conversation. A door slammed. Cassie stood, pushing aside a net curtain. Saved.

"It's Jan," she hissed at Nik. Saved by Jan from what had to have been the most embarrassing five minutes of her life. As long as her mother had enough sense not to continue the conversation in front of a stranger. She wasn't entirely sure she wouldn't. Blair frequently fell short of understand-ing socially appropriate behaviour.

"I'll get the door." She launched herself towards it, a convenient escape from the uncomfortable triangle in the lounge. Ushering Jan in, she crossed her fingers behind her back in desperation.

"Oh, you must be Nik's dad." Blair stood with a smile. "I've just been talking to these two—"

"He's not my Dad." Nik cut in quickly, flashing Cassie a panicked look. Nik's father or not, this conversation needed to end right there.

"Mum, this is Jan. He's the jeweller that Nik's been learning from. Lives up the road."

Her mother lit up, all thoughts of sex education pushed away as she focused on the visitor. "Oh, Jan Dravitski. I know of your work. Blair Tremayne—you might know of me as Blair Silvestri?" She stretched out an eager hand. Cassie knew that tone. It carried a suggestion of hope, an invitation for Jan to reply that he knew of her work, too.

But Jan stood there, rendered mute in her presence. Her mother had that effect on men. With deep copper hair and unlined skin, Blair still possessed the looks that she'd used to charm her way around South America at eighteen and lured Daniel Tremayne when she was almost thirty. Her beguiling smile and the flutter of her long, dark lashes were an instinctive reaction to men, even when she wasn't attempting to flirt. But right this minute it appeared a full-on effort to captivate, and it was working.

After a few beats, Jan came to his senses, grasping her hand and going in for the European double-cheek kiss, while murmuring "Good to meet you."

Seeing his means of escape arrive spurred Nik to his feet. "Better get on the road Jan. Mum needs her car tonight."

"Oh, ya, for sure," Jan replied. "Might have to call in another time, Blair." No one could fail to detect the note of interest in his voice. "Maybe you can show me your latest work?"

Nik leaned across to press an awkward kiss on Cassie's cheek while her mother and Jan continued to eyeball each other optimistically. "Oh my god, Nik, I'm so sorry," she said under her breath. Still mortified, she was barely able to get the words out. How could her mother have spoiled this day so utterly?

"Don't worry," he whispered. He placed one hand on each shoulder, dropping his head to meet her gaze, his face solemn. "I promise, no backseat of the car down at Riverhead."

He broke into a grin. She couldn't help but respond with an embarrassed giggle. If he could make light of this ridiculous situation, then maybe she could, too. And somehow even the thought of parking up in a secluded place with Nik seemed far removed from the last time she'd done that. Because Nik was a very different to the boy who'd driven her in his car on that night. She shivered a little. Was it remembered fear? Maybe, but with his gentle attention, Nik would help her move on from that. She preferred to focus on the quiver of anticipation as her thoughts spiralled down possible pathways where today might lead. As long as, when the time came, she could keep thoughts of her mother's voice, babbling on about condoms, out of her head.

She caught the glint of silver off her chest, drawing her hand to the pendant. She traced the little constellation with one finger. Another reminder of how different Nik was to anyone else she'd let get close.

He leaned in to her, tracing the curve of her cheek with his huge hand. If her mother wasn't worried about them having sex in the bedroom, then she wouldn't object to her kissing him in the lounge. As he was definitely about to do, his eyes focused on her mouth as he cupped her chin.

"Thank you for this," she said. "It's amazing."

His lips met hers, and they kissed slowly, the tender warmth of his mouth sliding across hers, making her whole body turn to thick, sweet liquid. When they parted, it was to face the intense interest of two pairs of eyes upon them. Jan and Blair gazed at them with twin benevolent smiles.

"Sure you're ready?" Jan said, tossing a wink at them.

Catching his lower lip with his teeth, Nik suppressed the grin begging to escape, and followed him out the door.

"Don't forget to call in for coffee sometime when you're passing, Jan," Blair called after him, with a girlish giggle.

Cassie slumped in the chair. She didn't want Nik to leave, but she was also glad he had, calling a halt to the humiliation. Her mother's smile turned her way, hinting at further awkward conversation. She leapt to her feet in panic. "Homework to finish," she blurted, and escaped to the safety of her room.

Chapter 12

Princess

Auckland New Zealand – July 2009

SATURDAYS TOGETHER BECAME WEEKENDS together; then weekends, plus stolen weekday evenings when Nik could escape his family after dinner. Cassie understood how precious this gift of his time was.

After working in Jan's studio during the day, or attending classes at school, Nik was expected to labour at the vineyard every afternoon. With the harvest season over, he worked indoors in the Francovic winery, where the team turned grapes into wines of deepest ruby-red or gold-tinged white. He'd gift a bottle to her mother every so often.

"Pays to keep on side with your girlfriend's mother," he'd said the first time, offering Blair a cheeky grin. Her mother thought him quite the best boy Cassie had ever brought home. Cassie couldn't argue with that.

Nik didn't challenge his mother's expectations, fronting up to night time meals with his family; a wise move given how often he borrowed her car. But the moment he was free from his obligation, he'd drive over to her place, staying long into the night as if not wanting their time together to end.

Tonight he lay on her bed, dominating the width, even though someone had chosen to wedge a generous queen size into the tiny room. She rested her head on his chest, feeling the steady thump of his heart beneath her cheek. She twirled one hand in his hair, while the other traced the shape of his stomach.

His hand slid up her side, moving to cup her breast in his heavy palm, his large fingers giving a gentle squeeze. And although he'd done it dozens of time before, and she'd liked it, this time, her hand seemed to take on a life of its own, roughly brushing him away.

"Sorry," she said, meeting his puzzled expression. "I don't know why I did that. It's OK, really." She took his hand, guiding it back into place, willing herself to relax under his familiar touch.

"Can I ask you something?" he said after a while. She felt the rumble of his words vibrate through her, like the strum of a bass guitar.

"Sure," she said. In the afterglow of making out with him, she always had this blissful feeling that washed over her, as they lay there and talked about everything and anything. So his question provoked only curiosity, not caution.

"You know, when you're lying here like this, I feel like you're so happy to be here. That you're comfortable with—well, you know, this, me touching you, you touching me."

"It's nice. I like it."

"But there are times, like just before, when it's as if you can't bear to be near me, or hate me touching you. I've felt you flinch sometimes. I know you can't help it, but what's that about? I mean, if there's something I do that makes you react that way, I want to know. I hate seeing that happen."

Nik was more perceptive than most guys, attuned to lots of little things in a way she'd never experienced. She should have expected this conversation would come. But she thought she'd hidden it so well. She sucked in a breath. If she trusted him enough to lay here like this, to let him touch every part of her body, she should trust him to know.

"It's OK, Nik. It's not about you. It's about me."

She rolled up onto him, wanting to meet his honest question with an honest answer, for him to see the truth of it in her face, that it was nothing to do with him. She drew in another deep draft of oxygen.

"Back down south, one night about two years ago, a guy tried to force himself on me. A guy I thought I could trust."

She could see the immediate flare of anger in Nik's eyes and the threatening set of his mouth. He didn't need to say it. She knew if it was in his power to dispense justice right now, he would, and it wouldn't be pretty.

"What happened?" he said, his voice low and thick with emotion.

"He picked me up one night, like he'd done a few times before. He was a lot older than me, and I kind of liked that I'd got his attention. Usually we just went into town, grabbed a burger or something. Sat and talked. But that night he drove us out of town, parked up at a lookout at the far end of the lake. I mean, it was naïve of me to not realise his intentions. He wasn't taking me down there to look at the view. And, well, things got out of hand. Fast." She couldn't conceal a shudder at the remembered fear. "I tried to fend him off, but he wouldn't listen. Called me a little prick tease. Said he knew I was gagging for it." She cringed at the words, so disgusting even coming from her own mouth. "I still wonder if another car hadn't pulled in right that minute..." Sometimes luck fell on your side and that night it sure had been on hers. "Anyway, he climbed off me, shoved me out of his car and left me there on the side of the road."

"Shit, Cassie," he said. "That's...that's just so fucked up. That's attempted rape. It's a crime. Did you lay a complaint or anything?"

She shook her head. "If it happened now, I would. But back then, I thought it was my fault. I've learned a lot since then."

"How could you even think it was your fault? No means no, right?"

"Yeah, he should never have assumed. And he should have stopped way sooner than he did."

"Bastard. I'd like to wring his fucking neck," he growled. "If you ever see him, you tell me. If he comes near you, I promise I will deal to him."

She absolutely believed him. And hoped their paths never crossed. One, because of the emotions that it would stir up in her at seeing his face again, and two, because of the outcome of Nik's rage.

"Not much chance of that. He went to Australia soon after. I talked to the school counsellor, and she encouraged me to do something about it. But I decided—what's the point? He's gone. I learned."

"I'm really sorry that happened to you. And I'm sorry that I asked. Bringing up those bad memories for you."

"No, it's OK. I'm kind of glad we got that out of the way. You understand that I do like you touching me? Just sometimes, I get like a flash of memory, and my body reacts without thinking."

"Don't worry, Princess," he said. "If it happens, I'll know it's just my brave little warrior scanning for a threat."

"Why *do* you call me that?" she asked.

"What? Princess?"

"Yeah, I mean, I don't exactly think I'm the usual princess type."

He'd played with that name for her since they'd first met. The thought of being some fairy-tale princess didn't fit. Not with her; she wasn't into froth and frills, or simpering eyelash flutters. Her vintage dresses were more 50s Hollywood starlet than Disney heroine. And she wasn't one of those high maintenance Barbie princess girls, all primping and preening, obsessed with their makeup and hair.

Nor did it fit with how Nik treated her; although he'd come to her rescue a few times back there at the start, he seemed to admire her strength, pleased she wasn't some helpless damsel in distress relying on him to sort out the world.

"You're *not* the usual princess type," he said. "But that first day when I arrived to find you in the middle of two aggressive little guys having a go, your hair flying, and you telling them what's what—well, the first thought that came into my head, was 'Oh my god, it's fucking Xena'. You know *Xena, Warrior Princess*? Lucy Lawless?"

She burst into laughter. She'd never felt powerful enough to consider someone might make a comparison like that. "For real?"

"Oh, yeah. You looked scary." He waggled his eyebrows, his face contorted in a caricature of fear. But he couldn't hold it and his laughter rumbled through his chest, causing it to ripple against the press of her breasts, almost dislodging her.

"Not scary enough to stop them scrapping."

"Maybe not. Not when they were so fired up. But anyone in their right mind would respect a girl who looked like you did. I considered standing back and leaving you to it. Princess," he said, tapping her on the nose. "You'd have sorted them out, I bet."

"I'm glad you didn't," she said.

"Me too. Otherwise I would have had to find another reason to introduce myself. I never thought I'd be grateful to two scrappy little Year 10 dickheads."

A softer laugh tickled against her ear. Then he moved to nibble at it gently. He rolled her off him, lowering her to the bed, crushing her body to him. She lay there, feeling his constant warmth against the length of her. He nudged a knee between her thighs, and she parted them, inviting him in closer. They lay intertwined, the only sound their breathing, almost in perfect unison, and she basked in the comfort of having him there, knowing her secret, and trusting him with it.

She always wanted Nik's body against hers. In fact, she wanted Nik's body inside hers. Each time after he left her, she'd lie in bed at night thinking about maybe the next time, going that step further. It was such a small step. They'd done practically everything but have sex. So it shouldn't be such a big deal.

She knew what it was like to have his hand stray into the band of her panties, and his fingers find that very spot that ignited all her nerve endings into a burst of sensation. Just as Nik's large hands could deftly shape a lump of jeweller's clay, moulding delicate shapes at his touch, so he touched her with an unexpected delicacy that sent her body insane.

She'd read enough books to understand what was happening to her, but she was in no way prepared for the explosions of white hot pleasure. Somehow she'd thought—no doubt because that's what happened in books—a proper earth-shattering orgasm would only happen at the hands of some older, more experienced lover, not her eighteen-year-old high school boyfriend.

She'd been prepared for his exploration to be hesitant, clumsy even. But Nik brought the same careful attention to her body as he brought to the task of handling the clay, watching intently to see the effects of his touch.

At first it had unnerved her, his eyes upon her, watching every twitch of her body, every expression on her face with a pleased scrutiny.

When she stroked at his penis, thick and ribbed with veins, yet with skin so soft, and watched it grow eager under the touch of her hand, she wondered what it would be like to invite it inside her. He was so much bigger than her, but when he rolled onto her, he always caged her a little, taking most of his weight so as not to crush her beneath. She welcomed the solid feel of him, blanketing her body with warmth and safety.

Even through their clothes, the length of him pressed hard against her. The thought of him pushing it into her sent shivers of anticipation. Between her legs, a little ache of longing for him to fill that empty space simmered away. But she wasn't ready for that yet, and sometimes she worried, knowing he was. She feared that despite reassuring him otherwise, when the day came—and she knew it would, as they explored further and further, edging relentlessly towards it nearly every time they were alone—that she'd freeze. And that would be beyond embarrassing. She'd already decided her virginity was Nik's to claim; if only she could convince her stupid brain to let him.

CHAPTER 13

Elephant In The Room

Auckland New Zealand – July 2009

SEX. IT WAS THE elephant in the room. Not a large benign presence like Burma, the resident elephant at Auckland Zoo, standing quietly in the corner swaying her trunk from side to side, content in knowing she would eventually get attention. No, this elephant trumpeted at them, demanding to be heard.

Bloody Blair Tremayne. He blamed her. No sneaking around. No fending off suspicious looks. For a guy of his age, it should have been a dream to have a girlfriend with an open-minded mother. It was a fucking nightmare.

They hadn't taken Blair's conversation as a reason to jump straight in. However, embarrassing as it had been, it had broken the ice. He and Cassie had discussed the subject with an openness that he'd never done before. To even talk about it beforehand was new. While he'd fooled around with quite a few willing girls, he'd only had actual sex with two. And both times it hadn't been him who'd made the decision to take things that far.

The first time, two summers ago, a girl his older cousin knew, had made it her goal to work her way through the guys in the extended Francovic family. At sixteen, he'd felt flattered to have caught the attention of a worldly eighteen-year-old. And stunned disbelief that she would suggest they go all the way after a few minutes of mutual pawing behind one of the packing sheds. Remembering it made him cringe at how overly eager he'd been.

The second time a girl he'd known since primary school had lured him in. A student at St Teresa's, the Catholic girls' school over on the North Shore, she'd asked him as her date to last year's Year 12 and 13 ball. It seemed losing your virginity had become an after-ball rite of passage for the St Teresa's girls. It had started with some awkward fumbling on both their parts. Every spare bedroom in the vast house free of parents held teenagers doing the same thing. Surprised when she'd whipped out a condom from her handbag—and intimidated by the expectation that he knew what to do with it—he'd hesitated a moment. But he did know what to do, and his body had begged him to. So he had. They'd not seen each other again. He'd served his purpose.

But this afternoon, with Cassie, the elephant pushed its way forward, despite his attempts to hold it off. Because of her past bad experience, it was a huge act of trust to even go as far as they had. And when they took that next leap, because it would be her first time, he wanted it to be good for her. And also because he wanted things between them to keep moving forward, not take a backward step. He worried a physical change in their relationship might change other things.

The surrounding house was silent, not only in the absence of sound, but in that deeper sense that indicated the absence of people. They were alone, the empty house offering freedom. No one else hovered outside this space. There was no chance anyone might overhear Cassie's soft mewling sounds under the touch of his hand between her thighs, or her small groan of pleasure as he slid one finger inside of her.

He always took care in his exploration, not wanting to hurt her with his inexperience, but determined to do more of whatever evoked this response. Her eyes were closed, head arched back against the pillow as he stole a glance. It seemed wrong to watch as if intruding on a part of her that he wasn't yet entitled to know. But he couldn't help it, entranced with the beauty of her face and the thrill of knowing he was responsible for that expression of blissful enjoyment.

Her eyes flickered open and her languid expression suggested his observation didn't bother her. She smiled, moving her body against the pressure of his hand, thrusting her small hips upward against it. His own groan poured out, morphing into a growl as her hand probed under the waistband of his jeans, slim fingers finding the swell of his cock.

He gently moved the finger inside of her, in and out, each time a little deeper, feeling the tiny flutters intensify. God, what it would be like to feel the clench of those strong muscles around him, the heat and pressure of her against his cock. The mere thought sent his mind pounding with need for her. But he pushed it aside, focusing back on her pleasure. He wanted her to enjoy this. He'd learned how to do that over these winter afternoons, studying her as carefully as he'd studied his craft. Good with his hands, he now applied those talents to a new purpose. He took pleasure in her response to his touch, adjusting ever so slightly as he saw something she liked, or something that didn't quite work. He knew her body well, and he loved what he could make it do.

With his free hand, he continued to massage outside of her, each circle of his thumb causing her to melt beneath it, as new surges of wetness engulfed her. They didn't teach you that in sex ed—that a girl could be so warm and wet. Probably just as well, given what the slick feeling of her did to his brain. Not that any explanation delivered by a slightly embarrassed teacher to a class of awkward teenagers could prepare you for the reality. The warmth and the smell, sweet and salty hanging thick in the air, made him want to lean down and taste her. But he would hold back from that. He didn't want his own crazed need to make him take a step too far. Not yet.

When she came against his hand in huge, rippling waves of pleasure, the powerful shudders rocked his body. It still blew his mind that he could do this to her, for her, with her. He almost came himself simply from the way she totally overwhelmed all his senses at that moment. Giving her what she deserved felt amazing, letting her be worry-free and just enjoy his undivided attention.

He leaned over her, capturing her mouth in his, her lips still curved in a wide O of delight, before dropping to nuzzle against her neck. He tasted the soft skin, lapping his tongue in the small hollow there, inhaling the smell of her like a drug, even though he couldn't yet taste all of her yet.

Her hand sought his erection, huge and stiff against his broad thigh. She too had learned, her strokes coming bold and confident.

"Look at you," she giggled as she settled into a rhythm, the power in that small hand reminding him of the strength inside her body. With each upward stroke, her thumb brushed the tip of him, tantalising that sensitive area. Each time, anticipating that touch drove him wild with need. He felt it glide across the little beads of liquid already leaking from him, making each new stroke even more smooth. Feeling the tight grip of her hand, he imagined her whole body tight around him, his cock gripped between those hidden muscles that pulsed and clenched—and he exploded with a rush, the thick hot spray soaking her hand and his belly. He sprawled back against pillows, each last small movement of her hand causing him to spurt some more.

"Sorry," he said, looking at the mess. "God, the bed is soaked."

"It's everywhere," she laughed and, grabbing the corner of a sheet, mopped his wet stomach a moment, before giving up on the task. The bed was awash with sweat and patches of sticky liquid. She snuggled in against him, one knee across his legs, the curve of her thigh against his hip, and it felt so damn good. Not in the way that massive explosion of sensation from moments before had felt good, but a comfortable warm feeling like he could simply lie there like this forever and never want for anything more.

"I want to do that with you inside of me." Her hot breath against his ear sent a renewed thrill of desire through him, and his slack cock, lying in a sad spent curl between his legs, stiffened a little, as if hopeful it could fulfil that request, even though he knew he couldn't usually revive it that quickly. "Nik, I'm ready. To do it properly."

"OK," he said. "Not today though."

"No. You probably couldn't anyway, right? Too soon?"

Oh, he probably could. In fact, he knew he could. But he wouldn't. He wanted her first time to be more special than a quick afternoon shag in her bed, all the while one ear listening out for the possible return of her mother, or Archie.

He wanted to start at the beginning, bringing her slowly and surely to the point where she wanted nothing else in the world but him inside of her, all other thoughts banished. Including the thoughts of that other bastard who'd come so close to grabbing her precious virginity for himself.

"Yeah," he lied. "Not today. But one day soon. OK."

"OK," she said. "Soon."

CHAPTER 14

Orbit

Auckland New Zealand – August 2009

"You look very smart, Nik."

"Thanks. Orbit's meant to be a flash restaurant. Thought I'd better make an effort for it." And for Cassie. She'd spent all afternoon getting ready.

His leg jiggled as he sat under the scrutiny of Blair Tremayne's cat-like eyes. In so many ways they were identical to Cassie's—an unusual amber, with small gold flecks, framed in dark lashes—but that knowing, calculating expression was all Blair. Cassie's mother had a definite edge that her innocent and less worldly-wise daughter lacked.

Today, those eyes held an extra spark, matching the way she spoke to him, her words almost too bright. Did she know? How could she? A mother's intuition, perhaps? It made him uncomfortable.

He sat staring at the television, pretending to pay attention to the six o'clock news while in his head he checked off all his arrangements. Cassie turned eighteen today, and he was determined to give her the best birthday ever. And then there was the other thing they'd agreed to.

Tonight they'd do it. Go all the way. He inwardly shivered in anticipation. After all this time of going slow and careful, pulling himself back when all he'd wanted to do was slip inside of her, tonight he wouldn't need to hold out any more. He hoped her mother couldn't read the thoughts of her daughter that swirled in his head right this moment. Shaking himself, he pushed them away, and tried to look interested in the sports news, dominated by that night's rugby test match.

He couldn't give a shit about whether the All Blacks walloped the Springboks in Hamilton. These days he paid little attention to the game, just keeping up enough that he could join in with his mates' conversation. Slowly but surely, his life had shifted. While to them, he might look like the same old Nik—a bit suspect with all his arty-farty jewellery-making shit—but a pretty normal West Auckland guy all the same; he was far from the same. Not since January when a bronze-haired warrior princess upended his world. She was his first thought when he woke in the morning and the last at night.

Footsteps sounded on the stairs, and he and Blair looked up in unison. Her mother beamed with pride. Although he'd seen the whole outfit laid out carefully on her bed, he wasn't prepared for the sight of her.

With a mother and three sisters obsessed with clothing, hair and make-up, he'd had a head start on learning about girly stuff. Lying on Cassie's bed on winter afternoons while she trawled through pages of magazines where women dressed like 1950s pin-up girls stared back at them, he'd learned a whole lot more. And now she stood here in front of him, like a cover model for her favourite 'Vintage Style' magazine.

The navy polka-dot wiggle dress clung to her curves, ending a little below the knee. Its sweetheart neckline directed his gaze towards the dip of her breasts. He also knew the little navy shoes were called kitten heels. Not the sort of knowledge most eighteen-year-old guys possessed.

This outfit wasn't one of the regular op-shop finds that filled her wardrobe. She'd earned this brand new retro designed dress. He'd encouraged her to enter a short story into a competition. With the unexpected win and a hundred dollar prize, she'd bought her own birthday present. Tonight, gift-wrapped in it, he couldn't help but imagine taking it off her later.

She'd coaxed her hair into sleek curves, no doubt with the help of the hair straighteners her father had sent from Arizona. Daniel Tremayne might be absent, working at some remote desert observatory, but he seemed reliable enough, phoning once a week, and ensuring the birthday present arrived on time. But Nik was grateful for his absence tonight, though. It was bad enough facing Blair, who already assumed they were having sex under her roof. He shuddered at the idea of sitting there in front of Cassie's father, knowing his plans for the night ahead.

"Darling, you look beautiful," her mother said.

The silver pendant dangled at her neck, little shards of light flashing off the inlaid gemstones. But nothing could compare to the girl who stood before him on the stairs, shining so bright it almost hurt.

Holding Cassie's hand as the lift plummeted down fifty-two floors to the base of the Sky Tower, he was still reeling from the unexpected kindness of the restaurant staff. Nerves had almost overwhelmed him as in a shaky voice, he'd given the booking name. He'd felt so conspicuous, sitting in the revolving restaurant, high above the blazing city lights, two high-school kids dressed like grown-ups in the middle of the Saturday night crowd. But Cassie had glowed under the spotlight of the wait staff's respectful attention.

It had cost Nik a whole four weeks of extra hours at the winery after school, but it was worth it. Worth spending hours in the dingy back shed, chopping up old pallets for firewood, unstacking and restacking barrels, and hefting rubbish into a skip. To see her enjoying all the special attention, the food, the champagne, and even a little birthday cake, he didn't regret the hours of his time taken to provide it. Yes, when she told her father, he would understand how much Nik cared for her.

She sat, eyes a little hooded, a languid, satisfied smile on her face as they spiralled up from the depths of the underground carpark. A turmoil of tension and uncertainty swirled inside him. He gripped the wheel with white knuckles as he navigated the maze of on and off ramps at 'Spaghetti Junction' and swung the car onto the North-Western Motorway.

While trying to keep his mind on negotiating the motorway traffic, still thoughts of her father, this unseen man, came back to trouble him. Daniel would definitely approve of the expensive dinner at Orbit. And as he detoured up the winding road towards Karekare Beach, he suspected Daniel Tremayne might not be at all understanding of what they intended to do next. But he was a few thousand kilometres away, and nothing would stop them. Unless she changed her mind. She might. And while his body even now struggled against that possibility, his mind and his heart would be OK with it. He could be patient. For her.

Because not only did he want to make love to Cassie Tremayne—he loved Cassie Tremayne. What would his friends say to that? He'd never admit it out loud to them. His mates pretty much still saw it as shagging, bonking, getting your rocks off, a quick fuck. Love was a word they feared girls might throw at them, with no knowledge of how to respond, except the unspoken rule that you didn't say it back. Yes, they lacked the vocabulary for this thing that existed between him and Cassie—because none of them had the experience of a girl like her.

Once or twice before, it had been on the tip of his tongue. Tonight, he wouldn't back away. He would say it. Whether she decided to go ahead with their plan and let him make love to her—he hoped that's what would happen—or whether she stopped him short as they'd done many times before—no matter what, he wanted to tell her. And despite his other fears—his lack of expertise; the threat that the lustful eagerness of his body would engulf him—he felt no fear in his decision to say it. As he pulled into the empty bush-shrouded car park, he rehearsed the three words in his mind: "I love you."

CHAPTER 15

Breaking The Rules

Auckland New Zealand – August 2009

"SO WE'RE FINALLY BREAKING Mum's rule, are we?" Cassie shot Nik a grin as they pulled into the empty car park at Karekare Beach. Her voice came out slightly high, as nervousness gripped her throat. "Parking up in out of the way places at night."

"Yeah, looks like we are," he said. "Is it still OK?" Sweet Nik, even now, he offered her an out. But she wouldn't go back on their plan.

"Of course. It feels like a night for breaking rules."

Feeling a little woozy, she climbed out and waited while he flipped open the hatchback. Inside sat two backpacks, one hers she'd smuggled out to the car the previous day. His own overstuffed pack sat alongside.

"It's kind of funny," she said, a hiccupping giggle forcing its way out. With him the sober driver, she'd drunk most of the bottle of champagne at the restaurant. She'd never had more than a glassful before, and now the effects of all those tasty bubbles were catching up with her. "Look at me. Getting out of one set of clothes, into new ones, just so you can take them off me again later on."

He grinned across at her. "Not much later on, I promise. Here, let me help you with that."

She let her hand fall from where she'd been struggling with her zipper. The brush of his hand across the bare skin of her back sent tingles of electricity. He trailed his fingers down towards the base of her spine, letting them linger in the hollow there, and she shivered at his touch. He peeled the dress away, exposing her back, before leaning his body against hers, wrapping her from behind. The warm, hard muscles of his chest pressed against her bare skin. He nuzzled at her nape with small nips of his teeth grazing the sensitive skin beneath. A hot surge of desire surged downwards, igniting heat deep in her centre.

If he suggested, right this minute, they have sex in the car, she'd probably agree. But he'd been so adamant this should be special, not losing her virginity in a quick tumble in the back seat. So, she stuck to the plan, damping down her need, stepping away from his embrace. She removed the dress, rolling it carefully, before tucking it away in her bag on top of the sweet little navy shoes.

In jeans and jumpers, with sensible trainers on their feet, they set off hand-in-hand along the bush track and then down the length of the beach. Around the curve of the headland, avoiding the crumbling cliffs, he made for a spot where once more low bush met the sand. He spread out a rug and dumped his backpack. While he scouted for driftwood, she unzipped it, pulling out handful after handful of the sleeping bag he'd stuffed inside. She lay it out across the rug, smoothing out the fluffy layers of down.

"Nik?"

He squatted by the mound of sticks as he attempted to coax the little fire into life.

"Yeah?"

"Ahh, how do you see this working?" The sleeping bag looked barely big enough to contain his large body, let alone the two of them. And then removing clothes, and—. He read her frown and laughed.

"Unzip it silly." Now she saw it. A small zipper ran right around the edge of the bag. She worked it undone all the way, and, with a shake, the mummy-like cocoon became a soft billowing blanket. She unlaced her trainers, tossing them and the socks in a heap. She flexed her toes in the silky sand. The cool grains soothed her feet, still tender from the confines of her pointy-toed shoes.

As the fire grew from a few shaky flames into a determined blaze, he tossed lumps of driftwood on top and came to sit alongside her. She studied his face, so serious in the flickering glow, as he tugged off his shoes. He lay back on the rug next to her, pulling her down beside him and shuffling the blanket up to their chins.

"See, I promised I'd take you stargazing for your birthday," he said. Sparks from the lively fire drifted skyward, merging with the swathes of stars that filled the sky.

"You did. Seems you're good at keeping promises."

"And I'm going to keep my other promise to you, too." His voice came low and husky, as he tilted her head towards him, catching her mouth in a slow, deep kiss. "That's if you're still OK with it?" he mumbled through more demanding exploration of her mouth.

"Yeah," she breathed, "I'm OK. I'm excited." Inside her, the fizzing bubbles of anticipation frothed up like the pink champagne.

"Oh, yeah," he laughed against her mouth. "Me too, if you can't tell."

"I can tell." With a giggle, she let her hand wander down to where she could feel him hard, pushing against his jeans. It sent a small thrill to think of that strength inside her, thrusting against her. She loved it when he moved his hand inside of her, bringing her to an orgasm that had initially caught her by surprise. It felt every bit as good as she'd imagined, perhaps more so, but still there was a remoteness about it. Just as when she'd used her own hands to work him into a frenzy before he came in huge, spurting pumps all over them; that was doing something to him, and for him, but as an observer, not fully part of it. She longed to do it *with* him.

"I've got what we need." He pulled his hand free of the blanket. Moonlight glinted off the foil packet.

"Good," she said. "I hope they're not the ones Mum gave you?"

"No." She saw his nose wrinkle. "Nope. Bought them myself at the mall pharmacy."

They'd both agreed there was definitely something 'ick' about her mother providing condoms.

"OK," she said, grabbing at his zipper. "How about we see if I can remember what they taught us in school?" Right now she appreciated the lessons, embarrassing as they had been. She knew what to do with a condom.

"Everything off first," he said. "It's never been you and me completely skin to skin. I want to feel that."

She did as he said, stripping off all her clothes, before they lay facing each other, warm under the blanket. They fit together so well, his large body cocooning her gently. She marvelled at the softness of his skin. Even his penis, so hard and erect, felt sleek and delicate. He shivered at her touch as she unrolled the condom carefully along its length.

"I love you," he whispered, before he rolled over onto her, taking most of his weight carefully on his elbows.

"I love you too, Nik," she said, tilting her hips upwards towards him, tugging him closer, not wanting anything, not even air, to come between them. And the words—it wasn't the first time she'd tried them out—but this time he'd said it too. And she believed him. This wasn't only the raw sexual need of two horny teenagers. They loved each other.

She bent her knees up, letting her legs fall apart a little, and guided him with her hand. He entered her part way, and she tried to relax, expecting pain and knowing it would be less if she could fight the overwhelming tension of need and anticipation and nervousness that gripped her body.

"OK?" he asked. Above her, despite the gloom of the night, she saw his concern.

"A-ha," she said, then tried to rein in her sharp gasp of pain as she took the full length of him into her, and heat rose through her body, swamping her with sensation, before she relaxed, meeting his rhythm with her own instinctive response. She closed her eyes, blocking out the spirals of stars and the slender crescent moon, the only witnesses to their first time.

CHAPTER 16

History Repeats

Auckland New Zealand – November 2009

"You know you don't need to go through with this." Her mother's bleak suggestion caught her by surprise. "Nowadays, if you don't want to have the baby, it's so much more straightforward..."

"I know, Mum. But you had the same choice, and you chose to have me."

Yes, back in 1991, her mother would have had to jump through hoops to arrange a termination, but Cassie truly believed that had never been an option. She'd always felt loved and wanted, not that she existed simply because the alternatives were inconvenient.

"Cassie, I was twenty-nine. I'd travelled the world, seen things, done things. You're eighteen years old, with everything ahead of you."

"Mum, everything *is* still ahead of me. Your life didn't end when you had me. Did it?"

Her mother's face rippled with a brief flash of uncertainty before rearranging into her usual confident, composed self once more.

"Of course not," she said carefully. "But it changed. It had to. And I wanted it to," she added quickly, "because it meant I could give you the life you needed."

"See, that's the thing, Mum. I had this plan of what my life would be like after high school. But it's changed. And I want it to." The words choked a little as she tried to find the courage inside her to justify her decision to the person she'd thought would support her without hesitation. The one person she'd thought would automatically be on her side. "Because I'm having this baby, and I'm keeping it. And I'm prepared to do whatever it takes for me to be a good mother to it."

The tears squeezed out. Blair reached for her, pulling her in close, and she lay with her head against her mother's chest, soaking the soft, woolly jumper. She breathed in the eucalyptus scent of wool-wash embedded in its fibres and the fresh antiseptic smell was strangely uplifting. Fingers stroked her hair, the gentle tugs as her mother twisted small tendrils, soothing her distress.

"And you will be my darling." Her mother murmured the words against her hair. "If that's what you really want, you will be."

They sat there for ages, lying side by side on her mother's bed, her tense body cradled in the safety of her mother's arms.

"Mum," she said after a while. "That's not all." She felt the slight stiffening in her mother's embrace. "Nik and I are going to get married."

Blair pulled back from her. The amber eyes met hers, a tender sadness there, as if reluctant to cause hurt, but unable to prevent it.

"Darling, you know I think Nik's a wonderful guy. And I truly think he loves you. It's no surprise that he'd want to do the right thing by you and this baby. He's not your usual eighteen-year-old. Dare I say it, he's even old-fashioned. But I would say the same, no matter who it was. You don't need to get married. Wait a little. Have the baby. Then if you still feel the same way, get married then."

"But why? If you'd met Dad when you were eighteen, would you have *not* married him?"

"I'd like to think I might have recognised he was the one."

Her mother's gaze drifted towards the three paintings on her bedroom wall. Blair had insisted these pictures of her father, Daniel, must accompany them to Auckland. Blair had painted them back when they'd first met, and they had always occupied their joint bedroom. Maybe bringing them with her was a way of keeping him close.

Cassie had always felt that way about them too, a constant reminder of the other most important person in her life, even when her father's work took him far from home. She'd sat in her parents' bedroom, staring at a younger version of her father, sometimes even talking to him, when the poor phone connections in remote places made the real thing impossible.

Apart from keeping his presence in their minds, these pictures were also special in that they were the only portraits her mother, a landscape painter, had ever produced. They would never be for sale—not that anyone else even knew of their existence to offer money, since they'd never left her room.

"Looking at those paintings of him, Mum, I think you would have." You could see the artist's love for her subject poured onto the canvas, the way she'd captured his smile, the angle of his head.

"I'm not so sure. My judgement as to the sort of men you might marry wasn't exactly great before I met Daniel. I was twenty-six when I first married and what a disaster that was. If sharing my own experience can save you that pain..."

"Mum, I know you don't want me to be hurt like you were." Even now, much as her mother would never admit it, there remained a small trace of the damage that shitty Italian guy had inflicted. Even years of her father's unfailing devotion hadn't managed to erase it totally. "But Nik would never hurt me. He's young, but he knows what he wants more than anyone I've ever met. Certainly more than anyone our age. And he wants me and he wants our baby. He wants us to be a family."

Blair reached her hand towards Cassie's face, tracing her jaw with a sad smile. "And I can see it's what you want. OK. I suppose we should call your father. Get the phone."

Might as well get it over with now while she still possessed the courage. She grabbed her mother's mobile.

Two hours later, she sat in her room fully dressed, ready to go. She worried at a loose tag of skin on one nail. The misty rain drifting through the trees intensified, and she closed her window against its rhythmic patter. The thick humidity hanging in the air dulled her brain. Sitting at her window, she waited for Nik, relieved that she'd navigated the first hurdle. She could put the rest aside until tomorrow.

They'd agreed he'd come at eleven and they'd head up to Jan's. Like most Saturdays lately, she'd sit and write while watching him work, something she found incredibly restful. Spurred on by a few small successes, where someone had actually given her money in return for the words she spun on the page, each keystroke felt like one more step towards their future. Meanwhile, Jan had sold a few of Nik's pieces on his behalf. He'd been so excited, depositing the modest profit in a newly-opened business account. It felt like they were already shifting into the grown-up versions of themselves; people who could handle the very grown-up responsibilities of marriage and babies.

When she sat there beside him, she could see her and Nik in the years ahead: he, an artist making his exquisite jewellery; she, an author, spending her days immersed in her imaginings; perhaps living somewhere like Jan's place, a cottage in the bush—although she'd keep house much better than Jan—with Nik's studio right next door; the two of them raising their beautiful child together.

At the sound of an engine, and the crunch of braking tyres on the gravel driveway, she leapt to her feet. "I'm off, Mum," she called as she reached the foot of the stairs. Blair had sought refuge in her painting after the morning's earlier upheaval. Not waiting for an answer, Cassie tumbled into the car, dragging her small laptop bag behind her.

"How did it go?" Nik asked, bringing her back to the hard reality. "I wish you'd let me be there with you," he said, squeezing her hand.

She'd insisted she do it alone. She wanted to take responsibility for this, not have her parents look to Nik and attribute blame. It wasn't either of their faults. An accident. Everyone knew it happened, no matter how careful you were: unplanned pregnancy. God, that was what had happened to her parents. She wasn't having anyone think she'd been a naïve party in this whole mess.

"OK, I suppose. They weren't exactly thrilled." Not thrilled was an understatement. Her mother's surprising thinly-veiled unhappiness at the choices they'd made, and her father's blatant disappointment echoing down the line all the way from America, had been hard to take.

"Your Dad's not leaping on the first flight back here to hunt me down and kill me?"

"No," she said. "He's working."

She missed her dad. And although her mother had been through all this herself, somehow she still didn't feel present in this situation, just as she'd never quite felt present in their lives. Maybe it was her self-sufficiency, or her single-minded obsession with her art, but Blair always remained a little remote.

Whereas her father, despite his frequent physical absence, had supported her every move, celebrated her accomplishments, and been there for her. Except perhaps this past year. This time his separation from her mother, and from them, had a sense of permanence about it. She wished she'd asked him to come home.

Tomorrow an even bigger hurdle awaited—they'd tell his parents, and what she knew of them caused the painful knot of dread to twist even more tightly in her stomach.

CHAPTER 17

A Family Of Your Own

Auckland New Zealand – November 2009

"You look beautiful," he said, appearing at her shoulder. But his calm voice and steadying presence weren't enough to stop her trembling hand as she attempted to swipe a trace of mascara on her lashes.

"Thanks." Her weak smile reflected back at them, despite her resolution to be brave. Nik had arrived at her house early and now patiently waited in her bedroom, watching her agonise over every tiny detail as they prepared to tell his parents.

She struggled even with this first decision—make-up or not. He'd told her his mother always wore it. Antonija Francovic took care of herself: facials, manicures, and an account at Smith and Caughey's department store, where the beauty counter staff apparently knew her by name. A little time spent on good grooming would be useful, even expected, when she met her future mother-in-law for the first time.

Perhaps this mask of make-up would help her appear older and wiser, and therefore more capable of being a mother to their grandchild, and a wife to their son. She reached for a lipstick, applying it as neatly as she could with shaky fingers. But the coral smear made her lips appear too bold.

Looking like this, they'd probably label her as some painted little tart who'd snared their golden boy by luring him into marriage with a baby. She wouldn't be the first to take that road. According to Grace, lots of the Westie girls around here trapped guys with pregnancy. She swore it happened all the time, and while it didn't always bind their man to them forever as they may have hoped, it at least ensured the regular income of a government benefit.

After dithering for a moment, she opted for compromise: the sheer layer of foundation, and the brush of mascara could stay, and she'd change the lipstick to a more neutral shade. She grabbed for a tissue, removing the bright splash of colour in one swoop. She'd only just perfected the second sweep of lipstick when Nik leaned in with a reassuring kiss.

"Nik," she complained, dabbing at the smudges around her mouth. "I can't turn up there looking like we've this minute tumbled out of bed."

"Might be best we deal with that then," he teased, pointing at her hair.

It was true: left to find its own way, it *did* look as if she'd just fallen out of bed. And that wouldn't be a good idea. The last thing she wanted was any association between her and beds—because look where that had got them. But if she scooped it back in a ponytail, rather than convey a sleek business-like maturity, it tended to make her look exactly what she was—an eighteen-year-old high school girl with hair tamed in regulation fashion.

Again she went for middle ground, using her hair straighteners to flatten it into neat waves. In her nervousness, she caught the tip of one ear-lobe on the plates and winced at the sharp pain. The slight whiff of burning skin hung acrid in the air. But surveying the end result in the mirror, she breathed a grateful thank you in her father's direction for the welcome birthday gift.

"It looks great," Nik said, as she fussed over a few last disobedient strands. "Honestly, it's perfect." He settled back onto her bed, grabbing the top item from that morning's mountain of discarded outfits. "OK, Princess, what are you going to do about this lot? It's like Cinderella getting ready for the ball."

"I wish," she said. They hadn't actually gone to the school ball. Neither of them were close to many kids in their year group. Nik had rolled his eyes in horror when Grace had mentioned he'd need a suit. And Blair had relaxed with a visible sigh of relief when she'd announced they probably wouldn't go. Her family wasn't broke, but the full cost—a dress and shoes, hair and nails, not to mention the ticket—added up to a lot for one event. Instead, they'd stayed home, watched movies and drank a bottle of the new Francovic sparkling rosé—sweet and light, like alcoholic soda—that Nik had smuggled out of the winery. They'd managed to evade the drama of ball prep, but this much more daunting task was unavoidable.

If it had been any other situation, he'd have laughed, teasing her that she'd morphed into one of those other princesses, fussing over clothes. But in his genuine concern for her distress, he leaned into the task, holding up one item after another.

"So maybe this?" he asked, dangling a brightly coloured top. She loved the genuine seventies swing top, with its bell sleeves, and floral patterns, a treasure found in a K-Road op shop.

"Yeah, well, at least it would cover my stomach—and stop your parents scrutinising my middle for evidence." She cringed at the thought of their judgmental eyes upon her.

"So, it's a maybe?"

"Yeah. Put it on the chair as a possibility." She sighed in frustration at how the extraordinary circumstances of this day made everyday tasks difficult.

"Or what about this? You look great in it." The stretchy lace top in a deep purple was one of the few non-vintage items she owned.

"Do you think that's wise? This," she said, lifting her t-shirt to reveal the small, rounded curve of her belly, "would be *very* obvious in that." She hadn't expected the baby to make its mark on her body so soon, but three months in, suddenly, one day, there it was. He leaned in and planted a kiss on her bare stomach.

"Not a problem to me," he said, the words humming against her skin. "Her being obvious. I love that she's already making her presence known." He'd decided the baby was a girl. They'd even chosen a girl's name—Brontë—after her favourite author. "I don't give a shit what Mum and Dad say. She's real and she's ours and I can't wait till the day we get to meet her properly."

"Thank you Nik," she said, threading her fingers through his hair. "For sticking up for her already. You know, Mum was pregnant with me before they got married. And they never hid that from me. But they always made it perfectly clear that, while I was unexpected, I wasn't unwanted. Never made me feel like I was some accident. I want that for her, too. To know she was wanted, from the very beginning."

So what would the Francovic's prefer: a discreet cover-up while still possible? Or proof this wasn't a crazy lie, made up to trap Nik into marriage? In the end, she went for the retro top. She always felt pretty in it. And she sure needed something to help her feel better today. The nauseating feeling in her stomach wasn't morning sickness. Thankfully, that had gone; if she'd ever actually had it. She wondered now whether most of that terrible swirling in her gut those first few weeks was driven by dread—that she was pregnant, that she'd have to tell Nik, and her parents, and his. The outcome of those first conversations should have bolstered her courage for today. But she knew—even though she'd never met them—that facing his mother and father would be different. And not in a good way.

She'd passed Francovic Wines many times, with its low arching Mediterranean styled building and terracotta tiled roof. Behind it rows of grapes marched in neat lines across the low hills of the main vineyard. Early-blooming roses punctuated the end of each row in bright pinks and reds. The open cellar door looked friendly and inviting, a sign offering wine tasting and food platters. But visitors wouldn't find the family welcoming them inside on a Sunday. Staff took care of everything while the family, minus Nik, went to Sunday Mass.

A few hundred metres later, Nik pulled into a driveway nestled in a small thicket of bush. They paused at the heavy gate of barred iron. She looked across at him, mouth dropped open in surprise.

"I should have warned you," he said. "We live in a prison."

Yes, he should have warned her. Now here she was. About to confront people who lived in the inevitable mansion that lay behind such a gate. Her stomach lurched uncomfortably, and she swallowed hard.

Nik stretched his hand through the open car window and punched in a code. Noticing her shocked expression, he grinned over at her.

"Don't worry, it's only a gate. We had a break-in a few years back and with all the home invasions in the news at the time, Mum went crazy at Dad saying she wasn't going to live all alone out here where just anyone could drive up to the house."

"Is there a camera?" Her hand automatically reached to smooth her hair, in case at this very moment Mr and Mrs Francovic were getting their first glimpse of her—their daughter-in-law to be. Then stopped herself.

They wouldn't be there yet; at least half an hour until they'd be back from the weekly church service at St Joseph's in Henderson. Nik had timed the meeting deliberately. It was a relief she wouldn't have to handle them greeting her at the doorway, all the while knowing what lay ahead. This way she could settle into the unfamiliar surroundings and mentally prepare herself to follow the script they'd rehearsed.

"Nah," he said. "No camera. Honestly, it's only for show. They figured if they made it look intimidating, any would-be burglars would move onto easier pickings. And if they didn't, the dogs would be scary enough to convince them otherwise."

The house beyond its bush-fringed frontage was large, but no haughty mansion. A surprisingly ordinary 1980s brick and tile, it too sat with the vineyard as its backdrop. As Nik climbed out of the car, two large German Shepherd dogs bounded across the lawn, barking furiously; their mouths spread wide in ferocious smiles, their dangerous teeth clashing.

"Nina! Otto!" They lunged at him and he fended them off with playful shoves, each dog dancing back at him, twisting and leaping in delight. "Don't tell Mum and Dad," he said. "They're always telling me off for encouraging them. But you love it, don't you?" The dogs barked in reply.

He crouched down now, spreading his arms wide, and they came in to nuzzle at him. He spoke to them like adored children, in low indulgent tones. And she had a flash of the future: him speaking loving words to a real child; their child, wrapped in the embrace of a doting father. It was going to be all right. They could do this.

As they headed for the house, the dogs continued to bounce in happy circles around him, nudging at her too. A spontaneous giggle bubbled up inside as damp noses snuffled against her hand.

"See, they like you. I told you they were soft," he said. "They'd lick a burglar to death."

"Yeah, they're sweet."

"Not what Mum says, especially if she finds them in here." He shooed them back from the hallway, closing the door firmly against their scratching paws. He led her towards the source of the delicious smell; Sunday lunch cooking. She caught a whiff of garlic and rosemary.

The aroma of roasting meat enveloped them as they entered the sunny kitchen. Nik opened the oven and slid out a huge roasting dish where a leg of lamb sat, golden brown and sizzling. He slid open a drawer and pulled out a knife. He cut a slice of the crisp outer and held it towards her. "Want some? These are the best bits."

She felt a wave of nausea at the thought of meat and shook her head. He tucked it into his mouth, licking the trail of meat juice from his lips.

Shoving the evidence of his crime in the dishwasher, he poured them a Coke each and ushered her through to the lounge. Vast leather couches angled towards a bank of ranch sliders offered a view of the circular turn-around at the top of the driveway. Nik slid the doors wide open, allowing air in. The sounds of the outdoors drifted in with it. In the centre of the driveway, water gushed from the statue of a woman in Roman garb, her pitcher poised to fill a small pool. The welcome babble of water filled the silence between them. They sat like two criminals waiting for sentencing.

A hulking Volvo four-wheel-drive appeared, coming to a halt next to the smaller car. One of those vehicles designed for families it had three rows of seats. Even so, Ivan and Toni Francovic would have been hard pushed to fit all their children inside. It had barely stopped moving before a stream of bodies poured from it. Nik's five siblings had yet to assert themselves as he had, all still complying with attendance at Sunday Mass.

The two taller girls, Ivana and Mila, were the first to alight. Cassie had seen them before at school, one a Year 12 and the other Year 11. They were close in age, and similar enough in appearance to be twins. Right now they wore identical sulky expressions as they strode towards the house.

"You can see how much my sisters love Sunday Mass," Nik quipped. "Can't say I blame them. Who wants to waste half the day in church?"

Two more Francovic children fell from the third row of seats, clambering over the lowered ones in front of them. The two boys—actual twins, Marko and Viktor, both aged twelve—ran towards the bounding dogs who had appeared around the corner. They sprawled on the grass in a joyful bundle, wrestling and laughing. It was hard to tell what was dog and what was boy.

"Hey!" An indignant voice sounded from the back of the vehicle. "Let me out." Even from inside, Cassie could hear the pounding of small fists against the window. Nik's nine-year-old youngest sister, Lana, trapped in the rear jump-seat, forgotten by her siblings, now demanded freedom. "Dad. The boys have shut me in again," she squealed.

Nik's father climbed out of the driver's seat. Ivan had that olive Slavic complexion, further deepened by years of outdoor work, and creased with lines of age. Threads of silver crisscrossed his dark, wavy hair.

It shouldn't have surprised her when he didn't spring out of the car with the same vigour as her own father might. Nik's parents were almost ten years older than hers. They'd married late and children hadn't arrived immediately. Now, when most people their age were contemplating being grandparents, the Francovics faced many more years of dealing with their own children. Of course, she realised with a start; they *were* going to be grandparents. Very soon.

While Ivan attended to freeing Lana, a frowning Antonija Francovic appeared from the front passenger door. She glared back at the bristling child. The girl stood, arms folded, still protesting to her father, who quietly ignored her complaints.

"It's not fair, Dad. They do it every time. Make one of them sit in the back."

"Svetjlana, enough." Antonija's clipped tone and use of the child's full name commanded immediate silence, and now she turned to survey the brawling boys. Her frown deepened as she took in the tangle of children and dogs that sprawled across the lawn.

"Marko. Viktor. Stop that at once." She turned to her husband. "Ivan. Get those dogs and put them away, will you?" she said wearily. "I've told Nik so many times and still he winds them up."

Having come to New Zealand as a seven-year-old child, she had retained the abrupt accented English of one not born to it. Her lips, outlined in a deep burgundy, set in a tight line. Her dark hair showed not the slightest hint of grey, belying her age.

"Told you they blame me," Nik said with a smirk. "I don't care. Otto and Nina love it. Marko and Viktor too. I can take the heat on their behalf."

"Ivan," his mother barked out again.

"Come on Toni. Let them be kids."

"Easy for you to say. You're not the one who has to wash the grass stains and dog prints off their damn clothes."

She stalked off towards the house, and soon the sound of her voice rang from the kitchen as she flung orders at the two older girls.

Ivan appeared in the lounge doorway, a wide smile on his face. "What are you two doing hiding away in here like this?"

"Avoiding Mum so we don't have to help with lunch," Nik said with a grin. "Dad, this is Cassie."

She stood, and he stepped in to greet her as Jan would, with the lightest brush of a kiss on each cheek. "About time this son of ours brought his girl home. I think your mother's forgotten you were coming." He leaned through the door. "Toni—Nik's in here," he called, "and Cassie."

Toni arrived in an overpowering cloud of spicy perfume. Her face bore an annoyed scowl at the interruption. She whispered a couple of words at her husband, wiped her hands on her apron, and stepped around him. The smile plastered on her face felt more disturbing than the scowl for its lack of sincerity.

"Cassie," she said, holding out a perfectly manicured hand, nails the colour of dried blood. When Cassie took it, the hard tips pressed into her palm, little dagger-like points digging deep, although the smile didn't leave the woman's face. "So lovely to meet you. Pretty too. Why on earth Nik's been hiding you away all this time, I have no idea. Well, I can't leave the dinner to Ivana and Mila," she said, her voice liquid smooth, "so we'll talk some more later?" The too-bright smile stayed firmly on her face.

"Mum, Dad, actually, we need a few minutes now." Toni frowned at Nik, conflicting emotions of annoyance and puzzlement crossing her dark features. "Please?" Nik said, and she complied with a begrudging huff as she and Ivan took a seat on the sofa opposite.

Side by side, the two were so alike they could have been brother and sister, not husband and wife. Same olive skin, and dark hair, just like all the other children—except Nik. Same smile, although hers lacked Ivan's open sincerity. Nik had warned Cassie not to be lulled by the apparent warmth of his mother's welcome. She swallowed down the sour taste in her mouth.

How could they have let this happen? The first time she'd met his parents, and it was to tell two strangers that she was pregnant. And they were to blame for that, at least. It was no accident that Nik had kept her away. Now she could see why. If they'd been more concerned with where he was and who with, they'd have wanted to meet his girlfriend. If they had created a more loving home, he'd have wanted to bring her into it. Ivan did, in fact, have a fatherly warmth about him. He seemed genuinely pleased they were here. It was Antonija's presence that, despite the touch of summer in the air, lent a touch of frost to the room.

"Well? What is so important that I need to leave the fate of lunch to your sisters, huh?" The smile didn't reach her eyes. They held a disconcerting, dark challenge.

"There's no easy way to say this," Nik began, swallowing audibly. His hand tensed over hers.

Before he even had time to get the words out, his mother's eyes flared with the knowledge.

"She's pregnant." Toni's harsh laugh barked across the room. He said nothing as she flung her outrage at them. "Why am I not surprised? Huh? Tell me why not Nik? Because you think you live this charmed life, where you just do as you please and everything will be fine. And now it's not."

Nik sat in silence, his face drained of all colour. He squeezed Cassie's hand so tight it hurt.

"Toni," Ivan warned, "I'm sure they didn't mean this to happen."

"No? Are you sure of that?" she flashed angrily at him before turning to Cassie. "And so, what do your parents think about all of this?"

She cowered a little under the hawk-like stare. "They…"

"They aren't exactly thrilled but…" Nik leapt in on her behalf.

"Nik, I didn't ask you. Let her answer," Toni threatened.

Cassie's words came out small in the huge tiled space. "As Nik said, they'd rather this wasn't the situation, but they will support us with what we've decided to do."

"What you've decided to do?" Toni repeated. "What *you've* decided? I would have thought the fact that this even happened shows you're certainly not mature enough to be making any decisions." Her hands danced in a flurry of angry gestures. "*Babies* are wanted. *Babies* are planned for. Not some accident because two kids couldn't control themselves." She lurched back in the couch with an exasperated sigh.

"Mum, it wasn't like that," he said, struggling to master an audible rising anger.

"No? Wasn't it?" she huffed. "So, are you're telling me you planned for this? That's even more disturbing. The pair of you, not even finished school and you—" She shook her head in disbelief. "You just decide it's a great idea to have a baby?"

"Toni, stop." Ivan's low growl halted the barrage.

She took two long, slow breaths and began again, this time in measured tones. "Well, abortion is absolutely out of the question. I won't have it. You made this child, you will bring it into the world."

Cassie found her voice. "I'm not having an abortion." She knew her mother's gentle suggestion had only been because she felt a responsibility to present all the options. Blair, also pregnant and unmarried, had chosen to give Cassie life. Cassie would do the same for their child. Toni's sharp look of surprise felt like a small victory.

"Good," she said. "There are so few babies for adoption these days. I'm sure some loving couple will be very grateful for your choice to go through with this."

"No," Nik barked out, leaning forward. His whole body grew as he curled a protective arm around her. "No adoption. We're keeping the baby. And we're getting married."

Toni laughed back at him. "Don't be ridiculous. Of course adoption is the best way forward here. My darling, you of all people should know how much an adopted child can bring happiness to a family."

"She *is* right about that Nik," his father added. "Bringing you home was one of the happiest days of my life. You and Cassie can give that gift to someone else."

Adoption? She felt stupid to have not predicted they'd suggest it. But Nik had never mentioned it, had never brought it up in their discussions as an option. There'd been hints—right back from that day in the car playing his silly fact and fiction game—that he didn't sit easily within his family. If she'd looked harder, she might have known how being adopted troubled him. Today, seated in front of his parents, and having watched his dark siblings spilling onto the driveway, it was obvious why he might feel like an outsider. But his violent reaction to his mother's suggestion of adopting the baby was the final proof.

What she couldn't understand was why he'd never talked more with her about it. They'd talked about everything, except for this one thing that lay at the root of his bitterness towards his family.

"We are not giving our baby to someone else. She's ours and we are keeping her." His hand fell across Cassie's stomach, as if defending his right to the life inside.

Heavy silence blanketed the room. Ivan studied his hands, picking at a ragged nail. Toni leaned forward, elbows on her knees. She pressed her lips against steepled fingers, resting with eyes closed. Finally, with a huge dramatic sigh, she rose to her feet.

"Well, it is your decision. And I can see nothing I say is going to change it." She surveyed the pair of them wearily. "And, I suppose..." Hard eyes fixed on her son. "At last now you'll have a family of your own, Nik. Since you don't seem to want to be part of this one."

Nik's face crumpled. Gone was the determined set of his mouth. His brows furrowed with hurt. It was like someone had taken a shiny new piece of paper and crushed it in a fist. She swore tears glinted in his incredulous eyes, and she felt a prickle of sympathy in her own. But in a flash, it was gone. With a fierce glare, a defiant tilt of his chin, and the tense set of his shoulders, Nik summoned his armour in an attempt to deflect his mother's cruel words. He said nothing.

Toni offered a stiff half-smile and stalked back to the kitchen. Across from them, Ivan looked unsure of what to do. Then, with an apologetic glance, he followed his wife from the room.

Nik wrapped Cassie in his arms, his grip so tight she could barely breathe. His head lay heavy on her shoulder. Dampness seeped through the fabric of her top as he sobbed, his body vibrating in huge silent shudders.

CHAPTER 18

Wedding Party

Auckland New Zealand – November 2009

THIS WAS NOT HOW she'd imagined being driven to her wedding: in a Mini Cooper, her mother at the wheel, humming away to one of the eighties songs that pumped out of Blair's favourite radio station in a steady stream.

In the seat behind them, Archie, lured only by the attraction of a day off school and lunch out, played games on his handheld PSP. The latest model, not yet available in New Zealand, it was his constant companion. This unexpected gift from her father, who'd been working in the USA for six months now, had catapulted Archie into instant celebrity status amongst his schoolmates.

A small box containing two hand-tied bunches of flowers sat on the seat beside him. The orchid grower up the road next to Marija's place was happy to oblige at short notice. Her mother had given Archie the job of looking after them, but that was the last thing on his fourteen-year-old mind. She'd thought her mother's insistence on the flowers was a little frivolous. Now, on the day, it felt important; part of doing this properly. In the years ahead, looking back on photographs, the day would appear special—planned, not a hurried arrangement made necessary by the child growing inside her.

This was also not how she'd imagined the first day of her life after high school. While all the other Year 13s enjoyed this sunny late November Friday morning, prize giving over, exams completed, she was getting married. While they lolled in bed until lunchtime, or headed for the beaches or shopping malls, she had been up since eight, once again struggling with the preening she was so useless at.

Her mother, although similarly challenged, at least had more years of practice. She'd tamed Cassie's hair back, leaving small wisps framing her face. Her skin glowed under the soft makeup, possibly one positive benefit of her pregnancy. Her mother fitted a pair of star-shaped diamond studs, an anniversary gift from her father one year. She finished by fastening her own starry pendant around her neck. It rested neatly in the deep v of her dress.

They pulled in to find a scattering of vehicles in the car park of St Joseph's Catholic Church. She recognised Marija's van. Near the parish hall, a woman in a blue uniform helped elderly people from a bulky vehicle emblazoned with the words 'Heatherbrae Retirement Village'. A group of three snowy-headed women slowly made their way up the pathway towards the building. Another car with a grey-haired driver pulled in next to the van. But nowhere could she see the little silver hatchback.

She wouldn't blame Nik if he bailed on her. Lots of guys would have. But she knew he wouldn't. She didn't doubt his fierce determination to care for her and this baby. Showing up at the church and marrying her was another way for him to show it. He was late, but then punctuality wasn't one of his best qualities.

They stood in a small huddle in the church foyer. Marija fussed over her, adjusting a strand of hair here, brushing a smudge of eyeshadow there.

"You look beautiful, darling. The dress is perfect," she said.

"Thanks to you." Giving in to her mother's nagging that she should at least look for a proper wedding dress, it had seemed a good omen when they'd found this in the Silverdale Hospice Shop. The low-lustre satin sheath dress hanging amongst a cluster of second hand ball gowns glowed as pristine white as if it were new. A few alterations courtesy of Marija's talented hands and it fit her perfectly.

"I'd swear it was made for you. I can't wait to see Nik's face when he sees you." Grace bounced excitedly beside her. She felt so lucky to have someone she could confide in, and a friend to stand beside her. She grabbed Grace's hand and gave it a grateful squeeze.

"You're looking gorgeous too. It's a shame Nik hasn't got some good-looking friend to be the best man." Grace's on-again off-again romance with Liam Keenan had finally imploded after she'd called him out on kissing Rachel Heath out the back of the school hall at the leavers' dinner. It would be good to see her find some nice new guy to move on with and put that jerk behind her. But sadly, she wouldn't find him here today.

Nik had, he said to protect her, told virtually no one about the wedding. None of his friends knew, and in a way she was relieved. It would only add fuel to the nasty conversations that swirled around them. In a high school it was hard to keep secrets, especially scandalous ones like theirs. To keep the gossip at bay, he'd only invited one person today. Jan would stand beside Nik as his best man.

"Yeah, I'm not totally opposed to the idea of an older guy," Grace laughed, "and Jan's pretty good looking for his age. You know, he's got the silver fox thing going on. But someone old enough to be my father—that's just gross."

Jan, engrossed in talking to her mother, fortunately didn't hear her comment. He'd arrived at the same time as them, scooping Blair into a hug. Now they were deep in conversation about some new arts collective starting up in Matakana. In those early days, she'd suspected her mother had her eye on Jan as a potential fling. She'd felt sick one afternoon when she and Nik had arrived at the studio to see her mother's car there. But they'd found them innocently sitting in his kitchen drinking the thick dark European coffee that he brewed in a little aluminium pot on the stove and talking art. Art lovers—not lovers—enjoying the companionship of kindred spirits.

Archie, grumpy because her mother had forbidden him to bring the PSP inside, despite his protests that he'd only play while they waited, ignored the conversation. He held the box of flowers with a sullen scowl. Marija seized it from him and thrust one bunch into Cassie's hands. Then, before handing the other to Grace, she freed a small orchid. The delicate scent wafted up to meet them. Tucking it into the loose, messy bun at the nape of Cassie's neck, she whipped a small mirror from her handbag to show her.

"See," she said. "Just what you needed."

Father Peter smiled warmly, watching the woman fussing around her. Unlike last week when she and Nik had met him dressed in sombre black trousers and shirt with the uniform white collar at his neck, today he outshone them all. He wore festive robes of cream edged in gold. The celebratory tone of the outfit felt reassuring, as if they *should* celebrate this wedding, even if it might be in less than ideal circumstances.

At five minutes to eleven, there was still no sign of Nik. She scanned every new car that pulled in: a white Toyota with two more white-haired women; a red Honda that circled once and left; and finally a dark blue wagon. A large young man with untidy hair of dirty blonde in a dark grey suit scrambled out. He ambled across towards them, and she felt a burst of joy. He'd made such an effort with his outfit. All for her.

"Sorry, I couldn't go as far as a tie," he said with a grin.

"What's with the car?"

"Ours. A wedding present. From Dad. You know, I bet he'd have come today, if it wasn't that Mum would never speak to him again."

"Does *she* know about the car?" She'd never have predicted Ivan would be brave enough to do something like this, even behind Toni's back.

"No, not yet. But Dad said it's important that we have a good safe car, and one that has room for a baby seat, and a stroller and all the other stuff we're going to need. I'm sure that argument will shut Mum up when she finds out. Much as she's pissed about this whole thing, she's not so hard-hearted that she wouldn't want the best for her grandchild."

Promptly at eleven, Father Peter beckoned them into the church. Nik and Jan went first and waited at the altar. Blair thrust her phone and handbag at Archie, motioning him forward to where Marija sat in the first pew. Marija bustled around in her mother's handbag, producing a small CD player. Propping it on the carpeted steps of the altar, she hit a button. Music floated back towards them, a mellow man's voice.

"Mum?" Cassie asked. "What is this? It's beautiful." The music, both sweet and haunting, echoed in the vastness of the empty church.

"Elvis Costello," she whispered. "It's called 'She'. From *Notting Hill*. You know how I love my Julia Roberts movies. But Julia has nothing on you, my darling," she said. "I think someone else feels that way, too." At the foot of the long central aisle, Nik stood, waiting. She melted under the intensity of his gaze. Never before had she felt so adored, so wanted, and any lingering doubt fell away. "You're beautiful," her mother said, fingering one of the delicate spirals of hair framing her face before turning to Grace. "Time to go, sweetie. You're on."

Grace took a deep breath and in slow, measured steps headed down the aisle. Despite its unhappy memories, she'd recycled her red ball dress. With her flowing dark hair and slight figure, the split in one side revealing shapely legs, she was stunning. How could idiotic Liam Keenan see her like that and then go sneaking around with someone else?

Her mother looped one arm through hers, and they followed Grace. Cassie's steps were unsteady, as if the ground hovered below her, just out of reach. She fixed her gaze on Nik. His smile was the sun, filling the dome of a summer sky, his eyes sparkling gold-flecked blue like the tumble of a friendly wave. And, as if sighting a safe place to anchor in the advance of an impending storm, her rapid heartbeats stilled a little.

At the foot of the altar, her mother brushed a kiss on her cheek, releasing her to face him, and he leaned in drawing her close, lowering his forehead to meet her, eyes closed as he inhaled.

"I'm scared," he whispered on a slow exhale, clasping his hands over hers.

"Me too," she replied, swallowing down a half-smile.

"It's OK, we can be scared together from now on." The last shreds of her nervousness fell away as he opened his eyes, his gaze steady as he tightened his grip.

She glanced up at the huge cross suspended high above the altar. A mournful Jesus stared out across the church with dull eyes. His expression of disappointment appeared directed at the pair of them, as if they'd let him down. Two kids who couldn't rein in their lust and now this was the result: a pregnant bride.

Father Peter cleared his throat. "Shall we begin?" She pushed away all negative thoughts at his reassuring smile. If God's representative could be happy for them, then she supposed it was OK. He nodded towards Marija, who fumbled to fade out the music.

"Just a moment, Father," a man called from the foyer. All heads turned towards him. "Don't be starting without me." She knew that deep Scottish voice. She turned to the tall man with bright red hair striding down the aisle towards them.

"Dad?" She'd only spoken to him yesterday; in Arizona, she'd assumed.

"Daniel!" Her mother's face exploded with joy.

"I might have missed you being born, but I wasn't going to miss my little girl getting married."

Nik's hands dropped from hers, his face turning pale. Father Peter's smile widened as her father's arms wrapped her tight, while familiar lips grazed her cheek. Releasing her, he stretched out his hand to a wary-looking Nik.

"Nik—I'm Daniel. I suppose I should call you son," he said with a grin.

CHAPTER 19

Loss

Auckland New Zealand – December 2009

"Here," Grace said, spotting a group about to vacate a seat. They dived for it, a refuge from the oppressive crush of people swarming the mall. Two days out from Christmas, it felt like half of Auckland had packed into this space.

Cassie sipped on her Coke, wondering if the choice of drink was wise. The rattling ice provided a soothing chill, but the fizzy liquid didn't sit comfortably on top of the two tacos she'd eaten in the food court. "I'm starting to regret lunch already," she groaned. "I'm getting a gut ache."

"Well, you and Nik would insist on fancy Mexican. A good old McDonald's cheeseburger and I'm feeling fine."

"I wonder if he's feeling crook too?"

"Probably. Five minutes in Kmart with all those people would be enough to make me want to throw up."

Nik had disappeared into the depths of the enormous store. Inside frenzied shoppers charged around like they were on a battlefield, the victors promised the best of the Christmas bargains as their spoils. It was packed, despite the steady stream of people emerging with laden bags. She felt bad, but he had insisted on braving it on his own. Adamant that, despite money being tight, he needed to find a small gift for each of his siblings today, Nik had plunged into the fray one last time in search of something for Lana.

Earlier, in the pharmacy, she and Grace had found cosmetic bags for the two older girls. The gaming store offered an easy gift solution for the twins. Like Archie, Marko and Viktor were mad about video games, battling each other on their game console every minute they could until their fierce mother declared enough. Only the problem of a gift for a nine-year-old girl remained, and Nik had decided there must be something suitable in the vastness of Kmart.

"Are you going with him to deliver the presents?" Grace asked.

"Shit no. Even Nik is wary of calling in there, so it's still a long way off before I'll be ready to face them." She shuddered at the thought. "Ivan's OK. I think he's secretly quite pleased at the thought of being a grandfather. But no. Toni's such a bitch. And Nik hasn't forgiven her for what she said to him. You know—about him finally having a family of his own? He's planning to go around this afternoon while she's out having her nails done before Christmas."

"How's it going at your place?"

"OK." She thought about the tiny cottage overflowing with people. Her father's booming voice filled the space. Her mother's exuberant laughter spoke of happiness. As did her flurry of painting. Blair had produced almost as much in the past three weeks since Daniel's return as in the whole three months prior. "Actually, better than OK. It felt a bit weird at first—the two of us in my room, Mum and Dad across the hallway—but it's good."

"So, is your dad staying? In New Zealand?"

"I think so. He's off to Christchurch after New Year. He's working on some arrangement with the uni. If it works out, in February, he and Mum will go home. Archie too."

"And what about you? You can't stay?"

"Not there. I don't think the next artist in residence wants to find us living upstairs. But Nik's looking for a flat for us. Something close to the art school. Dad's helping him."

"That'll be you guys next year." Grace pointed to a young couple seated by the mall Santa, her holding a toddler on her knee; him grinning down with pride at his offspring while the jolly man beamed at the camera with a practised smile.

"What? Scarring my child for life by making them face some weird old guy in a red suit with a huge scary beard?"

"Didn't do me any harm."

"What? Your parents did that?"

"Still do. Last week when we went to Lynn Mall."

"For real? Haven't they noticed you and the boys are a little old for Santa?"

"The boys like to pretend they still believe. Too scared to admit it in case the present supply dries up. It's hilarious. Mum loves to torture them, make them think she doesn't know. You should see them when she drops hints.

Sometimes she even questions them outright. They lie through their teeth every time."

"I can't believe you're still doing the Santa photos. That's crazy."

"I can't believe you haven't seen the pin board in the downstairs TV room. One for every year from my first Christmas. Newest one is there right now."

"Well, all I can say is, it's bizarre. Besides, I've always thought teaching your kids that strange old men are fine to approach because they promise presents is a little off."

Her stomach cramped again.

"In pain? The damn tacos?" Grace reached out a hand in concern.

"Yeah," she huffed out. "Do you know where the loos are? I hate to say it, but if I don't get to one soon, this could get ugly."

"Follow me." Grace led the way to a far-flung corner of the mall, where a patient line of women waited in the inevitable queue with resigned looks.

"You think they'd have more than five loos in a shopping mall this size," Grace grumbled, as they inched forward.

Hunched over in pain, Cassie didn't answer. Her friend's arm draped around her shoulder, Grace's small hand giving a consoling squeeze. No one in the stony-faced queue responded to her growing distress. No one took pity on her to offer their place. Minutes crawled by until finally they stood at the front of the line. When two doors opened side by side, they tumbled through them in unison.

The moment Cassie sat down, skirt hiked up, she knew something was wrong. The warmth between her legs felt as if she'd wet herself. Specks of blood dotted her underwear. When she mopped at herself with toilet paper, there was more. Bright red interspersed with ominous darker blobs.

"Grace..."

"Don't tell me. No bloody loo paper. Here."

She could hear handfuls of paper being furiously pulled from the dispenser and a hand appeared under the cubicle. She took it.

"Grace, it's not that. There's blood. A lot of blood."

"What?"

"Grace, can you come in here?" her voice shook. Another fierce cramp grabbed at her stomach. She heard the flush of water and she leaned forward, reaching for the latch.

"Oh, fuck." The word tumbling from prim and proper Grace's mouth jarred as much as the realisation that although neither of them knew much about pregnancy, both of them knew this was bad.

"Grace, get Nik," she breathed. "Get Nik." She sat doubled over, her breath coming in short pants. Beneath the stabbing cramps, a low dragging pain clawed at her back.

The collective gasps of shock from the women outside told her when he arrived.

"Which one?" His frantic voice rang out across the space. Squawks of exclamation echoed back. Someone barked an angry reprimand, another let out an astonished gasp.

"Piss off mate," someone said. No surprises there. Being confronted by a large young man pushing past to the front of the line wasn't an everyday occurrence while queuing for the ladies' loo.

"Here." Her voice came out a whimper. The door flew open and his bulk filled the frame. Wild-eyed, he took in the sight of her.

"Is it the baby?" She could only nod as tears shoved their way forward. "We need to get you to the hospital." He turned to where Grace's pale face bobbed behind him, flanked by a few curious women. "Grace, we need help here."

"The information desk is just down there," an older woman suggested helpfully. "Maybe they can call you an ambulance?"

Grace pushed her way back through the worried circle of faces that now hovered close to the cubicle. Despite the murmurs of concern, no one stepped forward with any practical help.

Nik jammed himself in the tiny space, pulling the door closed behind him. He clasped her head against his stomach, stroking her hair. It brought no comfort. She could endure the physical pain. But the tearing in her heart, and the gut wrenching agony of their combined silent sobs consumed her. She wasn't sure she could survive the day.

Chapter 20

Substitute

Eight years later, Tekapo, New Zealand - June 2017

THE CRUNCH OF THE crushed shell driveway beneath her feet brought back floods of memory. It was the soundtrack for so many comings and goings of her life. Her father, leaving for yet another expedition. And the joyful announcement of his return. The accompaniment to her slow trek towards the school bus to face another dreary day at school. And her quick steps towards a car, eager to meet a boy whose actions would tarnish her life. The backdrop for loading their belongings as she, Archie and Blair had set off for Auckland, crippled by fear that they'd never return to live in this house. She'd never come back for more than a visit, but her parents had.

Years of memories lay in this house, this town, and the family farm tucked away in the hills—not only her own, but her mother's, her grandmother's and those of the feisty great-grandmother she'd never met, but who lived on, larger-than-life in family stories. She wondered what memories they would make this weekend to linger long into the future. Her mother's summons, while delivered in her usual light, breezy tone, had an undercurrent of compulsion that filled Cassie with dread.

"How is she, Dad?" Daniel meeting her at the doorway rather than her mother wasn't a good sign.

"Tired. You know. The chemo takes it out of her. It's been a week, and she's usually bounced back by now. But this time..." He shook his head. Her father was many things: intelligent, determined, courageous, kind. And while all of these qualities found their usefulness when caring for a wife battling ovarian cancer, the constant barrage of emotion had taken its toll. "I'm sure she'll rally now you're here. She's been restless for days. Excited that you were coming."

He leaned back against the broad mantle, toasting his back against the fire that crackled day and night in the winter months here. She inhaled the familiar bursts of popping pine-sap and smokiness.

"So what's this all about, Dad?" She cast her eyes around the vast lounge. Paintings rested against every wall space. These were huge paintings, Blair's trademark landscapes bold and vibrant, a flurry of new works, all dated in the past month.

"She wants to tell you herself. As you can see, things have been happening."

"They sure have. I'd assumed she'd have been hardly well enough to paint. I never expected to find this."

The massive explosion of creativity surprised her. It also launched a jolt of fear. Was this her mother's swansong? Had she realised she wasn't winning against the cancer and intended to go out with a bang? That would definitely be her mother's style. Blair never did anything quietly. If she was dying, she wouldn't just slip away without a sound.

"What do you think?" Her mother stood in the arched doorway, framed by the dark carved-wood flowers and vines, beautiful still, but gaunt. The long, dark burnished copper hair that she'd always been so proud of, her one vanity, had streaks of grey that hadn't been there six months ago. It spilled in thin strands across her shoulders, no longer thick and lush. The sheen had gone, like a coin dulled from the fumbling of many dirty hands.

"You've been busy."

She laughed, that deep throaty sound that still hinted of wildness, even wickedness. God, no wonder her father had married her within months of their meeting. Even now, fighting illness, she glowed with that irresistible inner light that, no matter what she did, couldn't help but draw you to her. When she asked something of you, you did it.

Which is why Cassie had begged her boss for time off, shrugged off the spectre of two days' lost pay, and sucked up the huge hit on her credit card for flights and a rental car to get here. She hoped with a few subtle hints her dad might realise how broke they were and slip her a few dollars in compensation. Nik hadn't said a word about the expense. In fact, he'd told her she had to come. He'd have joined her if there'd been money to spare for two. He thought of Blair as more mother to him than his own.

"Busy. That's one way to put it. But I did hope you might note more about them than their number." She flashed an expectant smile as she took a seat in her favourite armchair. Its vibrant fabric looked as if designed especially for her. Somehow she appeared more her old self wrapped in its whirl of bright colours.

"Mum, you know they're good." Cassie took up her usual seat on the couch next to her dad. "They always are. I don't think you could produce a bad painting if you tried."

That laugh came again, with not a trace of humility. But then why should she be humble? Blair Tremayne's work had the power to strike people dumb. Art critics loved her. Even people in this conservative rural district, who'd normally disparage anything that wasn't a realistic representation of the world, defended Blair's work to outsiders. They claimed her as a local treasure; to those in some circles, a national treasure.

"Thank you. Call me vain, but it never gets old. Hearing praise. It's what spurs me on. Makes me want to do more."

"So, it looks as if someone's been heaping a whole lot of praise on you lately. If this is anything to go by."

"You might say that."

"Come on, Mum. Just spit it out. I know you can't wait to tell me. You're practically bouncing on that chair."

"Well, you remember Elias Sutherland?"

Cassie nodded. She'd never met the man, but Elias Sutherland, an eccentric Scottish art collector, and Blair's number one fan, had been a benign presence in the background for Cassie's entire life. He'd bought his first of Blair's paintings from a little gallery in London back in 1990. Back when she first started signing them as Blair Silvestri—the name she laughingly referred to as the only good thing to come out of her impulsive but short marriage to a flaky Italian. Elias's first purchase had spawned a long-term obsession with her work, and he owned dozens.

"He called me a month or so back. Told me he'd pitched an idea to a big fancy art gallery in Edinburgh. He's done it before with another artist in his collection, and he wanted to do it with me." Her waves of excitement flooded across the room. Traces of her illness slipped away, subsumed by the broad smile and the spark of life in her eyes. "A retrospective of my work.

His collection will form the basis, plus a few more he'll cajole from others. And then there will be a whole section with new works. These."

"Mum, that's incredible."

"Yes. It also gives me an incentive to hang in here. Damned if I want to be one of those artists whose biggest fame only comes after they're gone. This is big, and I'm determined to see it happen."

"So you'll go over?"

She shook her head. The veil of weariness slipped back over her eyes. "No. Short-term pain for long-term gain, I'm afraid. I need to stick with this treatment schedule. Otherwise, my next exhibition *will* be when I'm dead."

Cassie cringed at the word. The rest of them circled around it, never speaking it. But Blair, in her inimitable style, pushed back, naming her nemesis, and refusing to let it scare her.

"And, my darling girl, that's where you come in."

Cassie looked at her, puzzled. "I don't get it Mum."

"You go. To Edinburgh. In my place. It's not unheard of, family members overseeing an artist's work. Accompanying it to exhibitions. People love it. Not the artist herself, but another of her works—her daughter."

Cassie leaned forward, elbows on her knees. She brought her hands to her temples, massaging at the disbelief in her brain. Her mother had made some unusual requests over the years. She wasn't a regular mother. But this one was so unexpected.

"Wow, Mum. That's a pretty big ask." Her mind whirled. Scotland. The motherland. The mythical place her parents spoke of with dreamy reverie. The place all her fiercely loyal Mackenzie Basin family and neighbours still looked to as home despite it being the country abandoned by their immigrant ancestors. But she couldn't simply walk away from work. As a primary school teacher, leave during term time meant leave without pay. How would they cover the bills? The mortgage?

"It is," her mother said. "And I'd love you to go for the reasons I've already said. But there's another. Elias has asked for more. Things that I'd never let out of my possession. Unless I could give them to someone I trust to care for them."

She knew what that was. "The pictures of Dad."

"Yes, the pictures of Daniel."

Those three pictures that had always hung in her parents' bedroom were an enigma. Any time she'd asked about them, Blair had brushed it off as "Just some pictures I painted of your father when we first met."

But Cassie knew from the way she gazed at them when she thought no one was watching—her mother valued those pictures beyond anything else she owned. Hell, she'd wondered, if the house caught on fire, would Blair save her kids or the pictures? True, they were unique. Blair never painted people. Except she had, only once, some time back in 1990, when Daniel Tremayne had come into her life.

"How does Elias even know about them?"

"I sent him photographs. Years ago. Remember, Elias, more than anyone, understands my art. Worships it. Call it a perverse need to see what he might say if I threw something at him that didn't fit the view he had of me and my work. I wanted to rattle him a little." Her mouth turned up in a small, pleased smile. "He's been intrigued by them ever since."

"It's just the logistics of it, Mum," she spluttered. Then drew in a long breath. May as well tell her everything. "And the finances. The mortgage is killing us. Nik's business is ramping up. People love his work. They're buying it. But we're a long way from me being able to toss my job away. Why do you think I've held out so long against his desperate need to be a daddy?"

She regretted that final comment the moment she said it. It wasn't fair to belittle Nik's fixation on having a family. Like her, the hurt of losing their baby had never really gone away. The pain of Brontë's death simmered under the surface of their life and he saw another child as a possibility for healing that pain a little. He nudged her towards it at every opportunity, with small encouraging comments.

He'd gently suggested she overstated the challenges of being a working mother, pointing out other people who somehow made it work.

But as a teacher, she knew enough about child development to want better for their children than a mother who went straight back to a demanding job. Call it sentimental, but she wanted the childhood she'd had. Blair's parenting had been interesting, sometimes questionable, but she'd maintained a stable home with her constant presence not just in their early years, but beyond, always there to wave them off on the school bus, always welcoming them home as they walked in to sling school bags on the floor. No, for now, she needed to work, so babies were out of the question, as was gallivanting off to Scotland at the behest of a single-minded Scottish art collector.

"Darling, you forget. Elias is loaded, and doing things like this is his hobby. It makes him happy. He is quite prepared to throw whatever money it takes at this little endeavour."

"He'll pay me?"

She nodded. "Oh, he'll pay." Her smile became smug. "I think I missed my calling. Negotiated a very good deal. A generous salary. An apartment. A car. Business class ticket. Hold out for first class, I say. He'll pay."

"Mum...it's tricky."

"No, it's actually very easy, darling. All that's left is for you to say yes. Take leave from work. They adore you." It wasn't boastful to agree with that. She'd taught in only one school; started there as a new graduate and never left. The place felt more like family than work. "They're not going to let you slip away. And if they baulk at the suggestion, play the pity card. What's the point of having a mother with cancer if you can't use her for a little leverage?"

"So, how long would I be away?"

"The exhibition will open November 8th. But you'd need to be there before that. Accompany the works. Do a few advance publicity engagements. That's the norm for these sorts of things. They've got it pencilled in till December 9th. You could stay on for Christmas, New Year even. Just imagine—a white Christmas. It's magic. And for New Year, Scotland's the place to be, apparently."

"But what about Nik? I can't just leave him here." They'd hardly spent more than a day apart in eight years together. Never a week. No way they'd cope with three months.

"Air tickets for both of you. And before you tell me he can't work over there—I've checked it out. Jewellery masterclasses. Studio space for rent. Whatever he wants."

Her mother was right. She sure knew how to put together a deal. She'd covered every angle, every possible objection. How could they refuse?

CHAPTER 21

A Father's Wisdom

Tekapo, New Zealand - June 2017

THE OLD WICKER PORCH swing creaked beneath her. Air crisp with the breath of recent snow burned her lungs. She tucked her head into the folds of her coat. Her exhaled sigh billowed from under the collar in a wispy cloud. The numbness of her nose matched the pain in her exposed fingers. After years living in the north, she didn't even own gloves, but it was too soon to go back inside to borrow a pair. The freezing temperature, even now at almost midday, obliterated any nostalgic thoughts of childhood winters in Tekapo. How had she ever endured this searing cold? Perhaps her memories were coloured by the people; family, especially the woman inside who had wrapped them in her own warm, if slightly offbeat, brand of love.

Footsteps clomped across the verandah, the tired boards issuing small moans of protest at her father's progress.

"Shove over, kiddo."

She did as he said, wiggling across to make space. As always, she complied without hesitation, unlike her natural impulse to push back at her mother's requests. Somehow he'd been the easier parent to love, easier to please, easier to do as he asked. Pangs of guilt stabbed at her. She hadn't always been fair to her mother.

It had been easier with Dad because he hadn't been there. Like a single parent, Blair had done the tough stuff: made the rules, insisted on home-work, demanded chores of her and her brother. Not that she'd been as hard on them as some parents. But the mundane things had always fallen to her.

Whereas Daniel would breeze into their lives, a benevolent father with time to indulge his kids for a few months before heading off again. Even when he'd swapped roving for periods of tenure at the university, he'd stayed on campus most weeks, returning home on weekends. Yes, it had been easy to always do as he asked, because he'd asked so little of them, only making time to do the fun things dads did with their kids and none of the shitty stuff.

"Ouch, prickly," she said as his bearded cheek rasped against hers.

"The unshaven mountain man look serves me well over winter down here." He chuckled, deliberately nuzzling his abrasive face against hers some more. "So, kiddo. What are you going to do?"

She squirmed a little in his hug, feeling the weight of two people's expectations upon her. "I want to say yes, Dad. Do this for her. But..."

"But you're worried about how you'll make it work. Sometimes I wonder how two such impractical people as your mother and I produced such a sensible child." His amused smile warmed her cheek. "If you throw enough money at something, you can pretty much make anything work. And Elias has no shortage of that."

She sighed. With a niggle of betrayal, that she found it easier to talk to her father who'd been more absent than present rather than a mother who'd always been there, she decided to tell him. "I'm not sure Elias has enough money for this." Maybe being a man, a husband, Dad would understand. "It's not only the practical stuff, Dad. I'm worried. About Nik and me."

"Sweetheart, marriage is never easy. And with you two, you were both so young. You're still so young. Younger now than when your mother and I met each other. It was always going to be tough. You're different people from when you set out on this journey. You were just kids. Now you've grown up."

That was exactly it. They'd not only grown up. They'd grown into people who knew a lot more about what they wanted from life than two eighteen-year-olds ever could. And that was the problem. Their hopes and dreams *had* been the same: Nik would finish his diploma, start his business; she'd be a stay at home mother, write her book, get a publishing deal. But they were the dreams of deluded kids who had no idea what it might take to make them come true.

When Brontë died, it seemed as if from then on, everything they'd planned started to unravel. It wasn't that losing their precious unborn baby had caused them to abandon their dreams. Rather, it had exposed those dreams as unrealistic. The world demanded a more down-to-earth approach; patience; sacrifice.

Strangely, Nik had got most of what he'd wanted. And she'd willingly done everything in her power to give it to him. But for him to have those things, they needed her to work. Work meant children must wait. Somehow, he didn't see it that way. Every argument they had led back to this one impasse. That was the difference. He believed they should just go ahead and do it. Just figure it out as they went along. That they could have it all now. She had put her dreams on hold—her long-time dream to be a writer, and the dream that caught her by surprise, to be a mother—and was prepared to hang on that bit longer to make them come true.

"I don't know Dad. Sometimes I think it's not that we've changed. The differences were always there, but we were too blindly in love to see them. And now they're painfully obvious."

"Differences can be worked through, you know." This was the voice of experience. You could hardly find two people more different than her parents. And they'd had their struggles along the way—and worked through them. "It's not easy. It takes time."

His voice was low, tarnished with the hint of difficult memories. That year they'd been away in Auckland—it had been hard on him. Yes, her parents had given their problems time, and here they were, still together, still in love.

"Why don't you take up this offer from Elias? It might give you that time. The two of you take a break together. A change of scene. A chance to reset. Time to really talk, away from all the day-to-day stuff that gets in the way."

He might be right. Nothing she'd tried so far to stop this widening rift between her and Nik appeared to be working. However, pulling him away from the thing that meant everything to him—was that truly the answer?

"I dunno Dad. The timing isn't great for him."

"You worry me. The way you're totally focused on what's good for Nik, even if what's good for Nik, may not be good for you."

She had to look away from his earnest gaze, fearful he'd see in her eyes the truth in those words. Sometimes she wondered how she'd let it go this far. Nik didn't expect it of her. Was it a sign that underneath she still didn't trust him to stick with her, when a child no longer bound their futures together? But analysing her reasons was more than she could deal with right now.

"I mean, I'm not knocking having a commitment to the people you love," he said. "It's admirable. Although I know where you get it from. You're more your mother's daughter than you realise."

She laughed. "Me and Mum? I don't know…"

"When your kids are young, as parents, you shield them a lot. Especially from truths about your own relationship. It's not fair to lay your dramas on your children. But I think it's time. I don't think your mother would mind me telling you. Not if it saves you from yourself." He took a slow, deep breath. "When I met Blair, I thought I'd found my perfect match. In personality, it was a case of opposites attract. She was loud and a little brash—"

"A little?"

"Yeah, a lot." He chuckled to himself. "I was quieter and I think my whole brooding man vibe intrigued her."

"Not a lot of change there, either?"

"No. But the one thing on which we were in total agreement was our love of travel. Didn't want to be tied to one place. Didn't want to be trapped with one person, unless that person was prepared to live that free existence. When I met her, I'd just arrived at that conclusion. I'd come out of a relationship that imploded because I was never there. Then I met this woman who was not only amazing, but she'd left home at eighteen and gone ten years without ever spending more than a few months in any one place."

"But she ended up back here. And apart from that time in Auckland, she's never left. You kept moving, but she didn't."

"And when I saw her for the first time back here in Tekapo, even though she claimed otherwise, I thought staying here was what she wanted, too. I could see this was her place, her family, her home. Here. And I had this feeling that despite her protests, she really didn't want to leave again, even with me. That she belonged here. I decided it wouldn't be fair to take things further. To always be away and leave her in New Zealand without me wasn't an option. I'd tried that route and it ended badly." He sighed, as if the memory of that past failed relationship still haunted him a little. "So I tried to break it off with her. But she set me straight. She'd travel the world with me without hesitation. And we had this romantic notion that when kids came along, they'd simply come with us. A family of nomads."

"So what happened? That sure didn't."

"We were planning to head off when Blair found out she was pregnant. I'd committed to a couple of months in Australia and then a project in the wilds of South America. No proper facilities. High risk of disease. No place for a pregnant woman. So she let me go alone. Came back here from Australia. Gave up on the plans."

"Gave them up for you."

"No, sweetie." His weary sigh matched the exhaustion she read in his face. The lines of tension etched there deepened as he turned to meet her gaze. "This might be hard for you to hear. But believe me, I'm not saying it to make you feel bad."

How could she have been so blind? She knew. Maybe she'd known all along, but hadn't wanted to accept the guilt that overshadowed that knowledge.

"It's OK Dad, you don't need to worry. I get it. She gave it up for me."

He took her hand. "Yes, your mother gave up travelling for you. She was idealistic, but she wasn't selfish. Not where her child was concerned." His big fingers offered a reassuring squeeze. "But what you need to understand is, she didn't give up on her real dreams. Neither of us did. Much as we both might have spouted words about being free spirits, it was never really about that. Your mother's dream was to be a working artist. Mine was to have a career in astrophysics. We both got what we wanted. Sure, there were sacrifices made on both sides, especially when you and Archie came along. Blair tethered herself to this place. And I had to accept missing out on parts of my children's lives. That was the price I paid for my career, and believe me, there are times I regret that."

"It's OK, Dad. You did all right." He had been a good father to them. Not always there physically, but he'd maintained a diligent presence in their lives.

"Look, what I'm saying is, you don't have to live your whole life for someone else. And you don't have to give up on your dreams for Nik. Yes, like your mother, you were prepared to give up things for your baby. When it's a child involved, plans sometimes need to change. But even then, you don't always have to abandon your dreams for your children. Your Mum made some changes for sure, by staying here, but she was OK with that. It was what she wanted."

"Was it?"

"I'm sure it was. And in a strange way, it worked out. Life gives you surprises. Who'd have known she'd find the inspiration for her greatest work here?"

He was right. The international art world couldn't get enough of this landscape—the mountains, the steep high country, the lakes—all reimagined in Blair's bold, unique style,.

"The only sad thing, perhaps her only regret, is that this last couple of years, once you guys were all grown, she didn't take the chance to get back on the road again. It's mine too. After being apart, I just settled for having the two of us together in the same place. When we could have done some of the things we always talked about. And now it might be too late."

She laid her hand over his large, weathered one. Not the hand of a manual worker, but that of a man who'd braved the elements in every continent of the world in a thirst for knowledge of the universe.

"Maybe not Dad. Maybe she'll get through this." She patted his hand, trying to believe the words herself.

"So…" He swiped roughly at his face, batting away a rogue tear before adopting a brisk tone. "Perhaps leaving your teaching job, going to Scotland for the exhibition—well, perhaps it will be a step in the right direction."

"The hardest thing will be getting Nik on board with the idea. He's so committed to his business."

It felt like the topic of every conversation. At nights, he brushed off her invitations to join him in bed, letting her head off early without him, while he bashed away on his computer. And even when he slipped in beside her, often well after midnight, sleep didn't come, his mind refusing to put aside the problems of the day while he tossed and turned.

"Don't you worry.' He gave her hand another squeeze. "This is a time for us to deploy our secret weapon—your mother." He grinned down at her. "Let's get her to phone him, eh? Poor Nik. He won't know what hit him."

She grinned back at him. Maybe, just maybe, everything would be alright.

Chapter 22

The Cage

Auckland, New Zealand - July 2017

THERE WAS A DISTINCTIVE clomp of heavy boots on the stairs to the studio, and a few moments later, Nik's retail assistant, Annika, appeared in the doorway. Her normally pale skin glowed an even more deathly white than usual under the fluorescent lights, which with her huge dark-rimmed glasses and midnight-blue hair made her look like a character who'd leapt from the pages of a black and white comic book.

"Hey, Nik."

"You OK?" he asked, putting down the lump of jeweller's clay he'd been working on.

"Not really," she said. "I just threw up. Again."

Poor Annika was having a nightmare pregnancy. Even now, as her growing bump filled out her self-selected uniform of workman's overalls, she still faced daily bouts of morning sickness, and not just in the morning.

"You need to go home," he said. "Shut the shop. Honestly, at four-thirty on a winter Monday, I don't think we're likely to have any customers banging on the door."

In reality, he wanted that damn shop open every minute he could afford to staff it, maximising every opportunity to make sales. The lease on this trendy little renovated warehouse just off Ponsonby Road wasn't cheap. But in her condition, he wasn't about to make Annika feel bad for closing early.

"Go. Now," he ordered. "Beat the traffic. Or do you need me to drive you?"

"No, I'll be fine Nik. Thank you. I just hope this goes away soon." He could hear the weariness in her voice.

"The price you pay for a baby, eh?"

"Worth it though."

She offered a weak smile, and he smiled back. But inside, the words broke his heart all over again, reminding him of what he and Cassie should have had, but lost. He would give anything, no cost too great, if only she'd stayed. Their little girl would be seven now, if things had worked out. A school girl, going off every day with Cassie.

Then he remembered that if Brontë had survived, Cassie wouldn't have been in a primary school classroom these past four years; she would never have swapped her dream of writing for a teaching degree.

While Cassie never complained about her choices, it bothered him how easily she'd walked away from that dream. And guilt dogged him when he thought of how he'd simply carried on, staying on the path he'd mapped out for himself, while she'd veered off in another direction.

That was part of the reason he nagged at her to consider other possibilities and why he tried to shield her from the reality of his business as much as he could. However, despite his attempts at a veneer of calm, Cassie wasn't stupid; she suspected things were tough for him, even if she didn't know the full extent of it.

And so she still clung to the idea that she needed to work; that they couldn't afford to try for a baby. And no amount of gentle prodding on his part had got her to explore his suggestion that she again look to writing as a career.

Although recently there'd been a small glimmer of light on that front from an unexpected source. Since she'd come back from visiting her parents, Cassie was writing again, just a little each night, but it was a start. The sound of her fingertips flying across the keyboard, and the intense look of concentration on her face, transported him back to those days secluded in her tiny bedroom, where he'd fallen in love with her, intrigued by a sweet young girl weaving steamy romances in fantasy worlds. These past few weeks, sitting down at night, sipping a beer against the soothing rhythm of her keystrokes had been the perfect antidote to his crazy work schedule.

He went back to the clay mould—this one for a wide silver bangle—and, although of simple design compared to some of his pieces, it was special; a one-off. With deft strokes of the modelling tool, he leaned into the joy of doing what he loved the most: shaping the materials, knowing there would never be another like this, just as he had in the early days. And this one was extra special, a gift for Cassie.

Crafting bespoke jewellery like this was a rare pleasure these days, as his focus had turned by necessity to the design of items he could produce in quantity—limited editions for sure, but up to fifty or even a hundred of each. As his business manager reminded him, he needed to keep scaling up, produce more product. And, as he couldn't replicate himself, the answer lay in replicating designs multiple times.

When he was finally happy with the overall shape of the bangle, he slid it carefully into a rack. Tomorrow he'd work on it some more. The thought of getting into the finer details excited him. He planned to use a motif he reserved only for her and smiled at the thought.

Plus, working on the bangle would provide a welcome diversion from dealing with the other less pleasurable tasks that must be completed before leaving for Scotland. Now with less than nine weeks to go, sometimes he hung his head in his hands, wanting to slap himself for not trying to sidestep his role in Blair's latest manipulations.

But Nik couldn't refuse, not when she was Cassie's mother, not when she was so unwell, and not when she was someone he'd developed a genuine fondness for. He'd been lucky with his quirky mother-in-law. A fellow artist, she'd never once questioned his direction in life, or suggested he consider a more normal job with a stable income. Blair had his back in that respect, and he'd always been grateful for her quiet support.

But there was no denying that right now, reciprocating that support had created enormous pressure in his life. He mentally checked off the list: the new online shop to go live, the launch of his latest collection in time for the Christmas market, interviewing for a new retail assistant, as well as employing a couple more part-timers, all while waging the ongoing battle against his constant nemesis, the balance sheet.

He sometimes worried he'd fucked up; wondered if all this shit was punishment for being too ambitious; asked himself if he should turn his back on it all and follow Jan's path, turning out pieces on his own terms in a shack in the bush. But, for now, he had no choice. He was committed, with a three-year lease on this place, and supply contracts with a couple of small retailers in Wellington and Queenstown. If he could just get over these hurdles, surely it would get easier.

He glanced at the clock. Five to five. If he hauled arse, he too could beat the traffic. He closed his laptop on the unwavering lines and mind-numbing figures of an open spreadsheet, and locked the studio.

Downstairs on the street, he paused momentarily at the lighted shop window, drawn like a magpie to the gleaming silver and gold on display. Small perfectly angled spotlights highlighted the flowing curves, the ridges and valleys, the imprint of his hand on the metal. Seeing his work spread out before him like this offered reassurance that it *was* all worth it—the stress, the worries, the doubt—to see his dreams made tangible.

Twenty minutes later, pulling into the driveway of their little rental in Te Atatu, to his surprise, he found the house shrouded in darkness. Normally, by this time of night, the place would be awash with the red and orange hues of the little retro lamps Cassie loved, lit up like a psychedelic 1970s bar room. Unease crept across him. Where was she?

He'd left her in bed this morning, indulging in extra sleep on the first day of her school break, freed from the need to race to catch the early bus to work. She hadn't mentioned any plans. And with Grace working afternoon nursing shifts at Middlemore Hospital, there was no way she could have spirited Cassie away for a cheeky Monday evening drink at their favourite little wine bar.

As he warily stepped through the unlocked front door, a pale glow spilled from the kitchen, and he heard the staccato of neat nails striking plastic keys. The tension slipped from his body as he stepped into the darkened room.

"Hey, what are you doing working in the dark? I'm sure I paid the power bill."

She sat at the dining table, eyes still fixed on the laptop screen, with its white glow illuminating her features.

"Lost track of time," she murmured, fingers still moving.

"Writing?" He knew the answer. Nothing else lit up her face like when the words were pouring from her. He wondered if he had the same look when he drew, or sculpted.

"Of course."

He leaned in to look at the screen, wrapping his arms around her and resting his chin on her shoulder. Tendrils of hair brushed his cheek, and he inhaled the honey sweet fragrance of her shampoo. Her body was cool to the touch, the chill of the winter day settled on her in this icy room. She'd been in too deep to even switch on the gas heater, or seek a woolly jumper.

"You've been at this all day, haven't you?"

"Pretty much," she said vaguely, the dreamy bliss of her fictional world still veiling her face. He drew his arms tighter, and she leaned back into him as he pulled her back into the real world. He placed a kiss on her hair.

"Oh, I did go out," she said, taking another step into normality. "Just a walk. Went down around the inlet and stopped in to get milk from the dairy. Otherwise, yeah, this was my day."

"You know, every day could be like this."

"No, it couldn't, Nik. We can't afford…"

"Stop saying that, Cassie." He wrenched his arms away, stood there behind her, his back rigid, his fists clenched in frustration. "I don't know where you got this idea that you just have to keep working and working, and that somehow if you stop the bottom will fall out of our world. We'd get by."

But in his gut, he knew how she'd come to that conclusion. It was the times when he'd needed to vent about the cost of raw materials, or low margins on product lines. It was the days he'd spent deliberating over whether he should take on the lease, using her as a sounding board. While he'd really tried not to, he had laid too much of the shit on her. He'd brought this on himself. He vowed from this moment he wouldn't mention money to her ever again. It was the part of the business he hated the most. He was an artist, not an accountant, but to be one he had to be a little of the other, and sometimes it weighed so heavily upon him. However, this was a burden he could no longer share with her.

"It's eating at me, Cassie, seeing you go off every day to a classroom. You say you love it, and I know you're damn good at it. But you don't love it like this. You'll never be as good at it as you are at this."

It was like bloody Stockholm syndrome. Teaching had captured her and changed her in ways that meant now he wasn't sure she wanted to leave her captor, even if she could. She whirled on him, and even in the half light he saw the flash of anger, colour rising up her neck.

"How do you know that, Nik? You've never been in my classroom? How do you know?"

He reached for a switch, needing to cast light on the long overdue conversation, and let her see the hard truths in his face. He'd shied away from it, but this time, no matter how uncomfortable, they were going to sort this shit out.

"I don't have to go into your classroom to know. I've seen your face when you talk about the kids, and school, and I've seen you like you were when I walked in that door tonight. When you love something as much as you love writing, there's no doubt that you're better at it than anything else."

"Then you know exactly why I can't quit teaching," she breathed. "Because I see things too. Back on that first day when you took me to Jan's, showed me your drawings and your jewellery, when I saw the look on your face as you spoke about it, watched your hands as you messed around with a piece of clay—that's when I knew that you were meant for this, and that I would do whatever I could to help you."

"Starting with dragging me through Year 13 English," he said, tossing out the flippant comment, buying himself time, trying to put distance between himself and the uncomfortable knowledge he'd tried not to see. It wasn't just his whining about money, or sharing his fears and overwhelm as the business moved in new, uncharted directions. Cassie had been quietly denying her own talents so his might flourish and had been for years.

Her eyes flared in annoyance.

"Nik," she warned, "why do you always do that? Try to deflect the hard stuff. If we're going to talk about this, we're going to talk about this. I want to support you until the business is solid."

"OK,' he said. "If we're going for honesty—here's what I want. I want you to quit teaching. I want you to write full time." He didn't dare put into words the final thing he wanted from her; the one he wanted the most. Both of them were too fragile to speak of it, even now when they were laying everything on the table. If he could get her agreement on the first two, then when the dust settled from that, then they'd talk babies.

"Nik, the business is doing amazing. I'm so proud of you. But I know it's not quite there yet. Expecting it to pay for everything? I'd feel guilty putting that much pressure on you."

"God, Cassie, all this guilt shit. Anyone would think it was you who was raised Catholic, not me. You need to stop being the bloody martyr."

"Fuck you, Nik," she spat, and the spark of fire gave him hope that the girl he'd fallen for was still in there.

His wife had built herself an elaborate cage, and had inhabited it so long, she no longer knew how to escape, maybe no longer wanted to escape. But he was going to shake that damn cage, painful as that might be for both of them.

"Ah, there it is. That's more like it. My warrior princess is back. There's still some fight left in her."

"Don't you see, Nik," she said. Tears welled in her eyes, and her face crumpled. "I don't want to fight with you. Not like this. I want to fight for you."

Under the glare of the kitchen spotlights, her defiance faded. Tiny rivers edged down each cheek. She gulped in air, any words she had left trapped in her throat.

His resolve crumbled. He'd gone too far. He hated bullies and now he'd become one. Reaching for her, he crushed her against him, limp and defeated. He'd won some ground, but it was a hollow victory. Holding her to his chest, each heaving vibration of her small body was a blow to his heart, her muffled sobs soaking his shirt while he drowned in the mess he'd made.

"I'm sorry, babe, I'm sorry. I'm sorry," he whispered. "Please don't cry. I just hate seeing you dimming down your light so I can shine. You're Cassiopeia. You should be blazing bright in the sky. It's not me *or* you. It's me *and* you. We do this together."

After a time, she stilled, and he reached a finger under her chin, tilting her beautiful tear-stained face to his, and pressing a kiss to her lips, the salt tang a bitter reminder of the hurt he'd caused. He let his hand fall to her smooth skinned collarbone, traced the path of the silver chain, coming to rest on the circular pendant she never took off.

"Remember what it says," he said.

"We are all in the gutter, but some of us are looking at the stars."

She knew the inscription by heart and kept it pressed close there, but somehow over the years since he'd made it for her, she'd lost her ability to turn her gaze upward towards her dreams.

"Us," he said. "Not just me, not just you, but *us*. I'm not leaving you behind in the gutter, Princess. Promise you'll come with me?"

"I'll try," she murmured.

"Little steps," he said. "Don't be scared. Just take my hand and come with me. You're right, I can't do this without you. But I can't do this—I don't want to do this—if it means leaving you behind."

"Little steps," she nodded.

"You've already taken the first ones, babe. You're writing again." Feeling a subtle shift, a slight uplift of her shoulders, he nudged a little further. "And when we get back from Scotland, think about cutting back your hours at school. I'm sure they'd happily find you something part-time rather than lose you altogether."

She nodded again, and he could see her mulling it over. He'd succeeded in planting a small seed of possibility. And much as this damn trip to Scotland might be causing him grief, it offered Cassie the experience of life outside the cage. Once she'd tasted freedom, surely she wouldn't willingly go back inside.

CHAPTER 23

Cassiopeia

Edinburgh, Scotland - October 2017

THE IMMIGRATION OFFICIAL IN the booth ahead surveyed Nik with a wary eye. Cassie couldn't help but let a smile slip out. She'd seen that look before—people assessing if he was friend or foe. His sheer bulk confirmed he was the sort of guy that, if he wished to, might use his size and strength against you.

He swept back his overlong hair with a weary hand. She'd hinted that he might get a trim before they left, but he ignored the suggestion, preferring to wear it in the style of a seventies rock star, curling on his collar. The shadowy stubble on his chin only added to his untidy appearance. In his leather jacket and jeans, hands covered in chunky metal, all he needed was a gang patch, and he'd look like he'd stepped out of *Sons of Anarchy*. No wonder the Scottish border staff scrutinised him so judgementally.

If only they looked more closely, they'd observe the gentle clasp of his huge hand over hers. They would notice the protective arm that came around her when two boisterous teens scuffling in the line threatened to jostle her as they celebrated freedom from the confines of the plane by laughingly cuffing each other in a game. They would note the tenderness of the other hand that massaged her aching shoulder and how she let her eyes close in bliss at his soothing touch. Looks could be deceiving—she herself had many times marvelled at the contrast between the real Nik and her first sight of him.

Two lengthy flights plus a six-hour layover in Hong Kong Airport had taken their toll on both of them. Waiting in the arrival hall, she sat listlessly in an uncomfortable vinyl seat while Nik sorted the rental vehicle. With little sleep, the continuous stream of chimes from the airport intercom grated on her ears. Despite the lilting Scottish accents delivering announcements, she gritted her teeth in irritation.

Nik, by comparison, had bounced off the air bridge, simply relieved to be off the plane. Even the extra space and attentive staff in business class weren't sufficient to ease his claustrophobia. And because he'd been on edge, she'd been on edge too, worried about forcing him out of his comfort zone into this flying tin can; not to mention the huge leap of trust he'd taken, leaving his business in the hands of staff to be here.

A valet pulled up front with the vehicle, a hardy-looking modern iteration of a Land Rover. A Nik-sized vehicle. She wondered if they could ever afford something like this. They were still driving the compact family wagon his parents had bought them. A wedding gift given back when they wanted to ensure a safe vehicle for their grandchild, Cassie had always expected Toni Francovic might insist Nik return it. In other circumstances, he probably would have. While it might have come with a good safety star-rating and could comfortably fit a baby seat in the rear, Nik overflowed the driver's seat. But he endured the discomfort, mindful they had no money for anything more.

And now here they were in Scotland, already experiencing what it might be like to have wealth. From the roomy business class seats on the plane, and this modern, comfortable vehicle, to the room with an early check-in at a sleek airport hotel nearby, everything was easy. Evidence of Elias Sutherland's readiness to spend money to ensure the smooth running of his pet project infiltrated every aspect of their journey.

Even the merest suggestion of something from Blair and Elias magically made it happen; including booking the week-long holiday in the Highlands that awaited them. At Blair's request, he'd gifted them a brief peaceful interlude before they faced the onslaught of exhibition preparation, and the stress of the launch.

Cassie's phone chirped with a text. "It's Mum. Wanting an update."

Nik rolled his eyes, shaking his head in a knowing smile, as he put the stick shift in first gear and pulled out into the exit lane. "And so it begins."

***

Her dad had warned her about Castle Ruaidh Hotel, describing it as 'flash', but that hadn't prepared her for the reality of it. From the moment Nik eased the Land Rover under the portico and staff descended on them, it felt like they'd entered an alternate universe. The air crew in business class had been kind and responsive, but this felt next level. Here you only had to think of something and it materialised in front of your eyes.

In the entrance hall, weighty chandeliers bounced shards of light off highly polished wood. A heavy brass bannister led up a wide central staircase. Cassie noticed an unobtrusive maid travelling in the wake of guests, discreetly wiping away invisible fingerprints from its gleaming surface. Their accommodation was a sprawling suite with an enormous old-fashioned bath and a sumptuous bed that made her feel like she'd fallen into the story of the princess and the pea. And inside the dining room's wood-panelled walls, attentive staff presented a Michelin starred chef's reimagining of traditional Scottish dishes.

"Oh my god," she said as the young woman waiting at their table glided away into the shadows, her steps making no sound. "Nik, can you imagine Mum working here? Doing this?"

"I don't think your mother could even breathe quietly enough to hold down a job like that. And everything I've ever heard suggests she was at her loudest and wildest back then. Are you sure she's not spinning us a story?"

"Well, if it's a lie, Dad's in on it. But yeah, I have a new admiration for her if she did this. Even if it was only for a few months."

"So, how does it feel to be here, where they met? Where it all began? Before you were even a twinkle in your dad's eye, to quote him."

She laughed. "Excited. Grateful. That they found each other here. Not only because I'm in this world because of it, but for them. That people can find love and then make it last all those years. It's nice to think there are real life happily ever afters. That it's not just some unrealistic ambition. A fairy tale."

"Do you think we will?" he said. His blue eyes shot her a piercing glance. "Make it last?"

She had to look away. She studied the precarious stack of wafer thin parmesan and roasted vegetables on her plate. So easily toppled. Like them.

It would take so little to push their fragile marriage over the edge, leaving an ugly mess.

He'd spoken the question that neither had dared to voice. When they were younger, there had never been any doubt. They were soulmates, fated to be together and lucky enough to find each other early in life. No prior string of unsuitable others. No damage from broken hearts. No baggage of failed relationships. Childhood sweethearts who loved each other singly and fiercely. But was that the real fairy tale here? The myth that young love could be enough to sustain a lifetime.

"I hope so. Nik, I know it's been hard. I've been difficult…"

"And I haven't? Cassie, we're both struggling. You know, losing Brontë—it was tough, sudden, brutal. But these last few years…in some ways, it's been almost as bad. Like a slow torture. Just when I seize on a little spark of hope that things might be getting better, the next moment I feel like I'm battling again."

There it was. He'd finally admitted how tough it had been. The fact he'd always tried to shelter her from pressures and the worries of his work frustrated her. Why couldn't he share it with her? Why did he need to protect her from it? She could take it. She could help him.

"Maybe this break is what we need. Take some time to stand back from it all. A different perspective."

"Yeah," he said, a thoughtful hand grazing his chin. He'd allowed the growth of two days' travelling have its way. The beard suited him; an extra accessory for that sexy, slightly dishevelled vibe that never failed to stir something in her. "It's hard to find your way out of the shit when you're buried in it over your head. This might be a chance to step out of it and just breathe."

"You know, I think somehow Mum knew that. When she cooked up this plan. Everyone wins, but perhaps us more than anyone else. She believes in us. I believe in us."

"Cassie." His voice shook a little, low and hesitant. He took her hand, brushing his thumb back and forth, the rough touch of his skin beating a nervous rhythm. "I love you and I believe in us, too. If I didn't, I wouldn't be here. Although sometimes I wonder why *you* are. When I look at you, I still shake my head in disbelief that you chose me. And that you've stuck with me when there wasn't any reason for you to stay. I'm a grumpy bastard. Never happy. Hard to please," he said.

"Yeah, all of that," she said, with a rueful smile. "But choosing you wasn't just the decision of a naïve kid, Nik. We might have rushed into getting married, but we didn't rush into what came before that. And staying with you, that's a choice I gladly make every day."

"Like I choose you every day." He smiled across at her. "My lucky star. My north star. I'll always find my way back to you." He paused, reaching into his jacket pocket. "Perhaps this might be a good time. I've got something for you."

Placing the midnight blue box with its distinctive logo on the table between them, it felt like they'd already found their way back to each other. Inside, nestled in a bed of white velvet, a silver bangle glistened in the candlelight. Gold was more valuable, but silver was his material of choice, like sculpting the moonlight, he said. And across the curved band, picked out in diamonds, her constellation twinkled back at her.

Nik's business advisor had begged him time and again to bring out a signature range with the Cassiopeia logo, replicated in precious metals and diamonds. All the big jewellery designers did things like that. But Nik had refused. Told him the only woman wearing jewellery with that image on it would be her. She had the pendant, the gift that had marked the start of their relationship; the wedding band he'd made for her, back when two kids had stood in a near-empty church making weighty promises to each other, oblivious to how challenging it might be to keep them; and now this.

He reached over and picked it up, undid the clasp, and held it open. She lay her wrist across it, and he closed it with a small click. Bound. To him.

"Thank you Nik, it's beautiful," she breathed, twisting it so the candle-light caught it. Small rays danced off the diamonds.

"Nothing less for you."

She wanted to hang onto that expression in his stormy blue eyes, fix it in her mind for when the inevitable tide rose, swamping them again. She needed to remember and find the strength to believe in him and in them.

"I love you Nik," she said, to remind herself as much as him. Those words hadn't come often enough lately.

"Yeah, you and me, we are just one of your love stories," he teased. She could see his quiet pleasure that she'd been writing more regularly. After her father's gentle chiding about putting everything aside, she'd created a folder on her laptop and started to play with words again. Most of the time it was only a few minutes a day, but it was bliss.

"So my love," he said, pushing away his dessert plate, so bare he might have licked it clean when no one was looking, "how about we take a walk down to the castle? Check out where this other great love story began? Since it's a nice night."

"Good idea. I need to walk off this food." Her own plate still held a small sweet mound of raspberries and cream, but delicious as this concoction known as 'cranachan' was, she couldn't force another mouthful. Defeated by a Scottish dessert, she shoved it his way. Two mouthfuls and two minutes later and they were heading through the grand entranceway, all dark wood and tartan patterned carpet.

Off to one side of the hotel, leading away from its towering gothic spires, a pathway meandered towards the loch.

"You think they'd light it," she said, picking her way across the loose gravel.

"Maybe it's a deterrent. Stops guests from wandering around after dark. So they don't meet the ghosts of the Camerons," he said with a laugh.

He'd been on the internet reading up on Glen Ruaidh and its bloody history, revelling in tossing gory bits of backstory about warring clans at her. It reminded her of the boys in her class, devouring the *Horrible Histories* series, gleefully reading out gross facts about the past. In so many ways, her husband was just a big kid. Perhaps that was what marriage was like, forever tied to a man, while the boy he'd been always hovered beneath the surface.

A tiny prick of sadness came with the thought. Sometimes she didn't see enough of that boy, weighed down by the worries of the adult world. She made a silent promise to him, as they strolled beneath the stars, that on this trip she'd try not to crush that trace of the old Nik within him as she knew she so often did. He would be playful, and she'd respond with serious words, or worse still, brush it off. The demands of the world pressed heavily on both of them. Here in Scotland, they had a chance to push them back for a while.

They sat on a crumbling wall, the unseen quiet lap of black water a little beyond. Above them the stars blazed across a sky of indigo and navy, rendering small pockets purple and softest pink. Dark sky country. Like Tekapo. But not like Tekapo at all.

He shrugged off his jacket, laying it on the ground, before sliding down to sit on one edge. "Come here," he said, reaching a hand to hers. She slid down to join him and they lay shoulder to shoulder, the stars of the northern hemisphere blanketing them. "There it is."

The tremor of excitement in his voice echoed the thrill that surged through her body as she cast her eyes in the direction of his outstretched hand. Instinctively drawn to the wide W-shaped constellation, her arm strained towards it as if by some magic she might touch it, even though thousands of light years separated them. The pulsing stars of Cassiopeia lay above her, the matching diamonds on her wrist glistening as if dancing in time to the beat of an invisible cosmic drum. She had come home.

CHAPTER 24

Set Sail

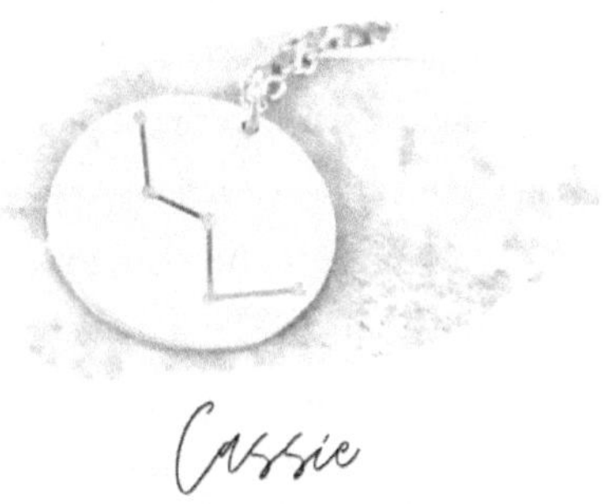

Cassie

Blackness, Scotland - November 2017

"I can't believe it." She rolled over with a groan and thrust the phone at Nik. Gallery owner Paula Orwald's bright breezy email message was not what she needed this early in the morning. Especially on the first day of a break from all the exhibition mayhem. "Look at this. I literally have two free hours on Monday morning—well, I *had* two free hours. Now I don't."

"Another radio interview, though? That has to be good, right?"

"Right," she agreed gloomily. Easy for him to say. He wasn't the one shoved out of his comfort zone. She felt her tiny introverted self literally dying under the microscope, with the entire Edinburgh arts scene focused tightly on her at this moment. Actually, on her mother, but it was her fronting up to the string of events and interviews surrounding this exhibition. She'd experienced others' excitement around her mother's work before, but not on this scale. And not with it aimed at her, a living, breathing, tangible part of the artist here for them to grab at.

She lay back on the pillow with a huff of dismay at the thought of the nauseating, anxious cramps that attacked her before every appointment. Her, talking to journalists. Her, on the radio. And then next week, how would she survive the opening night? A panel discussion with her, Paula and Elias, on a plush sofa on a stage, in the middle of the vaulted gallery, surrounded by strangers who expected a highbrow conversation about art. Instead, they had paid good money to hear her, the odd one out of the trio, bluffing her way through. She outwardly shuddered at the thought.

"Hey," Nik said, his hand massaging her shoulder. "You'll be great. You're a natural at this stuff. I saw how you handled that magazine interview last week. You were amazing."

"Thanks." She tried to put on a brave face. "Yeah, I know once I get there, I'll probably be fine. It's what it does to me beforehand. I almost threw up twice before that interview. Imagine what state I'll be in going live on air, with all the Edinburgh arty-farty people hanging on my every word."

"It's not live," he said. "Read the last bit again. *Taping* at ten. For the afternoon show."

"Oh, thank god. Presumably that gives them enough time to edit out my stuff-ups. And remove any paralysing silences."

"And she also says they're sending through the questions later today. So you won't be going in cold."

"Wonderful. Another thing to spoil my days away. Once I've read those, it will be all I can think about."

They'd planned the few days at this little B&B out on the coast near brooding Blackness Castle to provide a refuge from all of that. Just a spare room with a tiny attached bathroom in a quaint cottage—modest compared to the apartment Elias had given them in Edinburgh—it felt safe and peaceful.

Paula Orwald had frowned at Nik's insistence that she take this time out before the last pre-exhibition whirl. But Nik hadn't budged, and she was grateful. So far, it had helped. Except when she broke his number one rule, and made a quick check of her email, like this morning. Just as well the woman didn't have her mobile number.

"But you are *not* going to read them. You'll only spend the next four days agonising over the answers. Plenty of time when we get back to the apartment on Monday morning. No checking email again until then. Husband's orders."

"Yes, sir," she said, giving him a jaunty salute as she slipped out of bed. "You know, I think I might go for a walk before breakfast. Up to the castle. Take my mind off that message from Paula. Want to come?"

"No," he said. "A couple of things I need to take care of."

"*Nik*. I thought this was meant to be a no-work break?" She regretted her raised brow and the whiny edge coating her words the moment they were out.

"Come on Cassie. You know I can't just abandon the business. Do you still not realise what I put on hold so you didn't have to do this on your own?" Part of her conceded the point; she was being unfair. Part of her argued back. Was it really too much to ask this of him? A few days without work this week, when she'd put her entire life on hold for him for the last eight years?

Turning her back on his reproachful silence, she tugged on a puffer jacket, tied on a pair of trainers and left him glued to his laptop screen. She tiptoed down the narrow staircase, running her hand along the dark wood of the bannister, wondering at how many hands before her might have done the same. Everything in this country was old. Their host had gleefully told them they were staying in the newer part of the house, an addition from only a mere hundred and fifty years ago. And according to the friendly Mrs Morag Campbell, the castle she now headed for had stood sentinel on this windswept peninsula for more like five hundred.

"You're up early, love." Morag looked up from her pottering in a little garden beside the back door. "I can start your breakfast now if you'd like. I cut a little parsley in case you wanted the scrambled eggs."

Her broad round face, framed with a mop of grey curls, lit up in a toothy smile. Morag's ample breasts and rounded stomach pushed against a floral apron, evidence that she ate as much of her delicious cooking as she pressed upon her guests. Her sturdy legs, straight as fence posts with no ankle at all, disappeared into a pair of plush burgundy slippers.

One of those women who looked like everyone's ideal grandmother, Morag had welcomed them warmly into her home, as excited to have 'this lovely young couple, all the way from New Zealand' as if she'd paid them to stay with her, rather than the other way around.

"Thanks Morag, but if it's OK with you, we might have it a little later. Nik has a bit of work to do and I thought I'd walk up to Blackness."

"Oh, a lovely morning for it," she said, with a nod to the sun and blue sky that signalled a decent autumn day ahead. "The castle itself won't be open yet. So you'll want to go back later."

There was no doubt they'd be doing that—thanks to Nik's growing obsession with Scottish history. Last week, rather than wander aimlessly around the gallery while she thrashed out final details of the exhibition opening with Paula, he had ventured down the street and into a bookshop.

Later, back at the apartment, he'd spent that whole evening, and some of each night since, buried in a book—*Stories of the Stones: Scotland With The Castle Hunter*. You'd think he had Scottish ancestry, not her. And then with a jolt, she realised that wasn't entirely impossible. Nik was, of course, only Croatian by his parents' choice to adopt him. Maybe Scottish blood tugged at him too.

"He's good, this guy," he'd said, lounging back on the sofa. "Listen to this one."

His voice had carried an edge of excitement as he insisted on reading out the first of many passages about murder and mayhem within the walls of some remote castle. She didn't share his level of interest, but gave him her attention, simply because it was so good to see him distracted from the business. His singular focus wasn't healthy.

As for 'The Castle Hunter'? The title seemed a bit of an oxymoron. You didn't have to look too hard to find castles here in Scotland. One lurked around every corner. Like the one that loomed ahead of her as she followed the narrow pathway wedged between road and sea.

'The ship that never sailed'—that's what Nik said they called Blackness Castle. Standing staunch on a promontory jutting out into the navy waters of the Firth of Forth, it indeed seemed possible it might actually take sail today, as a lively wind whipped her hair across her face. She tucked it behind her ears and squinted up against the sun. She should have worn her sunglasses. The bright glare off the water jabbed at her eyes. She licked her lips, tasting salt spray.

The blunt-edged castle walls soared vertically from a jumble of rocks. Its brutal architecture echoed the treatment meted out to many of those who had dwelt as prisoners within its walls. Real people had suffered here, although she'd heard more about the fictional—one Jamie Fraser in particular.

Blackness had recently starred on film in her mother's favourite television series. Blair seemed almost as excited about the fact Cassie might visit some of the *Outlander* filming locations as the exhibition. She'd even registered Cassie to attend a semi-academic conference on the subject next month. Yes, it meant giving up a day of her life to learn the real life history behind the phenomenally successful television series and the books that lay at its heart. And probably a week to prepare the full blow by blow account of it her mother would expect afterwards. But she'd do it willingly. It seemed so unfair that disease had forced a vibrant woman like her mother to live so much of her life through others.

Hoping to bring a smile to Blair's face, she snapped a photograph, posing in front of the sinister-looking metal mesh that barred the low curved entrance way. She held up her phone to find a signal, sending a text winging its way to New Zealand. It didn't need words to accompany it. Blair would recognise the castle on sight and love that Cassie had sent it.

Past the barricaded entrance, a long pier stretched out into the sea and she meandered halfway along it before turning back. A chill had settled upon her, out there over the water, exposed to the full strength of the biting wind. She sought shelter tucked in by the castle entranceway, hoping to soak up a little of the warmth from the stones before heading back to enjoy Morag's breakfast.

Leaning back, eyes closed, a mournful sound drifting from the dark mouth of the castle ripped away her peaceful enjoyment of the heat against her back. She'd heard a sound like that before, one night when she was a kid, the whole household woken by the terrible noise. When her father had braved the darkness to investigate, he'd discovered one of the sheep grazing behind the house had become wedged in a drain, a leg broken in the fall.

Did some wounded animal lie within the castle walls? Maybe it had plummeted off the high walkway? Or become trapped in the rocks? She looked around, hoping someone with more practical knowledge might appear, but she was alone.

The rise and fall of it sent a shiver through her body, as Nik's folk-tale retellings played out in her imagination. Thoughts of her own wild imaginings reared up from the depths of her brain. The all-encompassing fear growing in her heart was more real than any of the stories she'd created. She'd plunged her characters into situations like this and revelled in their discomfort. Invisible forces. Unseen monsters. Inexplicable supernatural sights and sounds.

But as a writer, she could also come to their rescue. Real life offered no such escape. No omnipotent being would materialise to save her. Nor would she find some hidden inner power with which to fight back. Small, scared and insignificant, she pressed her body further into the alcove, while the sound raged at her, a howling creature, its menacing teeth sweeping closer with every breath. She sent out a silent scream for mercy, but it ignored her pain.

PART TWO – THERE

CHAPTER 25

Interview With The Vampire

Cassie

Blackness, Scotland - November 2017

"Are you OK?" The tentative question came from somewhere far above her. Cassie craned her eyes skywards, daring to lift her head from the confines of her puffer jacket like a hesitant turtle.

"Are you OK?" he repeated, leaning over her a little, his shape silhouetted against the sky, a smudgy outline, the details hidden in shadow. "Do you need help?" The deep male voice, sweet and rich like dark honey, with alluring Scottish vowels, washed over her. She basked in its calm, soothing caress, now the excruciating pain of that other sound had mercifully ebbed away.

He took a step closer. Looking up at the man's pale face framed with a sweep of blue-black hair, she might have fallen into an episode of *The Vampire Diaries*. She stared into fine angular features, the cheekbones sharply defined. His eyes were a startling shade of bright denim, in stark contrast to the pallor of his skin. However, in them she saw wariness that suggested he wouldn't be going for her throat any time soon. His dark brows knotted together in a frown that might be concern. He stood there considering her, his gaze intense, as if weighing his next move.

Surely, if he was a sinister creature of the night in search of a final victim before retiring to his rest, he wouldn't hesitate to act. This man appeared in no such hurry, perhaps needing time to assess why a woman should be here on her own, slumped against the wall of a castle.

And even if he moved towards her, she doubted she'd be able to spur her body into action. His sheer presence paralysed her. A creature from her imagination made flesh. He was beautiful—not like some fashion model, or movie-star—but with that ethereal, almost other-worldly look of some of the characters she'd written in her books.

Perhaps this familiarity had ignited an instant spark of attraction. Its mere existence was enough to unbalance her. When she'd woven that theme into her stories, it had always felt pure fantasy, that one could feel an overwhelming sense of connection to someone you'd just met. But there was nothing fictional about the feelings that bubbled up inside her from the mere sight of him.

She stared up, squinting against the glare of the early sun, still reluctant to stand and face him directly. This would require her to uncurl her body and leave the protection of the small hollow in the wall that had been her sanctuary. After the punishing onslaught of sound, she instinctively clung to her place of refuge, unsure of leaving herself vulnerable. But in his eyes, she read genuine kindness and relief as she mustered a small smile.

"No, I'm OK, I think." She needed to convince herself as much as him. "I just..."

How could she explain it to him and he not think she her mad? He already seemed to suspect there was something not right with her. And who wouldn't be, coming across a woman wedged tightly into this little alcove, arms curled above her head? In his position, she'd have assumed drunk or drugs. She had an immediate need to assure him otherwise, and grasping for an explanation, an idea pushed its way forward.

"Agoraphobia," she blurted out, waving a hand upward at the towering wall behind her. She'd heard of it. How some people freaked out around tall buildings, even large trees. She grasped onto her excuse.

That did it. Any final guardedness in those piercing blue eyes immediately softened, replaced by sympathy.

"That can't be easy," he said, smiling reassuringly. Any remaining trace of the crazy notion he was some supernatural being trickled away at the warmth in that smile. Just a normal human—no, not normal, because normal insinuated average, everyday, ordinary—and this was the most extraordinary man she'd ever met. Never, ever, in the space of moments had she felt such a sudden overwhelming need to know this person. Or the need to convince him to not turn his back and walk away.

"It's not," she said, hoping to engage him longer. "Not when you can't predict what will bring it on. But fortunately, it doesn't happen very often."

"Well, good on you for not letting it hold you back. Brave of you to venture out on your own. I'm pleased that it's nothing more, though. I'd have been bloody useless if it was. Not the best at first aid or practical stuff like that, I'm afraid. Especially not blood." He gave a small shudder. Definitely not a vampire.

"Anyway, I'm Simon." He stretched a hand towards her. She grasped the long slender fingers, and with unexpected strength, he hauled her to her feet.

"Looks like I took part of the castle down with me." She brushed at her clothes, the dusty fragments of crumbling stone rising in a faint cloud. "I'm Cassie Tremayne."

"So, what brings you out so early? Usually there's no one here but me."

"Just a morning walk before breakfast. That's how I usually start my day."

"Walk? From where?"

"I'm staying at the cottage down there."

"Ahhh, Morag's place," he said.

"You know it?"

"Yes, this is my home turf. My family came from near here. I inherited my grandmother's place—further back along this road. Right before the little village." She nodded. The cute village shops looked like something out of another time. A pub, the small general store and a gift shop blended seamlessly into their stone walls, their modern interiors hidden sympathetically behind well-maintained original exteriors. "You'd have passed it on the drive in to Morag's. Mine's the two-storey house, big oaks out front, tumbledown stone wall—and to my embarrassment an overgrown garden."

"Yeah, I saw it." How could you miss it? The huge brooding house with soaring honey-gold walls and slate tile roof loomed over the other buildings in the village. The garden, although certainly overgrown, added to the feeling that ancient magic lurked inside. Perhaps he was a vampire, after all.

"And you're a New Zealander? The accent?"

"Yes, doing the OE thing. 'Overseas experience'," she translated, noting his puzzled expression. "It's a kind of rite of passage for us colonials. To spend time in the motherland."

"So, what brings you to Scotland? A lot of the kids from the antipodes don't seem to venture further than London, apart from taking drunken tour buses around Europe."

She winced at the word 'kids'. Although perhaps she should take it as a compliment. After all, at twenty-six, she was now on the slippery slope towards thirty. If he thought her youthful, that was a good thing, right? Scanning his face more closely, she placed him as well into his thirties. Against that, she probably seemed like a kid.

"I'm a writer," she said. His eyes flared with interest. "So it's good to get out of the city. A crowded flat in London isn't exactly conducive to getting work done. And this sort of place," she waved a hand at the shadowy castle wall, "is definitely more the atmosphere I need."

He smiled at that, as if by praising the castle she also offered him a compliment. "And what do you write?"

"Fantasy romance." She automatically employed the well-practised defiant tone and set of her chin. It provided suitable armour against the disparaging reactions she sometimes got to that answer. Fantasy felt reasonably acceptable. In fact, given the obsession with turning fantasy books into hit TV series, it even brought admiration. But admitting to writing romance more often than not attracted embarrassed titters and derisory comments. This time, she received neither.

"Published?" he asked.

Again she steeled herself against possible judgement. "Yeah, I went indie." May as well admit it up front. No one could argue with her success at self-publishing. Sure, it wasn't enough to retire on, but five books in, she had a hopeful feeling that nights working bars might soon be a thing of the past. And if one of the big traditional publishers took note of her growing sales, her life might change forever.

"You make me feel rather inadequate," he said with a grin. "I wasn't born with your sort of courage. More the sit back and wait kind of writer."

Did he actually suggest self-publishing was a good thing, and not some deluded form of vanity? And he was a writer? "You write too?"

"Yes, not in the brilliant creative sense of someone like you. But yes."

He ducked his head, a modest flush rising on his neck. This shy awkwardness was a surprising contrast to his slightly haughty appearance. His every word, every gesture forced her to revise her opinion of this man. She cast him an expectant look, hoping to encourage him further.

"So...would I have heard of you?"

"Probably not," he shrugged. "I'm first and foremost a historian. And this..." He pointed up at the castle. "This is my specialty. Castles. Scottish castles, to be specific."

"And how did you become a writer?"

"Because of the interest in the topic, I get asked to do a few public speaking engagements. At one of them, a promoter put a label on me: 'The Castle Hunter'. It sort of took off from there. Suddenly, I had a name and a small fan base. That's how the book came about. I took my academic writing, distilled it into a more widely palatable form. And of course, my words got well-polished by an editor. Before I knew it, I was a published author. I'm working on a second volume now."

"This is research?"

He shook his head. "No, Blackness is an old friend. I've been coming here since I was a wee boy. Me and my cousins. My grandmother loved us kids coming to stay, but faced with the reality of a group of boisterous boys, encouraged us to free range as far and wide as we wanted to save her sanity. Up here at the castle was always where I wanted to come and play. And then when I was fourteen, we moved in with her." A brief shadow flitted across his eyes, but he pressed on. "From then on, I'd walk up here most days. Turned into a lifelong passion, I suppose."

"Sounds like a happy childhood."

"That part of it was." His upturned mouth stretched into a bitter, twisted line. In his eyes, she saw a flash of anger, quite at odds with the calmness he otherwise projected. But it was gone in an instant. As if realising he'd piqued her curiosity, he shut down the question that sprang to her lips.

"Well, how's that for a coincidence?" he said. "Two random people meet and we both happen to be writers." He seemed bright again—a little too bright, as if forcing himself. "How about I walk you back to Morag's? I'm sure I can wrangle a coffee out of her while you tell me some more about your writing."

"Sure. Thanks," she said, trailing him back along the pathway. Simon might not have wanted to reveal further, but she couldn't help but wonder what darkness had provoked that brief but dramatic change in him. Her childhood, although imperfect like most people's, didn't hold darkness.

"Ahhh, Simon." In the sunlit kitchen, Morag Campbell paused from scrubbing at a basin of clattering dishes. "So, I see you've found our Miss Tremayne."

"Stumbled across her by the castle," he said, and then, as if to say 'Your secret's safe with me,' threw Cassie a conspiratorial wink.

"Those look good," he said, peering over Morag's shoulder with the easy familiarity of someone who'd stood in this kitchen many times before. "Any chance of one with a coffee while Cassie has her breakfast?"

The tray of date scones not only looked appetising—rows of cloud-like mounds with burnished gold tops—but their sweet, warm smell filled the kitchen. His hand hovered teasingly above them.

"Simon Buchanan, I swear you're just as cheeky as ever," she said with a flash of her big-toothed smile, while flapping her tea-towel at him. "Go on then, sit yourself down next door and I'll bring one through. Cassie, love, would you like the porridge or the eggs? Or both?"

"Porridge again please," she said. The memory of yesterday's breakfast—salty grains of oatmeal, swimming in a lake of yellowy cream, and topped with a swirl of honey—made the choice easy.

"Ahhh," said Simon with an approving nod. "So we've already made a true Scot of you?"

"In the blood," she said as they made their way to the cosy dining room to sit at the square pine table topped with a cheerful red gingham cloth.

"Really? You're Scottish?"

"More than half. Can't you tell?" she said, pointing to the copper flush in her dark hair. "My Dad's Scottish. And my mum's family trace back to here. Believe it or not, I was born in the Mackenzie Country."

"Yes, well, side by side in the street, they'd pick you for a Scot over me," he said, pointing at his own hair the colour of midnight. "But I'm as purebred as my good Scottish name."

"Simon? Or Buchanan?"

"Both actually. Anyway..." There it was, that quick deflection as they strayed close to anything personal. "Fantasy romance. Am I right in thinking that's sort of *Game of Thrones* meets *Outlander*?"

"Pretty much."

"Sounds great. I've read both. Watched both too."

"I'm surprised at that. Somehow, I didn't think historians would be into make-believe stories. You know, playing with the truth rather than sticking to the facts."

"You'd be wrong there. Because after all, that's what history is really: stories. With my area of history—pre-twentieth century—there's no one alive to give you an eyewitness account. Only their stories remain. And even if they were here to tell the tale in person, it's still only a story. Like this morning—if you and I were to tell that story, it wouldn't be the same."

"Yeah, like I wouldn't use the words 'stumbled across her by the castle' to describe how you found me." She grinned at him. "More like, discovered her cowering in a corner."

Somehow, talking about it made the whole experience a little less frightening. Maybe her lie could be the truth. Maybe she did suffer some type of agoraphobia, but she'd never noticed it before. Castle-induced perhaps?

"Tell me," he said. "I'm curious. When I write I literally immerse myself in the subject matter. Spend my day trailing round castles, climbing the stairs, walking the walls, checking out all the nooks and crannies. Back it up with some online research and reading a few books. Then back to my room each night and write. So I've got lots of information to work from. How does a fiction writer do it? When you're just making it all up?"

She could easily have chosen to take that as a criticism. But she scolded herself, knowing she must try to move on from automatically becoming defensive when people asked about her work. So, trusting the question was genuine, she attempted to explain.

"You see, Simon, that's where *you're* wrong. Most of it isn't made up. Fiction is pretty much real life recreated on the page. But done in a way that makes it feel like something new."

"Is it your real life recreated on the page? Or someone else's?"

Writers always got asked those sorts of questions. Everyone was desperate to know if the female main character having rampant sex with the big brawny alpha leading man was, in fact, wholly based on you. But this time, it felt like genuine curiosity, rather than voyeurism. Strangely, his earnest attention spurred a sudden wicked urge to have some fun with him.

"A bit of both." He seemed so serious. Time to lighten things up. And if he read it as flirting, then he wouldn't be wrong. "I have to admit, I still need to use a bit of imagination for the steamy stuff," she deadpanned. "I can't claim to have done everything my characters do, although I'm working through the list," she said, struggling to keep a straight face.

"Steamy?" He frowned at her, uncertain. God, was she going to have to spell it out to a man maybe ten years older than her? And then as realisation dawned on his face, a racing blush of colour followed. It was really quite endearing. This rather severe looking man—who, if he wasn't the love interest in a *Twilight* movie, could be the main character in a billionaire romance—coloured up at the mention of sex like an embarrassed teenager. He smiled nervously, as if she was going to pounce on him and demonstrate exactly what 'steamy' meant.

She decided it would be kinder to rescue him. "I'm like you. I gather stories. And from that, I retell them in new ways. As they say, there's nothing totally original."

"You know," he said, as if grasping for a way to turn the conversation in a safer direction, "since you're writing fantasy, you can't go wrong with visiting castles for inspiration. How about I take you to a few? There are some fantastic ones around here." His face lit with enthusiasm. Here was a guy with a real passion for his subject. "It's only a short drive to Doune Castle. Winterfell in *Game of Thrones*, Castle Leoch in *Outlander* and a star turn in *Monty Python and the Holy Grail*."

"Oh, wow, Simon, I'd love that."

"Although, will you be able to ward off any more of those agoraphobia attacks? As I said, I'm not your man in a crisis."

"I'll be fine," she said. "I've got some rescue remedy somewhere. A few drops of that will help."

She silently thanked her mother's advice for the small stash of herbal remedies in her bag. It certainly wouldn't hurt to take some. Under the bright mask she put on for Simon, she still felt wobbly. And helpfully, it would support her spontaneous made-up version of what had happened to her at the castle this morning.

As for the real version? She'd rather not dwell on that for now. It sent a shudder through her just to think of the sound. She wouldn't be going to

Blackness Castle alone again. Even in Simon's company, with his genuine fondness for the place, she wasn't sure she could face it anytime soon.

Flood

Doune, Scotland - November 2017

IF ANYTHING WAS GOING to trigger a genuine bout of agoraphobia, it was the looming walls of Doune Castle. Cassie stood, head tilted back, struggling to see the top of the tower above her. Like Blackness, it was no fairytale castle, with bland, almost brutal stonework, the windows mere slits, and no hint of embellishment to relieve its severe expression.

Simon stood close as she peered upwards, steadying her with light, reassuring hands on her shoulders. His mellow voice, thick as treacle, came low in her ear.

"If there's any time you're not OK with this, just let me know," he said.

"I'm good," she said, smiling up at him. How could she not be with that handsome face inches from her own? "It's amazing. How old?"

"Built in the early fourteen hundreds, but if they excavated, they'd most likely find Roman era stuff. Such a strategic position, here where the two rivers meet, perfect for a fortress in any century."

"Incredible."

"OK, the tour starts here," he began, taking her hand. Still a little unbalanced by her previous castle encounter, she welcomed the safe feeling of being guided into its gloomy interior. He led her through the musty entry tunnel, its iron gate flung wide in welcome, no longer needed to repel invaders. Beyond it, at the top of broad stone steps, they entered the vastness of the great hall.

As Simon spun the story of its history, she could imagine the lords and ladies—kings and queens too, he said—seated at tables heaving with food, decked out in their medieval finery; the walls hung with heavy tapestries; a chandelier of interwoven antlers with blinking candles above their heads. It was as if she'd fallen into one of the fantasy worlds which, up until now, she'd created purely from images and words. Here she was, immersed in another time and place, and she sighed with pleasure at the sensation of stepping out of her normal life into something new, yet old.

"Follow me," he said, beckoning her through a high curved doorway. "This is the real heart of a castle." The purpose of the adjoining room, with its wide remarkably well-preserved hearths, was immediately obvious. "Can you imagine the chaos in this kitchen back then, producing food in quantity for demanding, noble guests with not a scrap of modern technology?" he said. She trailed her hand across the arched serving hatches, reminiscent of a modern day restaurant. She could almost smell the aroma of meat roasting on a spit. "Cooks yelling, and servants hustling, it must have been crazy."

"A little Gordon Ramsay, perhaps?" she grinned, thinking of the notoriously grumpy celebrity chef. "God, I love his shows. He's such an arsehole, but he gets results. Just as well he hasn't come up against me—no amount of shouting will help my lack of skill in the kitchen," she groaned. "A bit of toast and a boiled egg is about my limit, I'm afraid."

"It's OK, stick with me and you won't starve," he laughed. "I love cooking. And, apparently, I'm not totally rubbish at it." He paused a moment, leaning his elbows on the stone counter, chin resting on his clasped hands, while surveying her through the serving hatch with a thoughtful expression. "In fact, why don't you let me cook you dinner tonight? If I can prise you away from Morag's clutches?"

"I'd like that, very much," she said. "She's not expecting me for a meal tonight, anyway. I told her I wanted to try out the pub."

Mostly, staying with Morag was a delight, but being the only guest, after two days Cassie was finding the old lady's well-meaning but constant chatter claustrophobic. Craving a reprieve, she had planned to take refuge in the tiny village pub this evening. Fuelled by some bangers and mash and maybe a pint of beer, she'd been looking forward to some alone time, but dinner with Simon was an altogether much more attractive prospect.

"Good," he said. "You like Italian?"

"I love Italian."

"Great," and she could see the spark of anticipation in his eyes. She knew he had to see it reflected in her own. Something arced between them, and the little jolts of attraction were addictive. It was the first time in ages a man had ignited that small spark. Perhaps spending time over dinner might fan it into a flame.

"OK, time to head there," he said, pointing upwards at a small balcony. "Let's go meet *the* queen."

It was a surreal feeling, walking in the footsteps of the legendary Mary Queen of Scots, standing in her bedchamber with its tiny closet space that seemed hardly enough for a queen's finery.

"A private bathroom," he said, when she queried the purpose of the small alcove in one wall. "The royal throne, so to speak," he quipped with a deep, rumbling laugh.

She could get used to hearing that laugh; wanted to coax it out of him, bask in its surprising exuberance, see the little creases like rays of sunshine bloom at the corners of his eyes, watch his often serious mouth curve upwards with a hint that dimples might even lurk beneath his often moody expression.

"Beautiful," she said, as she stood at the queen's window, the tops of the trees laid out at her feet. Their leaves, heavy with colour, whispered of the approaching winter. In the stiff breeze, they swirled like molten metal, brass and copper, bronze and gold all captured in a huge melting pot, stirred by a giant invisible hand.

"It is," he said, and she turned to the sound of his voice. "Beautiful." His eyes swept over her, and there was no denying the meaning in his gaze. "My god, standing there like that, framed against the window, you could be her," he whispered. As if overtaken by a need to confirm this, he stepped towards her. "With your complexion, the hair."

He reached out long slim fingers, finding a stray piece of that wayward hair and tucking it behind her ear. She stood unmoving, sure that in the silence he might hear the fluttering of her heart, like the frantic wingbeats of a hummingbird.

"Might be worth checking the family tree," he said, not taking his eyes from her. "Could be some royal Stewart blood back there somewhere." She didn't need proof of royal blood to feel like a queen under Simon

Buchanan's admiring gaze. "Would you care to walk in the courtyard, your majesty?" he said with a shy smile. He extended his hand like a courtier, and she let him lead her to the stairs.

Pulling up at the cottage, Cassie didn't expect distraught Morag Campbell rushing out to meet them. She had barely climbed from the passenger seat of Simon's car when the elderly lady burst from the front door, pausing on the steps as if undecided what to do next. Her wild hair stood out in a grey halo. She wrung her hands in the folds of her apron.

"Oh, thank goodness you're back. What an afternoon!" Her ruffled appearance was a dramatic contrast to the calm, cheerful host they'd left this morning. "Come in, come in. I've got some rather bad news, I'm afraid," she said, her tone apologetic. "I should have had the plumbing attended to the last time I heard those strange rumbling noises. It's all my fault, really." She turned and wandered off inside, as if hoping to avoid the awkwardness of this admission. "And I'm not sure what we can do about it."

They trailed up the narrow stairs after her and into Cassie's room. Beyond the doorway, sodden carpet squelched underfoot. A pungent damp smell billowed up from each footstep.

She regretted not taking more time to tidy her things. This morning, gripped with an unexplained sense of anticipation at Simon's invitation, she had raced upstairs and rummaged through her belongings in search of a suitable outfit for scrambling around castles. Shoes lay on the floor where she had tossed them at the wardrobe. An explosion of clothes tumbled from her suitcase.

Embarrassment flooded across her as Simon took it in with a raised brow, a grin spilling across his face as she pounced on the froth of lacy underwear on top. His eyes lighted on the skimpy thong that somehow tangled around her fingertips and she felt heat rise in her cheeks. Under his scrutiny it felt like the more she tried to dislodge it, the more the damn thing seemed to tighten its grip.

"Need some help there?" he whispered, leaning close, while Morag prattled on with her blow by blow account of the plumbing disaster.

"No," she said under her breath, tossing him a grin that probably looked like a grimace. Finally managing to free her fingers with a thwack of the elastic, she scrunched the rebellious thong into a ball, and buried it amongst the rest of her wayward underwear.

At least it was clean underwear. And thank god it didn't include the stretchy nana pants she preferred for flights; the ones that didn't ride up your butt as you wiggled around trying to get comfortable in the unpleasant airline economy seats. *They* weren't the kind of thing she wanted a guy she'd just met to see; certainly not a guy she found very attractive; definitely not a man she already considered someone she possibly wanted to reveal her underwear to at some time in the future.

Turning his attention back to Morag, Simon took careful steps to avoid the worst of the wet patches, heading towards where she stood in the little bathroom. Cassie tiptoed after him, hoping not to soak her shoes in the puddles.

"It's the loo," Morag said sadly, looking at the lake of water that even now lapped at the rim of the toilet bowl. "I was cleaning it after you left. Who'd have known that last flush would be its last flush?"

The sheen on the bathroom floor came from a thin layer of water that remained, despite Morag's obviously valiant effort to clean it up. A mop leaned against the bath, next to a half-full bucket of murky water.

"I only intended to pop out for a few minutes. Just to take the scones up to the castle cafe. But of course that Dulcie up at the shop can talk. Her son in Belfast is having a terrible time of it, you know." She shook her head.

Whether her gloomy tutting was over the half-inch of water still covering the floor, or the fate of Dulcie's son, remained unclear.

"And then when I arrived back, Roy next door asked me over to give an opinion on what's been gnawing on his broccoli. Some nasty wee caterpillar, I think. Anyway—." She paused in the tale for a quick breath. "There I am in the kitchen, and I hear a strange sound and I say to myself, 'Morag, did you leave the tap running?' Because I did that once. When I came up here to see, there it was—water gushing from the loo. I tried to get it to stop. Bashed the button, but it kept coming."

"But you obviously did get it to stop somehow," Simon pointed out.

"No, *I* didn't. Thankfully, Roy is a quick thinker. Found the water main and turned it off. Then came up and took a peek inside. Says the fill valve has failed. I knew I should have done something about it sooner. There's been an odd sound for a while now. But I thought nothing of it. And that's not the worst thing. Young Jeff the plumber says he can't get here for at least a week. Some job up north on a new build, he says."

"You can't stay here for a week without water, Morag," Simon said.

"Oh no, no, it's OK. Roy disconnected something or other, then turned the main back on. So I'm fine here. But it's just this," she said, surveying the tiled bathroom floor still underwater, and the soaked carpet of the bedroom. "Cassie has paid for a proper room. And now all I've got is this."

"That's an easy fix, Morag. You're not to worry. I have a perfectly good spare room down at mine. She's welcome to stay there. If she wants." He looked at her expectantly and Cassie felt a new thrill of possibility at spending more time with Simon Buchanan. "That's if she can ever get all those clothes back into her suitcase." His mouth turned up in a cheeky grin.

"That's a bit harsh."

"I did offer to help," he said with a wink as his hand hovered dangerously over the jumble of bras and panties.

"Oh, that's so kind of you, Simon. And Cassie, I'll refund you, of course." An expression of relief mingled with resignation passed across Morag's face.

"No need at all. I've already paid the money." Morag obviously relied on renting this room and her daily baking for the cafe to supplement her pension. She wasn't going to take money away from the old lady. Especially as she now faced what could be a hefty bill. "And you'll need it to pay the plumber. It's not necessary. Unless Simon here is going to charge."

"Tidy guests stay for free. I only charge for messy ones. And double for those who bring trouble." He waggled his eyebrows at her and she couldn't help but think Simon might welcome some trouble—and she'd be happy to pay the price.

Morag appeared oblivious to the undercurrent in their banter. Amidst the playfulness, something arced between them. She sensed his excitement at the prospect of her staying with him. This morning, a strange twist of events had thrust her into Simon Buchanan's world. The result: a day spent with the most interesting and attractive guy she'd met in a long, long time. It was as if whatever forces had pushed them together, pleased with that outcome, had decided to shove her more firmly in his direction. She felt sorry that poor Morag had to bear the brunt of those manipulations. But she wasn't sorry at the opportunity to spend a few nights under his roof, even if it was a slightly spooky old manor house, with serious Addam's family vibes.

CHAPTER 27

Need

Blackness, Scotland - November 2017

SIMON HAD NO IDEA why he should be so comfortable with the presence of Cassie Tremayne hovering at his elbow while he did his best Jamie Oliver impression. Trying to appear nonchalant about the simmering bolognese sauce, he fired up another gas element to bring water to the boil, ready for the pasta. He attempted to move confidently as if this was no new thing, to have a beautiful woman here in his kitchen; a woman who'd spent an entire day with him, listening to him rabbit on about castles.

As usual when nervous, he'd vomited out words, facts and dates, all to avoid the frightening thought of having to make real conversation. But it hadn't deterred her. And as he'd slowly relaxed, she'd reacted to his less anxious self by coming in closer. Stayed holding his hand long after he'd helped her through a narrow part of the stairs. Tucked in against him out of the wind up on the wall walk. Shuffled along to sit right beside him in the booth at a pub in Linlithgow where they'd called in for a beer after visiting the palace.

And now here she was, in his house, in his kitchen, allowing him to cook her a meal, almost resting her chin on his shoulder while she peered over it, complimenting him on his skill at creating a dish he could almost make with one hand tied behind his back.

He thanked god for his grandmother's insistence on self-sufficiency. And how cooking had turned into something he genuinely enjoyed—and was reasonably good at. At least even if he disappointed her in other ways, Cassie's choice to eat here tonight rather than dining on pub fare at the little local wouldn't prove a disappointment. But he also felt a small optimistic flutter, that Cassie Tremayne liked what she saw in him beyond his culinary talents.

And he was pleased he'd spent so much damn money this past few years to make the front part of the house habitable. At least these rooms were somewhere you could invite a woman into without fearing it would all fall down on her head. As for the rest, well, she didn't need to see that part, with its walls crying rivers of damp and moss growing on the beams overhead. He preferred not to see it himself, given the eye-watering cost of dealing with it.

"I have to say that bears no resemblance whatsoever to the sorry spag bol that seems to be the mainstay of nearly every flat I've ever lived in," she said, eyeing the pan with admiration.

"It's not exactly difficult. Simply follow the recipe." The large Italian cookbook sat propped open on a wooden stand to his right.

"I think that's the usual problem—not using a recipe. I had no idea there was one. Thought you just fired random ingredients in and hoped for the best. It smells so good," she said, stepping around him to lean over the pan, inhaling the wafting aroma of basil and garlic, eyes closed. If he could create that blissful look on her face with food alone, what might he accomplish given the opportunity to do some of the things he'd been imagining all day?

"Taste?" he said, offering the wooden spoon, and immediately regretted the offer.

The sight of her pink lips pursed tight as she blew on the steaming sauce caused an embarrassing lurch of his cock. He was grateful for the apron. Her groans of pleasure as she lapped at the spoon only made it worse.

It was a long time since he'd felt this. And he was fairly sure it wasn't only his body's desperate need for a skin to skin encounter with something besides his hand. The self-enforced celibacy was the least important part of the distance he'd placed between himself and women since the debacle with Renee. It felt like the last remnants of the damage, the crushing lack of trust in another human being and the loneliness that sprang from his need to protect his fragile self, had finally lifted from him today.

Who could have predicted that the vagaries of ancient plumbing might deliver such a windfall right into his home? Not that he wished poor old Morag Campbell any ill-will, but he secretly hoped that Jeff the plumber had a jam-packed work schedule for a few days yet.

"Do you want to pour us some of that red?" he said, nodding towards the open wine bottle on the counter in a desperate need to extinguish her excruciating little coos of delight over the food.

"Sure," she said. "Glasses?"

"In that cupboard over there."

She hummed away to herself, busy pouring a generous amount of the delicious Primitivo while he tried to keep his mind fixed on stirring the pan with deft twirls of the wooden spoon.

"You know, I had the best time today?"

She handed him a glass, deep ruby liquid swirling inside it. He'd been saving this bottle for a special occasion. Tonight he'd reached for it without thinking, but noting the upward curve of her lips as she spoke of the day, he knew it was the perfect choice. This completely ordinary scene, in his kitchen, cooking, didn't feel the least bit ordinary. It felt like a special occasion, simply because of the extraordinary woman who not only filled the room, but something inside of him, with a sense of rightness.

"Me too," he said.

"Despite a less than auspicious start. God, you must have wondered what you'd done to deserve that—your morning walk spoiled by a crazy woman."

"No," he said quickly. "That's not what I thought at all. I was worried about you. That there was something very wrong. Thank god it was nothing." Stupid. He regretted the dismissive words the moment they tumbled out unfiltered from his mouth. He, of all people, should have empathy for the problems a fickle mind could conjure. "Cassie. Shit, I'm sorry. I shouldn't have said that. To diminish your agoraphobia..."

Her exuberant laugh cut him off. "Simon, it's fine. I want nothing more than to diminish what happened this morning. It *was* nothing."

"No. It wasn't nothing. You were in distress. And—this sounds bloody awful—but I felt strangely relieved that it was the sort of crisis that I could do something about."

She chuckled at that with a shake of her head. "And you did. What you did was perfect. Talked to me. Got me back to Morag's. And see—I was great for the rest of the day. Guided tours of two different castles and not one single incident of me spinning out. It seems you were just what I needed."

Just what she needed? A warmth flooded through him. To be what someone needed—he hadn't felt that way in a long time. Probably not since he'd lived in this house with his grandmother. And beyond family, had he ever been what someone else needed?

Not with a woman. Not like that. He'd needed them, needed love, acceptance. Their need for him had been for different reasons altogether. Selfish, grasping reasons with him a fortunate pawn in a bigger game. He shook off the jab of regret and focused back on this woman, who was so far removed from scheming Renee, that she might be a different species altogether.

"Who'd have known that I could be so useful?" He smiled back at her. Her delicious perfume already lingered in his bathroom. Now, close to him, mingling with the fragrant herbs, he breathed it in, basking in the smell of contentment. He hoped she smelled it, too.

***

"I may be useless at cooking, but I do know how to load a dishwasher, Simon. Go." Cassie snatched at his plate, still sticky with the remains of the decadent dark chocolate brownie Morag had pressed on them. "Although, that brownie was so damn good I'm tempted to do what my gross little brother would and lick my plate clean."

She grinned down at him as she teasingly put her own plate to her mouth, poking out her delicate pink tongue. He inwardly groaned at the sight. Was she deliberately flirting with him? Attempting to provoke images of what else she could do with that tongue? If so, it was succeeding in ways that were incredibly uncomfortable in the confines of his jeans.

"Don't let me stop you." The words came out contorted, his throat constricted as tightly as his cock. She didn't appear to notice, thank god.

"No, I'll be good," she said with a laugh. "Although she may have failed with Archie, Mum did teach me some manners. Go on. You promised to convince me about whisky. Why don't you get us one?"

He did as he was told, heading from the dining room to the library. He tossed some more wood on the open fire, then poured them each a decent splash of the 25-year-old Laphroaig. Another thing he'd been saving for a special occasion.

He reached a hand to the chess set on the side table, the game he'd abandoned last night. He pondered a moment, scanning ahead in his mind, then moved the black piece; rook to d7. Maybe she played? A real life opponent, no matter their level of skill, would be nice. Although drawing her attention to the game sitting there might also reveal the pathetic loneliness of a man who usually played against himself.

The shelves of books stared down at him. What would she make of this room? Probably realise that he was merely a dull university lecturer with nothing interesting to offer except an obsession with the past. Dozens of dusty old histories of castles jostled with works by his contemporaries. Their neat alphabetical order nurtured his need for regularity, but appeared aesthetically muddled. Amongst them, on the top shelf in the 'Bs', his thick leather-bound thesis sat wedged between a small book on Blackness his Masters supervisor had encouraged him to print, and the newest publication in the collection: *Stories of the Stones: Scotland With The Castle Hunter.* While the doctoral thesis had drawn expected compliments from his peers, he'd been ill-prepared for the success of this book.

He had fans. Even here, safe from their scrutiny, he cringed at the uncomfortable thought. At least his publishers had seen how immovable he was. He'd laid down his terms: no in-person events. He wasn't prepared to sign his name endlessly while making small talk with strangers—although his arm still ached in sympathy at the memory of an afternoon spent in his editor's back room autographing two hundred copies of the new special edition a few weeks ago.

And why on earth had he agreed to that damn *Outlander* thing at the University in December? Lured by his enjoyment of bringing history to the ordinary people, he'd said yes and now regretted it. He told himself it was just another lecture, no different to the ones he delivered to his history students—but it wasn't. He only hoped his Icarus self, flying so close to the blazing popularity of a wildly successful author and the television series spawned by her work, wouldn't be burned by the experience. Fame was something he avoided. Yet still it tried to poke its nose into his life.

The clatter of dishes, running water and Cassie singing quietly to herself, drew his attention back to this more pleasant intrusion into his safe, boring existence. He didn't recognise the tune, probably his ignorance because of the age difference between them. She was young for sure—but despite that, they'd found so much common ground.

He settled back on the couch and recognised the warm symphony that gathered in his chest as something more than the effects of the whisky. The homeliness of the dimly lit room with its dark panelled wood and overstuffed furniture; the heat radiating out from the smoky crackle of the fire he'd built, chasing away the chill winter night; the sound of her moving around next door filling the formerly sad empty spaces both around him and inside him with her presence—all of these things came together in one precious and recently rare word: happiness.

When she arrived to sit next to him, that glowing ball expanded. She clinked her glass against his and they sipped companionably, her hand straying to rest on his thigh. The simple touch pulsed through him, igniting a strong attraction, although he tried to damp it down and remain casual, as if this happened every day.

"Simon," she said slowly, her voice low, with a hint of caution. "This is going to sound weird. Which is not good after a whole day of me trying to convince you I'm not some deranged weirdo."

She looked at him with those beautiful amber eyes, the burnished colour of the whisky in the tumbler. They were a cat's eyes. Not that the description should have felt like a compliment. He wasn't overly fond of cats. But Cassie's cat's eyes felt different. They didn't have that desperate, hungry look of a wildcat. Nor the haughty, judgmental stare of his aunt's pedigree Persian with its scrunched face. Not the calculating expression of Morag Campbell's cat that followed your every move around her kitchen, weighing the odds of food falling from the sky.

Cassie's eyes held the warmth of a friendly cat that you might invite into your lap, and take comfort in stroking. He stiffened again at the thought of inviting her into *his* lap.

What he'd give to let his hands glide over that swathe of dark hair, the firelight catching red bursts of colour in its depths. Thank god for the dim light, hiding both his prominent erection and the lust that had to be written plainly on his face.

"If I thought you were deranged, I wouldn't have brought you home, would I? It's not generally wise to reveal your address to crazy people, let alone drive them right to the doorstep. Or cook them dinner."

"OK, well…I have this feeling—like I know you. Like I've known you forever. Even though we know so little about each other. It's the oddest thing."

She reached for his hand. He stroked her palm, tracing soothing circles, attempting to ease the small knot of tension he felt there. Or was it to soothe his own? This conversation headed in unexpected directions. She broke his gaze. With chin low, her voice dropped further.

"It's as if I've fallen into one of my own books." She let out a tiny giggle, soft and hesitant. "Or one of the latest bookstagram trends: my life in romance tropes."

"Bookstagram?" She was speaking a foreign language. "Tropes?"

"OK," she said, seeing his blank look. "So." She took a small breath, speaking slowly, with the patience of someone explaining to a small child. "Bookstagram is just part of Instagram. People sharing about their love of books online."

"Ahh, I see," he said, even though he really didn't. Yes, he did Twitter. It was useful for his work. But the rest of social media was like an alien planet he had no desire to explore.

"And tropes. Well, they're a sort of plot device." She looked back up at him, her voice confident as she drew on obviously well-known facts, explaining her craft. "It's a situation people enjoy in a book. One they often love to see over and over in what they read. And some writers have favourite tropes they like to reuse, but in different settings. It's certainly big in romance, but you get it in other genres too."

"So what are your favourite tropes?" he asked. This whole romance author thing was surprisingly sexy. The thought that she wrote all this stuff down made him wonder what might be going on in that head of hers at any given moment. She'd said she wrote 'steamy'. That thought didn't do anything to tame his wild thoughts. He tried hard not to imagine what steamy might look should the pair of them become characters made real.

"My first book was an enemies to lovers—rivals to an ancient throne—he's a vampire, and she's a witch. After months of fighting for control of the kingdom, they end up falling for each other and ruling together."

"Somehow, I don't think that's what's going on here." He raised a brow, and another of those delicious giggles bubbled over.

"No," she said. "Although I do confess to thinking vampirish thoughts about you this morning."

His own laughter spilled out helplessly. "Me? With my aversion to blood? That's ridiculous."

"Yeah. It is now. But this morning, even though I was still feeling woozy, I was *very* relieved when you admitted that." Her broad grin softened, and her hand reached for him. "No, it was this," she said, sweeping her fingers through his hair, letting them linger a little, and he shivered as the neat tips of her nails brushed his scalp. She trailed them down his temple, along his jawline. "And this. Your skin. So pale. Flawless."

She wasn't the first girl to make playful vampire jokes. And the broody moods that gripped him more often than not probably helped the illusion. But with her, it was no joke, more like worship as her hands traced his features. And this woman—it was she who felt like some mythical being, some beguiling creature of legend, ensnaring him with her magic.

He leaned in, pressing his lips against hers. A small groan escaped as she responded, her mouth admitting him, her hand cupping his head to her, forcing him to deepen the kiss.

She tasted sweet and smoky, the whisky merging with the lingering chocolate. He wanted to taste more of her, all of her. Trailing kisses down her neck, he nuzzled at the base of her throat, inhaling the faint soapy smell of her skin.

"Bite me?" she said through a laugh. He responded with a small nip and then another as she shuddered in his arms.

"There's more of you I'd like to taste," he murmured, sliding her jumper down, his lips grazing the bare shoulder, its skin velvet smooth. "And touch."

"I'd like that too," she said, guiding his hand downward. He snaked one arm under the loose hem of her jumper as she leaned back, allowing him admission.

His hand found pert nipples that tightened into hard buds at his touch. She lay back with a moan and he pulled the clothing up, exposing a lacy bra. While his mouth sought out the peak of her beautiful round breast, so warm beneath its web of lace, he let his hands coast lightly across the bare stomach, tracing the slight curve, taking in the sight of the slight jut of her hips visible above the band of low cut jeans. The thought of removing those jeans took hold, and he reached for the zipper. She brushed his hand away.

"Tricky these," she said. "Vintage seventies. Buttons. Let me do it." With deft fingers she unbuttoned them, shimmying them down and tossing them onto the floor. "Sorry," she said. "You know I'm not tidy."

"You are welcome to throw clothes anywhere you like."

She stood, and unable to hide his admiration, his eyes swept across her half-naked form, silhouetted in the firelight. She laughingly stripped off her jumper, flinging it aside, standing there in the tiniest of lace panties, and the flimsy bra that left nothing to the imagination.

"Time to get messy?" she said, as she scrambled back onto the couch. He nodded, with a grin at her clothing littering the lounge floor. "In that case, these need to go too." She pounced on his zipper with determined hands, while his whole body thrummed in anticipation. Things were about to get very messy.

He knew before he fumbled in the drawer that he'd not find anything there. Yes, in his Edinburgh flat, there'd be condoms in the bedside table, and in the bathroom too. But here, somehow, the respect he'd shown his grandmother by not bringing home girls and shagging them in his bedroom—there'd always been other options—had meant he'd literally never had sex in this house. And so he wasn't the least bit prepared for it to happen now.

He sat massaging his forehead, wondering what to do while Cassie was in the bathroom. The flush of the loo told him he'd run out of time. He was hungry for more, for all of her and she for him. While his body still pulsed from the memory of what they'd done to each other with hands, and lips, and tongues, it wasn't enough.

She emerged totally naked, the sheen of sweat on that pale skin glistening in the dim light. He stiffened immediately and her sly grin at observing his very obvious erection only made him more despondent that he had no solution to the problem.

"Slight problem," he mumbled. "No, scrap that. Large problem."

"Large, but not a problem," she said, crawling across the bed and stroking him all the way from base to tip with a light, teasing brush of her thumb. He pushed back a moan, knowing he had to tell her now.

"Not that. The problem is no condoms."

"Oh," she said. "No worries. I absolutely have that covered. No pun intended." She flashed him a grin as she headed to the next-door bedroom he already thought of as hers. Not that she'd be using it tonight. Maybe never. Moments later, she returned, the silver strip glinting in her hand.

"Three enough?"

"You come well-prepared. Luckily."

"I learned young. To be very well-prepared." Her eyes briefly lost their playfulness, and she took a deep breath, audibly sucking in the air while he saw thoughts flash across her face. "I learned the hard way. I was pregnant at eighteen. An accident with my also eighteen-year-old boyfriend."

"Wow, that must have been tough."

"Yeah. We did all the right things. But like I said, it was an accident. They happen. So now, I make extra sure they can't. I get the injection, but

I always have condoms, just in case. And you know, in case people haven't been tested recently. I have, by the way."

"Good for you. I haven't. Hasn't been the need. No action to speak of. Not for some while." She nodded at him. He studied her face, moments ago, so alight with fun, now serious, eyes glistening with perhaps a hint of tears.

"I lost the baby. In case you were wondering. People usually do. And they're surprised to hear I was more sad than relieved. But anyway, I moved on. If I do have a child, I want it to be planned, not an accident."

He took her hand and drew him to her. "I'm sorry," he said. "That you had to go through that. We don't have to do this, you know."

"No, no. I want to." She sighed. "I'm sorry that I even brought it up. Bit of a passion killer, eh?"

"No," he said. "The fact you'd trust me with something so important makes me want you even more, in ways I can't even put into words."

The overwhelming tenderness he felt towards her swamped him, as his mouth met hers and she melted into him. His body coursed with need, not only physical, but a deep emotional desire to connect with her that sprang from a part of himself he didn't know he possessed. It was as if he by joining with her, with two of them against the world, neither need ever face their hurt alone again.

He relaxed back into the pillows as she skilfully unfurled the condom with deft hands, while her mouth never left his, hungrily drawing him to her. She pulled back a little, then eased herself over him, her hips moving with a powerful rise and fall that left him helpless under her touch. Within her, he found home.

CHAPTER 28

Instalove

Cassie

Blackness, Scotland - November 2017

THE OLD-FASHIONED CLOCK ON the bedside cabinet beat a steady rhythm as the hands inched towards midnight. This time last night, lying in the cosiness of Morag's cottage, Cassie had felt no premonition of the chance meeting that would upend her life. Even a few hours earlier, while she'd sensed something was brewing between them, in the end it had happened so quickly.

Without hesitation, she'd plunged into this with Simon Buchanan, and now she wondered whether that was wise. She hardly knew him, but there was that strange and undeniable feeling, like she'd known him forever, as if she'd slipped out of his life for a moment before falling back into the centre of it.

"So it seems like our story got a little steamy." She rolled over to drape herself across him, smiling into the warmth of his chest. His heart still thudded in a rapid staccato against her ear. "Not that I'm complaining."

"Does this mean I'm going to be material in your next book?"

"You specifically—no. But you certainly gave me plenty to draw on for love scenes." She giggled into the dark thatch of hair, and he cupped her bum, playfully pulling her in, as she wrapped one leg across his still sticky thigh.

"Good," he said. "I prefer not to feature. I've been in that situation before and it wasn't good. I don't want people who don't know me to read about me. Or the people who do, for that matter."

"In a book? Someone wrote about you in a book?"

"No, no, not a book. Fodder for the newspapers. What you hear about the tabloids in Britain—it's all true. And when you're in the middle of it—" His voice became thick and low. "It's more brutal than you could ever imagine."

"Simon, that's awful. What happened?" She regretted the question immediately. Who would want to relive something that had obviously been traumatic? "No, it's fine. You don't need to tell me."

"I think I want to. You trusted me with things that hurt you in the past. Now I offer the same trust to you."

"Only if you're sure."

He fixed his eyes on the ceiling, blinking furiously, his mouth set in a tense line. She propped herself on one elbow, her other hand stroking his chest while under her palm she felt his heart quicken, thumping wildly as he spoke.

"My name isn't actually Simon Buchanan. Buchanan was my mother's maiden name. I was born Simon Knight. My parents met at university—St Andrews. Both taking law. My mum, Pamela, was Scottish." She noted the past tense, and the hitch in his voice as he spoke her name. "A Buchanan. Grew up in this very house. A modest branch of the Buchanan family. Some of them have land, huge farms and vast manor houses that make this one look like a crofter's cottage." She blinked, thinking of this impressive house. Sure, Simon's renovation was obviously a work-in-progress, but to her it seemed a mansion. "One lot even have a castle of sorts. Not us. We're merely the poor relations."

"And your father?"

"He's English. From a 'good family'." The sarcasm dripped heavily. "Not nobility, but moved in the right circles, rubbed shoulders with all the right people, went to all the right schools. That's why he came up to St Andrews. Even before Prince William and Kate attended, because of its age and reputation alone—it's six-hundred years old, the third oldest university in the English-speaking world—it's always attracted students who want connection to the upper echelons of society."

"That's incredible. Six hundred years ago, my country was barely inhabited. But you didn't go there, right?"

"No, they offered everything I needed, but it's the one university I would never go to. No way I'd follow in my father's footsteps." He let out a bitter laugh. "I've taken some extreme measures to avoid being linked with him."

"Like changing your name."

"Yeah. For what it was worth. Not sure that will even protect me in the end." He took a deep breath. "My father was intelligent and charming. He and Mum both graduated with good degrees, secured jobs in notable law firms in London, and worked their way up quickly. Both real high flyers.

He specialised in commercial law. He made truckloads of money with rich clients. But that wasn't enough for him."

He paused, his hand tightening and loosening itself reflexively over hers. With each tight squeeze, she felt the tension pulsing through his body. She tried to allow it to flow into her. She could feel the huge burden of his past weighing heavily upon him. Desperate to let him know she would willingly share his load for a while if he'd let her, she offered her own reassuring squeeze. As if sensing her silent support, he took a deep breath and went on.

"Behind the scenes, he was making more. A lot more. He got involved with some powerful but dishonest people. And if he'd kept his head down, he might have gotten away with it. But when people started making noises that he should run for parliament—offered him a shot in a nice safe Tory seat—he took up the opportunity. Vanity, I suppose."

That low, bitter laugh ruffled her hair again. It was hard to believe modest Simon had been raised by a man like that. She waited as he took time to gather his thoughts.

"Or perhaps his puppet masters thought he'd be useful in the House. He got in, but within three months, a journalist who'd been tracking him for a couple of years finally found the last piece of the puzzle. His chanelling of dirty money laid out in the tabloids for everyone to see. The scandal was huge. He should have gone to jail. But those powerful people protected him. Spirited him out of the country before he could spill everything. I think he's somewhere in Spain."

"How old were you when this happened?"

"Fourteen. The news beat my mother to my posh boarding school in Kent. Everyone knew. She picked me up, and we made a run for it to Scotland. To this house, with my grandmother."

"She had to leave everything behind?"

"Yeah, they seized it all. Proceeds of crime. She didn't fight it. There were some that wanted to take her down too. Said she had to have known. She didn't. He was clever."

"So she lost her career too."

"Yeah, she lost everything. Husband, house, money, job, her reputation. But the thing that broke her was his betrayal. That he could do all of this stuff with no regard to how it might impact the people he said he loved. I don't think he loved us. If he had, he'd have stayed and faced it."

"That's simply awful, Simon. For you. And your mother. It's just awful." She had no experience that let her even begin to understand this man's actions. Her own father's adoration of her mother, and his dedication to her and Archie, were so far removed from Simon's story. But she didn't need to have experience to understand the damage he'd done. She could feel the hurt coursing through the man lying next to her.

"That was the beginning of the end for Mum. Physically and mentally, she retreated into this shadow of herself. I think it's what killed her." The painful crack in his voice stabbed at her. She couldn't imagine what it would be like to lose your mother young.

"I mean—although doctors might argue otherwise—it felt like that was the root cause. She was diagnosed with this rare immune disease. Two in a million people. Just her bad luck with those odds. Damaged her kidneys." His voice ebbed to a whisper. "She died on the waiting list for a transplant."

"Simon, I'm so sorry. I can't imagine how hard that was—that is. To lose your mum."

"Yeah, especially when he was responsible. Although the doctors say there's no identifiable cause for the condition, I blame him and what he did to her. I was twenty when she died; at the University of Glasgow, doing law. Following her—not him," he said with a vehement tilt of his chin.

"But you changed to history later?"

"Yeah, and that's a whole other part of the saga. We Brits can never leave well alone. Like to dredge up the dirty little secrets in everyone's past. First, they did it to Mum. Every so often, some journalist grasping for a story would write a nasty piece—you know the sort of thing, 'Does Pamela Knight know where her husband is?', or 'Secret messages between Pamela and Graham'. Then one day it happened to me: photographs of me going into work, my first job in a law firm in Glasgow, and the headline, 'Like father like son?'. I wasn't going to let them crucify me the way they did my mother. Quit my job, changed my name and disappeared back into the safety of a different university, and a part of history that doesn't include me or my family."

"That's huge Simon. And brave."

"You think so? I sometimes consider it rather cowardly. Maybe I should have held my head high and proved that I'm not my father. But it's worked for me. Mostly."

"Mostly?"

"Well, I still have—" He sighed. "I suppose you'd call it 'major trust issues'. I'm trying to overcome those, but it's a battle. Probably should see a therapist, but you know, must be my British half—stiff upper lip and all that." He rolled to face her, his muscular arms wrapping around her, drawing her close. He whispered the words against her ear, his breath warm. "And that's why I'm damned if I know why I trust you. But I do. You're different. I feel like the universe knew I needed you, and here you are."

"Maybe the universe knew I needed you too," she whispered back, twining her fingers in his hair, as they lay, heartbeat to heartbeat. "This, us, it is different—although it goes against everything I know. After only one day, I have to know where this story leads."

"Our story," he mused, pushing his troubled past out of the conversation. "What tropes do you think it will be?"

"Well, we've already got friends to lovers in there. We are friends, aren't we?"

He nodded up at her with a grin. "Very good friends," he said. "Friends with benefits," he added, nuzzling against her neck, offering small, playful nips that sent a charge of electricity all the way to her toes. "Any others?"

"Meant to be," she said. "I don't normally do this. Jump straight in. But from fairly early in the day, I had this sense of... inevitability. That everything was leading to this. And strangely, it didn't trouble me. Who'd have known this morning that I'd end the day in an instalove book?" A spontaneous giggle toppled out. She'd always looked askance at the concept.

He quirked one dark eyebrow. "Instalove? As in 'instant love'?"

Heat bloomed on her cheeks. She'd been comfortable with the first 'l' word—lover—because there was no doubt about the magnitude of what had physically happened between them. It came naturally to think of him in those terms: a new, and to her delight, very capable lover. But that other smaller 'l' word, that was in fact the big one. And now she'd gone and clumsily dropped it into the conversation between them.

"Yeah." She fumbled over the words. "An immediate overwhelming attraction."

"Instalove." It didn't seem to bother him. "Instalove," he said, trying out the word again. He pressed his mouth to hers, the kiss warm. "Sounds good to me," he smiled against her lips, and she breathed him in, a small inhale of relief that she may not have scared him after all.

CHAPTER 29

Night Writer

Blackness, Scotland - November 2017

HIS FINGERS SNAKED ACROSS the space beside him, seeking evidence of her existence. His mind demanded a sign this wasn't simply the lurid dream of some sex-starved, affection-deprived man. He found little in the rippled bedsheets, although perhaps he detected a small curved depression in the centre close to where he lay, right where a warm body may have tucked in to wrap itself around him in the chill autumn night. No trace of that warmth remained to confirm the possibility, although his body recalled the sensation of velvet-smooth skin radiating heat against his.

While darkness and the absence of tangible evidence might suggest she didn't exist, other senses argued otherwise. The smell of a soft perfume mingled with the distinctive aroma of a woman, and the earthy musk of sex hung in the air.

He lay his head against the pillow, inhaling deeply and a picture of her sprang to life as if projected on the back of his closed lids: a tumble of dark brown copper-infused hair, faint freckles dancing across the bridge of her nose; eyes dreamy with blissful arousal and a slurred smile of pleasure on her face as she leaned over him; her body rising and falling in a slow, insistent rhythm. His erection raged stronger than ever at the image.

Not only did the fragrance of her tantalise his nostrils, but as he swallowed down his rabid need to take hand to cock and deal with his hard-on, he could taste her. He licked his lips and the distinctive sweet saltiness conjured a sudden vivid recollection of his tongue seeking warm, wet places, while the echoes of her gasping for air in between stuttering yelps of delight bounced around his brain.

As if triggered by the memory of her vocalisations, his ears reached out into the inky blackness, searching for an audible trace of her in the usually silent space of his home. At first he detected nothing, beyond the slight shudder of the old refrigerator from downstairs and the one drip of the bathroom tap that he'd neglected to fix.

He really must deal with it before he left for the Edinburgh apartment on Sunday, otherwise on his next visit he might find a flood rivalling Morag's unfortunate episode. Stretching further beyond these regular household rhythms, he detected another. The faint tapping was less like the steady beat of a pop song, and more the slightly random pulse of improv jazz.

Opening his eyes, they adjusted in the darkness, allowing him to pick out the familiar shapes of the bedroom he'd known since childhood. He made out the gaping outline of the doorframe. He never slept with the door open, but here it was ajar; and beyond it, not the expected blackness, but a faint pale glow reflected from the room across the hallway.

Not pausing to throw on clothing—strewn around the floor, tangling at his feet—he struggled towards the door. Here was another sign of something amiss; the neat habits of his bedtime routine rarely deserted him. Even when pissed, he usually managed to wrangle his clothes into some semblance of order on the dresser.

In the adjoining bedroom, the rectangular light of a laptop reflected off her face, illuminating the serious focus of eyes on the screen, and dainty fingers flying across the keyboard. Dressed in his alumni sweatshirt—it dwarfed her—the hood gave her the appearance of a hunchback huddled at the computer. He stood at her shoulder a moment before she paused, acknowledging him, tilting her face upwards. He slipped one hand into the v of the hoodie, cradling the curve of her collarbone, brushing the smooth skin beneath his hand as if to confirm this wasn't a dream.

"You inspired me," she said, reaching one hand to stroke his fingers where they lay.

He tensed at her words. His self-protective brain lurched in an ugly direction. What the hell was he thinking? He'd brought a virtual stranger into his home and then into his bed. Lured by some uncanny and totally illogical feeling that he knew her better than people he'd known for a lifetime, he'd let her in close. She knew truths about him few other living human beings understood. And here she was, writing. Despite her assurances, his mind roared the accusation: *she's writing about you.* He swallowed hard, feigning nonchalance as the words struggled out.

"Can I read it?"

"Worried you'll Google Simon Buchanan and find you're a lusty knight in a romance book?" The light teasing words jarred against the fist of fear that twisted in his gut. He battled to find a calm response.

"Will I?" he croaked out.

"Simon?" She twisted towards him, a frown creasing her forehead. "Are you OK?"

"Yeah," he lied. "Going to head back to bed. Leave you to it." His voice came out flat, the speech of a robot-like automaton who, with measured steps, followed the same instinctive programming that had protected him before.

He fled. Like he'd done as an overwhelmed teenager, desperate to block out the sights and sounds of the one person he loved most in the world, grappling with physical and mental pain, he sought the safety of his bedroom. This had always been the place completely his own where he could shut the door and keep the world at bay.

But it wasn't his own anymore. He'd invited her in; and now she followed. The small footsteps padded after him, the wooden floorboards creaking slightly even under her slight weight.

"Simon, what's wrong?" She slipped into bed beside him, bracketing his body with her own. With a gentle hand, she tipped his head towards her, cradling it against her chest. Her small palm smoothed his hair, like a mother soothing a frightened child. His breathing stilled a little at the reassurance of her touch. "And don't say 'nothing'."

"Hard to explain," he said. Even in the darkness, he could sense the intensity of her gaze upon him.

"Try me. I'm a good listener. And I think I've done a pretty good job so far."

He swallowed. She knew the most potentially damaging stuff about him already. Why not tell her the rest?

"There are other reasons why I was wary this morning. Why every so often throughout the day you probably noticed me pull back. Trusting new people is hard for me, but especially women. One—Renee—" Even saying her name felt like someone had grabbed him by the throat. "—she really messed me up, and since then I'm constantly scanning for hidden motives."

"She was your wife? Girlfriend?"

"Girlfriend." He choked out a bitter laugh. "I thought she might be my wife someday. And so I trusted her with everything. We clicked from the very first. A bit like us." He couldn't help his mouth creasing upwards in a faint smile. "I met her about three years ago. She came and sat beside me in a booth in a coffee shop one morning. I had my laptop out, working. It was crowded, with no tables free, and she asked did I mind. Of course, when you're single, rather lonely, and an attractive woman approaches, you don't mind at all.

"Anyway, things progressed from there and before I knew it, she was living in my apartment. Stupid of me. I thought she worked in advertising. And she did. But I didn't know that she also freelanced as a journalist, working away on stories after hours, selling one now and then. She never told me and when I found out, saw an article with her name, I freaked out.

"Suddenly there's an investigative journalist who knows Simon Buchanan is really Simon Knight. It wouldn't make big news these days, but it would still sell. Sometimes I think I might have been too hasty, ending it. But the fact she didn't tell me upfront, when she knew the things I told you tonight—I had to assume she might use them against me. I dunno, I just had this feeling in my gut that one day, it would happen. I still do."

"I swear, Simon, I'd never tell anyone what you've told me. Or write it down. You can trust me on that." Still reeling that he'd revealed so much, her desperation to reassure him damped down the fear that swirled in his stomach.

"I know," he said, trying to shake off the last shreds of it. "You're different from her. And how I know that, I can't say."

"Simon, you are *not* in my story. Not by name and not in any recognisable way. I promise." She'd made the leap of understanding, working out the reason for his sudden flight.

"I know. I'm sorry." He was such an idiot. "I doubt either would transfer well to Ilveria, anyway," he joked, trying to lighten the moment.

She'd revealed the incredible fantasy world of her imagination yesterday and it was impressive; every minute detail carefully mapped out: a bold and brawny race of warriors, and a mystical order of freakishly tall knights. She'd gone so far as the creation of a language.

"Simon Buchanan sounds a little ordinary compared to what was it? Your morally grey hero—Cazimir?"

"Yes, Cazimir Lamordieu."

"Yeah, Simon just doesn't have quite the same ring about it."

"No Google there either," she said. "Medieval tech only."

That word again. He had to tell her. "That's a relief. To be honest, that's another thing that sent me spinning out."

"Google?"

"Yeah. Google. Have you ever Googled yourself?"

"Yeah, now and then. It's nice to see my books showing up. Reviews and stuff. Waiting for the day it tells me I've made Wikipedia." Her chest vibrated with a light giggle that ruffled the hairs on his head. "And you?"

"Every day."

She shuffled up on an elbow and he could feel her questioning eyes on him through the darkness. "Every day? But why, Simon?"

Would she think it vanity? A desire to see that he rated? That he was 'someone'? Proof that the world noted his existence? In reality, it was the opposite.

"Longest 0.6 seconds of my morning." How did he explain the dread that loomed over him while he waited out that minute snippet of time? He couldn't. But he could explain the reason. "Followed by the happiest moment of my day, when I see the usual results: Simon Buchanan, History Department University of Edinburgh; Simon Buchanan, 'The Castle Hunter'; 'The castle as a social construct in late seventeenth century Scotland' by Simon Buchanan PhD—my doctoral thesis. Me, interspersed with all the other Simon Buchanans—and there are hundreds of them, some much more notable—but all of us with a name common as muck. I get to hide in their midst."

"Impressive. To have such a popular name."

"Predictable. Safe. You see, Simon Buchanan *is* safe. But if I put in Simon Knight." He swallowed down the name, burying it deep in the pit of his stomach. "It's all there. Each sordid article about my father, my mother, the ones about me. And, if anyone should put two and two together..."

"This life you've built is over."

"Pretty much. So each day I go to Google and get the same repetitive list of Simons. And heave a sigh of relief that for another day no one has stood the two of us side by side and recognised we're the same person."

Without words, she shuffled in until no space existed between them, her breathing in sync with his own, her hand stroking his arm.

"So, I have to warn you, Simon Buchanan is complicated, I'm afraid." She needed to know what she was getting herself into. It was the only way this could be anything more than a one-night stand.

"Complicated is interesting," she whispered against his chest. "Complicated is fine with me."

CHAPTER 30

Game Over

Blackness, Scotland - November 2017

SHE REACHED A HAND across the bed beside her. Cool. Empty. This was a novel experience. Waking up to find the guy you'd just spent the night having great sex with had slunk off come morning was something she'd heard about, even written about, but never faced.

Unlike some of her friends, she chose carefully who she invited into her space. She made sure it was someone she'd be comfortable waking up next to in the morning, and someone she felt confident wouldn't run at the thought of her face meeting theirs across her bed by the light of day.

Except this wasn't her bed. And Simon had nowhere to run. Besides, he seemed more the sort of man who might be downstairs this moment, preparing to surprise her with breakfast. She strained her ears for evidence of him in the house. And there it was. Not the rattle of pans or the hiss of a kettle. Not the banging of plates on the countertop or the faint rustle of butter searing in a pan. A solid sound, but unfamiliar.

Focusing her attention on the faint thwack brought frustration. Sometimes it found a rhythm—one, two; one, two, three; one two—like the first steps of some old-fashioned dance. Even now she cringed at the memory of clammy-handed boys clumsily steering her around the gym in compulsory dance lessons before her Year 6 school social, their steps tentative. But this sound had a confident, purposeful tone. Even when the rhythm faltered, the pauses and unpredictable beats resembled the muffled words of some free form poetry.

Drawn to investigate, she reached for clothes. The sun hadn't yet emerged to push back the chill of the autumn morning. But when she nudged aside a heavy curtain, the full moon remained low in the sky. It lit up the garden below, gilded every leaf, uncovering every shadow.

On the bedroom floor, the silvery beams picked out Simon's shirt. She reached for it as the easiest solution to her nakedness. She held it to her nose, inhaling the smell of him, a smell that already provoked a comfortable lurch of familiarity. Finding it still buttoned up, she pulled it on over her head; obvious evidence of their frenzy last night. He was definitely of the 'remove clothes carefully' sort. Perhaps even 'fold neatly' or at least 'stash in the laundry hamper'. Not lying discarded on the floor in a crumpled heap, arms and legs twisted, unbuttoning abandoned.

But only speed had mattered, with that first kiss on the sofa like a starting gun, triggering a sprint to the inevitable finish. They'd followed it up with a more leisurely exploration of each other's bodies. And each other's minds. Maybe today they'd relax into that slower pace. The thought of enticing Simon back to bed for some languid early morning lovemaking had a definite appeal. For that, she'd need to find him first.

Downstairs, she followed the sound to a door off the entry hall. She turned the large brass knob slowly; and it rewarded her care with only the slightest click of the latch. She nudged the door open, hoping not to disturb him.

The dim glow of a bare bulb bathed the windowless room in a soft light. It lit up pieces of gym equipment—a set of weights stacked in neat rows, a bench, a spin bike—all the answers to the question of those muscles she'd traced, that lay hard beneath the leanness of Simon's lithe body. And the answer to his shapely arms—more substantial than she'd expected when she'd run her hands across them, memorising their contours, stronger than she'd anticipated when he'd caged her against the wall of his bedroom, insistent that she needn't bother to resist—lay in the object of Simon's intense focus for his fists. The red punching bag glowed beacon-like in the corner.

Simon faced it, bare to the waist. He wore only a pair of sweatpants. They hung low on his slender hips, barely covering that neat butt. The black-gloved hands pummelled his sturdy opponent, with one slight hesitation in a flurry of punches the only hint he sensed her intrusion.

Standing in silence, she respected that she'd invaded his space without invitation. She suppressed the impulse to greet him. She pushed back the questions that sprang to mind. The sight of this gentle man attacking the bag with such aggression only emphasised how little she really knew about him. She sensed there were shades and depths to Simon that might take a lifetime to uncover. He harboured secrets, only to be revealed in snippets as he built trust.

And yet in the dark hours between making love and giving over to sleep, he'd trusted her with some heavy stuff. Perhaps the decision to do so was why he now couldn't sleep, battling this tangible opponent rather than his thoughts.

The dull light also revealed another of Simon's secrets. A tattooed lattice of lines criss-crossed his shoulder blades, a chessboard. The regular squares picked out in black ink, already distorted by the contours of his back, rippled as he continued to rain blows on the punching bag.

The three-dimensional image was at once both fantastical and realistic, defined so vividly that she wondered how her fingers hadn't detected its lines as she'd frantically grasped him to her, urging him deeper inside. How had her hands not felt the curves of the chess pieces, the black and the white, paused forever, game over?

Flowing below the board, she could make out tiny words in neat capitals. She peered at them, trying to make sense. Although obviously French, they meant nothing to her: EN PASSANT. And next to the words, the oddest thing, some sort of strange code: 'hxg6#'.

Somewhere beyond the rhythm, he shifted his attention to her presence. With one last definitive smack at the punching bag, he turned. He blinked, his dark eyes shifting focus from the task to her face. "Sorry, did I wake you?"

"No. Yes. Maybe. But it's OK."

He moved to close the space between them, pressing his body against her, muscles still taut with effort. He crossed his gloved hands behind her neck. Even through the fabric of his shirt, the leather warmed her skin. He dusted a kiss over her lips, and rested his forehead on hers, eyes closed. Peace dwelt in that stillness, such a marked contrast to the violence of his thrusting fists.

"Good," he mumbled. "I needed this."

"This?" What was this? A daily routine? An escape?

"This is my therapy." It made sense. Sometimes she'd found calm in walking, the drumbeats of feet on the pavement a soothing backdrop. Solace could be found in handing your body over to the physical. It stilled a busy mind.

"Hmmm," she hummed against his cheek. "And you need it because of me?"

"Yes," he whispered. "And no. Maybe."

"It's OK," she said. "A lot has happened these past twenty-four hours. I'm struggling a little myself."

"It's OK," he echoed. "Well, it will be."

"And what's this?" She ran her hand across his shoulder blade, fingertips seeking the lines and finding perhaps the slightest hint of the artist's work beneath them.

"A reminder. That the small can overcome. That the least powerful can outmanoeuvre the mighty."

"In chess."

"In everything."

"Show me."

He turned to let her see. She traced the lines of the tattooed board. Her fingers drifted across the elegant curves of the pieces, painted in black and white, across his pale skin. He shivered a little under her touch.

"The pieces on the board represent the end point of a famous chess game. Back in 1928, in Australia."

"And the words?"

"The winner used a move called 'en passant'. It's when a passing pawn captures another. In this particular game, the move allowed a white pawn to check the black king. "

"I see it," she said, tracing the outline of the brave pawn, standing in the path of the sinister black king, preventing its advance.

"That's me," he said. "I might have been only a pawn in the game. But in the end, I outplayed the people who would hurt me. By making myself small so they'd not even notice me."

"And these other letters?"

"I can tell you're no chess player."

"No. My dad tried to teach me once. He gave up in frustration." She didn't possess the logical thinking required. Despite her father's patience, she couldn't see the patterns or predict the path she should take. "My mind doesn't work that way. So is this chess language?"

"Exactly. It's a code that represents the last move in that game; the checkmate."

She clasped her arms around him, folding into his sweat-laced body, and placed a kiss at the nape of his neck. The sharp saltiness reminded her of other kisses in the dark, and she smiled against the warm skin.

"It's beautiful Simon."

He stood for a moment, still and silent. She let him take her weight a little, enjoying the reassuring support of his body. He felt so solid, so dependable, so right. She hoped he felt it, too. That she was right for him. That he'd not take fright and end this.

He dropped his head, dotting delicate kisses along her forearm, before twisting inside her embrace so they once more stood face to face.

"I'm hot and sticky," he said, pressing another kiss on her forehead. "I'm going to jump in the shower. You want to make us coffee? You can handle that little stove top coffee machine?"

"My cooking skills might be almost non-existent, Simon, but I *can* make a passable coffee. In my house, Dad expected us to wrangle one of those from an early age. But no, I don't want to make us coffee. Not yet. I think I might need a shower first myself." She raised an expectant brow at him. He took her by the hand and led her back upstairs with a knowing smile.

Chapter 31

Creature

Cassie

Blackness, Scotland - November 2017

She hated being less than truthful with him. He'd been let down so badly by another woman's sin of omission that she struggled with her own. But her little white lie bore no resemblance to that other larger lie, in that it had nothing to do with him.

It was silly, really. How could it hurt to admit that she didn't actually have a diagnosis of agoraphobia? To tell him it was a label she'd pulled out of the air in a desperate need to make sense of the incomprehensible wasn't a big deal, was it?

But somehow it felt worse to do so now, after three days. And especially after seeing his vulnerability to anything less than complete honesty. Best to just play along, swallow a squirt of good old rescue remedy and plant a plucky smile on her face.

It wasn't totally an act. Thoughts of events at the castle still disturbed her and revisiting the place triggered an unsettling nausea in the pit of her stomach. She'd felt brave strolling along the road from Simon's house towards it, the faint warmth of a winter sun overhead, buoyed by his presence at her side. But now, as they entered the castle grounds, unease came back to plague her. She placed her hand in the safety of his as they walked to the gaping mouth of the six-hundred-year-old entrance tunnel.

"Face the fear? My friend Trina, over in the psychology department, would say that's a good move."

She nodded at him. "I think Trina might be right."

They halted at the entrance, where today the iron grilled gate—no, the yett, as he'd corrected her—lay open, allowing them inside. Despite its age, it had a dull, rust-free shine.

"So, this," he said, launching into one of his adorable nerdy professor spiels, "is called a caponier. Only one of three surviving in Scotland." He pointed at the tunnel curving away from them into the gloom.

"No grand entrance? I feel like I've arrived at the side door set aside for tradesmen."

"Function trumps form," he said. "Everything about this castle is designed for defence." She followed him inside, swallowed up by musty black air. As her eyes adjusted, she found herself in a small cavernous space that swung to the left.

"Difficult for an attacker to charge through." He made his way towards the light, stopping a little beyond where the tunnel exited into a rough-floored courtyard. "And if they did—well, look up."

She did as he asked, scanning the soaring walls, feeling the vulnerability of being down here. Above, castle defenders would be in the perfect position to rain down arrows or gun fire.

"Wow, impressive," she said, swaying a little as she took it all in. His hand shot out to grasp an elbow, while he placed himself close behind.

"Sorry," he said. "Shouldn't have said that. Don't want you having an attack."

"No, Simon," she smiled. "I'm fine. Who would have known you are the perfect cure for agoraphobia?"

"Are you sure? We don't have to do this."

"I'm absolutely sure. And we do have to do this. I'm not missing a tour of Blackness on the arm of none other than its biggest fan, the legendary Castle Hunter."

He broke into a boyish grin, the joy of his passion spread wide on his face, and relief in those blue eyes, the dark depths a mirror of the lapping sea beyond.

"Come on, then." Leading her into the centre of the courtyard, he took her on a journey back in time. Spending time with Simon consumed her life right now; listening to him also fed her other passion. Her days of researching background details for her books might be over, with her very own, extremely willing history expert at her beck and call. What detailed fantasy worlds might spin from hearing his real world knowledge?

And observing that fire inside of him ignited a blast of attraction. She couldn't help the sweep of her eyes from head to toe, taking in this perfectly packaged, beautiful, intelligent man and thanking the universe for dropping her in front of him. Her gaze came to rest on his mouth, soaking up the velvety tone of his voice, while appreciating the curve of his lips that had tasted her all over.

"What?" he said. A small smile played around his mouth as he stopped mid-flight. "You look like you want to eat me."

"Oh I do," she smirked. "Has anyone ever told you how sexy smart is?"

"They don't need to. All I need to understand that, is to look at you."

A flush crept up her neck. "Oh no, Dr Buchanan. The little bit of success I've had with my books is nothing compared to holding your own in the academic world."

"Don't put yourself down, Cassie. What's so different about what you and I do? We both take in facts and ideas, turn them around in our minds and send them back into the world with our own spin on them. We're the same, you and I. I've worked with some amazingly intelligent and talented women over the years. You'd hold *your* own with any of them. And crush most of the men."

His laughter echoed off the courtyard walls, a deep, warm sound that filled her with a burst of joy. He grabbed at her hand and led her towards a narrow staircase that twisted upwards into darkness. They emerged on the wall walk, where a brisk wind off the sea lashed her hair. Standing out at this furthest point of the North tower, it was easy to imagine standing on the bow of a ship. From a flagpole, the Saltire slapped in the wind, the white diagonal cross and deep blue of the flag crackling in broad ripples against the sky.

In a flash of spontaneity, she leaned forward between the twin pillars of stone, right at the 'ship's' prow, where only a metal railing prevented her from toppling onto the rocky shore below. She spread her arms wide, the wind carrying her laughter out across the waves.

How many others had stood here and done this same thing? The navy waters of the Firth of Forth, although a little choppy today, weren't quite the Atlantic Ocean. And unlike *Titanic*, this 'ship' had endured, standing strong against the onslaught of the elements.

"Come on Simon. Play the game." He stood with a puzzled expression. Really? How could he not know this scene? "Simon, please tell me this is simply a lapse of memory. Surely even you have some knowledge of popular culture beyond the seventeenth century?" Still a blank look. "Oh my god, do you honestly not know? *Titanic*? Jack and Rose? It's only the most iconic scene from the second biggest movie of all time."

Dawning recognition rippled across his face, and he stepped in close behind her, placing his hands at her waist. "Is this what you mean?" He nuzzled at her ear, conjuring up memories of the last time he'd done that. Heat bloomed between her legs at the thought of where that had led, waking up this morning to the sheets of his bed drenched with the scent of their lovemaking.

Somewhere out in the haze, Edinburgh, and his apartment, awaited them. Thoughts of sailing towards a life there with Simon, although equally vague in its details, caused her skin to tingle in anticipation of the future.

It wasn't that she hadn't achieved anything in these past few years since finishing her degree. With her parents' encouragement, she'd travelled; lived and worked, and learned about the world outside her tiny home country. And she'd stuck with her decision to be a writer, even though almost everyone else she knew had opted for more traditional paths. She'd seen the amusement in their eyes, humouring her ambition as if it was a naïve dream she'd grow out of. She was proud that she hadn't settled for less, and proud of those five brave indie-published books.

But in some ways she'd drifted rudderless, never spending long in any one place; making friends, sometimes finding lovers, but always moving on. She had a sense that, if she was to really reach for her dreams, it was time to anchor herself to something more safe and solid, to find somewhere she could call home, and to know there was someone else who would support her. Out beyond the dancing waves, Edinburgh beckoned her forward into a life with a man she'd only known for three days.

"Can you ever see the city from here?" she asked, peering into the distance.

"No, it's tucked around to the right. It's such a great wee city. I so want to show it to you—seeing it through someone else's eyes for the first time." He paused, then whispered into her hair. "How long do you think you'll need to go back to London for? I don't know how long I can wait."

"Not long if I can help it. Maybe a week." She had the problem of sorting the flat, but it wasn't a big one. The others should fill her room quickly enough. And she had few possessions of note. "I've been living fairly simply. The most important things are already here. My laptop for a start."

"I'd like to think I'm on that list?" He grinned down at her, but she could see the faint question in his eyes.

"Yes, of course you are." She poked a finger at his chest. "Number one." She could understand his need for reassurance that this wasn't simply a whim, given the sudden decision they'd made to throw their lives together and see what happened. "Crazy to think that three days ago, I never even knew you existed. How is it already my life before seems vague by comparison?"

"It's the one time I'm glad someone discovered me."

"I think it was you who discovered me. In a heap on the ground."

"Best discovery of my life—my favourite person in the world at my favourite place in the world."

His lips met hers, warm despite the cool air, and she gave over to them, drowning in this overwhelming connection. She couldn't help but think it seemed a lot like love.

It was essential they stop at Morag's on the way back to Edinburgh, even though Simon was keen to get away early and be in his city apartment before dark.

First, the old lady, determined to mother them, had insisted they should leave with that night's dinner pre-prepared. It would appear churlish to refuse the gift of the cottage pie she'd baked. And given the contrast between Morag's sumptuous cooking and Cassie's own lack of skill, it solved one problem when they arrived at Simon's apartment.

The second reason was, however, more important: somehow she'd left behind a precious tartan scarf, still wrapped in its brown paper gift shop bag, in her room. Her mother had asked one thing of her on this trip to Scotland: an *Outlander* souvenir. When she'd seen the scarf in the Doune Castle gift shop, she'd known it was perfect.

Their shared love of books was one place where she and her sometimes distant mother connected. The first *Outlander* book had been Blair's escape from the stress of being a new young mother, battling with the demands of a fractious baby Cassie on her own while her astronomer husband remained in South America on a scientific assignment, having missed the birth of his child. The following seven books had accompanied Cassie's mother through a tumultuous thirty years: a second baby, raising two children virtually single-handed, the loneliness of life trapped in a tiny town far from the art scene she loved, a tense year of separation when she'd on a whim moved them to Auckland, followed by the intense rekindling of her parents' relationship.

Blair had urged Cassie to read every book and watch the more recent television series. She'd enjoyed them, but even more so the opportunity they'd provided for some common ground between the two of them. Receiving one *Outlander* patterned tartan scarf in the post would mean far more to Blair than its monetary value.

"I'll wait here," he said. "Morag can talk the leg off a chair. You've got a better chance of escape if she knows the car's still running."

"Don't I know it," she groaned. "OK, I'll do my best to be quick."

Already, at just on three o'clock, lengthening shadows of trees criss-crossed the pathway leading to the rear of Morag's cottage. She shivered a little as the tendrils of cold penetrated her jacket. She'd most likely find the old lady in this part of the property, either in the garden or the kitchen, her favourite spots.

The tabby cat appeared, sliding out from between two leafy bushes, twisting a sinuous body around her legs, while fixing her with a hopeful stare. She bent down to pat the sleek-coated moggy, and it let out a satisfied meow, before adding in a rumbling baritone purr. She liked cats. Growing up, she had always befriended the neighbour's farm cats. In the country, they proved useful for dealing with the hordes of mice that ebbed and flowed in number according to the seasons.

But now, over the top of the cat's amiable purring, another sound caught her attention. It too, had an animal-like quality. She froze in recognition, bile rising in her throat. It was back. The castle wasn't the only place inhabited by this invisible creature with painful claws of sound.

She paused, torn. Which direction provided escape? Morag's kitchen was closer, but Simon had been her saviour last time. She struck out toward the car, but it was as if the thing smelled the fear rolling off her, and became emboldened. Its voice rose in power as it grabbed at her ankles, preventing forward momentum. She struggled towards the corner of the house, hands now plastered over her ears. If she could diminish that noise, even just a little, she might make it to where Simon could see her.

The cat, startled by her sudden flight, streaked across the path in front of her. She swerved to avoid it, overbalanced and tumbled to the ground. The sound swept across her as if taking delight in this fortunate accident. She clasped her hands across her head, seeking protection from the onslaught.

PART THREE: HERE

CHAPTER 32

Restart

Blackness, Scotland - November 2017

Two faces stared down at her. Apart from the identical frowns of concern, they were as different as two people could be.

The elderly woman, with lips stretched tight across prominent teeth, looked vaguely familiar; even down to the legs gnarled with varicose veins pressed into a pair of fluffy slippers that tickled Cassie's ear.

Nik, long-lashed eyes wide, mouth aghast, dropped to the ground beside her. "Cassie? Are you OK?" A curious cat swirled around from behind him. It sniffed at her hand as if asking the same question.

"Ah…," she huffed out a breath. It struggled past her dry throat, tight from the effort of sucking air in panic. Tiny threads of that panic still pulsed through her body. Her heart thumped as if she'd been running. But there seemed no trace of anything that might have triggered her flight. She sensed no hint of injury. No pain. Only a dullness, like she had used every ounce of energy and had nothing left to give.

"Let's get her inside," the woman suggested. The voice triggered a memory. Morag. This was Morag's house.

"Yeah, come on, let's get you up." Nik's strong arms tucked beneath her, and he levered her onto still shaky feet. "Can you walk? Or shall I sling you over my shoulder and carry you?"

Underneath the teasing tone, she still read worry in his eyes. It stayed as he supported her into the house. She saw it as he helped her out of her clothes. And it even lingered as he tucked her into the big antique bed.

"You've been doing too much," he said. "Get some sleep."

He slipped out of the room. She had no problem doing as he'd asked. Sleep found her quickly, but it didn't last. When she awoke in the dark room, the clock showed six p.m. She groped in the dark, finding her robe slung over a chair.

The small apple-shaped logo cast a pale glow from where her laptop sat half-open on the corner of a desk. It beckoned to her and, unable to resist, she complied. She sat down moodily, swivelling the screen towards her with a sigh. No doubt there'd be emails from Paula to deal with. Back to Edinburgh tomorrow, so she couldn't avoid them any longer.

She jiggled the mouse and the screen burst into life. But it was the bright white surface of a document that dominated the screen, not the demanding subject lines of her email browser. From the formatting—Times New

Roman font and double spacing—it appeared to be part of her unfinished first book. Long-neglected lines of text stared back at her, while the cursor blinked accusingly in the centre. She frowned at it. Another thing she had no recollection of. She couldn't remember touching this document for months; no, years. It sat in an old folder of work, not the one where she'd saved the playful exploration of recent months.

She started to read. The words drew her in. Images both strange but also possessing an eerie familiarity swamped her. The male main character appeared to have taken on a life of his own. This wasn't the man she remembered. This dark-haired stranger, poised on a castle wall, offered a declaration of love. The woman in the story rushed to him, finding refuge in his arms. The description of their desire triggered an echo in her own body, the heat flowing through her as if her own passion ignited on the page.

She startled as Nik's hand pressed down on her shoulder, squeezing tenderly, massaging the tense muscles there. "It's so good to see you writing again," he said. He leaned in, peering at the screen.

She'd long ago become comfortable with him reading her words. Not since they'd been simply new friends had she flinched at him stepping into the intimacy of her creativity. She'd allowed him into the very centre of it, just as he'd welcomed her into his, watching him draw and create. There was no one else in the world she'd let see her newly written words. But tonight, an unexpected prickle of discomfort rippled through her as his eyes roved down the screen.

"It's good," he said. "Really good."

"Thanks," she said, accepting the praise, yet feeling she hadn't earned it. Not for words she couldn't recall crafting.

"And it's exciting to see you back in Ilveria. I love that world. God, to think you created it when you were only eighteen." He went back to rubbing her shoulder. "Maybe it's a sign?" She could hear the hope in his voice.

"What? That I should get back into this book?"

"Yes," he said, pausing. "And maybe it's a sign that we should both get back to where we started—before..." His voice caught a little. He still avoided saying her name. Brontë. They both did. "Cassie, this time eight years ago, we had plans. Big plans. Beautiful plans. You were going to be a mum. You were going to write. We had that ripped away from us. And since then, bit by bit, every year we stray further away from those plans. It's like we've lost our way."

He drew her against his warm bulk. His large arm wrapped across her chest, and she relaxed into its safety. "Let's do it all again. Start over. Try for a baby. And you don't go back to school at all. Not even part time. Quit teaching. Stay home and be a mum and a writer."

She felt herself wince, the memory of their most recent conversation on the subject of her future still raw even though months had passed. That night, Nik had seemed angry, frustrated. This time, the words seemed to come from a gentler place. And maybe this time, far away from home, and their problems, distance gave a different perspective that made it easier for her to hear them.

"Are you sure all those plans weren't simply the way two naïve kids coped with a tricky situation?" The practical side of her that had ruled her life ever since still demanded to be heard.

"No." He shook his head. "We were idealistic, I suppose. But in some ways, when you're young, you see more clearly. Before the world comes in to cloud your vision with everyone else's opinions."

"Yeah, it seems like everyone has an opinion. Funny thing is, Mum and Dad would agree with you. They suggested much the same when I was down home. I kind of wrote it off at the time."

"I think they're right." A slight note of excitement crept into his voice. "We can do it."

"I don't know…"

He fell silent again, staring hard at the screen, while images of books and babies swirled in her head alongside the nagging voice of doubt.

"Cassie, I've been doing a lot of thinking." He swallowed hard, his voice coming low against her ear. "Since that fight back in July, it's been bothering me. And then, after this afternoon." He planted a light kiss on her hair. "I've been unfair. You carry all the weight of your own problems, and then you have to carry me as well. No wonder you get to where it's overwhelming."

She said nothing. It was true.

"I know I go on about the business. And god knows I've been trying harder not too. But I feel myself always on edge, as if it's struggling, and really—it's not. I think my expectations have been so high. When I stand back and look at what I've achieved, it's going better than I could have hoped for.

"I'm nervous about the money side because I hate that part of it. Because I'm not good at it, I worry. I keep thinking if I take my eye off it, one day I'll turn around to find I've made some massive miscalculation and the whole thing will go down. What I'd give to hand it all off to someone else. But for now I have to be too hands on with all that shit. And I offload all my fears and frustration about it onto you."

"Isn't that what a wife should do? Share the load?" She turned her face to him, wanting him to see that, despite its truth, she forgave him for it. She reached one hand to trail the stubble, feeling the tension as he spoke.

"Yeah, but not to the point she puts everything of her own aside for it. Cassie, we can get by. We don't need much. I just need you. I want my old Cassie back."

She closed the laptop and stood, wrapping her arms around him. "You've got her."

Paula's emails could wait. Her book could wait. If this strange, unremembered blast of creativity had produced words on the page once, then it would happen again. In this moment, nothing was more important than him; than them.

He was strangely quiet as they left their refuge the next morning, heading towards Edinburgh. While Morag's cottage was humble in contrast to the city apartment, it had offered blissful days of peace and comfort. Except for her brief odd episode of yesterday.

"I've got some news," he said as he swung the car onto the main highway.

His quiet voice caused her to stiffen. She tensed at the hesitancy. "Not good news, I take it?"

"No," he said, through tight lips, eyes fixed on the road ahead without a glance her way. "Mum rang this morning while you were in the shower."

Well, that said everything. Nothing good ever came out of calls from Toni Francovic. Trust the woman to pick the exact moment she was elsewhere to phone. It made her feel shrewish, but usually she made Nik put his mother on speaker when she rang. It served two purposes: one; she knew Toni hated it, and that gave her a perverse pleasure; but two, and more importantly, she also knew Toni reined in her acerbic comments a little in the hearing of others. She was still a bitch to Nik, but she wouldn't do her worst with someone listening in, even if it was only Cassie.

"And? What did she want?" Toni never phoned unless it was to complain or to ask for something.

His hands tensed on the wheel, his knuckles white. He took a sharp intake of breath. This was not good.

"She wants me to leave Scotland earlier."

"Nik!" she sputtered. "Please tell me you're not about to race back to New Zealand on the whim of your mother. God, you can't expect me to believe she's missing you so much that she needs you back. Fuck Nik, tell me you said no."

Body upright and rigid, he stared straight ahead, eyes fixed on the road, unresponsive.

"You said yes?" Heat flared in her cheeks. A sharp, angry tear prickled at the corner of an eye, then escaped. "Why Nik? Why? I need you here. It's bad enough you're leaving me here for half of December."

She immediately regretted the sulky words. That was the deal, and she knew it. He had left his business at the most important time of the year, for her and for her mother. They'd agreed he would help her through this first bit, all the daunting publicity, the opening, the first few weeks of exhibition events. Then he'd fly back to his team to make sure all was in place for one of their busiest months of the year. They must capitalise on the Christmas rush. But the bitter twist of anger still roiled in her stomach. The manipulative bitch had reached out her claws across the miles to rip him away even sooner.

He looked across at her now, his face sad and apologetic. "I know. I'm sorry. But it's not that she wants me to go home early. She's asked me to go see her parents in Croatia. I'll need to leave on the twenty-third."

"Why doesn't she just get on a plane and come see them herself? It's not like she can't afford it. There's nothing stopping her from jumping on a plane." Her voice came out tight and shrill, painful even to her own ears.

"She's too stubborn. She has never forgiven them for leaving her and Svjetlana in New Zealand and going back to Croatia. I mean, the girls were in their twenties, but neither of them ever properly got over it. They were both married, tied to New Zealand. Family is everything to Croatians. They could never understand why their parents would abandon them." Never mind that Nik was now going to abandon *her* five whole days earlier than they'd agreed. She fumed at the thought. "Svjetlana has been over to visit a few times, but Mum never."

"So, to fix her guilt at not doing something *she* should have done, something she could still easily do, she sends you."

"I'm not doing it for her," he mumbled. "I'm doing it for them. They're in their nineties. It must hurt that they'll never see their child again, that she won't make the effort. Perhaps seeing me will help a little."

She said nothing, not wanting to state the obvious, but he did it for her.

"Yeah, I know. There's no blood connection between me and those two old people. But they don't know that."

She looked at him, stunned. "Your mother never told them she adopted a child?"

"No. Never. And I'm sure she threatened Svjetlana with her life if she ever told them. Mum saw being unable to have a baby as a flaw. Fortunately, one she eventually overcame. Anyway, I'm not going to Dubrovnik for her. I'm going for them."

She flipped the visor down. A tear-stained face stared back at her from the mirror.

"Just as well, this is a radio interview," she said, tracing a finger along the hollows under her eyes. Etched there in purple shadows were a lack of sleep and the trauma of these last twenty-four hours.

"That's the other bad news," he said.

"Oh, what now?"

"Paula sent me a text. Said you've been ignoring her emails." She had. "Late this afternoon, they've got you a slot on an arts show. Nothing big. Pretty much the same ground you'll cover this morning, but on TV."

She couldn't believe she was hearing this.

"TV? Please tell me you're joking?"

"Sorry. I wish I was. Don't worry. I'm sure they'll have a hair and make-up person to sort you out."

She looked down at the faded jeans and tired sweatshirt she'd thrown on this morning and desperately went through a mental checklist of her suitcase contents. Nope, more of the same. Just when she thought the day couldn't get any worse.

Chapter 33

Wayfarer

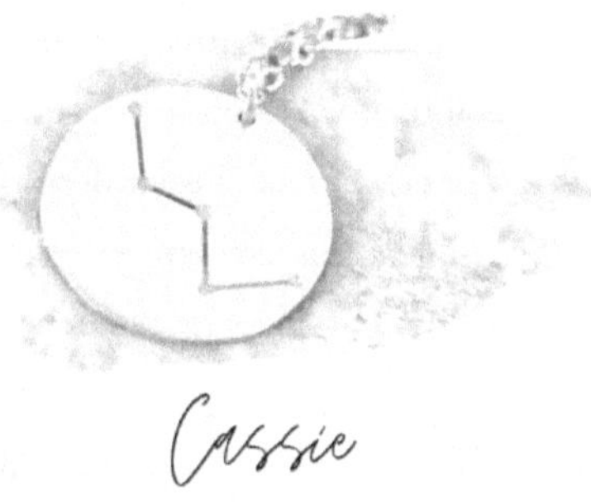

Two years later, Edinburgh, Scotland - September 2019

CASSIE STOOD AT HER husband's back, the two of them a small blot of grey misery amid a rainbow of happiness. The cramped cafe overflowed with chatter and the smell of coffee. The air felt thick with excitement, the anticipation almost palpable, as eager tourists fuelled themselves. Parked in neat rows outside, a multitude of tour buses, with signs showing destinations all over Scotland, patiently awaited their passengers.

The queue snaked between the maze of tables and around past cabinets of tempting food, moving towards the till at glacial speed. She saw the reason ahead of her: the horde of foreign visitors first struggling to read the blackboard menu, then straining to interpret the heavily accented woman taking their orders. Her Scots brogue baffled even those for whom English was their first language.

Cassie smiled to herself, finding it rather charming. Along with the tasteful splashes of tartan, it gave the cafe an authentic feel. It was a welcome contrast to many places they'd been in the past few weeks, where they were as likely to meet a fellow New Zealander behind the bar, or an Australian waiting tables; or young people from practically every country in Europe, all funding their overseas adventures with casual hospitality jobs.

With a cheery expression and incredible tolerance, often repeating herself several times, the woman extracted each person's request and passed it to the kitchen team. She glimpsed them scurrying in the background, laden with steaming bowls of porridge and plates heaped with a traditional Scottish fry up.

"Quick, nab that table." She gave Nik a discreet nudge. She didn't want to alert anyone else to the imminent departure of two women sitting knee to knee at a tiny table made for one. Right by the doorway, anyone sitting there would need to endure the jostling of the endless stream of people. There must be at least fifty already wedged inside the Wayfarer Cafe at seven-forty-five am on a crisp autumn morning. But today, any table would be welcome.

She enjoyed the brief rush of pride at successfully noting who of the diners had finished their food. By studying their body language, she'd determined the exact moment they would stand to leave. Silly really, to take pleasure in such a small thing, but it was a useful skill in crowded pubs and bustling tourist spots.

But Nik ambled slowly between the waiting customers, prompting anxiety that some new arrival might beat him to it. He was, predictably, in a foul mood and not particularly willing to follow any instruction from her this morning.

"Hurry up." Muttering to herself helped to push away her annoyance that even now, on this last day of their holiday, a day that meant so much to her, he was being difficult; irritating, but understandable. This was Nik's coping mechanism; by retreating into a surly, scowling version of himself that lurked behind the boisterous, playful boy she'd fallen in love with.

In reality, it had been a mistake to come to the UK. But she wouldn't deny her mother's request. Had Blair hoped, with the clarity of one knowing she wouldn't live to see it, this trip might be the thing to save them? Cassie knew that a month ago, boarding a plane at Auckland International Airport, each of them held a faint hope that maybe, freed from all the stresses of everyday life—the mortgage, work pressure, and of course the battle with infertility they'd fought and lost—perhaps time away might help them shore up their crumbling marriage. Last time they'd come to Scotland, two years ago, they had returned to New Zealand happier. But this time, the country had failed to work its magic on them.

The tears that had lain beneath the surface these past weeks ambushed her now, welling over. First one, then another, made a silent trail down her cheek. She fumbled for a tissue, hoping to wipe them away before anyone noticed. After today, they would face twenty-four hours of travel cramped in economy class, and then arrive home to face the unpleasant truth that their marriage was over.

Rather than bringing them closer together, four weeks in each other's company 24/7, without visiting friends or family to provide a reprieve, had only emphasised how little remained. The love between them had seeped away. Now she wondered if they might even struggle to remain friends after the inevitable uncoupling. She winced as the thought provoked another lunge of stabbing grief deep in her stomach.

"Mornin' luv, what can I get ye?" She realised with a start that the queue had made a sudden leap ahead and it was her turn to order. The woman flashed her a smile. Cassie marvelled she could maintain such cheerfulness in the face of the never-ending stream of customers.

"Are ye on one of the eight-fifteen tours, dear? Because if so, I'm afraid I could only do cabinet food."

"No, nine o'clock—Outlander," she replied.

"Aye, that's a popular one. All the lassies looking for Jamie Fraser, even though most of them are old enough to be his mother." She lowered her voice and offered a quiet aside. "I'll let you into a secret—he's actually out the back there." She pointed to a door emblazoned with the sign 'Toilets.' "Look out for him when you go to the bathroom."

⸻

Cassie only picked at her food when it arrived, even though it was good. Either excitement about the tour or Nik's brooding presence had killed her appetite. The thick sourdough toast, smeared with melting butter, provided a bed for two poached eggs cooked to perfection. She dabbed at them listlessly. Even the coarse Scottish square sausage, a new favourite, couldn't tempt her. It lay there rejected, with nibbled corners looking as if a rat had been at them. She dumped her knife and fork on the half-finished plate and slugged down the last of her lukewarm coffee.

"Just going to duck to the loo." She shoved her chair back with a clatter. Nik acknowledged this with a grunt, but didn't look up from his phone.

She dallied in a wood-floored foyer, walls lined with a jaunty plaid wallpaper, the backdrop for a mini-gallery of framed pictures. It gave her something to look at while she waited. Only two toilets for such a busy place. At least she wasn't in a hurry.

She scanned the pictures, ticking off in her head many places she'd been in Scotland: Eilean Donan Castle, Stirling Castle, Edinburgh Castle, Holyrood Palace. She'd loved every one of them. Although Nik was adamant, he was all castled out and wouldn't be venturing in any more. A shame, as today the itinerary would take them to several rather special ones. But she was beyond caring if he missed out. Served him right for being so sulky. Anger at his mood reared up. It wasn't as if he was the only one hurting here, and for her, the other hurt layered on top of it made it even more painful.

Amongst the landscapes and portraits, a familiar face jumped out at her. Jamie Fraser, 'the king of men' as portrayed by the actor Sam Heughan. *A gift from the artist*, said the small plaque below. A bloody talented artist who'd captured his likeness accurately. Seeing it, her throat tightened, sadness welling up. She thought of her mother's bucket list, written by hand in that flamboyant looping style, little joyful hearts drawn next to each item achieved. But this one—do an *Outlander* tour in Scotland—languished unembellished in that notebook, now bequeathed to Cassie to fulfil.

So today she'd immerse herself in all things *Outlander*. She hoped as they ventured to the beloved spots from the books and TV series, it might soothe the outrage she felt at the unfairness, that having beaten cancer once, it should continue to stalk her mother in stealth, then in a sudden ambush, steal her away. Maybe from wherever she was now, Blair Tremayne would watch quietly at her shoulder as they travelled around these places.

Little tears prickled at her again. As a woman emerged from behind one of the navy blue doors, she quickly wiped them away, embarrassed at how close to the surface her emotions were today.

When she stepped back into the cafe, the woman at the till glanced up, tossing her a wink and a knowing grin, as if to say "Told ye Jamie was out there". The small gesture was just what she needed as she made her way through the crowd, vowing to enjoy the day as her mum would have wanted.

"And the fun begins." Nik, unable to repress his sarcasm, cast a withering look at the queue of people politely arranged behind a small sign on the pavement with the words 'Outlander 9:00 a.m.'

Cassie surveyed their companions for the day with a kinder eye. The group was fairly predictable in its composition. Four pairs of women, all forty-plus, giggling and chattering like excited school girls. One American couple, the wife trying to jolly along her unenthusiastic husband by reading him the itinerary. He'd possibly be company for Nik—they could commiserate over the waste of a perfectly good day. A single woman, probably in her late twenties, the tag on her backpack suggesting she was a fellow New Zealander, engaged in conversation with an older lady wearing a jaunty felt fedora.

And a step ahead of them, a dapper gentleman with a neatly trimmed white beard and twinkling blue eyes. He wore a vibrant kilt of aqua and emerald tartan, solid walking boots, a bag slung over one shoulder, and a set of bagpipes cradled in his arms. Dressed in those clothes, he had to be their driver and tour guide. But when he opened his mouth to speak, Cassie's own mouth dropped open in surprise.

"Guten morgen, I'm Tomas. From Berlin." He extended a hand, beaming at them.

"Cassie, from Auckland, New Zealand. And my husband, Nik." Nik mumbled his own hello and shook the man's hand.

"So, you are both fans?" he said.

"No." Nik jumped in quickly. "Cassie is. I'm just along for the ride."

"Ah, yes," Tomas replied with a wry grin. "Not too many men like the *Outlander*. But me, I'm big fan. Big fan."

"We can kind of tell," she said, casting an admiring gaze over his outfit.

"Yes." His tinkling laughter matched the merry eyes. "And the ladies love it too, you know, something about a man in a kilt," he said with a wink.

"Fucking hell, now I've seen everything," Nik said in a low voice as the cheerful Tomas made his way to greet some others in the line. "I can't believe I agreed to spend the last day of our holiday on this lame bloody tour."

She whirled on him. "Well, fuck you too Nik," she said, not caring if anyone heard her. Anger surged inside, a flush of red heat spreading across her face. "No one's making you come on the tour. I told you I'd be perfectly happy to go on my own while you sloped around Edinburgh. Or you can always go back to the apartment and spend the day with your fucking phone." Years of working as a teacher meant she usually had a pretty good filter on what came out of her mouth, but he'd pushed her over the edge.

"Calm down," he hissed. "I'm sure the rest of them don't want to hear your potty mouth."

She glared at him. He stared her down, with his face like a slapped arse—that's what her mother would have said. If it wasn't for the presence of the rest of them, she might actually have given *him* a slap for good measure. That she'd even consider hitting him startled her. Her emotions were quite out of control. But contrary to what he thought, no one else had noticed how pissed off she was, or heard their conversation. They were all too engrossed in making the acquaintance of brightly clad Tomas, who provided a fortunate distraction.

"I've paid to go on the tour, and I intend to go on the tour." Nik crossed his arms in front of him with a belligerent sneer as he showed his stubborn streak.

"OK, well then, perhaps you might let the rest of us enjoy it," she said, turning her back on him.

A boisterous young Scottish man arrived. Also clad in a kilt, he interrupted the hum of conversation. He wore the authentic *Outlander* tartan, matched with rustic boots. He made his way along the row, checking tickets, welcoming them with a cheeky grin and waving them onto his bus. Once on board, he ensured everyone introduced themselves to their fellow tour members, Cassie answering on behalf of herself and her sullen husband.

Then they were off, navigating the cobbled streets as the driver, Evan, revealed he'd inherited the Scottish skill of telling a good yarn, even extracting smiles and laughter from Nik, who appeared more cheerful despite himself.

Shaking off the city, they were soon crossing the broad expanse of the Firth of Forth on a soaring bridge. Plunging down into sprawling countryside, trees already in vibrant autumn colours punctuated the lush green fields. They wound down a narrow road into the quaint village of Cullross, piling off the bus to see the first film location.

Nik trailed behind, in conversation with the other reluctant husband dragged along against his will. This left her to enjoy the guided walk, reimagining scenes from the TV series in the company of other fans. Two stereotypically loud but cheerful American women adopted her at once.

"Come along with us," said Ruth, linking one arm in hers. "Did you know my friend here has an *Outlander* tattoo? Show her Edie."

Edie complied, rolling up her sleeve to reveal the words 'Dinna fash Sassenach' inked on the inside of her wrist. A slightly drunken looking dragonfly fluttered away from them towards her elbow.

"Ah, very nice." Cassie feigned polite admiration, but in her mind vowed to never let someone mark her body permanently unless she could be sure the result wouldn't be so clumsy.

"And I met herself last year," said Ruth proudly. "We were in Scottsdale visiting family and I saw this bookshop, with a lovely display of the books in the window. So I said to my husband, Charlie, you wait here. I'm going in." The image of a harried looking husband dawdling on the sidewalk leapt to mind. "Well, I couldn't believe my luck. I see Diana Gabaldon disappearing through a door behind the counter. They'd called her in to sign books, so I asked and she kindly signed one for me. Personalised." Ruth's eyes sparkled with excitement.

"Wow, that is special." She'd never before been in company where she could openly share her enthusiasm. None of her friends were the least interested. With her mother gone, she missed the fun: a watch party for the new TV series, shared rereads of their favourite books, little trinkets and collectables, even an *Outlander* themed cake for her twenty-seventh birthday last year. She'd spent much of her life feeling her mother as a slightly remote figure in the real world. Who would have predicted that in these last couple of years they'd bond over a fictional world? She was determined to extract every ounce of pleasure from this day.

Following Ruth and Edie into the little walled area known as 'Claire's garden', she walked among unruly flowers and strident herbs that overflowed the confines of the beds, resisting the gardener's attempt to tame them. The fresh green smell filled the morning air, making her feel alive.

She stopped to photograph a stray, late blooming sweet pea, inhaling its delicate perfume. She'd filled her phone with photos, recording memories to be little bright sparks of happiness in the future. She'd need them to survive the unpleasant time in her life about to unfold when they left for home tomorrow.

Reading the details of the next stop on the itinerary, Cassie suspected Nik might renege on his threat to avoid castles. She was right. The bus had barely come to a halt before the driver's question lured him in.

"Right folks," said Evan. "Doune Castle is not only Castle Leoch, a mecca for the *Outlander* fans. Do we have any *Monty Python* fans here today?"

Nik's face broke into a spontaneous smile, and he waved a hand. He had a fondness for the insane British sense of humour, cultivated over nights in his teens, when he'd kept Jan company watching old TV programmes.

"Ah, see I wasna lying when I told ye there'd be something for everyone today. Well, just for you, Nik, this is the home of *Monty Python and The Holy Grail*. Be sure to get yerself the audio guide. An' while the ladies here will enjoy Mr Heughan's dulcet tones," he said with a wink, "ye'll find most of the recording is by Terry Jones himself."

Keen to make the most of this unexpected bonus, Nik was first off the bus, and soon weaving around the castle wearing a set of small headphones. It was a relief to see the upturn of his mouth, and from time to time even bursts of laughter, as he made his way to each numbered stop.

Freed from fretting over Nik's unhappiness, Cassie moved from room to room with a feeling of lightness. Despite its gloomy exterior, inside the castle felt welcoming. She wandered through the expansive halls, marvelled at the well-preserved kitchens, and, standing in the private chambers, let her curious mind reach out to those who had stood there before her. She imagined those nebulous others looking out these same windows, commenting on the beauty of the view across the surrounding woodlands, drinking in the soft sunshine of an autumn day. In some rooms she was sure she felt them still there, standing lightly at her shoulder. Once or twice she swore she heard the voice of a man, and soft laughter, but when she turned, there was no one. But, rather than disturbed by ghosts of the past, she took unexpected comfort in their presence, sensing familiar friends offering a warm greeting.

Glancing at her watch, Cassie saw it was almost time to head back to the bus. With a silent, reluctant farewell, she left the past inhabitants of Doune behind, and made her way downstairs. Stepping out into the courtyard, she spotted Nik emerging from the gift shop. He'd found a wide smile and a souvenir t-shirt inside.

"Got this for Jan." He held it up for her to see. With its picture of an armless knight bleeding profusely while proclaiming 'Tis but a scratch', she knew Jan would appreciate it—but the real gift here was the rare opportunity to see her husband's face lit up like a child.

"He's going to love it," she agreed. Seeing his lightened mood, she even risked asking him to photograph her with one of the American women—and a giant cardboard Jamie Fraser the woman had insisted required his own seat on the bus. How her mum would have loved the idea of Jamie coming along for the ride.

Only a short journey away, the bus crawled up a walled driveway, leading to Linlithgow Palace. Nik announced he would once more stay on the bus; that there was nothing to interest him there. She rose from her seat without a murmur of protest, noticing relief sweep across his face as he retreated into his book. She would never understand how he could read on that damn phone. She loved the feel of proper books, the smell of their pages intoxicating and addictive. But at least it kept him occupied. Happy to leave him to his own devices, she moved to follow the group of women who were fast becoming friends.

"So The Four Marys at twelve o'clock?" Their driver had recommended the place for a lunch stop in the centre of Linlithgow as they drove in. She flung the question at him, but didn't wait to check his acknowledgement. If he turned up well and good.

———

Heading along the coast towards Blackness Castle that afternoon brought a tumble of memories. The bus ambled past the cute cottage that had been their refuge for four peaceful days back in 2017. She smiled, thinking of sweet old Mrs Campbell and her sumptuous Scottish breakfasts. Had it really only been two years? The brave, hopeful plans made there felt so distant.

Even before they alighted, the tangy salt of sea spray assaulted her nostrils. Small pinpricks of water peppered the windows, carried by a howling wind off the waves. Here on the small promontory jutting out into the sea, its bleak dark walls exposed to all the Scottish weather could throw at it, the castle projected a menacing strength.

"Now I know this is a very significant spot for ye," said Evan. They all nodded, visualising the horrific television scene staged here, where the villain Black Jack Randall flogged Jamie Fraser. Even though she'd only watched it once, the graphic special effects had etched the scene in her mind as if it were real.

"So, we've a tad longer here, so ye can have a good explore. And if it gets too wild for ye, the little shop here does a good coffee and scones."

"What about the pub back there by the village shops?" Nik asked.

"I tell ye what—if you wanna wander down there, I'll pick ye up on our way past." Obliging Evan didn't hesitate to accommodate a request from his least enthusiastic guest.

"See you later," Nik called as he set off at a brisk walk toward the pub, leaving her to follow the others, who were making a beeline for the castle entry.

She was glad of the wide tartan scarf, her mother's precious *Outlander* memento. She wrapped it tight, an extra layer against the wind's chilly fingers that tried to prise their way under her coat, and plucked wildly at her hair.

The entrance only enhanced the castle's sinister feel. Stopping inside the curved dark tunnel, she laid her hands on the stone walls, thinking of what they had witnessed over the centuries. She could even taste their damp mustiness as she breathed in the scent of time.

In the central courtyard, no trace of the movie set remained. With the whipping post gone, the courtyard floor itself had returned to the ruinous state of the rest of the castle, bleak and empty. The rough ground was tricky, and she carefully picked her way across, avoiding the sharp-edged rocks that snapped at her ankles. Although the steep walls blocked out the sun, they also provided shelter, and she unwound the scarf, draping it through the handle of her tote bag. Following a map in the little brochure, she headed for the tower where they'd kept prisoners—the unfortunate ones on lower floors in windowless rooms, those of more noble lineage in the upper storeys to serve out their sentences in reasonable comfort.

Coming in from the daylight, at first, absolute darkness engulfed her. She saw nothing, stepping into a black void. Feeling her way, she pressed her palm against the wall, hoping the curve would show which way to turn. Her eyes adjusted to the gloom, revealing a tight and steep stairwell, more so than any other she'd navigated so far. There would be no room to pass another person coming down. She strained to listen above the whistling wind, checking no one was above her.

Bracing herself, one hand on each wall, she took the first step. As she climbed, the noise of the wind amplified, the whistle becoming a cascading roar, and although she couldn't feel its angry breath, the sound engulfed her. The very air vibrated with it and panic rose in her throat.

When she looked up, the walls loomed inwards, threatening to crush her, trap her there forever. She sank to the ground, hands pressed against her ears but failing to keep out the sound that whirled both around and within her. She drew herself into a ball, a desperate attempt to protect herself as the world folded in.

PART FOUR: THERE

CHAPTER 34

Flicker

Blackness, Scotland - September 2019

"Cassie. Cassie." Her name came from above. "God, are you all right?"

The hideous sound had evaporated, leaving only the blare of the wind off the sea overlaid with a frantic Scottish voice. Cold stone pressed against her cheek, and the dusty odour of other feet that had passed over it drifted upwards. The sour taste in her mouth, as if she'd almost thrown up, matched the clench of nausea in her stomach.

His hand rested on her shoulder. Like a periscope scanning for danger, she lifted her head, swivelling her neck in his direction. She looked up into Simon's concerned sea-blue eyes.

"Oh Cassie, thank god. When you didn't appear—and then to find you lying here."

A surge of embarrassment swamped her. It wasn't easy to explain that you'd flung yourself onto the floor in a panic. She'd never been claustrophobic, but this is how it must feel. And the sound had left now. Maybe it had never been. Perhaps it was some projection of her scrambled brain as it switched into overload, overwhelmed by the dark confining walls that had threatened to trap her. But she had a fleeting memory of it. Somewhere, in her past, she'd heard that sound before.

"Are you hurt?" He crouched beside her now, perched on the narrow step, his tall body wedged uncomfortably against the wall. She did a quick mental check. No obvious pain, except a slight area of soreness on one knee, probably bruised as she'd fallen to the ground.

"No, no. I'm OK." She gave him a weak smile. "Except for feeling rather stupid. I think I've just had some sort of panic attack. Not sure what brought that on."

"It's not stupid." He reached out a soothing hand to stroke her hair. "We all have our fears. You know I can't stand needles, pathetic as it sounds. Nearly passed out when I had to have my jabs before I went to Egypt."

"Yeah, but it took me by surprise. I've trailed round heaps of small dark places with you and it's never happened before."

"But you have had something similar. Surely you haven't forgotten the day we met? The agoraphobia? Do you think it's that again?"

At this moment, she could barely remember what had happened mere minutes ago, let alone two years earlier. And yet how could she admit to being vague about meeting the man who was her everything? The man who frowned at her now, while scanning for signs of injury, a long delicate finger tracing a smudge of dirt on her cheekbone.

"I remember," she said, as she struggled to find equilibrium. Because she did remember—not much, but she remembered that sound.

"And yet you've never had it since. What is it with this castle?" He shrugged. "Ah well, let's get you up, eh?"

He stretched out his large safe hand, and she clasped it tightly. With one fluid movement, he had them both on their feet. He planted a tender kiss on her forehead, and she felt a surge of love for this kind, gentle man. The universe had smiled on her that day at this very castle, two years ago.

Yes, she remembered now. Crouching in that little hollow in the wall, desperate for escape but with the nearest possibility, the narrow passageway blocked. She pushed that nauseating image aside and focused on what had come next: a dark, handsome Scot named Simon Buchanan had seen her distress and stopped to help.

"I'll help you back down, then," he said, placing a protective arm around her waist and turning her towards where the stairs led back to the entrance.

"No," she said. "I'm fine. I'm not going to miss the best bit." She looked forward to these days out, interludes of calm amongst their busy lives; time to share the things they were passionate about. These castles were his passion. And if you intended to spend the rest of your life with someone known to the outside world as 'The Castle Hunter'—and she did intend to spend the rest of her life with him—then it was pretty important that you got used to clawing your way up, down, and all around places like this one. And she certainly wouldn't deny him the chance to stand in his favourite place in all the world.

"It's wild up here," she called to him, as the blustery wind buffeted them, whisking her words away. There was no escape from it on the wall walk. 'The ship that never sailed'. This castle bore the title proudly, with its tapered bow jutting out into the water. Photographs of it from above emphasised its slim shape mirroring the curves of a large ship, cutting a swathe through the choppy waters of the Firth.

They stood out on the furthermost point, and she suppressed the ridiculous urge she always had standing here, to do the *Titanic* movie re-enactment. He'd indulged her once. She wouldn't push him again. Not today when they were surrounded by the now ever-present tourists.

He stood rugged up against the chilly blast, the collar of his dark charcoal coat turned up to deflect the wind, like some benevolent vampire. The dark hair, sensuous mouth, and his elegant profile against the insipid sky reinforced the image. A layer of high cloud shrouded much of the blue, with tiny rays of sunlight peeking through gilding faint blue lights in his hair. In the moment, he was beautiful, and she lifted her phone, framing him in a photograph.

"Simon." She said his name, and he looked towards her. She snapped a second photo, this one capturing his languid smile and the deep blue of his eyes, the colour of the sea deprived of sunshine.

"I can take one of the both of you if you'd like." In the voice behind her, she heard the drawl of the southern states. "Go on, honey, give me your phone. Nice to have a shot of the two of you." She turned to see a tall woman with a tumble of blonde curls and a large, immaculate grin.

"And then perhaps we could ask you to do the same," suggested her friend, slightly smaller but displaying similar picture-perfect teeth, her bobbed red hair topped with a jaunty tartan beret.

"Thanks, that's kind of you. What a good idea."

She handed over her phone and nuzzled in under the protection of Simon's arm. He always felt so warm, and solid, as if his physical presence reflected the steadiness he'd injected into her life, no longer adrift but grounded.

She knew the photo would show the happiness that bubbled over in her spontaneously whenever they were together. Even the smell of him, his own Simon smell, overlaid with the woody aftershave he splashed on each morning, made her relax in its comfortable familiarity.

"Thank you," he said, as Cassie stretched out her hand for her phone. "And now I'll take one of you then?"

"Ahh, a genuine Scot," said Mrs Tartan Beret, nodding at him. "But you're not. Australian?" she suggested, looking at Cassie.

"No—a New Zealander."

"Now, *that* looks like a beautiful country. We'd love to go there some time, wouldn't we, Davina?"

Davina nodded with enthusiasm. "If it's good enough for our Graham McTavish, then it must be all right."

Cassie raised an eyebrow.

"You know—the *Outlander* actor."

"Of course. Dougal." She knew. It brought back bittersweet memories of evenings spent on the phone, talking with her mother over the intricacies of character and plot.

"Oh, so you know *Outlander* then?"

"I do," she said. "My mum loved it." And Simon had been rather chuffed that his favourite Scottish castle had become an international celebrity on the back of the television series.

"We're on the tour," said Davina, pointing down at a small bus parked over by the coffee shop. "It's been a wonderful day. Right Judy, give him your phone." The two women huddled together, arms wrapped around each other, their backs to the wind, while Simon snapped a stream of photographs for them.

"Enjoy the rest of your day, ladies," he said as they disappeared into the tower.

"Oh, we will for sure," one called back, "and thanks for the photographs."

"That is exactly why this castle has to be included in the television programme," he said. "This and Doune, Midhope, and of course Eilean Donan. Popular appeal."

This was the problem uppermost in Simon's mind at the moment, wrestling with the difficult task of narrowing down the list of castles from the hundred or so in his book to around twenty. It was now only two weeks before he'd have his chance to punt the concept for a TV series, *Scotland With The Castle Hunter*, to the people at BBC Scotland.

"Not so nerdy?" Although she found his nerdy intelligence extremely appealing.

"Yeah, nothing like TV to make history sexy enough for the masses."

"I'm sure you're going to make history very sexy," she said with a grin. It had certainly worked for her. Not that she disliked history, but since she'd been with Simon, seen the way his face lit up when he talked about the clan feud here or the rebellion there—well, it was hard not to fall in love with the things he loved.

She wondered how she'd feel if women out there—seeing the same light in his eyes, and that handsome face on the TV screen—took a fancy to him. God, he might even have fans lying in wait for him when they went out places. She shuddered a little inside. She hoped that, while she wanted him to be an enormous success, he didn't become so famous it became tiresome.

However, she didn't fear losing him to those prospective fans. Cassie was confident that, no matter what, Simon was hers. Only her he would take into his bed at night. Only her to whom he would do those things that made her shiver with ecstasy. Only her who would elicit those groans of pleasure from the muscular body hidden under those conservative layers of clothing. She blushed a little that she should even think those things in public, thoughts that surfaced unbidden, fuelled by the exquisite desire that thrilled inside her simply from being near him.

"You know it's freezing up here," he said, pulling his coat tight. "Perhaps we should come back another day. I think I've got enough notes for now." He frowned over his small notebook, where he'd been scribbling away. "If we leave now, we could swing by Midhope on the way back. I want to check it out at this time of day. I've got a feeling it will look its best in the afternoon."

She followed him down the stairs of the south tower. Its wide passage allowed her to descend without confronting the frightening confines of the other stairs. She held his hand for reassurance, anyway.

As they emerged from the castle, to the right, a small crowd seemed to be hovering around his car.

"Oh god, please tell me they're not waiting for me," Simon said, his mouth drawing into a tense line. Had her thoughts of fans acted like some summoning spell? He was already known for his book, and the odd person approached him from time to time, recognising him from his author photograph. But never this many.

The possibility this whole group might be lying in wait triggered a rush of anxiety on his behalf. While she considered the prospect of fans an annoyance, for Simon, it was the one large blot on his enthusiasm for the television project. To him, fame was best avoided. And yet, now he was marching steadily towards it. Lured in, even though he knew it might burn him, only because a starring role offered the opportunity to save the one thing he had left of his family, the old house down the road.

Stepping into the Buchanan family home, just a short walk away, was like entering a building on a movie set. Simon had slowly restored the front of the seventeenth-century house, shoring up aging stonework and replacing the leaking slate tiled roof. Inside, modern plumbing and new wiring made it a well-functioning home. But beyond that façade, the remaining rooms were virtually derelict. And Simon was losing the race to finance their repair before they started to crumble, and ruined all the hard-fought improvements he'd made.

That was until his cousin Calum, already a successful documentary maker, had pointed out that Simon's book would be the perfect springboard for a TV programme—and could also make him a lot of money—although it came with risk.

As they drew closer to the group, Cassie spotted Davina and Judy giving them a friendly wave, and to her relief, realised it was just the *Outlander* tour party gathering for a photograph. Seeing them arrayed in all their *Outlander* merchandise caused her to notice the absence of her own, the special tartan scarf, bequeathed from her mother.

Damn, she knew she'd put it on when they left the car. And she had a fair idea of when she'd lost it—in the horrible stairwell where she'd had that embarrassing claustrophobic experience. But there was no way she could leave that scarf behind.

"Simon, I have to go back. I've dropped my scarf."

"Do you want me to go? I don't mind."

"No, it's fine. I won't be long," she said, seized by a strange determination to face her unexpected fear, alongside the need to retrieve her precious scarf.

"OK, I'll grab us a coffee to go." She watched his black-coated figure navigate the crowd as she took a deep breath and turned to set out on the recovery mission.

The tourists had all filtered their way back to the carpark, leaving the castle empty. She picked her way over the rocky courtyard, scanning the area in case she'd dropped the scarf there, hoping she had so she need not venture into the stairwell. But there was no sign of it. She stood at the stone arched doorway of the tower, mentally preparing herself for the blackness, and plunged inside.

The interior was far less sinister than she'd let it grow in her imagination. Yes, it was dark, but as her eyes adapted, it wasn't so bad the second time around. She traced the curved wall, trailing her hand over the rough surface, and headed upwards. One step, two, and then her foot scuffed against something soft. Her scarf, its blue and browns almost blending into the grey stone floor.

As she bent to pick it up, there came a low hum. It seemed to emanate from inside the wall itself and the rough stones drew her hand, as if to confirm the source. As she made contact with the wall, the vibrations leapt into her fingers, streaking up the length of her arm in a surge akin to an electric current. It reminded her of the time her cousin had tricked her into touching an electric fence on the farm. The sensation was the same; although not exactly painful, it provoked a nauseating feeling. And there was a drifting ozone smell overlying the cloying mustiness of the dank air.

The accompanying sound rose in intensity, enveloping her; an almost tangible presence. Overwhelmed, she instinctively dropped to the ground in the somewhat vain hope she could escape beneath it. But the black wall of sound swamped her, despite clamping her hands on her ears in a futile attempt to hold it back.

PART FIVE: HERE

CHAPTER 35

Shadow

Blackness, Scotland - September 2019

SHE JUMPED AT THE firm hand on her shoulder, startled by the touch. She tentatively let her hands drop from her ears, aware of the near silence, apart from the hiss of the wind and the distant swish of the sea. And then a voice, urgent and concerned.

"Cassie, are you OK? What the hell are you doing down there?"

She opened her eyes to see Nik's blonde hair. Then her eyes focused, registered his blue ones boring into her, and felt surprised to read worry within them. He still cared for her. As she did for him. So much shared history since they'd laid eyes on each other as half-grown seventeen-year-olds. But marrying your high school sweetheart, while a romantic notion, hadn't turned out so well in reality.

"What's wrong with you? You look like you've seen a bloody ghost."

She offered a weak smile. "Didn't see one. Might have heard one, though."

Then, seeing his exasperated look, she decided there was little point. She wouldn't attempt to explain. And to be honest, she couldn't really explain it herself. Her head was thick, her mind foggy. At least he put out a hand to help her up, and she took it, grateful for support as she tested the steadiness of her feet.

"We'd better hurry. They're all waiting for you." They? Of course—the bus tour. "Although they'll probably forgive you for going back for your *Outlander* scarf." She clutched it tightly in one hand. So that's what she'd been doing.

"What are you doing here?" She remembered now. He'd gone to the pub.

"Walked all the bloody way there to find them closing the doors. Not a proper pub anymore—only a cafe, really." He sounded pissed off. "Got myself a Coke from the shop and walked back. Just in time to find the tour bus filling up and no sign of you." She wasn't sure if he was more annoyed with the absence of alcohol or finding her missing. Probably the latter.

"Well, you found me." Energised by her irritation, she strode away from him, tumbling up the steps of the coach to a round of applause from the rest of the group. "Sorry," she said, offering them an apologetic smile.

"No worries, luv," said Evan. "I'll just put me foot down a bit and we'll soon make up the time."

True to his promise, Evan sped along the narrow country roads, navigating them with the confidence of someone who'd driven them many times. While Nik remained engrossed in his book, she relaxed back into the seat, lulled by the voice-over on the episode of *Beautiful Scotland* playing on an overhead screen. The backdrop of casual chatter from the other passengers jumped in volume as they turned onto a side road. A single sign pointed out their destination: Midhope Castle.

"And now, something special," Evan said through his microphone, flicking off the video. The haunting sounds of the 'Skye Boat Song', the *Outlander* TV series theme, floated from the speakers, prompting a collective hush as the passengers let it wash over them. The bus wound along a metal driveway, where trees gilded with late afternoon sun crowded right to the edges, before it opened out into a wider car park area with a rustic ticket booth. The sign said 'Closed'.

Evan parked, announcing, "No tickets needed, all part of the tour. And no one else here at this time of day. Ye've got it all to yourselves."

"I'll stay here," said Nik, still grumpy, as if he considered her tardiness at Blackness a personal insult. But Cassie wasn't about to let him tarnish the highlight of the day. She followed the others as they tumbled down the steps, gathering at the bottom of the pathway, speechless in awe as the castle of their dreams, Midhope—or to them, 'Lallybroch'—peeped through the trees. They moved towards it as a group, in a slow reverent procession, although Cassie sensed from the waves of excitement pouring off them some would have preferred to break and run.

"Here we are Mum," she said under her breath, and in the slight breeze felt the faint brush of her mother's answer in her ear. "Here we are, darling."

Once near the castle, the group fanned out in all directions. The curved stone archway drew some. They ran their hands over it as if absorbing the history, feeling the echoes of those who had passed underneath it. Others made for the grassed areas, snapping away, capturing picture postcard images—although nowadays they were more likely to appear on Facebook or Instagram. Cassie had seen the online groups filled with excited posts from fellow travellers, proof they had found their way to this sacred spot.

The earlier high cloud had cleared and now the gold tinged stone towers stood in sharp relief against a sky of brilliant blue. A small informal queue formed near the steps leading up to the weathered wooden door. Politely waiting in turn, every person, some on their own, others in couples, took a moment to sit on the steps and recreate one of the most poignant scenes from the TV series. She and her mother had ugly cried through it time after time, captivated by the grief of a fictional character mourning her lost love, and the other people she'd known in her journey two hundred years back in time.

Cassie offered to take pictures for others, capturing their expressions of delight at sitting on the hallowed ground of 'Lallybroch'. When her turn came, she stepped forward and took her place on the step, an involuntary smile spreading across her face at the thought of actually being in this spot, despite the tinge of sadness. She'd never expected to be here alone, without her mother. And at that moment, as if in response to her mood, a melancholy note rang out.

Tomas, the German tourist, had put bagpipes to his lips and launched into his own rendition of the "Skye Boat Song". It was so achingly beautiful Cassie found tiny drops of emotion sliding down her cheeks. She glanced across at the archway where TV Claire had seen the remembered image of her husband Jamie through her tears.

There, to her surprise, stood a man. Tall like TV Jamie, but he was dark-haired, not ruddy, and wore dark jeans, not a kilt. Wrapped in a black winter coat, he stood like a vigilant shadow. Not part of their group, he hung back as if cautious of intruding. He leaned on one pillar, pausing there, perhaps listening to the music, as they all were. Even through the teary fog that clouded her vision, Cassie noted his finely sculptured features and a sensuous mouth that turned up in a slight smile.

There was something almost familiar about him, but she brushed the thought away, attributing it to where he was standing—in Jamie's special spot. Their eyes met, and she smiled back at him, a moment of shared enjoyment at the mesmerising rise and fall of the pipes. Then he turned and strolled off.

A round of spontaneous applause erupted around Tomas as the last notes faded away. He grinned, his cheeks flushed with modest pleasure. It was a perfect end to the day.

Not even Nik's grunt of acknowledgement as she climbed into the seat next to him on the bus could spoil her mood. Evan put on some music, a Scottish woman singing haunting ballads. Cassie relaxed back, eyes closed, letting the Gaelic lyrics drift over her, not needing to understand the words to appreciate the stories of love lost and longing they conveyed.

She dozed a little, her mind wandering with the music, finally settling on an image she then couldn't shake. The stranger in the archway. She nudged him away. She had one man in her life she still needed to deal with before letting any other further complicate things.

CHAPTER 36

Crazy

Edinburgh, Scotland - September 2019

HIDDEN TREASURE LAY BEHIND the apartment building's historic brick façade. Beyond it, a dingy tunnel led to an incongruous 1970s spiral staircase. It soared up out of an unkempt garden. The climb to the third floor was steep and treacherous, even when not hauling suitcases. But the surprising view once inside the apartment was worth the risk.

Cassie sat in a comfortable armchair, staring out at Edinburgh Castle. Darkness had come, but she didn't want to draw the curtains. No one would want to shut out that view: the ancient stones floodlit, the battlements aglow against the clear indigo sky.

Nik appeared from the bathroom, freshly showered, rumpling a towel through his damp hair. "Thought I might head over to the Royal Mile. Spotted a restaurant and bar over there that does some good whisky tasting flights. You want to come?"

"Nah, I don't think so. That pub lunch was massive. I'd be happy with a snack. I might eat the last of the cheese and crackers. Otherwise, we'll have to toss it."

"Sure. OK. I'll only be a couple of hours." He looked slightly relieved that she'd declined. Pulling on a jacket, he grabbed his wallet and hurried out as if worried she'd change her mind.

She savoured the empty room, peaceful after the tension of the day. Over the next hour, she read a bit of a book while chomping her way through the odorous but tasty cheese and the whole packet of wafer thin crackers, as well as making a dent in their last bottle of wine.

Feeling full once again, she sprawled back on the sofa, mulling over what tomorrow would bring—an early taxi to the airport, followed by almost two days of immigration queues, wasted hours in transit halls and long flights cramped in economy class—all in the company of an unhappy Nik. It filled her with dread.

Because at the end of it, she'd be back in New Zealand and the need to face her old life. No—not her old life. They would separate. He wouldn't argue otherwise. But who knew how long it would take to untangle their shared lives? It wasn't easy to pull apart ten years.

Whether it was her mind's desperate search for a way to avoid her immediate future, or the realisation that for the first time in her adult life, true freedom beckoned—whatever the reason, she sensed a niggle of potential. The chance to throw away the script. Create her own path.

She wandered to the window. Looking out at the street below, where old buildings hugged modern pavements, she made a decision: she wasn't going home tomorrow. Sure, it would be a surprise to some of their family and friends; those who hadn't thought to look beneath the veneer of normality they'd shown to the world. But Dad wasn't stupid. He knew things weren't right in her marriage. And he'd long since shrugged off the need for his children's attention, pulling himself back into life with determination after Mum's illness. No, he didn't need her running back to New Zealand on his behalf.

She grabbed her phone and flicked off a text message to their Air BnB host, on the off chance that it might be possible to stay on. Otherwise, her first immediate problem would be accommodation. The reply was instant.

Rosina

> Hey, Cassie. Your lucky day (and mine). My next booking cancelled two hours ago. You can have it for the next week. I'll even do you a good deal. Late cancellation means I don't have to refund. Jump on the app in 5 minutes and I'll have the availability updated.

Cassie took that as an omen. Seven days to craft her new life. She'd need money and a job. With the rounds of failed IVF and then this trip, their accounts were skint. While she'd had cause to question her decision to become a teacher over the years, at least it was a portable qualification. A quick internet search and she found that substitute teaching was a viable option. She gave quiet thanks for her father's advice; her British passport opened all the doors she'd need to create a life here. She relaxed back on the couch and poured the last of the wine. Staring up at the Saltire, Scotland's bold blue and white flag, fluttering over the castle, she raised a toast to the country and her new life.

The turn of the key in the latch disturbed her from a wine-induced doze. "Sorry," he said. "Didn't realise you were sleeping." He perched on the sofa beside her, his face a little flushed from the whisky. "You ready for the morning?"

"Yeah, well—about that." She hesitated, but in his eyes she could see he knew. "I think I might stay on."

"Good for you," he said, barely raising an eyebrow at the news. "Your boss is going to be upset."

"They'll survive without me."

"I'm wondering how I will." He shot her a small, sad smile. "But I know I need to. It's run its course, hasn't it?"

"You'll survive," she said. "More than that, you'll thrive. You have got so much good stuff ahead of you."

"So have you. No more playing the understudy to me, OK? I want to hear you're doing something better with your life. Promise me, no more excuses. Finish that bloody book for a start. Promise?"

"Promise." In that moment, she knew she would still always love him. Not in the way she needed for them to stay married, but his gentle concern for her welfare erased all her recent doubt that they could remain friends beyond this parting.

"I'll personally come over and kick your arse if you don't."

"You know, I don't regret us, Nik. Not any of it. But you're right, somehow we've arrived here. Time is up on this part of our lives."

"I don't regret you either. I still need you. As a friend. Do you think you can do that? Might be hard to imagine after the grumpy bastard I've been today."

"I know I can do it. I need you too, you grumpy bastard. Besides..." The huge tight ball of hurt that she always buried deep inside began to unravel, extending its painful threads, and then tightening around her chest, her throat. "Besides, you're the only one who understands…"

"About Brontë." He always was the one strong enough to say her name. "Yeah." He smudged a tear from her cheek. "No matter what, no matter when. If you need to talk about her, you call me. And you'll do the same for me." She nodded. "You stay strong, my little warrior princess. And when you can't, I'll still always have your back. You know that, right?"

"OK." In that moment, she, who always had so many words, had none. How could mere words capture it all? Grief, love, gratitude, relief, sadness, freedom: they swirled inside her in a messy whirl of conflicting emotions. She could only trust the reflection in his eyes, evidence he fought the same battle.

He let her hands fall from his and stood. "Right, as you don't need to be up early in the morning, you should take the bed, and I'll sleep here. So I don't disturb you."

She tried to raise a feeble protest, but he insisted. And it made sense. He moved all his stuff from the bedroom, leaving her to sleep alone.

This was how it would be from now on. Alone. But alone didn't have to mean lonely. She knew what loneliness looked like. Without Nik's brooding presence, his antisocial habits, and the fence he'd built around the two of them, she had freedom to make new friends. This isolating past couple of years, she'd been lonelier with Nik than she might be without him.

She awoke early, abandoning sleep as thoughts of her momentous decision and its immediate consequences came charging in, overrunning the previous night's surety as doubt and hope battled inside her brain. The empty space beside her served as a full stop on her old life. Now it was up to her to carve out a new life on her own.

Nik had been considerate, leaving around seven with only the quiet click of the apartment door and the soft whirr of the suitcase as he made his way along the landing and down the steep stairs towards the taxi waiting below. By now, he'd be checking in. Within an hour, the airline would mark her as a no-show. Maybe they'd offer her seat to some grateful person on standby.

She lay listening to the sounds of the waking city. A distant hum of traffic, the clang of a rubbish truck with creaking hydraulics, hoisting a skip from behind the restaurant next door. She'd love an inner city apartment like this, where she could feed off the energy. The next few days were going to be busy, but despite her sudden decision, she felt a calm belief that it would all be OK. Her current lack of a job or a roof over her head were not insurmountable problems.

On the bedside table, her phone pinged. She reached for it to see the airline notification: *Flight QTR609 check in open now*. Without her. She closed the message, then tapped on the camera icon. She had dozens of photographs from yesterday. It would be fun to share a few with the Kiwi Outlander Facebook group, letting those who weren't lucky enough to travel to live vicariously through her pictures.

'Living the dream' she typed, then started scrolling looking for suitably recognisable images to accompany her post. One of the market cross in Cullross, a great shot of Doune Castle. She definitely needed one of Blackness. And that is where she paused.

Photographs don't lie, they said. But if so, a disturbing truth lay in this one. And the next. And the next. Sandwiched between a snap of the rocky courtyard of Blackness Castle and a view of the tree-lined approach to Lallybroch were three impossible photographs, images that challenged everything she knew to be true.

The first was odd enough: a dark-haired man in semi-profile, captured in outline against the upper wall of Blackness Castle. In the second, he looked directly at her. A faint smile played around his wide mouth, as if about to speak. He had high cheekbones and a smooth unlined face that looked as if hewn from marble.

The photographs were on her phone, but she had no recollection of having taken them. And yet the face felt familiar. Her heart pounded, blood pulsing, a throbbing vein in her temple. She searched her memory for an answer. Then, noting the black upturned collar, she found it. He was the man she'd seen at Lallybroch, paused in the archway while Tomas's bagpipes filled the air with sound. Maybe he had somehow walked into a shot as she took it. Perhaps, but there was no sense of movement. He looked like a sentinel, standing guard, motionless. And surely she'd have seen him, with his gaze turned towards her.

The third photograph unsettled her the most. In this one she stood facing the camera, one hand holding her hair back against the wind, her face lit up with a happiness that she'd not seen or felt in a long time. With an arm around her shoulder—he was so tall she only just reached his armpit—stood the same man. His smile mirrored hers.

To anyone else, it might be simply a picture of a young couple caught in a shared moment. To her, it presented an enigma. One that made her entire world tip precariously. Her stomach lurched in physical pain, a dull ache deep in the pit of her gut. And then her frantic mind pushed forward a name. *Simon*. Of course, that couldn't be his real name. Somehow her brain had tried to make sense of the incomprehensible, naming him to add normality to the abnormal.

Later she sat in the Grassmarket, making up for the lack of breakfast with a slap up pub lunch. An actual fire crackled in the hearth, the faint whiff of smoke and pine giving a homely atmosphere. Cosy inside, like all British pubs it gave the sensation of being enveloped in a warm hug. The beef pie, perched in a nest of fluffy mashed potato ringed with peas, was the comfort food she'd unknowingly craved.

After the shock of the morning, for a few hours, she'd felt numb. Now immersed in the comforting ordinariness of a busy tourist spot, she found a better frame of mind. She had bought a small notepad and sat making a list of all the things she needed to do to avoid returning home with her tail between her legs.

She'd sent her boss an email. A hard conversation awaited her later when he woke up to find that in his inbox. Seeking reassurance, she'd fired a text to Grace. Then another to her work friend, Gina, not expecting the sudden and emphatic reply.

Gina, up in the night battling with a vomiting toddler, had sent back two words—*You're crazy*—maybe not unexpected, from a conservative mum with a husband, two kids and a dog, in a cosy nest in the suburbs. Crazy she might be—the incident with the photographs hinted she might truly have lost her mind—but she wasn't going back.

While sitting at the leaner, Googling a list of teacher supply agencies, once again, unwelcome thoughts of the mysterious Simon took up residence in her mind. Deciding that if Simon was determined to pursue her like this, maybe she should pursue him back, she typed in a search: 'Simon+Blackness+castle' and Google delivered her results at lightning speed - 6,222,000 results in 0.51 seconds it informed her with a satisfied smirk.

The first hit was, as expected, Blackness Castle's own website. But she wasn't expecting to find Simon in the very next: Simon Buchanan, university lecturer, historian, author, affectionately known by his followers as 'The Castle Hunter'. An expert on Scottish castles, with Blackness a particular favourite. And his bio pics left no doubt that this Simon was her Simon.

She chided herself —'her Simon'. She didn't even know him. But a picture on her phone and a feeling that resonated deep from within her, a feeling so powerful that it frightened her—these things said she did know him—intimately.

The Castle Hunter. The words felt familiar, and she rolled them back and forth in her mind, hoping to dislodge a memory. When it came, it brought along with it a slew of uncomfortable emotions: a crowded lecture theatre, a beguiling dark-haired man, an immediate and all-consuming obsession, a forbidden desire pushed back into the dark where it belonged. She knew him.

Star Power

Blackness, Scotland - October 2019

SIMON BUCHANAN LEANED ON the rough stone wall, his dog-eared notebook open. Old school, but that was how he liked it. He scribbled frantically. His usual neat hand deteriorated into a rather untidy scrawl, but so many ideas tumbled through his mind, he wanted to get them down without delay.

He hoped the attention to detail he'd developed through his PhD, as well as his much-lauded book on Scottish castles, would make this venture a winner. The thought of bringing his passion for the past to an even wider audience sent a thrill of potential. If only he could do it justice. But sharp teeth of worry gnawed at him. Plunging into the fast-moving world of television both excited and terrified him. He had never felt so conflicted.

If they were to save this country's fast-crumbling relics of the past, they needed a new generation of people committed to the cause. To capture the imagination of younger people required modern media, and people to front it who were more their age than the fusty historians who generally inhabited the territory. People like him.

But, who was he kidding? While he tried to justify his decision to create this television series as part of some noble cause, when it came down to the bare facts, it was really about the money. His own crumbling home, the last surviving tangible piece of his personal history, demanded urgent attention, and with it eye-watering sums of cash that were well beyond his modest academic salary. The TV series offered a lifeline.

But clutching at it came with huge personal risk. His agent, Jasper Everitt, had left him in no doubt that things would change. God, he had an agent—how the hell had that happened? The ebullient Jasper had wasted no time spelling out exactly how the spotlight would fall on him. Even though the plan was to get the local people telling their stories, his face would be front and centre in each of the six episodes. He still shuddered at the thought.

"You're perfect, Simon," Jasper had said, with all the weight of his ten years in television. "They're going to love you. You have the authenticity of an expert, but a sense of what interests the ordinary person. And the rest of the world is going nuts for Scotland right now." He'd paused and added with a knowing grin, "Not to mention your obvious physical attributes.

You really should consider a kilt. By god, the sight of a Scot's knees is enough to make women throw their panties at you."

Simon knew Jasper's rather crass summation of the situation could well be right. He wouldn't be the first documentary maker to find popular fame, gathering female fans along the way. His cousin Calum was a perfect example. Who'd have thought a Scottish bloke climbing up mountains while rambling on about it could catapult a man to celebrity status? But his relation and childhood mate was living proof of the power of television. Yes, Calum would have some advice on wrangling TV groupies if it happened.

And that might not be so bad. With a TV star persona on board, maybe he'd be more confident with women. Perhaps it would open up the opportunity to meet someone special. In his daily work, he brushed alongside many women—students, teaching assistants, colleagues—but all of them pretty much off limits. The university, very wisely, frowned on stepping across the line between professional and personal. And up until recently, he'd been comfortable with not straying over it, not wanting to complicate his life by navigating a tricky relationship.

But this last year, a slow, creeping awareness of his loneliness had settled in alongside him on the long evenings when he sat in his Edinburgh apartment, with only work for company. Sure, he had friends, but at his age, the inevitable fork in their paths, as most found marriage and then children, meant they didn't see each other often. And out in the huge country house, its many empty rooms only emphasised he was alone.

This new direction had the potential to take him down personal paths he'd not ventured along for a while. That would, however, mean addressing the large problem of his lingering mistrust. Surely enough time had passed to put Renee behind him? He wouldn't know for certain until he put it to the test. But he knew he should, unless he was prepared to be single forever.

Of course, the bigger fear was of someone dredging up his past. The thirty-six-year-old Simon Buchanan reflected in his shaving mirror each morning bore scant resemblance to twenty-three-year-old Simon Knight. The grainy newspaper photos, the only permanent record of that turbulent time, would now be relegated to some microfiche. The gaunt young man pictured in them wore a cheap ill-fitting suit, struggling to pull the jacket over his head while he fled to the safety of a car. He looked nothing like the well-groomed, self-assured university lecturer he'd made himself into. He must trust in the illusion. And hope more recent scandals would remain of far greater interest than some politician's dirty business dealings of twenty years ago. He'd be a fool to turn down this opportunity. It was time to step out from beneath his father's long shadow.

Simon gazed out over the navy expanse of the Firth of Forth. From here, it surrounded him on almost all sides. The always spectacular view from Blackness Castle was far more enjoyable today than on his last visit when the wind off the sea had ripped at his face, chilling him to the bone. Despite its unpredictable weather and brooding demeanour, he loved this place. Growing up nearby, this castle still spoke to something deep inside him, setting it apart from the others.

A young woman emerged from the stairwell, and maintaining a polite distance, took up a similar pose, taking in the sea views. She closed her eyes, face lifted to take in the tang of salt carried on a slight breeze, and enjoying the caress of the midday sun that, despite it being almost winter, had a pleasant warmth. In her bright green swing coat, she might have stepped straight out of the 1960s, a vibrant slash of colour against the blue of sky, and mellow golden stone.

He realised that without thinking he had taken a step towards her, and then checked himself. Sensing his presence, maybe hearing him take that step, she opened her eyes. As her gaze met his, the most uncanny wave of recognition swept across him. He encountered dozens of people in his work. The university was an endless bustle. So it wasn't unusual for people he'd met to surface in other places.

She had a pert prettiness about her; shoulder-length dark brown hair that might have been ordinary on a dull day, but today shimmered in the sun with chestnut and copper. And in her golden eyes, focused on him with an unexpected intensity, he thought he saw her own recognition of him.

"Stunning day," he said, unable to suppress his very British habit of opening every conversation with the weather.

"Sure is." Even in those two words, he knew she wasn't Scottish.

"Hi, I'm Simon." He extended a hand.

"Cassie Tremayne," she said.

"New Zealander?" he ventured, realising he'd held onto her hand a little longer than necessary.

"Yes," she said with a light, breezy laugh. "Good guess. But hopefully I'll be able to say I'm Scottish in a few years. Got the passport, but I'm having trouble letting go of my Kiwi accent."

He wouldn't want her to do that. He found its exotic drawl absolutely charming. "Living here now?"

"Yeah, teaching in Edinburgh. Primary school. Loving it. Although it's only been a month. But no regrets so far."

The sensations triggered simply by speaking to her were intriguing. It was strange, this feeling he knew her. Yet he'd never been to New Zealand, and she was a new arrival here.

"How about you?" she asked.

"I'm a historian. Castles are my specialty. Up till now, I've been a university lecturer." Suddenly, he had an urge to tell her. "But I'm about to go into television. Apparently people love Scottish castles."

"Oh definitely. That sounds exciting."

He decided to be bold. Act like the TV star he was about to become, according to Jasper. "It is. Can I buy you a coffee and tell you about it?"

She gave a beguiling little laugh, her eyes crinkling as the small band of freckles on her nose danced in time. "Why not? If I'm going to be properly Scottish, best I swot up on my history."

"So what brings you to Scotland?" Not the most scintillating conversation starter, but he was genuinely curious. Simon reached across to pull out a chair for her at the tiny table. He'd sat at the tables in this cafe many times, but always alone, reading, or jotting down ideas. He had never noticed just how small they were. He and Cassie would be practically knee to knee. But he wouldn't object to the forced intimacy—what man wouldn't want to get close to this woman? He hoped she didn't find it awkward brushing up against a stranger.

She hesitated for a moment before taking her seat, as if no guy had ever offered to hold a chair for her before, then slid into it, suppressing a small smile behind her hand. He felt a rush of pleasure, that the old-fashioned manners drummed into him by his grandmother could still impress a young woman.

"Oh," she said, blinking, with a shake of her head, as if realising she'd not replied. "Um, me, being in Scotland?" He nodded, watching the upturn of her mouth fade a little, and a subtle shadow pass across her eyes. She rallied quickly, her bright words almost too bright. "Well, I came for a holiday, loved it and realised I had no reason to go back to New Zealand. So, here I am."

"But you have family here? The British passport?"

"No, Dad's Scottish—hence the passport—but he's still working in New Zealand. I like to think that me living here might be an incentive for him to come back to Scotland. I know he misses it." He was pleased to hear the sense of permanence with which she spoke, as if this was now her home. "And your mother is a New Zealander?"

"Yes. She was." She closed her eyes and swallowed. This time there was no disguising the emotion on her face. "She died seventeen months ago."

Simon suspected if he asked her how many days it was, she'd be able to tell him. He remembered that rawness, when you ticked off the painful emptiness in small increments, hours, days, weeks, months, and slowly, years. No matter how much time passed, he would never not feel the gaping space created by his mother's death. He wished he could tell Cassie Tremayne that one day it would be OK, but he'd be lying. But he could tell her he understood.

"I'm so sorry," he said, his hand moving spontaneously to cover hers. He noted the neat fingernails, painted a vibrant orange. "You always think you'll have them forever, don't you?"

"Yeah, fucking cancer," she said, the hideous words slipping from her sweet mouth. "Yours?" she asked gently.

"Immune disease, kidneys failed, not enough time to find a donor."

Cassie nodded her acknowledgement, and they sat, neither needing anything more than the comfort of human touch.

Until, with her usual lack of subtlety, dear old Dulcie Grey appeared beside them.

Grinning at Cassie like a loon, she tossed Simon an approving look and a sly wink. He cringed inwardly, hoping Dulcie wasn't about to offer some embarrassing information about him as a kid, or comment on this being the first woman he'd ever brought into the cafe. He may no longer have family here, but these women of the district still took a healthy interest in his welfare. Now one had spotted him in the company of a pretty girl the gossip would be all over the village by the end of the day.

With shaky hands, Dulcie placed two large bowls of coffee before them. They rattled in their colourful saucers and foam overflowed in puddles.

"Generous here," Cassie said. Dulcie beamed at the compliment, floating back to the kitchen for the rest of their order.

"Wait till you see the scones," he said. "A lady down the road bakes them fresh every day. They are seriously impressive."

"This is your home turf, then?"

"Yeah, I grew up here. I have an apartment in Edinburgh too. Need it for work, but this is home."

"Might be a good place for a famous TV star to hide out too," she laughed. He tried not to wince at the suggestion. "Tell me more about this thing you're doing."

Her enthusiastic response as he rambled on about castles, and clans, feuds and battles, helped him to push back the lurking tension. It also supported his earlier optimism that, freed from just being a boring professor in the university history department, the new Simon Buchanan offered something far more appealing. The spark of interest in her eyes was not just his overactive imagination—she liked him.

Staring at her over the space of two more cups of coffee, and some complimentary Eccles cakes Dulcie insisted they must try, he found himself often lost in those eyes, the colour of a pint of ale, golden brown and enticing. And then he'd have to scramble, trying to pick up the threads of the conversation, hoping she wouldn't think him a bumbling idiot.

He liked her too; a lot. They shared an easy connection, even though she hailed from a country thousands of miles from here, and they had practically nothing in common.

At five to three, Dulcie's pointed table-clearing and glances at the clock signalled this blissful interlude was over.

Cassie stood outside, keys in hand, beside a shabby Ford Fiesta, a stark contrast to his shiny black Golf gleaming in the afternoon sun. He wasn't a great catch, but at least he could offer a decent car.

"Back to Edinburgh?" he said. God, he was hopeless at intelligent small talk.

"Yes, I've got a teaching day booked tomorrow. Pays to have an early night before facing a strange mob of unruly kids. And you? Staying at your house here or back to the city?"

"Yeah, back to the city for me, too. I'm covering lectures for a friend. Unruly undergrads. Not so different from your lot, I imagine, just bigger and uglier."

He hesitated a moment, before sticking to his earlier vow to be more decisive where women were concerned. There was something about this woman that wouldn't allow him to just let her drive off out of his life.

"I don't suppose you'd like to grab dinner? There's a fantastic Middle Eastern place near the university. Promise not to keep you out too late."

"I'd like that," she said. "I haven't been out much since I've been here. You know, still getting to know people."

"Well, now you know me. I can pick you up if you like," he offered, hoping he wasn't overstepping the mark, or sounding over-eager. "Parking in the city is always such a pain. And it would save you a taxi fare."

"Thanks, that's great," she said, offering him her phone. "Put your number in here, and I'll text you the address."

He took out his own phone and scrolled past the flurry of texts from Jasper. Just as well he'd had it on silent, otherwise his bloody agent would have completely spoiled the afternoon. The man couldn't seem to leave him alone.

"Oh, Canonmills," he said, as her text flashed on his screen. "I've got an apartment in Stockbridge. We're practically neighbours."

"Well, neighbour," she said with a smile, "it's been good to meet you."

She stretched out a slim hand. He noted that while this one bore a chunky art déco ring, the other was bare. Another good sign. Driving home, he was as excited as a stupid teenager, the evening ahead full of promise.

Chapter 38

Secret Mission

Two years later, Edinburgh, Scotland - October 2021

"Such a great choice. I know you're going to love them." Cassie sealed the brown paper bag with a satisfied pat, the small burgundy and gold 'Dreams In Ink' sticker trapping three books inside. "And when you've finished this *Shades of Magic* series, you've got so many others to look forward to. You know how people ask which books you'd love to read again for the first time?" The young woman nodded back at her, a knowing smile on her cherubic face. "Well, some of hers are like that for me."

"Good to know. Thanks for your help in choosing." She turned to leave, the precious parcel tucked under her arm.

"Oh, and one other thing—she lives here in Edinburgh, too. You might even get to meet her one day. They're talking about a book signing some time."

"I'll look out for it," the girl said, heading out into the brisk autumn afternoon beyond the cosy haven of the shop. Cassie stared after her, dreamily imagining how one day soon it would be her books plucked from the book store making their way to someone's precious shelves. In her mind, she could hear the shop assistant's voice:

"Did you know she lives right here in Edinburgh? How about one of these gorgeous signed special editions?"

A warm ripple of optimism flowed through her. Within mere months, the book sitting with final revisions complete on her laptop would occupy shelf space right here, amongst those of the authors she loved and recommended. The dream was so close now she felt like she could reach out and touch it. With the encouragement of two inspiring women from her writers' group and their innovative little indie publishing house, the characters who had journeyed with her for years would soon step out into the world.

A flash of bright red hair caught her eye, a blaze of colour against the grey day outside. She shook her head from her reverie, feeling her eyes widen, and her mouth slacken in shock as she recognised the man walking towards her with a small suitcase trundling behind him.

"Dad?" she said. "What are you doing here? Is something wrong?"

Worry flared at the sight of him. For her father to arrive unannounced, especially given the difficulties of travel that remained, she assumed the worst. That he would even contemplate navigating the red-tape and inevitable delays of a still pandemic-affected world suggested more than just a hankering to see his daughter. Besides, they talked face to face all the time. Daniel, with colleagues all over the planet was a veteran of virtual meetings from long before it became a necessity. His sudden urgent need to be in Scotland in person troubled her.

"It's OK, kiddo," he said, studying her face, circling his large reassuring hand on her shoulder. "There's nothing to worry about. I'm fine. Bit of a long story." He crossed his arms over his chest and sighed. "I'm here on a mission for your mother."

Cassie shook her head, biting at her lip to suppress a smile. Even more than three years after her death, her mother's wishes had a way of infiltrating their lives. In the final months of her life, in between a last desperate flurry of painting, Blair wrote. Filling her journal with lists, writing her family notes, sending emails with suggestions of things they should (or shouldn't) do in a future she wouldn't be part of. None of them minded. Rereading her words and sometimes filling those small demands brought a sense that she was still with them. Joking about her ability to still order them around, laughing at how even now Blair could manipulate the world into a shape she would find more pleasing, took some of the jagged edges off their pain.

But most of these requests had been little things.

Archie, I hate to say this about something permanently etched on your body, but that latest piece—it's a little clumsy. Please, promise me you'll try to find a different tattooist for your next one.

He had.

Cassie, the other day online, I met a woman who is a literary agent. Here's her number. When the book is finished, make sure you call her.

She hadn't.

Daniel, I've prepaid the cemetery cleaning company to maintain Granny's headstone. Please check they are doing it as in the contract. I suspect they are not.

They weren't.

Nik, here's the entry details for the Aotearoa Art Innovator Awards. I really think you've got a good chance of winning the Jewellery Art Design category.

He did.

None of the requests Cassie had seen were the sorts of things that might propel her father across the world, travelling for thirty hours solid. Whatever wish he needed to fulfil on behalf of his wife, it must be important.

"Anyway, aside from that, let's say this time, I had a hankering to shake the hand of the man who put an engagement ring on my little girl's hand before he married her." He beamed at her, the dimples that had so charmed her mother dancing on his cheeks. "Come on, give your old dad a hug."

She stepped round the desk into his arms.

"Then why didn't you tell us you were coming?" she murmured against his broad chest, inhaling the family spicy smell of his aftershave. "We could have met you at the airport."

"I suspected you might do what everyone at home has been doing—tell me I'm mad. To be honest, I've had raging cabin fever. This being locked inside our own country for months on end was messing with my head. It's the longest I've been in one place since I left home as a teenager. Besides, I've already had the bloody COVID, so between that and all the vaccinations, I think I'm fairly safe."

She wouldn't argue with him. Biology might not be his field, but he was a scientist. If he thought there was sufficient evidence travel was safe, then who was she, an ex-primary school teacher, yet-to-be-published author and book shop assistant to argue? Besides, he looked as vigorous as ever, his face still relatively unlined, and his hair vibrant without the silvering that dulled so many red-heads as they aged.

"I'm nearly finished for the day. We're on winter hours already. Closing at four."

He glanced down at the chunky watch on his wrist, a Tag Heuer, bought not for status but because it was sufficiently robust to survive his still frequent escapades in the outdoors. "Anywhere I can sit for a bit and stash this luggage?"

"Nice pub two doors down. Why don't I meet you there? And I'll send Simon a text to come and get us in the car. We don't want to be dragging that in the dark. Give it here." She tucked the compact case behind the counter, turning a smile on the next customer, who patiently waited for her attention.

She arrived at the bar to find him propped at a leaner, a tall glass of his favourite Tennent's lager in front of him, and deep in lively conversation with another man. Travelling the world solo had made Daniel Tremayne adept at finding company in strangers, despite a natural shyness.

He raised a hand, and her heart leapt at that smiling face she knew so well. It *was* good to have him here. More than two years since she'd seen him, except on grainy FaceTime calls or the family zooms he'd tried to coax a reluctant Archie to join from his grungy Auckland flat. It *had* been too long.

A pang of guilt stabbed at her for abandoning him. But two years ago, when she'd made the decision to stay, he'd agreed it was the right thing; insisted that she shouldn't come home for him, that he was doing OK. And then suddenly she couldn't, anyway. Closed borders and a crazy lottery to get back into New Zealand with almost impossible odds had left her trapped here in the UK, grateful for a second country that she could claim as her own as a refuge. She'd found safety with Simon just in time—before the world went mad.

She'd tried to assuage her guilt at staying by holding tight to thoughts of all those years her father had been self-sufficient in some far-flung part of the world away from family. He was a resilient man. But in those days, he'd always had the thought of Blair waiting for him, and her, and Archie. Now he was completely on his own.

He pointed towards a vacant booth near the back of the bar. "What will you have, love? Glass of wine? Beer?"

"A glass of red would be nice, thanks Dad." She shuffled into the seat, like a soft leather cocoon, wrangling the case in with her. Luckily, her father's wandering days had also given him the ability to travel light.

She'd barely downed one mouthful of the slightly acidic house wine he'd handed her when Simon arrived, looking harried. Parking anywhere in central Edinburgh was enough to test most people's patience. "Might as well have bloody walked," he said, stooping to kiss her. "I'm sorry, the car's a good three blocks away. Best I could do."

Her father stood. Dr Daniel Tremayne extended his hand to Dr Simon Buchanan. They'd spoken, of course; even seen each other over a screen when she'd pressured Simon into a family zoom. Including the day just a month ago after Simon had proposed, and she'd said yes. Facing him in person was different, and way out of Simon's comfort zone. His usual strong handshake, confident when meeting with his academic equals, faltered a little in the grip of his girlfriend's father.

This was only the second time ever she'd introduced her father to someone. The first was nervous eighteen-year-old Nik, uncomfortable in a suit at the altar of a church next to a pregnant teenage bride. What a contrast to this meeting with sophisticated Simon in his button down and well-cut wool coat. But here was her father, once again his solid presence standing behind her choices. In the same way he'd once signalled acceptance of a nervous Nik, Daniel pulled Simon into a fatherly hug.

"Simon, great to be here," he said. "Let me buy you a drink."

"I'll get it," she offered, leaving her two favourite Scots to get better acquainted.

CHAPTER 39

My Darling Girl

Cassie

Edinburgh, Scotland - October 2021

SIMON INSISTED ON TAKING care of the dinner dishes, although, as usual, he'd cooked.

"Go on," he said, planting a kiss on her forehead as he shooed her away. "Spend some time with him."

In the little lounge room, her father sipped on a whisky, his eyes half-closed in blissful appreciation.

"It's good, isn't it?" Even at this distance, the smoky molecules drifting towards her tantalised her nose. She could probably identify which bottle it had come from by that alone.

He grinned at her. "So this Scotsman has made a whisky drinker out of you, too?"

"He has."

"And other things as well, I see. Like happy."

"Yeah, Dad, he has."

"Well, that's good."

They sat in silence, the words not needing to be spoken. She and Nik had been happy, too. And then they weren't. And she admired both of them for the way they'd dealt with that realisation. Young Nik and Cassie, emotionally turbulent and wildly in love, had become older, wiser Nik and Cassie who'd navigated their parting with a sad resignation. They'd got out lightly, escaping the type of damage that some people carried with them for life. Her first love, while not enduring, had found its home with a good man. And now another good man had fallen into her life.

Her father cleared his throat after a minute, setting his glass down, and reaching inside his ever present leather satchel. Scuffed from years of bobbing along at his side, it had been a constant companion on jaunts everywhere from the sub-Antarctic islands to the deserts of Northern Africa. Inside, he carried his stash of notebooks and dog-eared papers. In recent years, he'd made space for technology by adding a light-as-air laptop. He pulled out a cream envelope. She read her name inscribed on the front in the indigo ink of her mother's favourite old fountain pen.

"Do you know what's in it?" she asked.

He nodded. "Roughly. I needed to know. You'll see why."

His face had remained fixed in a crinkle of pleasure for almost the entire time since his arrival. But now his mouth set in a small tense line, knowledge of this envelope's contents casting a serious shadow over the evening.

She flipped open the envelope and pulled out three sheets of heavy paper, filled with her mother's flowing cursive script.

My darling girl

The fact that you're reading this means that events I feared, and maybe others I hoped for, have happened. Your father promised me that should the time come when you needed to hear this, he would do this last thing for me. Know we both love you so very much, and want nothing but happiness for you.

If you have this letter, then what you and your beautiful Nik had, has ended. Even just thinking of that possibility now as I write this, when it isn't a reality—when it is still something that may never happen—makes me incredibly sad.

The moment he walked into our house, I knew he was the one for you. I think he knew it too, even though it took you a little longer to realise that. I hope the circumstances of your parting haven't caused you too much pain, and that you might still hold on to a little piece of that past love. They were good years, Cassie. Don't let whatever has divided you erase the memories of the things you shared.

But it isn't you and Nik who are uppermost on my mind. It is you and the man who you now seek to build a future with. A man I will never meet, can know nothing about, except this—he is also the one for you. Because I believe the people we need are sent to us.

Your father agreed that should the things you are now living come to pass, we owe this to you. He promised me that should he even suspect there is a chance that your life's path might mirror our own, he would arm you with the knowledge we gained along the way. We understand the experience, because we have lived it.

You will recall the story of how your father and I met and fell in love. A man with stars in his eyes and a wandering artist, a chance meeting at a castle in Scotland and, as they say—the rest is history. But there are parts to the story that are not quite as we told it.

I still lack the words to describe what happened back then in 1990, in that place. But then I'm the dreamer, and perhaps your father, the scientist, may be the better one to explain. Although I think the events surrounding our meeting still challenge everything he knows about the universe, and that's saying something, as you well know, with that formidable mind of his.

But he believes the truth of our story. We have talked through it so many times, and, while the theory of what happened is hazy (you can imagine how much Daniel hates that!!), the evidence that it did indeed happen is real and tangible.

You know how I have always been so protective of the paintings of your father that hang in our bedroom. You know how I lived in dread that something might happen to them when I impulsively agreed to let Elias have them for those few months.

There is a reason for this, and it's not only my own sentimentality. The fact is Cassie, those three paintings are not of this place and maybe not of this time. Those paintings are the only evidence that your father and I shared a life elsewhere. Rather than drive ourselves mad seeking more support for our story, we have, for the most part, simply accepted the truth of it. Although I know your father still craves answers in science. Who knows, he may yet win a Nobel prize for his quest.

I'll leave him to share the rest of our story. But I wanted you to know that it was my wish for him to do so. And to reassure you that your father hasn't descended into senility with these crazy claims.

My darling, if Daniel and I have indeed lived other lives, I hope with all my heart that you (and Archie) were there in other versions of our family. It comforts me that there are versions of myself who got to see you have your own child, got to be the crazy old granny.

I love you, to the moon and back, to the stars and beyond.

Blair

Through a fog of tears, Cassie neatly folded the pages, trying not to blot the blue ink with her damp hands. Her mother was right. Simon had been sent to her. From some other time and some other life, destined to be here with her in this one.

"So," her father said, with an expectant look. "You know I have a story to tell. What I want to know is, do you also have a story to tell me?"

She nodded and reached for her phone. Flicking open the photo montage, she scrolled back to a day in late September two years ago, and thrust the screen at him. For the first time, she had someone to share those pictures with who wouldn't think her mad.

"And I gather you don't recall these?" he asked.

"No. On September 25th, 2019, I was on the Outlander tour—with Nik."

"You were at that castle?"

"Yes, Blackness. It was one of the stops."

"And Simon? Do you know where he was?"

Even now, under her father's gaze, she flushed with embarrassment, knowing how she'd acquired the answer to that question. Nosing through Simon's notebooks with their carefully dated entries, all lined up on in the shelf in his office in careful chronological order, she'd felt like a traitor, but compelled to find out. And she had.

"At Blackness Castle. Alone."

"And he doesn't know?"

She shook her head miserably. Keeping the existence of the photographs from Simon had never sat well with her, but how could she tell him? Even with her father's reassuring presence; even with him lending his reputation as a man of integrity to support her claim that the photographs were no illusion; tearing away the veil of dishonesty she'd hidden behind—that should be torn away—terrified her.

How could she tell a man who trusted so few that she hadn't been completely honest with him? Simon loved her. He'd found those words early in their relationship. But she feared love might not be enough to carry them through the turbulent time ahead. Or to allow her to keep a secret from him forever.

———

Cassie lay back in their bed, propped up by a mountain of pillows, the heavy covers pulled tight against the slight chill in the air. She braved pulling her left hand free, twirling the beautiful antique engagement ring. Even after a month, it felt strange to once again feel a ring sitting on her third finger, and she kept needing to touch it, confirming it was really there.

She had tucked away those other rings that told of her life with Nik, deep in a drawer. She was unsure what to do with them. Unlike the previous owner of this ring, she could never part with them. They remained a reminder of the innocent love of two kids, and the happiness they had found for much of ten years together. Besides, tarnished by one failed marriage, could they cast a shadow over another? Once she would have scoffed at such fanciful notions, but in the last two years she had become comfortable with the unexplained. And she was about to take a gamble that Simon could be comfortable with it, too.

She was sure her father's sudden need visit an old friend in Aberdeen for the weekend, was his way of giving her space to do what was right. She couldn't go into a marriage with Simon with secrets between them, even if this secret had the potential to flip everything they knew upside down.

Her mother had taken such a risk. Her father had admitted to his struggle with the knowledge, but the evidence of the paintings and his love for her mother had got them through. She had to believe those photographs and the love of a man who wanted to spend the rest of his life with her would sustain them in the same way through the fallout from this strange impending conversation.

Small noises drifted in—the chug and hiss of the stove top coffee maker; the fridge door closing with a slight puff; George the cat offering a disappointed yowl as Simon lightly scolded him for demanding treats—and his soft footsteps as he headed back to the bedroom.

She took the warm cup from him, placing it on the bedside table, while he slid in beside her. He snuggled up to her, and she jumped at the chill of his feet.

"Sorry," he said with a smirk. "But they did get that way making you a coffee. Maybe this will take your mind off them." His hand snaked down across her waist, edging closer to her thigh, and she shivered at the touch and let out a gasp.

"Shit! Cold hands too!"

"They won't be for long," he said, grinning up at her. She could feel the hard length of his erection against her lower back.

"God, you're bloody insatiable."

"You didn't seem to mind last night."

"No, not at all, but maybe we could come up for air long enough to have a coffee and perhaps breakfast? After all, we've got all day."

Sundays were bliss. The other six days of the week Simon was always busy, juggling lectures, marking assignments, publicity for the upcoming TV series and research for his next book, while she was tied to the bookshop. She loved spending time there, amongst antique shelves straight out of *Harry Potter*. And she needed the money. Her own book wouldn't launch till spring and even then, this author thing was a long game. She didn't expect to be an overnight success. So, for now, Sunday was the only day guaranteed totally for them.

"Hmm," he hummed against her neck. "I wasn't planning to spend all of it in bed, tempting as it is."

"Oh?"

"Well, I wanted to take a drive out to Blackness. There's a minor question that's been bothering me, something I'd like to check. And I thought it might be appropriate, having just got engaged. Go back to where it all started. God, I still remember that day you appeared. It was as if you somehow belonged there."

Now was her opening. Who knew what the outcome of this conversation would be? But she couldn't carry this strange secret on her own any longer.

"Simon." Her throat tightened. Anxiety surged. "There's something I need to show you."

"Sounds ominous." He raised one dark eyebrow. "I hope you're not about to tell me you've changed your mind."

Her laugh came out small and nervous. "No, I definitely have not changed my mind. But there's something that's been messing with it."

CHAPTER 40

Flight

Edinburgh, Scotland - October 2021

SIMON WATCHED, INTRIGUED, AS, with a shaky hand, Cassie reached for her phone. She began scrolling through photographs, her finger finally settling on what she was looking for. She held it out to him.

"These three," she whispered.

He took the phone, puzzled by her hesitant expression and the un-expected hint of fear in her eyes. He flipped back and forth through the innocuous images, unsure of what he was meant to be seeing.

"So. Me. Me again. Me and you at Blackness. Although I can't remember who took that," he said, peering at the last one.

"Nor can I," she said. "But it's not so much who took it, it's when."

He checked the date. September 25th, 2019.

"Do you remember the date we met? It's not a test," she added, with a tense smile. "Promise I won't give your ring back if you get it wrong." She always made jokes when nervous. He smiled back, wondering why all of this was unsettling her.

"Of course I remember. Not only because it's etched permanently on my heart," he teased, sensing a need to keep things light. "I also know the date because I'd had the phone call that morning to say the TV series was all go. Who would have predicted that the two biggest moments of my life would happen on the same day?"

"And that's not the date." She pointed to the screen.

"No," he said, his brows creasing into a frown. "That's odd. It's almost a month before. There has to be something wrong with your phone set-tings." He swiped up, closing the photographs, and tapped the settings icon.

She took a deep breath and exhaled with a sigh.

"No, Simon. There's nothing wrong with the phone. There are some things I need to tell you."

———

He lay back on the bed next to her, stunned into silence.

After years of plunging into old books, trying to extract the truth from amongst the fiction and folklore, Simon was used to strange stories. He just wasn't used to ones that included him. Surprisingly, perhaps, for a person who dealt in historical facts, over the years his work had led him to develop an open mind to all kinds of possibilities, and a belief in the existence of things beyond human understanding. So, Cassie's story, while bizarre, wasn't something he would simply reject out of hand.

But it wasn't thoughts of impossible photos or mysterious premonitions that troubled him. Even notions of half-remembered other lives and convoluted ripples in time didn't bother him. He'd read articles where reputable scientists tossed around theories that suggested such things couldn't be ruled out.

More disturbing was the knowledge Cassie had not only kept secrets from him, but these were secrets that went right back to the very heart of their relationship, from the very first day they'd met—well, the first day they'd met in this life, if this whole 'other life' thing was true.

"That first day at Blackness. You knew who I was? You *knew*?" Some angry creature inside took hold of him, and he flung the words at her like an accusation.

Eyes wide, her voice rose in response. "I knew you were Simon Buchanan. I knew you were a university lecturer. I knew you were 'The Castle Hunter'. Nothing more. But I also knew you were the man in these photos. And that I had no choice but to find you."

"Stalk me, you mean," he spat. Some bitter, twisted part of himself had taken control.

"Simon, when I found these photographs, and saw us there, happy, in love—just as the first love of my life was about to climb on a plane, leaving me feeling like that was my lot, and I might never have anyone love me like that again—could you *blame* me for needing to find you? Should I have just deleted them as some aberration? In my position, Simon, what would you have chosen to do?"

He ignored her question. "But once you found me, you had a choice, too. The choice to tell me the truth, Cassie."

"I'm telling you now, Simon. And if I'd done it any earlier, would the outcome have been any different? In fact, what could I have done differently?"

He had no answers. He could see the fight go out of her in reply to his silence. The tears she'd bravely held back, biting at her lip, now forced their way out.

Fight or flight. That's what animals did. He didn't want to fight with her anymore. The only other option was to get the hell out of here before he did any more damage.

"I can't deal with this right now, Cassie. I need some space."

He grabbed a duffle bag from the wardrobe, grasping at a few clothes, rolling them in tidy bundles, neatly adding underwear, socks, and some toiletries.

"Simon, this is ridiculous. I know this stuff is crazy. It's making *you* crazy. Talk to me," she pleaded.

"I have to get out of here."

"Simon, why are you doing this? Why?"

"I'm going to head out to Blackness. I'll stay over." He picked up the bag.

"Simon," she said. He saw her renewed courage as she leapt from the bed and stood, hands braced in the doorway. "You can go, if that's what you need to do. But not until you give me an explanation. You owe me that, at least. Simon, no matter what you think I've done, I deserve to know why you're behaving like this."

It was his turn to admit defeat. She was right to stand up to him; to call him out. It wasn't fair to just walk away from her. That simply made him a coward, like his father. He dumped the bag on the floor, and pulled over a chair, taking a seat opposite the bed.

"This won't take long," he said. He waved a hand at the bed. "But you still might want to sit down." She moved to sit on the bed, back rigid against the headboard, knees drawn up to her chin, sheet pulled over them, the edge scrunched tight, her hands twisting and untwisting the fabric in anxious knots. She surveyed him with wary eyes.

"My real name is Simon Knight. My father was an arsehole with a high public profile, a coward who left my mother and I to bear the brunt of his immoral and illegal actions. Including leaving us in the firing line of our wonderful British tabloid journalists. And ever since I've done my best to keep under the radar, because there are people out there who love nothing better to dredge up the past, to make insinuations about me, who would have me believe I'm destined to be just like him..."

He choked on the words. Deep inside, he held this fear, one that although he knew it to be completely irrational, he still couldn't let go of. Despite trying his best to be a better man than his father, he suspected he carried some inherited weakness, some deep flaw. And he worried the day would come, when he'd be labelled his father's son, and have no means to dispute it.

"But Simon," she whispered, "I'm not one of those people."

"My last girlfriend was." Her eyes widened, flooded with realisation. A small nod of her head confirmed he didn't need to explain further, not for now, anyway. Cassie understood that today, as she'd revealed her duplicity, she and Renee had become one in his mind.

"I'm so sorry, Simon."

"So, you can see, I've got the double whammy; daddy issues and trust issues. Which makes me a complicated bastard. And sometimes, like today, I'm just a bastard."

"No, you're not," she said, stretching her hand to curl over his. He gently pushed it aside.

"But I am," he said. Guilt at what he'd just put her through washed away any anger he might have felt towards her. Overcome with shame, he still needed to leave. Through a fog, he grabbed at the bag,

"I'll call you," he said. He laid a hand in farewell on the ginger cat curled at the foot of the bed, oblivious to the fraught air in the room. Simon hurried downstairs, trying to steel his heart against the guttural sobs wracking her body, a sound he knew would haunt him as he drove out to his other house, and keep him awake tonight alone in his bed. He felt a stab of unease that what he'd come to think of as theirs might soon be just his once again.

CHAPTER 41

Refuge

Blackness, Scotland - October 2021

SIMON STRODE UP THE road towards the castle, hoping to make it beyond Morag's place undetected. He couldn't face a second day of awkward questions and the lies that spilled from his mouth in response. But no, it was too late. Morag waved at him as she shuffled down her garden path. It would be rude not to stop, particularly in the light of the slow progress she made towards him on unsteady legs.

In the six months he and Cassie lived here in 2020, the lockdown had thrust them together all day, every day. The neighbours in this row of rural cottages had offered some reprieve from that intensity. Cut off from the world, friendly conversations between locals had been a lifeline for all of them. But especially for two people feeling their way in a relationship, both new and thrilling, yet daunting from the overwhelming speed with which they'd fallen into it.

And from those conversations, Cassie and Morag had formed an un-likely but firm friendship. Morag repaid their companionship with gifts of scones and muffins passed over the fence. And, as they'd realised they were safe here in this refuge, the clandestine visits began. With no one to dob them in for breaking the rules, he'd found Morag in his kitchen, teaching Cassie to cook with a patience he didn't possess. He smiled even now at Morag's resilience. And Cassie's persistence. He was sure she'd only done it for him.

"Simon, I've got some gooseberries for you to take home to Cassie. It's the very last of them. Tell her to whip up one of those pies for your dessert one evening. Or she can pop them in the freezer to use later if she hasn't time. Nothing nicer on a cold winter night—a slice of gooseberry pie with a dollop of cream."

She flashed him her wide, toothy smile. As always, her face crinkled in pleasure at offering gifts from her garden. "I'll just leave them here." She tucked a container inside the letterbox. "Grab them on your way back from your walk."

"Thanks Morag, they'll be grand."

"Well, I know how that girl loves to cook for you. Just as well I taught her how to make something that won't give us all a bellyache." She tossed him a conspiratorial wink. "Don't tell her I said that, will you? Hate to knock her confidence."

"I promise." He plastered on a smile. Behind it, dread nagged at him. When would he see Cassie again? Was he ready to face her yet? Would he return to Edinburgh before the damn gooseberries turned to mush, or would he continue to hide out here? With what he hoped looked like a cheerful wave, he turned and headed towards Blackness.

At this time of day, before the tourists came, he had the castle all to himself. This place had always been his bolt hole. These days he'd forged such a good relationship with the trust who ran it, he even had after-hours access. It had started during the months of isolation on discovering the yett blocking the caponier unlocked; the padlock closed but not clicked in properly. He'd become an unofficial security patrol of sorts, and they were happy for that to continue.

He traced his usual morning route, out to the point first, then back into the castle proper, through the gloomy tunnel before bursting into the light of the brutal courtyard; up the stairs of the north tower, then out onto the bow. He loved this spot where in the distance, sea met sky in a golden haze; it was where he'd met Cassie. Or she'd met him. Thoughts of that morning, now with other unpleasant associations, came barrelling in, slapping at him with a mix of anger, fear, and guilt.

It was the last emotion that pushed its way forward today. Perhaps it was Morag's blithe assumption that they were still a couple, madly in love, her baking up culinary treats for him, happily playing house back in Edinburgh. The only thing standing between him and that blissful scene was him.

Him and his reaction to a woman who'd done nothing but offer him honesty—despite the cost. But to go beyond that required him to forgive. And what she'd revealed yesterday, the subterfuge, the internet stalking—my god, the outright bloody lying in wait to pounce on him—had seemed unforgivable.

He abandoned the rest of the walk, each miserable step taking him back over the same old ground, and the same harrowing thoughts. He didn't know how to fix this, or even if he had the capacity to do so. At the entranceway, he pulled the grilled gate closed behind him, not bothering to lock it. At nearly quarter to nine by his phone, it wouldn't be long before the first tourists arrived by car. Usually, the trail of buses snaked up the road around ten. Being here early gave him precious time alone with the stones and his thoughts.

Except that looking down the road, today another early bird approached on foot. Maybe Morag had a guest. They came in a fairly steady stream even now, as the season turned towards winter.

The man walking towards him was tallish, broad shouldered and covered the path between them with the ease of someone well-accustomed to hiking. The morning sun bounced off his bright red hair, a sight that should also have been a red flag, but wasn't.

Remaining absorbed in his troubles, it was only as they came within feet of each other he became aware that the man was fixated on him. He came to a halt as he registered Daniel Tremayne's hand extending towards him.

"Good morning, Simon. Up and about early, eh?" The paw-like grasp of the handshake tugged away any shreds of equilibrium he'd found on the castle wall. At least the guy hadn't hit him, because even pushing seventy, he reckoned Daniel Tremayne had the air of someone who could throw a handy punch. Not that anything in his body language suggested belligerence. But given how Simon had damaged the heart of his only child, anything was possible.

"You're staying at Morag's?"

"Morag's?" Daniel looked puzzled.

"Yeah, the B&B."

"No," he laughed. "Overnight dash down from Aberdeen. Maybe you'd shout me a coffee? God knows I need one."

While Daniel appeared relaxed perched on a stool at his kitchen counter, Simon's hands shook as he retrieved the little Italian stove-top pot from the pantry. "Sorry, only this old thing."

"Don't apologise. For someone of my generation, those were a lifesaver. Got us away from the bloody awful instant which most people offered you back then."

Daniel grinned at him, but even that and the usually comforting smell of coffee brewing did nothing to reassure him. The jiggle of the large cup on its saucer betrayed the tremor in his hands. Daniel didn't appear to notice. Perhaps he'd assumed his future son-in-law to be a little clumsy. That's if he and Cassie made it back to a place where that future still awaited them.

The silence hung between them. The ordinary sounds—the hiss of steam, the burble of liquid poured into cups and the rattle of a spoon as Daniel heaped sugar into his—provided a welcome backdrop to their lack of small talk. He settled himself onto a stool beside Daniel, preferring not to face him directly. Whatever was coming, it wouldn't be easy.

"Milk?" he offered as an afterthought. Daniel shook his head, stirring the spoon lazily in the blackness of his coffee.

"Simon, I'm not here for Cassie. She told me you were here, but she didn't ask me to come. I'm here for you." As expected, Daniel Tremayne didn't beat around the bush.

"Saving me from myself?"

"No, not at all. I'm saving from you having to go through something I went through alone. And telling you, I'll stand beside you as you weather what might be one of the most difficult things your mind will ever face. You and I are men of facts and figures. And none of that will help you now."

Simon couldn't help but frown. What was the man on about?

"What might help," Daniel said, stirring some more in the opposite direction, "is to start by accepting that those photographs are real, despite their impossibility."

He'd been so fixated on Cassie's deceit, he'd spent little time thinking about the photographs.

"And what if I do?" he asked, curiosity piqued.

"I'll tell you a story," he said. "And maybe within that, you'll find a way out of this whole damn mess. Might take a while. Perhaps we should settle somewhere more comfortable?"

Daniel poured his large frame off the stool and, without invitation, headed for the open door of the lounge.

He couldn't think straight with Daniel Tremayne in his house. Thankfully, the man let him off the hook. Gone by lunchtime, claiming an appointment with an old science faculty colleague back in Edinburgh, Simon breathed relief at his freedom, no longer obliged to offer further hospitality.

In the upstairs bedroom, he spotted one of Cassie's socks lurking under a chair. She was so bloody untidy, but he'd learned to live with that. He dropped it into the laundry hamper in the ensuite before slumping on his bed. That's what it came down to really: there were things about another person you could learn to live with, and then there were the non-negotiables.

He'd always believed honesty to be one of those non-negotiables. There was no room for shades of grey, only the black and white truth of the matter. Yes, that's what he'd believed, bloody hypocrite that he was. Because he hadn't been honest either. She had kept secrets. But so had he. He'd kept so much from her. Big things.

How could she have known that such a small betrayal of trust was huge in that fucked-up brain of his? Sure, she knew he struggled with letting people get close to him. She understood his nervousness at being the face of a TV series, becoming recognisable. But she didn't know why. He'd never told her the truth. Damn it, she didn't even know his true name till this blew up between them. Names held power, yet he hadn't trusted her enough to hand her that power.

Cassie thought she understood the reason he pummelled that bag in the gym every morning. But she was wrong. Attributing it to the battle against the same general pressures that dogged everyone in this modern world—work stress, anxiety over money, the normal day-to-day problems—she was oblivious to the reality. He fought the demons of his past. She hadn't known that his demons had names: Mark Fremont, tabloid journalist; Renee Kingston, untruthful girlfriend; and Graham Knight, a father who had never made the effort to reach out to his son, not even once.

And the image on his back? To Cassie, it was simply an intriguing piece of artwork. He'd played up the notion that it was just a wry juxtaposition of his outwardly conservative exterior with the tattooed body that lay beneath the neat button-down shirts and sports jackets. He'd never hinted that it was anything more; never opening up to explain its presence as a metaphor for the extreme measures he'd taken to reclaim his life.

He should have told her upfront. She was braver than him. He knew the most intimate depths of her past. He'd held her close while she dampened his shirt with tears for a lost baby. She'd led him through the story of her marriage, how it had not only sprung from necessity but a sincere, although youthful love. He'd clasped her hand as she described its slow decay, torn between supporting her husband while denying her own needs. His heart had ached for her pain, watching her face crumple as she questioned if she might have done more to save their marriage. Although he'd inwardly struggled, he'd supported her when she sent a tentative email to Nik, in the hope of salvaging a friendship, and tried to appear pleased for her when he'd responded.

He wondered if she might reach out to her ex now? If he and Cassie couldn't repair things between them, might she go to him? That prospect triggered confusion. A surge of bitter jealousy battled with the thought that at least she wouldn't be left alone. Disappointment that she might replace him so easily mingled with despair at the thought of going back to a life without her.

Just like her mother before her, Cassie had faced the fear. She had revealed all, even this bizarre secret of a shared past that neither could recall. Meanwhile, he'd cowered behind this facade he'd built until she'd forced him from behind it. He hated himself for it. And the only way out of this descent into self-loathing was to stop thinking and take action.

She didn't answer immediately. He almost expected the call to go to voicemail.

"Hey." The word came out small and hesitant.

"Hey you. Everything OK there?"

"Yeah, you know. George is camped by the fridge, looking hopeful." Damn cat, so typical of him to take liberties while he was away. "Oh, and I can hear that dripping sound you thought might be a leak in the loft again." He really must take a look up there. "But yeah, apart from that, it's OK. How about you?"

Simon hesitated. Was it better to keep up the small talk? Ease into more important subjects through mundane conversation? Or tell her now what she needed to know? He should have planned this better.

He took a deep breath. "I'm on my way home."

CHAPTER 42

Explosion

Edinburgh, Scotland - December 2021

SIMON WOKE IN A tangle of limbs, his massive hard-on nudging at Cassie's hip, her breath tickling his neck, and small needles rhythmically piercing the skin of his lower back.

"Piss off, George," he said, reaching an arm behind him to sweep the cat off the bed.

"Poor George," Cassie hummed against his skin. "He only does it to show he loves you."

"Like hell he does," he said. "He was taken off his mother too young. It's some bizarre feline self-soothing ritual, nothing to do with me."

The brush of her warm chuckle felt good, as did her lips murmuring against his collarbone. "You're such a nerd, Simon Buchanan. You've only been awake two minutes and you're psycho-analysing the cat."

"Forget the cat," he said, the words hoarse, as she lightly rubbed her warm centre against his thigh. "There's another pussy demanding attention here. You are so damn fuckable, grinding that sweet clit against me."

"God, a filthy-mouthed nerd," she groaned, pressing her mouth to his with an inviting thrust of her body. The warm folds brushing his skin commanded his cock to full attention, as she cooed breathily against him. "You are so my type."

It never failed to bring a smile to his face when she was like this; the contradiction was delicious. He'd never have guessed at the smut this sweet little thing concealed in the pages of her writing; or predicted the delight she took at him talking dirty to her within their private world beyond the bedroom door. Nor would he have ever imagined how that knowledge would provoke words spewing out of his mouth that he'd never previously thought himself capable of uttering aloud.

With a shove, he flipped her onto her back, and she lay there sparkling up at him, breath coming more quickly, eyes dancing in anticipation. He ran a finger lightly down between her pale breasts, so soft and full and languid, in contrast to the erect nipples that begged for his touch. He circled back giving each one a playful tweak. She shivered as he traced the curve of her stomach, lingering there for a moment, drawing lazy spirals on her skin, watching her body come to life under his, and her mouth slacken.

"Enjoy resting those beautiful lips," he said, lifting his thumb to brush across them. "They've got work ahead of them." His hands went back to their quest, trailing along the velvet skin inside her thigh before seeking the warm wetness he knew lay beyond. "But for now, shall we let mine do the work, eh?"

He dropped his head to her stomach, lapping at the salt-sweet taste of her skin all the way down until his tongue was buried deep and she mewled like a hungry kitten and writhed beneath him. *Perfect Sunday morning.*

"My god, you're a dirty wee girl, Cassie Tremayne." She grinned down at him from her perch, still firmly astride his fast fading cock. "And fuck I like it."

"Just as well," she said. "Would be a pity to have spent all that energy if you didn't." She rolled off him amongst a small flood of sticky bodily fluids. "This dirty girl might go and clean herself up a bit," she said, planting her bruised lips on his, before swinging her legs over the side of the bed, hands grappling on the floor for her robe.

"Make me a coffee too?" he said as she tied the garment loosely, leaving a tantalising peek of those breasts that made him want to free one and suck hard on the still swollen bud of a nipple pressed against the fabric.

"Sure," she said.

"And see if the Sunday paper's there?" he called after her as she padded towards the bathroom. His eyes followed the gorgeous sway of her arse. He still wasn't ruling out abandoning the newspaper in favour of repeating other Sunday morning indulgences.

She returned after a while, a coffee in each hand and her iPad tucked under her arm.

"No paper yet?"

"No," she frowned. "It's late. Maybe the press broke down again."

"Maybe," he said, feeling a little peeved. He loved the ritual of the Sunday paper. Usually they divvied up the sections, except for the sports section—it held no attraction for either of them—which they relegated to the floor. It came in handy to place under George's litter tray.

He sipped at his coffee, while beside him Cassie sat with knees drawn up, iPad propped on them, scrolling through her social media. He couldn't see the attraction himself. But she thrived on it. She hummed away happily, checking her beloved Bookstagram, smiling at the screen as small stabs of her finger triggered blasts of music.

"Oh." She paused, tilting her head to one side. "Did you hear that? I'm sure that was the sound of the newspaper hitting the doormat."

Amazing she could hear anything over the damn Bookstagram symphony.

"I'll go," she offered. "Top up the coffee?"

He shook his head.

She returned a few minutes later, distributing the parts of the newspaper between them like a dealer laying cards on the table with a well-practised hand.

He grabbed up the main section, immediately drawn to an international relations opinion piece. Like the author, he found the images of Russian troops massing on the border with Ukraine rather disturbing.

Meanwhile, Cassie flicked through the Leisure & Lifestyle section, where she always turned straight to the latest book reviews, no doubt imagining a day very soon where hers might feature.

"My god, Simon. Listen to this." The excitement in her voice jarred him out of the gloomy world situation. "It's an article in the TV section, '22 New Shows for 2022'." She folded back the page and began to read.

"*Darling of the Scottish history community, Simon Buchanan—*" She laughed, casting him a sideways glance. "Darling? What have you been up to behind my back?—*the University Of Edinburgh professor aka 'The Castle*

Hunter' brings to life the much-lauded book of his meanderings around Scottish castles. Expect spectacular landscapes, stories of brutal battles and, of course, captivating castles, all delivered to the screen with the dry sense of humour that has kept Buchanan's book solidly in our non-fiction Top 100 list since its 2017 release. Production company, Caledonia, reports filming of the project, working title 'Stories of the Stones', will begin in February, for an October release."

She looked at him, eyes wide. "It's happening Simon. It's really happening. There's even a picture of you. The one from the book."

He cringed. *And so it begins.* He closed his eyes and tried to take slow breaths to steady himself while talking this through in his head. This was to be expected. It was the first, and there would be more, but he must have faith in the production company and their PR team to roll out this sort of publicity in a controlled and predictable build up. There would be no surprises, just careful press releases feeding into articles like this one. He'd read it for himself later, but there was nothing to worry about here. He opened his eyes, picked up the local news section lying on the bed next to him, and forced himself back to reading.

"Simon."

"Mmmm," he said, not really listening, now buried deep in a lengthy article detailing local outrage at the council's plans to close the central streets even earlier for this year's Hogmanay celebrations.

"Simon." She thrust the page at him, her face pale, mouth tense and eyes wide, some unspoken fear lurking there. "Simon." Her voice was barely a whisper. "You need to read this. Just below the bit about you."

Her finger rested on the familiar picture of him from his book, resting on the wall at Blackness. His eyes flicked to the story below, the name 'Knight' hitting him from between the lines of print like a knockout punch.

In an interesting coincidence, Simon Buchanan's father, Graham Knight, features in another 2022 release. Caledonia this week also announced plans for what will be a riveting docudrama on the 1997 Docklands Scandal. The revelation of links between sitting members of parliament and organised crime almost toppled the government of the day, and provoked an unprecedented crisis in the Conservative leadership. The planned mini series will follow one man's quest to bring the three disgraced politicians involved to justice, including Knight, the only one of the trio never apprehended.

He swept the paper onto the floor.

"Fuck," he said. "Fuck. How did they know?" Her eyes were bleak. She had no answers. "Those bastards at Caledonia—how did they find out?" He choked back the bile rising in his throat. "And then—to put it in a press release as a salacious titbit to tout their damn docudrama."

He collapsed back against the pillows, jaw clenched, his chest heaving. It was as if a giant hand had plunged into his body, taking hold of his organs and twisting them in a cruel grip. Maybe he was having a heart attack.

Cassie moved to wrap her arms around him, but it brought no comfort. An irrational anger towards her surged in him, and he tried to damp it down. *Don't shoot the messenger.*

He allowed her to twine her fingers in his hair, accepted the soft press of her lips on his shoulder, and eventually, acknowledging defeat, let her absorb the panic, releasing the tension in his limbs and forcing his breath to slow.

The monster had arrived, ambushing him in the safety of his home, and there was nothing he could do to send it back into the darkness. From now on, he must live with its presence in his life. Unless he found a place beyond its claws.

He wondered if the creature pursued him in that other parallel life. In those mysterious photographs, he and Cassie both looked so happy. Did the wreckage of his family not exist in that time? Or had it just not come crashing down on them yet? He suspected even if they could flee to another time, there was no guarantee of safety.

He gently pried Cassie off him. She scanned his face, her eyes wide with concern.

"Just going to take a shower," he croaked out. He flung open drawers, snatched at clothes, only pausing to survey himself in the mirror. His father's face stared back at him. He cursed the genetic accident that had denied him his mother's rounded features and tumble of red hair.

He turned the water up as hot as it would go, and plunged into it, the scalding droplets searing his skin. Standing under the blast, in the billowing steam, a whispered suggestion found him. He made the decision to follow it.

Still glowing from the heat of the water, he tugged on jeans and a jersey. He didn't return to the bedroom. Downstairs, he grabbed his favourite wool coat, the keys for the Golf, pocketed his phone and left.

CHAPTER 43

Fall Out

Edinburgh, Scotland - December 2021

CASSIE STARED AT THE glaring white ceiling of their bedroom, eyes circling the curves of the ornamental plaster roses that surrounded her favourite spherical floral lampshade, as she rotated the options in her head. Although a grey day outside, the harsh midday light reflected uncomfortably off the pistachio-green bedroom walls. Even the rhythmic hum of the cat snuggled up in the hollow of her waist didn't soothe her as it normally would.

Simon was a haunted man, and today the ghosts of his past had come charging into his present, and possibly wiped out their future: the ghost of Simon Knight, a frightened man trying to hide in the shadows; the ghosts of tabloid journalists seeking a couple of dollars and five minutes of fame, uncaring of the damage they wrought; the ghosts of other people he'd trusted with his secrets who had let him down with their dishonesty. And now she'd opened the door and let them all back in. Worse than that, she feared she might soon become one of them. Just someone in his past.

Today she'd found an undetonated grenade, knowing she must handle it with care. She'd thought she had. But no, it had exploded in her face, obliterating this life they'd made, as the man she loved ran from her, the one person he could count on.

She'd had no choice but to show it to him. He'd have found out, anyway. Better that she was the one to sit alongside him as he read the poison woven through a seemingly innocuous article about a new television series. But entertainment journalists were as bad as the rest, always on the lookout for a shocking backstory or a scandalous past. And as for the production company's betrayal? She was unsure. Was it that they didn't know what the revelation might do to Simon? Or they didn't care?

"What shall we do, George?" The cat stretched lazily and fixed her with a haughty stare, as if channelling his noble namesake. Simon had pretended to not want a cat at first, even though they now had a firm bromance going on. He'd agreed to her keeping the spiky ginger kitten on the condition he could name it—George, after Sir George Crichton, the man who built Blackness.

"That's where he is, isn't he, George? At Blackness?" George appeared to nod in agreement, before indulging in an enormous yawn and tucking himself back into a sleepy ball.

She was sure that's where he'd have gone. To the safety of his grand-mother's house and the constancy of the castle he loved. She could follow him, to show she couldn't bear his absence, even for a day. But pursuit frightened Simon. Her pursuit of him two years ago was at the heart of him fleeing to Blackness last time. Or she could wait for his summons—or his return.

But what if neither of those came? She couldn't face that risk. Spurred into action, Cassie grabbed her bag from the wardrobe. She flung clothes into it in an untidy heap, squashing down jumpers to wrestle the zip closed. The predicted first big winter storm, when it came later today, would pummel the coast near Blackness as mercilessly as Simon pounded his punching bag.

She pulled on wool-lined boots and a padded jacket and checked George's automatic food and water station was well-stocked. He was, thankfully, a self-sufficient creature and probably wouldn't miss her one bit, although she paused to give him a last farewell pat.

The overcast sky matched her bleak mood as she trudged along the cobbled curve of St Stephen Place. A parking permit was simply that, not a guarantee of a space, and yesterday she had only found a spot for her car several hundred metres' walk away.

As she walked, she grappled in her pocket, gloved hands eventually finding her phone. She hesitated, unsure. Simon didn't like surprises, and today he'd been surprised in the worst way possible. But if she told Simon she was coming, would he run again? She sent the text anyway.

Cassie:

> You don't have to do this alone. I'm on my way.
> xx

Her heart leapt when three little dots immediately appeared on the screen. She sat in her car, praying for words to follow. But none came, and so, blaming it on poor reception because of the weather that was now rolling in from the west, with turbulent clouds gathering in a looming steel grey wall, she turned the key. The engine sluggishly turned over twice, and she held her breath, releasing it in a grateful hiss when the tired battery fired the car into life.

Forty minutes later, seeing no car in the driveway of the old stone house, she drove on past it, to Blackness Castle. There wasn't a single other vehicle in the car park. No one there. Unwilling to give up hope, she stepped out into a fierce wind that shoved her roughly towards the tunnel entrance. The courtyard inside offered a respite, and she stood, scanning the wall walk above, her ears searching for a human sound above the high-pitched scream of the weather.

And then she saw it, a figure entering the stairs at the top of the north tower. She stumbled across the angular rocks. Hope soared like the seagulls wheeling in the breeze above, riding the breath of the storm with their piercing calls.

She arrived at the lower tower entrance at the same time as the man coming down, colliding with him in the doorway. He wore a National Trust rain jacket, and a Blackness Castle badged hat pulled low on his head. One of the staff.

"You're keen, love," he said. "Didn't pick the best day, I'm afraid. I'd make sure you're out of here before that lot arrives." He tilted his head to the west, where the first distant stab of lightning ricocheted off the approaching bank of cloud.

"Is there anyone else here?" she asked. There was no time to search every room and level, not now, as a threatening crack of thunder echoed off the stone walls, loud enough to be heard over the violent waves pounding the rocky sea wall. "I'm looking for Simon."

"Nah, love, sorry. Haven't seen him today. You come here with him sometimes, don't you? His girlfriend?"

"Fiancé," she said, feeling a need to correct him, as if labelling their commitment to each other confirmed it still existed.

"Oh, congratulations, I hadn't heard. A wedding here maybe?" he said with a grin.

"Maybe," she said, trying to force a smile on her face, even though his words escalated the painful spinning sensation in her stomach.

"But no, Simon's definitely not here now," he said. "And if he was here earlier, I didn't see him. Time we got out of here, too." He tugged up his jacket hood, as the wind delivered the first spits of rain, dancing in the billowing air. A sharp ozone smell whirled around them.

In the few minutes it took her to get back to the car, a more insistent rain had started to fall. She sped back down the road, windscreen wipers on full power now, their desperate rhythm echoing the futile pounding of her heart.

As she dived from the car, beyond the sheet of water tumbling from the rooftop, she saw the door of the neighbouring house edge open. Through the gap, Morag waved at her and mouthed words, but the wind swept them away.

"Simon?" Cassie yelled back, but even that single word was lost on the wind. Morag frowned, gave a puzzled shake of her head, another hesitant wave, and wisely shut the door.

Inside, out of the weather, Cassie stripped off her sodden jacket, leaving it sprawled on the hallway floor. Then, remembering Simon's despair at her untidiness, she went back to place it on a hook.

She traced a futile path through the house, even checking the derelict rooms at the back, the ones whose sorry state had lured Simon into this whole damn television thing. She glared at them, hating that they were empty, hating that he'd sacrificed so much for them.

Upstairs, she took refuge in their bed, curled tight in a foetal position, and finally let her tears fall in silence as if instinct told her that there was no one to hear or care about her pain. After hours of restlessness, exhaustion won out, and she slept.

Cassie woke in a dull fog, heavy limbs pinned to the bed, as if some unseen hand had played with the settings of the universe, turning up the dial on gravity. Only the call of a plover fractured the eerie quiet left in the storm's wake. The bedside clock glowed; three am.

Here, with not a single streetlight for miles, sometimes the darkness was complete, so thick you could touch it. But not tonight. The weak light of a crescent moon slanted through the window. She got up to draw the curtains on it, even its feeble light painful to eyes still aching from crying. She stood one hand on the heavy drapes, the other pressed to the glass. Simon was out there somewhere beyond that window—but where?

Below, the sleek shadow of Morag's tabby cat appeared out of some scruffy bushes near the road. She followed its progress up their driveway, and it was then, as it approached the house, she caught the hint of a reflection—the faint moonlight bouncing off a solid shape. The black paintwork of Simon's Golf. He was here.

She found him in the library, asleep on the broad leather couch. He lay on his back—she'd never known anyone else who could sleep like that—his unlined skin almost white in the half light, his face calm and untroubled in sleep. He resembled one of those stone effigies, in one of his beloved mediaeval churches, a long-dead knight, his last battle fought. But Simon's battles were far from over.

She sat in an armchair, fighting the urge to wake him. As if sensing her presence, he stirred.

"Cassie." He rolled up on an elbow and shuffled over, patting the space he'd made beside him. "Come here."

She lay next to him, face to face, his deep blue troubled eyes so close that even in the darkened room, she could see the little grey flecks like silver. The black brows furrowed, either side of a small tense crease.

"Where have you been, Simon? I was so worried."

"Driving."

"For fifteen hours? Where did you go—John o'Groats?"

"No. Glen Ruaidh."

"Glen Ruaidh? Why the hell would you drive all the way up there?"

Glen Ruaidh. The name felt like a bad omen. The place where her parents had found, but then lost each other. And where she recalled having the first nagging feeling that she and Nik were losing each other, too.

"I don't know. I didn't really plan it."

"Why didn't you stay the night? Instead of driving all the way back here?"

"Do you know what they charge to stay in that hotel?"

She did, but she wasn't going to tell him how she knew. She sensed there were times the mention of Nik fed Simon's insecurity. The last thing he needed right now was dredging up the ghosts of her past, too.

"When I got here, and you weren't—Simon, I was worried sick. And with the storm..."

"Yeah, I'm sorry." He closed his eyes, and she felt the deep sigh run the length of his body. "I did it again, didn't I?"

"It's OK. You're back now. It's all OK," she whispered, her lips against his. "You don't need to run away."

She felt him tense; his eyes flew open, darting from side to side, as he studied hers; his tongue licked at his lips. Under her fingertips, the pulse in his neck quickened. Her own heartbeat stepped up in response as a slow, creeping dread edged forward. Even the hairs on her arms stood up, alerted to a threat.

"Cassie," he said, smoothing her wild hair with tender strokes of his hand. "I can't keep doing this. It's not fair to you. And I'm not getting better. I need time to figure this out." She closed her eyes, knowing what was coming. At least she could block out the sight of the words on his lips, even if she couldn't escape them. "And I don't think I can do it here. I need to leave for a while. Get right away from everything."

"Even me," she whispered. She forced the words past a ribbon of pain that ran down her throat and twisted in an agonising knot in her stomach.

"It's not like that, Cassie. It's not you. I know that might be hard to believe, but it's not. And I know it might seem this is more of the same old cowardly Simon. Running away. But it's not."

"So what is it, then?" she said.

"I thought a lot about it yesterday, sitting in my car up there, by the loch at Glen Ruaidh. Asked myself why I run; why I don't face up to things, stand and fight? I've spent years of my life on high alert. Fearing what's hiding in the shadows. Checking around corners to make sure nothing's lying in wait for me. That voice inside reminding me to always be careful, that 'it' could happen any time, and when it does, it will be catastrophic. Of course, my rational self tries to argue back; it says don't be so bloody ridiculous; it asks me what's the worst that could happen. But like yesterday, when I'm blindsided like that, instinct kicks in and all I know how to do is run to a safe place."

"I could be your safe place."

He traced the shape of her cheek with his thumb.

"Cassie, I love you, but that's not the answer. I have to get myself away from everything—even you," he said, "and then I can work out how to beat this stuff. While immersed in my life, I can't see what's broken. And because of that, I don't know how to fix it. I need space, time to stand back for a bit. I'm going to get Jasper to call a halt on this television shit, too."

"What about the contract?"

"Fuck the contract. They can try to sue me for all I care. I haven't got anything left to lose."

"You've got the apartment. And this house."

"Yeah," he said. "This house that got me into this mess in the first place." His eyes swept around the room, and she knew how much the thought of losing it pained him. But there was more at stake here than a house. "Still, it may not come to that. I'll see if I can push the timeline out a bit. Might keep them off my back."

"Where will you go?" she asked.

He shook his head. "I don't really know. Or for how long. But I'll leave in the morning."

She tightened her arms around him, as if she could change his mind by anchoring him to her. He unwound one, then the other,

"Cassie, go back to bed. Go upstairs. And stay there. Pull the curtains."

"But why? I can't just let you go like that," she protested.

"That's exactly how I need to go. I don't want a goodbye. I don't want you to watch me leave. Because if I turn around—and much as I tell myself I shouldn't, I know I will—if you're there watching me go, I won't be able to go through with this. And I have to."

He rolled away from her, and reading the finality in the rigidness of his back, Cassie did as he asked, not looking back at him either.

Chapter 44

Hanging By A Thread

Edinburgh, Scotland - December 2021

"Cassie."

She jerked her head up in surprise at Celia's sharp rebuke.

"Sorry Celia," she mumbled, tucking the offending phone under the sales desk as heat flushed in her cheeks. Celia, who'd been so good to her, more than simply her boss at the bookstore, deserved better. When her break came, Cassie removed the temptation further, burying her phone deep in her handbag even though she knew the need to check it would nag at her all day.

Since Simon left, she'd become one of those people she despised, wedded to her phone, relentlessly scanning the screen for notifications. But while others were less selective, happy to get that dopamine hit from any text or message, she sought only one. One that never came. Four days since he'd left. Four days of silence.

For now, this compulsion to look at her phone constantly was the only outward sign of the turmoil that had taken up permanent residence inside of her. Otherwise, she existed in a state of numb shock. She went through the motions of the day on autopilot. She wrote, she went to work, she ate, remembered to feed the cat. It was like living in an alternate reality, a life where Simon had never existed.

And so, in a desperate need for some proof of life, she begged Celia for an early finish and headed over to the university. She sat on the leather couch in the history department reception amidst the smell of musty books, stacked floor to ceiling on the shelves behind her. The same aroma filled Simon's office behind the locked door opposite and hung in the library at his Blackness house. She inhaled it, as if to capture the lingering presence of him there. And felt sad, realising it was not the same. Without the layer of his own smell—the fragrance of sandalwood and cinnamon, like a woodland grove in autumn—the room just smelled old.

"Hey, Cassie." Simon's colleague, Malcolm Shaw, extended his meaty hand, offering a smile that dissolved into a frown. "Wasn't expecting you. I thought you'd be off with Simon."

"No, not this time," she said, choking out the words through the knot of tense hope in her throat.

"Well," he said, fumbling to brush back his untidy shock of hair. "So where is he, anyway? Suppose he's taken off somewhere warm. Left us all here in this bloody Scottish winter weather."

"I don't actually know. I was hoping you might."

She had no plans to follow him. But just to know where he was. To look at a place on a map and think of him there. Such a small thing, but it would be better than what she had now—nothing.

Surprise and sympathy battled for control of Malcolm's face.

"Sorry Cassie, I can't help you there."

He exchanged a puzzled look with the department secretary, Cara Winterbottom, who left her desk, coming to hover at Cassie's elbow.

"Wherever he is, he's OK, Cassie," she said, with an instinctive gentleness. "He's sent several emails these last couple of days. And I know he's been in contact with his grad students."

"Emailed on Tuesday asking me to pick up the last few lectures for the 702 paper we do together," Malcolm added. "You haven't heard from him?"

She felt the heat rise in her face, embarrassed at exposing this rift in their relationship. Simon would hate that she'd revealed something so personal to his work colleagues.

But there was also relief. He was alive, somewhere, carrying on at least one part of his life as normal. Of course, he wouldn't neglect his responsibilities to his precious grad students and university colleagues.

Not in the way he'd dropped all responsibility for anything to do with the television series. He'd blocked Jasper. So now the agent pestered her daily with texts and phone messages, demanding she get Simon to call him. She hadn't responded.

Simon had eliminated the source of his distress. Without him, the project couldn't progress further. That he'd walk away from it was no surprise. But to walk away from her, to leave without a trace. Was she too a source of distress?

"No," she said. "I didn't really expect him to get in touch. Just wanted to know that he hadn't dropped off the edge of the earth." She forced a smile.

But inside, the kind expressions on their faces as they studied her provoked bitter envy. They had a direct line to Simon, while, at his request, she'd severed hers.

Back at the apartment, she sat down at her computer and broke the rules. The email she sent to Simon's personal address had no subject line. There was no message. Instead, she attached a short story, one of several she'd written after her book was complete.

Over the last month, she'd given in to the voices of the side characters from the main book who begged her to tell their story. There was unrestrained delight on the faces of her publishers when she'd shown them.

"Perfect," Anthea had said. "A companion anthology, set in the same world. Let's set up a preorder in January. Release it a month after the book. Do you think you could give us eight stories?"

"Keep going honey," Stephanie had encouraged. "If the words are there, just keep going." So she had.

And although Simon had abandoned her, she couldn't abandon the fictional people she'd created, or the real ones like Anthea and Stephanie, who were counting on her. Words still poured out of her every morning. With the real world crashing down around her, she sought refuge in the fantasy world she'd created.

Now, she wanted to let Simon know that life *did* go on without him. He hadn't taken all of her when he'd left. The writer in her endured. And if he too broke the rules, and opened one of those emails, the little 'Read' tag would show up on her screen, and she would know he heard her voice, even if it wasn't saying the words she wanted to say, the words she wanted him to hear, asking him to come home.

Next she phoned Grace. Strangely, letting Malcolm and Cara into her secret gave her the strength to admit out loud to someone else that Simon had left her.

"Oh, honey, I'm so, so, sorry," her friend began. "I wish I was there with you."

"Yeah, me too. I'd like nothing better than to drown my sorrows in some wine bar with you and wake up with a headache so bad there'd be no room for anything else in my brain."

Grace had toughened in her attitudes towards men over the years, disillusioned when real-life love hadn't matched the love she'd found between the pages of her endless romance books. And so now, having offered the expected sympathy, she pushed it aside for brutal honesty.

"You know, Nik had his faults, but he'd never have done this to you. I know you think you love this guy, Cassie, but I have to wonder—I mean, you'd only split from Nik a couple of months and then suddenly you've met this guy on the rebound. A month after that, you're living with him."

"I told you Grace. The moment I met Simon, I just knew we were meant to be together. We've been together for two years. It's not just some crazy fling."

"But for one of those years, you lived in a little bubble. And you know, the lockdown did weird things to all of us. It was such a strange, intense time." She wondered how Grace would react if she told her the full story, a stranger fiction than anyone could imagine. "Is it possible you just got caught up in the romance of it all? Written your own little fictional love story? Hunkered down in an old stone house with a dark, handsome Scotsman? And now you're out in the real world, it's—"

"I love him, Grace." Cassie's anger flared, and she leapt to her own defence. "Do you think I'd be so stupid as to go headlong into a second marriage, unless I was confident this one wouldn't fail?"

"OK, OK," Grace said. "I'm sorry. You're right. I shouldn't have said that." She paused, and Cassie heard the slow intake of breath. "But hun, I know you, and I don't know him, so, I have to ask—*does* he love you?"

"He does. I know it may not seem like it. But he does."

"OK," she said. "So, let's say he does. Even so, you know he's still being a jerk, hun. If he shows up, you gotta make him earn you back. Don't let him assume anything."

Cassie gritted her teeth. "Sure."

It had been a mistake to call Grace. She didn't understand; Simon wasn't some selfish man, hard and unfeeling, and careless of Cassie's emotions, like the ones who'd messed with Grace's heart. This was a damaged man, putting up a wall around himself and retreating to the safe solitude that had served him well. And damned if she'd turn him away when he found the courage to come out from behind it.

Cassie steered the remaining conversation into safer territory. She babbled on about her book, the weather, and the cat. She didn't want this one friendship that had supported her through so many hard times to falter now. Grace bore her own scars and saw the world through a less gentle lens. She needed to cut her some slack and look for what she needed elsewhere.

After the battering at Grace's hands, Cassie sought someone who might bring a less emotional perspective. She phoned her father. Usually, her father's first instinct would be to take her side. But he and Simon shared a unique bond. And so, unlike Grace, he straight away argued Simon's position.

"Give him time, darling. He's had a rough couple of months. This thing he's grappling with, it's bigger than any of us."

"Yeah, I mean Mum was always in the spotlight. You too, now and then. But only for good things. To have your father a wanted man, someone the public would love to see brought down. I can't imagine how hard it is for him."

"And remember, kiddo, he hasn't had family and friends there like you have. No one there to catch him when he falls. Now he's got you. He just doesn't see that yet. Give him time."

She checked her laptop one more time before bed, clicking to her sent box, and there it was. 'Read'. That one small word that meant so much. Seeing it, she resolved that, difficult as it was, she would do her best, follow her father's wisdom and offer Simon the gift of time.

But Grace's words still echoed in her mind. Did Simon really love her? Because if he didn't, even her best wouldn't be good enough.

On Christmas morning, she woke to a blast of Shihad from her phone. "Ignite" might be a great song, but this early in the day she regretted making it Nik's ringtone.

"Merry Christmas, Princess," he said. "Hope I didn't wake you?"

"It's seven a.m. here, Nik. Of course you woke me."

"Sorry," he said. "Still can't get my head around this time zone thing. Hope your man isn't pissed off with me for destroying his sleep time."

"It's OK," she mumbled, already scrambling her thoughts. Nik was the last person she wanted to know that she lay in this enormous bed alone. "Merry Christmas. How was your day?"

"Great. Exhausting. We all went to Mila's. She wanted to show off her new house. Ivana's kids are fucking relentless. It seemed I spent the day either wrestling with them, or with Marko's dog."

She laughed, as happy memories of an exuberant Nik with the family dogs fell out of the past.

"You should get one," she said. "A dog."

"Yeah, maybe I should. Good company. And another way to annoy my mother."

"How was she?"

"Not too bad. You know, give her a bit of alcohol and she mellows. And the grandkids seemed to have wormed their way into her black heart. Anyway, what does your Christmas Day look like?"

"Cold, and dark still. But they say it's going to be fine when the sun eventually comes up."

"It's been hot as hell here. Thank god it's cooled off a bit. So, plans for the day?"

"Yeah, my publishers, Steph and Anthea—they don't have any family here—so they're doing the whole big traditional Christmas dinner. Invited loads of people, so it should be nice."

"Sounds fun. Enjoy yourselves. Well, I won't keep you," he said. "Going to have a few beers with Viktor and Marko. They should be here any minute. Jan's coming over too."

"OK, well say hi to all of them from me."

"Will do. You take care Princess."

The moment she put her phone down, once again, Grace was in her head. She was right—Nik would never have just walked away from her like this. And now, after three weeks of making excuses for Simon—to herself, to everyone else—she was tired. Tired of the lies she told on his behalf. Tired of the sympathetic looks that told her no one believed her lies. And being tired made her angry.

Behind forced smiles and hollow laughter, she sat through the Christmas lunch consumed by this new emotion. The Christmas season might encourage goodwill to all men, but right now, thoughts of Simon brought a simmering, white-cold rage. How could the bastard do this to her? It consumed her day, and it took all her self control, when people gently asked her how she was doing, to not drop the pretense and simply rant at the unfairness of it all.

She couldn't muster a repeat performance a week later, declining invitations to New Year's Eve celebrations. While others toasted the new year with hopeful dreams, she sat home alone grieving the past one. Over the past week, the brief flash of anger had trickled away. As people babbled on about plans for the year ahead, she had dwelt on regrets—mainly that she'd loved Simon so hard, that his turning away from her hurt so much. Once again, she'd given herself totally to another person, and this was the result.

But, as if taking a perverse satisfaction from revisiting the pain of this gaping wound, she'd still sent him her latest story, and once again he'd read it. The invisible thread that bound them together, even across time, might be stretched thin, but it was still there. She could feel it. She wondered if he did, too.

CHAPTER 45

Manhunt

Roquetas de Mar, Spain - January 2022

SIMON'S HEAD AUTOMATICALLY FLICKED up from his laptop when he glimpsed the dark-haired man strolling along the row of beachfront cafes towards him. He ignored the concerned expression of the woman at the table opposite, who seemed troubled by the intensity of his hawk-like stare. Perhaps she suspected him an Interpol officer hunting a criminal, or a hit man looking for his target. Either way, she clutched at her purse as if considering whether it might be time to leave before he invited chaos into this peaceful little cafe by the sea.

He couldn't help it. Yesterday, he'd taken the decisive step of officially quitting the hunt for his father. But one day wasn't sufficient for him to abandon the habits of his month-long search.

In retrospect, it had been a stupid idea. Arrogant of him, really, to think that he, a historian, could succeed where the police had failed. Sure, he had years of practice at sifting through documents and records, scrutinising maps, following obscure leads and tracking people, even those who, it seemed, didn't want to be found. But he now knew finding the dead was far easier than finding the living.

And he was certain his father was alive. Simon believed he'd know in his gut—would feel some sense of relief, or joy—when Graham Knight no longer inhabited this planet. Maybe that feeling was all he was going to get—one day, when the bastard was dead. Maybe it was best that way.

At the beginning, when he'd left Scotland, he was sure that the future lay in finding his father, accosting him with an eyewitness account of the damage he'd inflicted on his wife, and confronting him with irrefutable evidence of the damage he'd done to his son.

But as Simon accepted the futility of traipsing around Spain—such a vast country that he'd barely covered a small corner of it—it was replaced by a growing sense that at least having tried was enough. By rehearsing the words in his head—sometimes even saying them out loud, as he drove mile after mile—the blunt truths he needed to tell his father had found their way into the universe, and the universe had accepted his outrage, leaving him strangely calm.

The approaching man slowed his pace, surveying the cafes with interest, pausing to scan a menu board at one. Sunglasses obscured his eyes, but he was the right height, with a slim, angular face, framed with dark hair exactly like Simon's own, except threaded with silver, as might be expected of someone who was close to seventy. The man stopped outside, mere feet from Simon's table. After reading the menu, he stepped inside the cafe and took a seat. The young woman waiting tables approached, notebook in hand. He swept off the dark glasses, revealing a pair of smiling, warm brown eyes.

"Buenos dias," he said. "Un cafe, por favor?"

Simon took a sip of the acrid liquid that passed for coffee and lowered his eyes back to the screen. He skimmed through emails from three of his Masters students. He'd got lucky with this bunch—smart, self-sufficient, competent researchers, no hand-holding needed—just how he liked them. Today there were just a few updates, with nothing more than acknowledgment required of him.

The fourth email was another from the frustrating PhD candidate he and Malcolm were supervising. He sighed, filled with dread at opening it, then noticed she'd sent it to Malcolm, and merely copied him in. Thank god for Malcolm. He could sort her out. Simon moved it to a folder he'd labelled 'Selena P'— 'P' for Padrutt—but he preferred to think of it as 'Pain-in-the-arse'.

Next, he clicked over to his personal inbox. Most days since he'd blocked Jasper, it was empty. Cutting the agent off like that was extreme, but necessary, given the man's mistaken belief that hounding Simon daily could convince him to come back. The TV show was on hold, and that's where it would stay, until he was ready. When, or even if, that time would come, he still couldn't say.

He gazed fondly at the four from Cassie, one for every week he'd been gone, one every Thursday, subject lines blank, no message, but each with an attachment. When the first arrived, he'd left it unopened, angry that she'd already broken their agreement, and fearful of facing the aftermath of his leaving written there in black and white. But later that night, lying alone with his dark thoughts, curiosity had won out.

She'd done exactly as he asked: no conversation, no news of her life, no questions about his. This was simply a short story, a few thousand words. He gratefully accepted those words, drawing him into another time and another world, as Cassie wove a tale of other people's lives and offered an escape from his own—a gift that showed she understood what he needed right now.

He moved on to opening today's single new message, pleased to see it was a reply from his cousin Calum MacFarlane, currently thousands of miles away in New Zealand filming a new series of his wildly successful television show.

```
Simon,
The offer of a bed stands, man. Unless
sunny Spain has still got you in her
grip. I know the flight's a killer,
but I reckon a catch up is long
overdue. If you need to get away like
you said, you can't get much further
than this. Send me your flight number
and I'll pick you up at the airport.
Calum
```

Five days ago, Simon had seen the arrival of the New Year while watching fireworks in a crowd of people at the waterfront, yet totally alone. Then consoled himself with a whole bottle of cheap Tempranillo back in his room. Fuelled by inebriation, he'd fired off an impulsive email to Calum, wishing him a happy New Year, and filled him in on the bare facts of his situation.

The two of them had been close as kids and right through their teens. Their lives had diverged at that point until eighteen months ago, when Simon had reached out to Calum for advice on his own foray into TV. Since then, he'd been a useful sounding board.

And now, he was perhaps the only person in the world Simon could count on to understand why he was sitting here in the south of Spain, having turned his back on everything he loved and why he'd wasted a month searching for a man who didn't deserve even a minute of his time. He pulled out his credit card and started searching for flights.

Nausea rose and fell in Simon's stomach, matching the heaving of the ocean just beyond the glassed-in front of Calum's house. The tang of salt hung in every breath. Out in the waves beyond Seatoun Beach, a brave ferry struggled towards the entrance of Wellington Harbour.

"For a man who's just spent a month in Spain, you're looking a bit fucking pasty. Here, get this into you," Calum said, offering a generous tumbler of whisky. It probably wasn't the wisest, off the back of two long flights, and on top of the churning in his guts, but he took it anyway.

"Nothing to do with lack of sun, mate," he said, taking a sip of the smooth amber liquid, the product of the MacFarlane family distillery. "I can't think of any other capital city in the world where they'd even attempt to land a plane in those conditions. And that runway? So damn short, the pilot just about stands it on its nose to stop in time."

Simon wasn't religious, but he'd nearly joined the other three hundred people in praying as the 737 rode a wind straight off Antarctica like an unruly bull before the pilot seized the opportunity to dump it on the ground.

"You get used to it," Calum grinned. "Just be grateful it's summer. Otherwise it'd be raining as well as blowing a hoolie." The familiar Scottish expression seemed gentle in contrast to the gale hammering the small waterfront cottage. "And be pleased we're not staying," Calum added.

"We're not?"

"Nah, I'm heading down south tomorrow. Need to get back to the filming schedule, I'm afraid. But I thought you'd be OK with tagging along? We can still spend time together, have that catch up. But might also be useful for you to see what goes on behind the scenes once you're actually in production. Don't worry, I won't drag you up any mountains with me."

"So, if we're going to the South Island we need to fly?" There was no way in hell Simon could face getting back on a plane so soon.

"Nah mate, it's all good," Calum said. "No wild plane rides. We'll just catch the ferry across the strait and then drive from the other side," he said, with a cheerful nod at the Jeep Wrangler parked out front.

Simon's guts performed another elaborate somersault as with dismay he turned his gaze back to the interisland ferry, tossed like a toy on towering navy blue waves.

———

The small town cafe faced a stunning view. The mountains of the Southern Alps towered in the distance beyond dramatic hill country that reminded Simon of home. He sat in silence sipping a second coffee, an interested observer.

The local reporter sitting opposite him tucked away her laptop. "I'll send it through for you to have a look at tonight," she said, shaking Calum's hand with a smile, before leaving the cafe.

Two women had been hovering to one side. One now braved coming forward. Calum made relaxed small talk with her before signing a photograph of him. She left with a broad smile on her face, gushing to her companion at how he was 'even nicer in real life'.

"So, how do you cope with it?" Simon asked. "Being in the spotlight like this? People ambushing you wherever you go? People writing about you online, in the newspapers?"

"Yeah, it wasn't easy at first. Took me by surprise, I suppose. But it's not as bad as you think. Not in our game. In fact, most of the time, I quite enjoy it."

Simon frowned. He couldn't imagine ever liking his privacy invaded like that.

"Look, I know what you're thinking. You've been exposed to some pretty tough shit, Simon. But it was a long time ago. And it was a totally different situation. When you're making this sort of feel-good TV, people come up to you because they *like* you. Journalists write about you *because* the people like you."

"So you're saying no one has ever written anything bad about you?"

Calum laughed, his large body relaxing back in the small chair, arms crossed over his chest.

"No, I'm not that bloody good. There have been a few less than complimentary reviews. But hey, you can't please everyone." He folded his hands on the table, leaning towards Simon. "The secret is taking control."

"How can you control all of them? Out there? It's impossible."

"That's right. You can't control what *they* say about you or write about you. But you can control how you react to it. That's what you do. Take control of what you can. Forget the rest."

"When did you become so fucking wise?" Simon scoffed.

"Not my wisdom. I didn't invent it. But I sure live by it. You should too."

Fuelled by curiosity about the place Cassie had spent her childhood, this morning Simon had dropped Calum with the camera crew and headed for Tekapo. Sitting parked in Calum's Jeep by the iridescent water of the glacial lake, he could feel her here. He imagined her small determined form walking the shoreline, with a haze of dark hair gleaming bronze in the sunlight; a golden limbed creature dripping pearls as she emerged from the icy turquoise depths; a laughing woman, head tipped back, sitting cross-legged on the impossibly green grass.

He didn't stop in the town itself. It was so small that, even filled with summer tourists, there was a high chance he might stumble across Daniel Tremayne. He couldn't face that possibility. Not after their last encounter. It was bad enough that time, but now? Although he was grateful for the man. He wasn't sure he'd have found acceptance of the strange machinations of time and place that had thrown him and Cassie together without Daniel's calm reassurance that none of them had lost their minds.

His phone chirped with a text; Calum letting him know he was heading back to the hotel, the day's filming done. With reluctance, he fired up the Jeep, and left Cassie's past behind.

He found Calum in the bar. His cousin waved him across to where two whiskies already sat on the table. He'd drunk more in this last week than he'd drunk in a year. But it was hard to turn down when it was a MacFarlane's whisky.

"So, you went to Tekapo," Calum said, taking a sip of the viscous liquid. "Got her out of your system, then?"

"No chance of that," Simon said with a gloomy shake of his head. "Probably made it worse, if anything." He took a too large slug of the whisky, the jolt of alcohol taking his breath away.

"Then what the fuck are you going to do it about it, eh?"

"I can't go back. Not until I can be sure I won't do this to her again."

"Then you can't go back. Ever."

"What do you mean?"

"If you're thinking this woman only deserves a perfect version of yourself, then it's never going to happen. Come on, Simon, you and I both know there's some damage that's not fixable."

"Yeah, well, guess we both have our fathers to thank for that, don't we? Fucking up our lives." It was his father's absence that had messed Simon up. Calum's father's brooding presence had cast a shadow over his life for years. The end result was the same.

"Sure, as kids, they fucked both of us up pretty bad. But we're adults now, Simon. We understand what they did to us in the past, and we can choose to not let that define us in the future."

"Some Calum wisdom this time? Been moonlighting as a therapist?"

"Yeah," he laughed. "Don't worry, I don't charge for family. Look, when Hamish died last year—" Like Simon, Calum never referred to his father as 'Dad'. Neither man deserved that title. "—somehow it gave me permission to move on, and I am. But I wish I'd done it sooner. I didn't need him to be dead, for him to be dead to me. All those years, I made the choice to give him power over me. And I'd always had the choice to let it go, I just didn't know it."

"Fucking Graham's still very much alive, I'm sure."

"Maybe. But he doesn't have to be in your life. Not unless you allow him in."

"I'm frightened that no matter what, he'll always be in it. DNA doesn't lie. Blood will out," as they say.

"Bullshit," Calum spat at him. "Fucking bullshit Simon. You are *not* your father. I am not mine. That is what this is really about, isn't it? You think you'll hurt her like he hurt your mother?"

"Well, I've done a pretty good job of that so far."

"Man, you are fucked up if you think taking a break because you're spinning out a bit comes anywhere near close to what happened with your parents."

"No. But what if one day—"

"For a clever guy, you can be really fucking slow, Simon. You have the power. You have the choice. You've always had them. And you always will." He let out a frustrated huff. "Fuck, I feel like I'm Obi Wan Kenobi to your Skywalker."

Simon sighed. There was no arguing with those emphatic green eyes, or the blunt common sense. Leaning back in his chair, he thrust his fingers through his hair. Who would have suspected his mountain-man cousin might see right to the heart of the problem? Or could zero in on the lies Simon had told himself to justify his behaviour? Or call him out on them?

Graham Knight didn't lie in wait inside him, like some evil parasite that would one day take over its host. No, *he* had power, and *he* had choices. But he wasn't sure what to do with this awakening self-awareness. Sure, Calum was right; he didn't need to be perfect, but Cassie deserved someone far less broken than he was. He needed fixing, and he had no idea where to begin.

"OK Doctor MacFarlane, while you're dispensing advice—what do I do now?"

CHAPTER 46

Homecoming

Edinburgh, Scotland – February 2022

THE HUGE WINGBACK CHAIR embraced her in a reassuring hug. Next to her, on an oak side table, a glass of ruby-coloured wine glowed in the warmth of an old-fashioned lamp. Cassie took a small sip, the velvety spiciness filling her mouth. Opening the foil-embossed cover of the book in her lap, she prepared to read aloud.

In the little enclave of the lamplight, she could easily pretend she sat alone in a cosy library room, the gentle, companionable presence of book-filled shelves her only observers, simply reading for herself. The small crowd lay beyond in the shadows, still and quiet, ready to be lulled by her words.

She exchanged a smile with her father, visible in the front row. He looked brighter tonight. Daniel's age was beginning to show, taking a little longer to shake off the weariness of travel, something that had always been part of his life and he'd always loved. She had tried to protest that he needn't come for the book launch, but he'd been adamant.

"Do you really think your mother would let me get away with that? I'm damn sure she wouldn't let me have any peace." Even now, Blair Tremayne loomed large in their lives. Cassie could feel her presence now. Did she stand at her husband's shoulder, with a proud smile and wearing a smug expression because she'd always known this day would come? Or did she hover here alongside Cassie, offering her support, knowing how terrifying and wonderful it was to offer your creations to the world?

Cassie breathed in the fragrance of the flowers surrounding her. When a colourful bouquet had arrived with a card from Archie, she'd sensed his new girlfriend's influence in the background. Grace may not have had enough money for the airfare, but she'd still gone all out with an enormous bunch of Cassie's favourite peonies. Being out of season, they must have cost a fortune. A gentle, old-fashioned sweetness drifted from the tightly-clustered petals of pinks and pearls.

Cassie brought her hand to touch the gleaming curve of silver pinned to the lapel of her colourful 1970s Biba jacket. She traced the pattern of the diamonds, the familiar zig-zag shape of the constellation. The words on the back gave her strength. 'Princess, I always knew one day I'd look up and find you in the stars.' It was a sign that she could always count on Nik's quiet love in the background. It endured beyond the differences that would always divide them.

She swallowed down the painful lump in her throat. If only she could see some sign that Simon still loved her, and there was a future for them. But for now he remained unreachable, still deep in the battle to force his past back to a place it couldn't hurt him anymore.

Seeing Anthea's questioning nod, she took a deep breath, pushing away the thoughts of the man who'd inspired these first paragraphs of her book, burying the sadness, and began to read.

A hush fell across the assembled Ilverian court as the stranger swept into the dining hall. It was as if he brought the night with him. He paused beyond the doorway, pushing back a wayward lock of hair, its threads as dark as the starless winter sky. His unlined skin glowed in the torchlight, pale and ethereal in contrast to the swarthy complexioned Ilverian natives. Smoothing down the upturned collar of his charcoal coat, he cast an appraising glare across the room, his mouth tensed in an arrogant sneer.

A couple of men standing by the door dropped into low bows. Someone should slap sense into those fools for stupidly feeding his ego like that. Astara would happily be the one to do it. Except she couldn't. Trapped behind this table, unable to free herself from between her fawning sisters, escape was impossible. Just as escape from the dictates of protocol also held her back from such impulsive action.

"Who the hell is that?" Meiryn hissed against her ear.

His eyes fixed on Astara. They had never met, but a powerful jolt of knowledge arced between them. He surged forward, then hesitated for a moment, halting his progress at the base of the steps. She caught the slightest flicker of wariness in those storm-blue eyes. Then it was gone as he advanced towards them once more, his stride confident, the contours of his angular face set in stony resolve.

"That," she said, tilting her chin in defiant challenge, as he stood in front of her, refusing to drop his head in acknowledgment, as he should, "is Cazimir."

At the end of the chapter, Cassie laid down the book. The patter of applause rippled towards her in warm waves. She basked in its appreciative rhythm for a moment before rising to her feet. Anthea Leonard stepped forward, clasping her hands in congratulation, then faced the audience packed into the small bookstore.

"And so, I'd like to offer some final thanks. First, to Celia of 'Dreams In Ink', for hosting this launch tonight. You've certainly turned it on for us. Love the food. Love the wine." She raised her glass to a beaming Celia. The audience applauded.

"To all of you who've come along this evening, braving our beautiful Scottish weather, thank you for sharing in the launch of this book. We know it is only the first of many for this undoubtedly talented author—Cassie, we can't wait for Book Two."

"It's coming," Cassie promised with a smile, and one of her advance readers in the audience let out a whoop of joy.

"Tonight is also a first for our little publishing house." Anthea stepped towards her wife, looping an arm around her waist. "Stephanie and I would like to thank Cassie for her faith in us; for trusting us to deliver this stunning debut into the world. And I'm sure you will all agree—even if that first chapter is all you've heard of it—it is stunning." Another enthusiastic surge of applause filled the bookstore.

"Now, if you'd like to purchase a copy, Celia here is all set to take your money." She pointed toward the sales table, where stacks of the gilt-edged special editions sat alongside their more humble paperback cousins. She could still hardly believe these books existed, the dreams of her teenage self made real.

"And then once you've got your book, head on over to this table. Cassie is going to do some signing for you all."

Cassie took a seat as a queue hurriedly assembled in front of the sales table, while another line formed in front of her, each woman clutching a copy of the book. The sight of these wonderful people who'd already read it and then turned up here tonight for her to sign the title page felt surreal.

She didn't mind as the ache developed in her right hand. Unused to much effort beyond the tapping of a keyboard, writing personal dedications for person after person was physically demanding, but satisfying. Anthea sat on one side of her, beckoning each new person forward. On the other, Stephanie distributed tote bags and bookmarks.

She was pleased she'd splashed out on the swag. Seeing her characters brought to life in pictures by a local artist, it had seemed a shame to limit their use to inside the special edition. As each woman walked away with a tote over her shoulder, Cassie experienced a thrill of pride that her words had inspired such beautiful images.

"Oh my god, it's him." The strident gasp of a woman near the door rang out, booming across the background hum of chatter and soft music. Hearing her words, the room paused, every person turning their eyes in that direction, and then taking a collective breath at the sight. "It's Cazimir," she said.

"Oh darling, this is sheer brilliance," Anthea cooed in Cassie's ear. "Well done. Although you could have let *us* in on the secret, you know. But I appreciate you might have wanted it to be a surprise."

A man with dark hair and eyes of deep sea blue stood casting a wary gaze at the assembled women. They remained transfixed by his appearance. He turned down the collar of his black coat and made his way through the crowd, awkwardly stepping around the women who had turned to stone in his presence.

Cassie sprang to her feet, jostling past Stephanie. She ignored the concerned looks of the women in the queue who perhaps suspected the book signing might suddenly be over. Only one thing mattered. She must get to him.

Simon captured her in those muscular boxer's arms, his grip so tight she could hardly breathe. He lifted her off the floor and spun her around, and the world became a delirious blur. The crowd of women, sensing something momentous happening, broke into another round of spontaneous applause as he kissed her.

"Cassie." He breathed the words into her hair. "I need to come home."

"You already are," she hummed against his neck. "I'm your home."

"I'm so sorry," he whispered, dropping his head to her shoulder. "I've been such an idiot. Running like that. Not talking to you. Not letting you talk to me."

"But I did talk to you. I wrote you stories. And sent them to you."

"And I read them. I listened."

"And in case you didn't understand what I had to say, I need to say it again. Look at me Simon." He lifted his head and locked eyes with hers, emotions swirling across his face. He looked small and vulnerable and she realised the power she could wield with words. Now he was back, she was going to use that power to forgive him and save them both.

"Simon, I can't imagine a life without you in it—whatever version of you that is. None of us is perfect. And I'd rather have a life with an imperfect Simon than one without you, because if I don't have you in my life, I'm alone." She cupped her hand to his head, tilting it to press his forehead to hers. They stood, eyes closed, with only the sound of her voice low and soft, just between the two of them. "You were there in my past and there's no one else in my future. Simon, you were always meant to be the happy ending for my story."

No one else in the room could have heard, but somehow every person there sensed this was the ending of a real life love story happening right before their eyes. As his mouth came to hers with a desperate hunger, cheers erupted around them. But amongst the noise, all she could hear was the explosion of relief inside her.

CHAPTER 47

Forgiveness

Edinburgh, Scotland – February 2022

SIMON LOBBED A SMELLY, dried sardine at George, who batted at it with a paw, before crunching it happily between his pointy teeth.

"I see some things haven't changed," he said as he soaped up his hands at the kitchen sink before rinsing away the fishy odour.

It was difficult to describe how something as ordinary as having him stand in the kitchen, feeding treats to the cat, could cause Cassie's body to fill with a happiness so great she might burst. An hour earlier, in one unexpected swoop, the universe had delivered a beautiful normalcy back into her life. It smudged at the edges of memories of lonely winter nights, trapped in this house, wondering if he would ever come back.

"Doesn't take much to win over that cat," he said. George twisted his appreciative body between Simon's legs, hoping for more. Just like her.

"He's pretty forgiving."

"So are you," he said. "To even let me back in here." He took a tentative step around the counter, and then one more, closing the space between them. His eyes fixed on hers, and she responded to the hopeful plea in them, extending a hand to trace his jaw. God, she'd missed him.

Now for the first time since they'd left the bookshop, he risked touching her, his hand grazing her face, as they stood, each a mirror of the other. She closed her eyes, relaxing into the familiar caress, soothed by the smell of him, the same woody aftershave mingling with the earthy masculine muskiness. When he stepped in close and his arms bracketed her, she inhaled it, like a diver surfacing after running out of air, gulping in precious breaths.

"God knows, I don't deserve any of it." He dropped his forehead to hers, his voice hoarse. "I'm not sure how you can even find it in yourself to forgive me after what I did. But I swear, Cassie, I'll make it up to you. Even if it takes the rest of our lives."

"I'm not saying you didn't hurt me, Simon," she whispered. "But I understand."

"But that's just it," he said. "You had the capacity to understand that way back at the beginning. When you sent your father to me. Except I was too fucked up to offer the same. Too stupid. And now I've squandered months working it out. Months wasted..." His voice cracked as his head drooped to his chest.

"Simon, look at me." He raised his head, blinking rapidly, eyes glistening. "Perhaps you need to forgive yourself, too?"

He lifted his mouth to hers. When their lips met, the warmth of his kiss triggered an explosion, like tiny stars fracturing into millions of pulsing shards. His tentative hands trailed across the curve of her hips, gaining confidence as they moved to burrow beneath the fabric of her shirt, finding their home on the mounds of her breasts.

Her own hands reached to cup him to her, pressing his firm arse close and allowing her to bury her nose into his shoulder, inhaling a breath of lemon scented freshly washed shirt. How could such an ordinary smell be so intoxicating? It beckoned her to explore what she knew lay beneath; the lean body she longed to press against the length of her own.

She pulled away from him, offering her hand and tugging him towards the stairs.

"Come with me," she said. "I've missed you. So much."

"Would it be OK if I didn't come straight up?" he asked. "If I just sit here for a bit?"

"Sure," she said, unable to suppress a raised brow. Warily, she worried he might be second-guessing his decision. What if he turned and bolted again? "You need some time to think?"

"No," he said. "It's you who should take some time to think. Think if this is what you really want."

She nodded, holding his hand, reluctant to let it go, as if once losing contact, he might evaporate. She didn't need time to think. She'd had plenty of that. Too much, in fact. But she did as he asked.

Cassie slipped into the comfort of Simon's Egyptian cotton sheets, soft against her bare skin. For three months she'd climbed into this bed naked and alone, pretending he was only in the bathroom next door; or maybe feeding his need for order doing a last sweep of the kitchen; perhaps finishing up some work before he joined her. Unable to grab at the elusive threads of sleep, each night she'd lay here, her mind seeking evidence of him. Tonight, she did the same, but overruled by exhaustion, lulled by wine, and trusting that he really was here, sleep found her.

She woke expecting a cool body pressed against hers. Her skin burned with need for him. But he wasn't there. Her mind reached out into the darkness, desperate for any sign; fearful of finding none. The distant noise of a vehicle drifted in from outside; beyond it the city slept. Inside, only silence echoed back at her; but still she sensed something within it, a quiet presence she'd not felt for a long time. It beckoned her, and she followed, not bothering to even stop for a robe.

He lay on his back on the broad couch. Seeing him in the half-light, sprawled there in that strange way of his, couldn't help but bring a smile to her face. It was only in sleep that Simon completely relaxed; lying there, one arm by his side, the other draped casually across his thigh.

Outlined in the slanting streetlight, she marvelled at the pale surreal beauty of him, like some creature of the night with his hair so dark it merged into the shadows. His angular features suggested the hand of a Renaissance sculptor, chiselling marble with long-lost skill, rearranging the blunt rock into the fluid lines of a more pleasing form.

A light hiss of breath between the fine symmetry of lips betrayed this as a living being. Simon's chest rose and fell in a gentle rhythm. She took a step closer, and he stirred a little. Wedged in between the back of the couch and his waist, George slept in a tight ball. She edged herself in on the other side, placing a hand on his chest as if to confirm he was real. His eyelids fluttered and opened. A slow smile spread across his face, and he lifted a hand, capturing hers beneath it.

"Come to bed, Simon," she whispered. He sat up, running a hand through his untidy tumble of hair. She'd never seen it this long, but the dishevelled look suited him. He nodded, and she took his hand and drew him up to follow her.

Seated on the bed, she watched him undress, his eyes locked on her with a calm intensity. He removed each piece of his clothing with care, folding it neatly in the nighttime ritual that she had always teased him about, but had missed so much. In the gloom, her eyes roved across the lean muscles, scanned the long limbs of his legs, followed the dark dusting of hair on his chest where its symmetrical lines merged above his navel before plunging low into the waistband of his jeans. She drank in every inch of him.

He turned to place his clothes on the dresser, and her eyes traced the tattooed lines curving across his back. And then she saw that there were more now, on his left shoulder. She stood and went to him, her hand drawn to the chess pieces, so exquisitely executed in three dimensions they might have been real.

On this board, the white queen stood beside the king. Before them, a black knight lay toppled, as if vanquished.

"Simon," she breathed, "it's beautiful."

"I had it done the day I knew I was ready to come back. That's us. The king and the queen. And him, the knight," he said, "we beat him. And we'll beat all of them. Together."

He took her hand and led her to the bed, a light press of his hand on her shoulder, urging to sit on the edge. He knelt on the floor before her like a supplicant. Tilting his head up, his earlier wariness had gone, his expression one of confidence, as if he knew this was exactly where he should be. She reached a hand to his hair, threading fingers through the dark strands.

He sat back on his haunches, letting his head drop between her outstretched legs, dotting kisses along her thighs. She closed her eyes, as little audible gasps of pleasure bubbled up from inside her. Pulsing need surged through her body, and she pulled him in, a shudder of anticipation as his mouth ventured to explore familiar places.

They made love like it was the first time all over again. He approached her with the same respect he'd offered her back then, when he'd invited her into this bed. Memories flooded back of the tender reverence he'd shown, knowing that only one other man had ever touched her. But boundaries had fallen quickly, and soon she'd struggled to recall that there'd ever been anyone but Simon who could respond to her needs in such creative and exquisite ways.

Tonight, they fell back into that well-known dance, responding to each other's bodies in an intuitive rhythm. Tonight, it was as if the months of separation had been a bad dream.

Afterwards she lay on her back, exhausted, but in a state of languid bliss. He burrowed low in the bed, nestled under her armpit, head on her chest where the delicious warmth of his soft breaths tickled at her skin. She stroked his cheek, and her fingers felt something more beyond the sheen of sweat—tears. She traced their trail, so unexpected.

"I'd understand if you still want me to go," he said, his voice hushed and small. "I don't deserve to presume anything."

Her heart lurched. Hadn't he felt it, as she gave over all of her body to him, she had also given him her complete forgiveness?

She knew too well that holding a relationship together took work. And even then, despite all the effort on both sides, sometimes love became so tenuous it slipped through your fingers, life's problems wrestling it from your grasp.

This relationship would take a different sort of work. The world had been unkind to Simon. People he'd thought loved him had been cruel. People he'd trusted had betrayed him. Fierce determination seized her to be the one person who didn't let him down; the one who protected him; the one who loved him, even when his fragile self made him unlovable.

She leaned down to kiss his cheek, tasting the damp saltiness. She murmured into his hair, so soft and sleek against her lips.

"I used to think it was enough that you didn't tell lies," she said. "But now I know it's more than that. Both of us held onto our secrets. We have to learn to trust each other with all of it. No matter how weird or frightening it might be."

"You already know how to do that," he said. "As for me…"

"But you can learn. Simon. I'm not saying this is going to be easy. To get back to where we were. For either of us. But I need us to try. I love you more than I ever thought I could love someone."

Her younger self hadn't known how the heart's capacity to love only grew with the years. Or how it could come back from difficult times, expanding not only beyond the limits of what had been, but beyond any concept of what seemed possible.

"And I know you love me, Simon. You wouldn't have fought past all this shit that's been weighing you down to come back unless you did. I think people believe trust automatically comes with love. It doesn't. You and I we just have to learn to trust each other."

"You're too charitable. You say 'we', but really it's me." His thumb brushed her lips. "But yes, I can learn. In fact, I've made a start on that. Therapy. I spent some time in London these last couple of weeks. Found someone there. He's good."

"Really?" She'd done a lot of thinking in the aftermath of that terrible morning three months ago. The cause of their parting lay in deep-seated pain, and layers of damage accumulated over years since he was a small child. And for that reason, she knew simply loving him would not be enough. Over years working in schools, she'd seen children, damaged like Simon was, and she'd seen what the right expertise could do. But she'd been in no position to make suggestions—hoped perhaps he'd come to it on his own. Now he had.

"I think that's amazing. That you've reached out to someone who can get you beyond this."

"Yeah, I've got my cousin Calum to thank for that. He made me realise that my emotions and my messed up brain were liabilities that would always be there, no matter where I went or what I did. That I'd never be completely fixed, but it might be possible to retrieve a half-decent person from the wreckage. He told me if I didn't get some help, I might as well walk away from everything—you, my job, the TV series—because dealing with it on my own wasn't working and never would. So I thought I might as well try. I had nothing to lose. Not when I'd already lost the most important thing in the world."

"You hadn't lost her, Simon. I was always here. I was never going anywhere. I never will."

"We haven't talked about this yet. And I think we should." She reached for her phone. At her touch, the screen glared as it leapt into life in the dim early morning light that nipped at the edges of the bedroom curtains. Lines of photographs flowed beneath her fingertip. She scrolled to the exact row in seconds, the location etched in her mind from dozens—no, more like hundreds, perhaps even a thousand—previous visits.

This bizarre knowledge hung between them. It couldn't be ignored. Like her parents, it would run like an invisible thread through the rest of their lives.

He took the phone from her, his slender fingers settling on the photo of them both, stretching it wide. "Us, happy, in love," he said. "What more do I need to say? That's all that matters."

"I know you Simon. You'll never be able to leave this alone."

A faint smile tipped the corners of his mouth. "This is where your father and I are alike. Questions excite us. We ask why and how. You're right. I want to know more—and also to know who."

"Others like us?"

"I'm sure there has to be. Like us, like your parents. In the present. In the past. I'm going to find them."

"You do realise how that sounds? What if they don't want to be found?"

A small huff of amusement brushed her ear.

"Hypocritical? Probably. But this isn't some witch hunt. I'm not about to out them, or us. Why would I want to reveal us to the world and have everyone stare at us like some freaks? But I'm not sure your father would show the same restraint if he ever cracks the case."

"I think he would," she said. "If I asked him. He's not a vain man. Like you said, questions excite him. I think the answer would be enough."

"And if I don't find any answer—*you* are enough for me. Right here in this life. And in all those other possibilities, those other versions of our story—it's the same." He brushed a kiss on her hair, and she breathed him in. He filled her like oxygen, air to sustain her when life threw a rogue wave at them, threatening to swamp her.

Her turbulent young love for Nik had been like swimming in the breakers at a wild, New Zealand west coast beach, exhilarating and yet frightening. Her love for Simon was like slipping into the deep waters of a Scottish loch, a caress on sun-parched skin, cool and soothing. She let herself fall into the depths, trusting in their safe embrace.

Epilogue

Edinburgh, Scotland – February 2023

SIMON FLINCHED AS THE first flash went off. His arm looped around her waist, tightened momentarily and then relaxed.

"You OK?" she asked.

"Yeah, all good," he said, the wattage of his smile not dimming the slightest, as the cameras snapped away frantically. The flurry of activity caught the interest of people filing in through the double doors of the theatre, as they handed off coats to an attendant. A larger-than-life image of Simon watched down on them from a promotional poster for *Secrets of the Stones*, drawing eyes toward the man standing beneath it.

There was nothing for him to be afraid of. This was all planned. No surprises. A ticket-only event, limited press access, all questions submitted in advance and the soothing presence of the production company's PR person, Lily Stanton, hovering just out of shot; all these precautions seemed to steady him. Although she could still sense Simon's nervousness simmering beneath in the slight awkwardness of his words, and a fleeting wariness behind his eyes. But she doubted anyone else would notice.

Some men might feel uncomfortable in the high-end suit and bowtie, but Simon wore it with a casual ease. Her floor length dress of emerald green satin gleamed under the foyer chandeliers. Sourced from a vintage clothing store, its genuine 1950s provenance spoke of old Hollywood glamour. With pinup girl makeup and hair tamed into a sleek French roll, she felt beautiful. She might have been a starlet, dazzling on the red carpet.

But tall and suave with a Bond-like presence, Simon dominated the scene. As he should. This was his concept, his words, his passion brought to life, and tonight the rest of the world would get its first glimpse.

"Are you sure you don't want me to come backstage?" she offered, as Lily herded him towards a door to one side of the foyer.

"No, I'm fine," he said. "You go in. I'm in good hands. I think."

Simon tossed a grin at the man beside him. Some might feel intimidated by the reputation of this tall kilted Scot, whose fame had spread well beyond his home country. But Simon had known Calum MacFarlane since they were kids. His mother and Calum's mother were cousins. At dinner last night, they'd spent hours laughing about boyish pranks and teenage dares. She'd sat back, delighted to be a just a spectator, as they threw jibes at each other and told stories in earthy language. Simon had other friendships, but none with this ease. She was so happy to see this one blooming again.

Calum's reality TV show, *The Kilted Climber*, had launched him into the world of celebrity. So he was the perfect person to help shy Simon navigate the limelight, especially tonight. But beyond that, Cassie harboured profound gratitude for Calum's wisdom. It had been the first step in giving Simon back to her.

Inside the theatre, she spotted her place alongside Jasper. He beckoned her in, patting the seat next to him. The agent, still overblown with pride in his protégé, babbled at her in excitement before she'd even had a chance to sit down. She nodded and smiled good-naturedly. Let him enjoy the reflection of Simon's success. Wasn't that what they were all doing tonight?

Two empty seats to her right awaited Simon and Calum. Before the premier screening, there'd be a live interview. Fifteen minutes of scripted conversation; five questions from the audience—made to appear spontaneous, but all planned—and then they'd come down into the row beside her.

The host, Maddie Whitelaw, arrived on stage. Cassie had seen the pert, pretty brunette on breakfast TV. She took a seat, microphone in hand, well enough known for the crowd to offer enthusiastic applause at her appearance. However, the noise was nothing compared to the roar of welcome when Calum stepped onto the stage. He waved a large hand, grinning broadly.

After a little banter between the two, Maddie invited Simon to join them from the wings. He appeared looking self-assured and elegant in his suit jacket. But where were his pants?

Cassie stared in shock as she registered they'd been replaced—by a smart grey kilt. Like Calum's, it was of a modern design. She had to admit, while unexpected, it was perfect. Her gaze swept from the polished black shoes to the discreet leather sporran as he took a seat, carefully smoothing the kilt to rest modestly between his thighs. Thankfully, they'd also supplied him with some suitable long socks to cover his hairy legs. Pale knees poked from beneath the hem as he settled into the chair. Delighted laughter bubbled up inside of her as she joined in the thunderous welcoming applause.

Jasper laughed too, tossing her a wink. "Told him he needed to get his knees out."

The interview flowed along as planned, and Simon never missed a beat. Perhaps he drew on the fact he'd faced large groups of people before. Helpfully, his interviewers also stuck to the pre-planned script. No surprises. That's how he liked things. When it was over, he followed Calum, striding off the stage with one last confident wave, and made his way to the seat beside her.

"You were brilliant," she said, squeezing his hand as the applause continued to echo all around them.

"I was, wasn't I?" he answered with a grin.

The lights dimmed, and the screen filled with the opening images of episode one. Through the magic of drone photography, they flew across landscapes, circled battlements and plunged in low to skim along ancient castle walls. In the background, mournful music hinted of past sorrows as Simon's mellow voiceover sounded through the theatre.

"Nothing is more romantic than a castle. When writers, and indeed filmmakers, take us to a castle, they're tapping into our fantasies of times past, of bold heroes and despicable villains, of sworn enemies and passionate lovers."

The first time she'd heard those words, and that voice, she'd felt herself falling in love with a man who was a stranger. Confronted and confused by thoughts of illicit desire for someone who wasn't her husband, she'd pushed it away, a shameful secret to be buried down deep. This time she allowed herself to fall for him all over again, knowing there was no need for secrets. Simon was hers and she was his, and in this time and in this place was exactly where they were meant to be.

If you enjoyed this book, I'd appreciate it if you have time to leave a review
on your favourite retailer, review site, or social media.

Tangled In Time, the story of Cassie's parents, Blair and Daniel,
is the prequel for the series. Find it on my website, along with other bonus
content for both books.
www.carolinecorvin.com

While you're there, sign up to my newsletter to receive bonus content as
well as future updates and information on new releases.
For details on all books in the series, turn over a few pages
to see more from Caroline.

Acknowledgments

THIS ONE'S FOR MY readers...

A couple of years ago, I wrote a short story about a young couple, Cassie and Nik, struggling to face the slow, painful demise of their marriage. That story went on to become a novella, in which, through a flicker in time, we meet Simon, and the possibility of a second chance at happiness for Cassie.

Without reader interest, the story might have simply stayed a little novella, offered as a glimpse into my writing style. But knowing thousands of people had downloaded it on their e-readers encouraged me to tell the full story. And this is it!

I'm so grateful for the part you, the readers, played in getting the story of these three beautiful people onto the page, allowing me to reveal their hopes and dreams, joys and sorrows, as Cassie navigates two lives and two loves.

Once again, a huge thanks to my developmental editor, Jackie Cangro. To talk with you in person about this book over coffee in a Brooklyn café, as well as indulge our shared love of romance in the cutest bookshop, was a highlight of my trip to the USA. I love how you push me harder with each new book. Working with you is a delight.

To the others who play such important parts in turning a manuscript into a real live book, I thank you. In particular, my cover designer, Jules, deserves a personal mention. I thought I'd tossed you an extra tricky brief this time, but you brought elements of the book to life in this stunning result. I'm in awe of your talent.

And finally, to my real life romance hero, who knows all about teen love and what it takes to grow beyond that and still be together, thank you for encouraging me, like Nik and Simon encouraged Cassie, to follow my writing dream.

Love to you all.

Caroline

More From Caroline

Now you've read Cassie's story, check out the others. While *Tangled Past* is the fourth book in the series, each book listed here can be read as a satisfying standalone.
Stop by my website to check out more details, and be sure to grab a copy of the prequel, *Tangled In Time*, the story of Cassie's parents, Blair and Daniel.

www.carolinecorvin.com

Tangled In Time

**A free-spirited artist, a wandering astronomer,
and an instant connection.
Is their future painted in the stars?**

Landscape painter Blair Silvestri hasn't time for stargazing —or love. It's her immediate, more precarious situation that she needs to focus on for now. Daniel Tremayne spends his life looking skyward. Maybe that's why he's made such a mess of all his relationships so far. A trick of time throws them together, but also threatens to tear them apart.

Tangled Threads

**What if her future lies
in a time tangled past?**

Now the last of those who loved her are gone, there's nothing left for young teacher Kate Moreton in New Zealand. It's time for her to forge a new life. Pinning her hopes of finding friends, family—and maybe even love— elsewhere, she heads for the bright lights of London. What Kate doesn't know is this journey will lead her to two men, two loves, and two lives. And offer a future lifeline when her world falls apart.

Tangled Paths

**"In a world full of limitless lives,
of endless possibilities, I will always find you."**

Sarah Mitchell always put family first. Now, freed from self-imposed exile in her hometown, she's ready to jump back on the academic path she sacrificed for others three years ago. It's her time to choose a path. Or is time going to choose for her? When Sarah's future seems destined to be defined by loss, will time's tangled paths deliver her a second chance at happiness?

Tangled Hearts

**Two loves, two lives. One heart shattered.
Can a love from another time heal the pain of the present?**

Young emergency room doctor, Layla Angell, is living the dream: in the perfect job, surrounded by friends who are like family—including the man she's always wanted to be more than a friend. Life is full of potential. But the future is never promised. Caught in a time-twisted love triangle, Layla's connection to two men, across two parallel lives, offers a second chance at happiness beyond tragedy—if she can learn to accept the impossible.

About the Author

WHEN NOT WRITING, YOU can usually find Caroline with her nose in a book from any one of an eclectic mix of favourite genres. While officially a resident of Auckland, New Zealand's stunning City of Sails, she has become adept at juggling her love of writing alongside her other magnificent obsession of travelling the world. Caroline didn't set out to write romance, but her characters took control the moment she let them loose on the page, reminding her that finding happily ever afters are the reason she's one of those people who sometimes reads the last page first, just to be safe.

**Follow Caroline Corvin on all your favourite
social media or review sites!**

Visit her website: www.carolinecorvin.com

9 781738 598168